The Veil of Gold

ALSO BY KIM WILKINS

The Autumn Castle

The Veil *of* Gold

Kim Wilkins

A TOM DOHERTY ASSOCIATES BOOK
NEW YORK

THE VEIL OF GOLD

Copyright © 2005 by Kim Wilkins

Previously published in 2005, in somewhat different form, under the title *Rosa and the Veil of Gold*, by HarperCollins*Publishers*, in Australia.

Book design by Spring Hoteling

A Tor Book
Published by Tom Doherty Associates, LLC
175 Fifth Avenue
New York, NY 10010

www.tor-forge.com

Tor® is a registered trademark of Tom Doherty Associates, LLC.

ISBN-13: 978-0-7653-2006-3
ISBN-10: 0-7653-2006-1

First U.S. Edition: July 2008

Printed in the United States of America

0 9 8 7 6 5 4 3 2 1

Luka,
Net mesta takovo zhe strashnovo i takovo zhe chudesnovo,
kak voobrazhenie rebyonka.

Acknowledgments

I would like to acknowledge the assistance of the following people.

For help with my research, my sincerest thanks to Dr. Andrew Gentes, Dr. Sonia Puttock, Professor Elizabeth Warner, Samantha Tinker, Tanya Martin, Andrei Nekrosov, Vladislav Nekliaev, A. J. Rochester, Caroline Yates, Carmen Roberts, Meg Heaslop and Kate Cuthbert. I claim all mistakes and bent truths as wholly my own.

For writing support, I'd like to acknowledge Paul Brandon, Mary-Rose MacColl, Verity Morgan, Sean Williams, Rebecca Sparrow, Louise Cusack and, of course, Selwa Anthony. I'd like to pay a particular debt of gratitude to Kate Morton, for going on this journey so closely with me: what a fine traveling companion you are, BF. The practical help offered by Mirko Ruckels, Elaine Wilkins, Nicole Ruckels and Ian Wilkins gave me the time and the space to write. Folk at HarperCollins who are never acknowledged fully enough for their positivity and goodwill are Stephanie Smith, Linda Funnell, Airlie Lawson, Alison Urquhart and Karen-Maree Griffiths (kisses to you, KMG).

A special thanks and hello to the staff of the Fryer Library, University of Queensland. Thank you for letting me work with the lights off.

Thank you also to Faye Booth, for her tireless work on my online community.

So much of the research on this project was done with the help of those who are impossible to talk to, but whose versions of Russia are the most vivid and evocative. So a special acknowledgment, presumptuous though it may be, to Tyutchev, Blok, Pushkin, Lermontov, Akhmatova, Tolstoy, Tchaikovsky, Rachmaninov and mad, mad Prokofiev (where would this book have been without his sleigh ride?).

And for Luka Nikolai, a special thank-you and the dedication of this book. You inspire me simply by smiling, and you have enriched my world beyond measure.

The Veil of Gold

Prologue

All the years I have lived in this world and in the other I have been known by many names: Koschey the deathless; the Siberian wolf; the mad monk; Chyort, the Devil himself.

But today I am simply Papa Grigory, for that is what my little Totchka calls me. I see her now; she stands in a ring of young daisies and the sun is on her dark hair, and her arms are stretched out like a swan's wings. Inside this old house of stone and wood, the glazed stove burns warm and the dried nettles at the windows keep away the encroaching shadows. I watch my little girl and everything dear and bright is already with me. Hush, and hear the silence of a contented man.

Perhaps . . . perhaps the silence will never break.

This morning I was holding Totchka while I brushed her hair. She complained and wriggled, and I became fascinated by the contrast of my hands—mottled blue with age, gold rings trapped forever below swollen joints—against the supple flesh of her white arms. I am old, and Totchka is young. Totchka is young, yet will not grow old. How is that so? I ask you this: how are many things so?

How is it that Totchka, this speck of a girl whose real name is lost to the years, is mine yet not mine?

How is it that I was stabbed, poisoned, shot, drowned and buried and yet I still live?

And why does the Snow Witch want the Golden Bear?

I rush ahead. You don't yet know of the Golden Bear. You don't yet know of Rosa Petrovna Kovalenka and the young man who loves her and the thrice-nine lands they both must wander.

I know many things that I will not tell, not yet. I am a storyteller, and any good storyteller knows not to give too much away too early. I will tell you some things now, some things later. Then, at the end, when all is revealed, you need not feel guilty or sad or responsible for terrible things. *You did not know.* Yes, *I* know. Let it be my burden.

Totchka runs toward the house. Clutched in her hand is a bright flower and she is calling my name. I must go to greet her.

As for you now, look around you. You are in St. Petersburg with its wide, overgrown squares and decayed splendor. In an old bathhouse—long imagined a place where magic is conjured—something rare and mysterious is about to be found.

PART ONE

Across the secret world of spirits,
Across this nameless chasm,
A veil of gold has been draped
By the will of the great gods.

—FYODOR TYUTCHEV

One

Rosa Kovalenka was beautiful and clever, but nobody knew the truth about her.

Not Daniel, not Uncle Vasily, and certainly not the American foreman who caught his breath from the run up the stairs before speaking.

"There's been an accident," he said.

Rosa leapt up from her desk. "Is anybody hurt?"

"Not that kind of an accident." He removed his hard hat, revealing sandy curling hair. "I'm sorry, Miss Kovalenka, but we've mistakenly knocked a hole in one of the walls." His eyes flicked around nervously. "Is Vasily here?"

"No, Jamie, Uncle Vasily is at lunch." She offered a reassuring smile. "Show me. Maybe it's not so bad."

Rosa followed Jamie from the office and down the worn stone steps to the street. She had been working in Uncle Vasily's business for the past six months, and she knew his temper was legendary, which accounted for Jamie's anxious body language as he strode ahead of her. Two doors up stood the bathhouse. A nineteenth-century structure that had been boarded up for forty years, it was the current object of Vasily's unstoppable desire to transform every old building in St. Petersburg into luxury apartments.

"It's the sub-contractors," Jamie was saying in embarrassed tones. Rosa knew that Jamie nursed a crush on her and revealing this lapse of judgment clearly pained him. "We speak English, they speak Russian. Something got lost in translation and they started pulling out a wall."

"Well, they'll have to put it back," she said gently.

"They've destroyed the plaster work, cracked all the tiles."

"Uncle Vasily won't be pleased."

"The men were hoping you'd tell him." Jamie pushed open the door to the bathhouse; inside was dim and cold. One wall remained uncleaned, the mold of centuries gathered in its antique crevices. The tiles imparted a glassy echo to every sound.

"There's something else," Jamie said, leaning close, his clear green eyes holding her gaze. "Inside the wall."

"What's inside the wall?"

"We didn't want to move it. But it looks like gold."

Rosa brushed Jamie aside and hurried to where the assembled crew stood scratching their heads, arguing in Russian and English. A bright spotlight had been angled directly into the gaping hole. She snapped at the crew to stand back, and leaned in.

Rainbow colors, golden mist, swirls of starlight patterns. An old song, half out of tune. A falling sensation beneath her ribs, an extra breath pressed into her lungs.

Rosa blinked. She had always seen things others didn't see: the magical world was laid bare to her, where it remained cloaked to most. This hollow in the wall was brimming over with magic. She peered closer and saw why. Shoved upside-down between two bricks was a bear made of gold.

Rosa gasped. "It's beautiful," she said, reaching into the cavity. Dust and mold blackened the lower three inches of the bear, but the top half was clean. Rosa's fingers brushed against it and electricity snapped up her hand and forearm. She snatched her hand away.

The workmen exchanged nervous glances.

"It's enchanted," she said, then repeated herself in Russian for the benefit of the locals. One or two of the crew snickered, probably the Americans.

The door to the bathhouse flew open and Vasily stood there, outlined by the sunlight from the street.

"What has happened!" he shrieked in Russian.

"Uncle Vasily, calm down," Rosa said, hurrying over and taking his fleshy arm. "I think the damage is not so bad, and they will be able to fix it easily. Come, you must see. A wonderful object has been found."

Vasily shook his head. "Ay, Roshka. Can I not go to lunch without a disaster befalling me?"

"It's not a disaster, Uncle Vasily. It's a blessing. You'll see."

She led him to the cavity and reached in for the bear. This time there was no electricity. The bear had already marked her. She drew it from its hiding place and Vasily hushed.

"Do you see?" Rosa said. "A hole in a wall is easy to repair. The bear wanted us to find her."

"Is it gold, Rosa?"

"I think so."

Vasily touched it and Rosa noted that no electrical charge passed between the bear and her uncle.

"Is it very old and precious?" he said.

"Perhaps."

Jamie, obviously made curious by their hushed Russian, broke in "You should take that to a museum."

"What did he say?" Vasily snapped, though Rosa suspected he knew what was being said. He was too proud for misunderstandings, instead relying on Rosa for precise translations.

"Jamie suggests a museum."

"It is mine!"

"I know, Uncle Vasily."

Vasily turned on Jamie and roared in darkly inflected English, "I am developer. I am not historian."

"It's all right, Jamie," Rosa said to the foreman. "We know what to do. Get your men to fix this wall. Uncle Vasily thanks you for your honesty." She slipped off her jacket and wrapped the bear, then put out her hand to Vasily. He took it firmly.

"I won't take it to a museum, Roshka," he said as the door to the bathhouse thudded shut behind them.

"I know," she said, then tried to cheer him out of his temper by teasing him. "Uncle Vasily, how is that dark cold place ever going to be made into luxury apartments?"

"You sound like your mother," he muttered, and Rosa's heart tumbled.

"Skylights?" she said, mock-brightly.

"Skylights. And heaters. And thick carpet. Somebody will buy them. Somebody always does."

She pushed open the heavy wooden door to their offices, and followed Vasily up the bare stone stairs. The first floor was an unfinished demolition site. The second floor was carpeted in green and wallpapered in cream and gold. Behind a partition, draftsmen and secretaries and engineers and accountants worked quietly. Vasily ushered Rosa into his private office and closed the door.

"Show me again," he said.

Rosa carefully unwrapped the bear and stood it on the desk between the piles of plans and the streaming in-trays. "I think it's very old, Uncle Vasily," she said.

"Why do you think it, Rosa?"

Rosa wouldn't say that she just *felt* it, because her mother had *felt* things and Vasily already spoke too much about Ellena Kovalenka. Her sad shade seemed always in mind.

"The face on the bear looks odd, almost like a human face," she said.

Vasily ran his fingers over his chin, pulling his bottom lip. His black hair, heavy with hair oil, flopped over his left eye. "Yes, yes," he said. "She could be worth a fortune."

"We should find out how much. We could ask a museum—"

"It's mine, Rosa. I won't hand it over."

"I don't want you to hand it over. I want you only to authenticate it. They won't take it from you. It was on your property."

"I don't trust historians!" he exclaimed, shooting out of his chair and adopting his customary brooding frown. "I don't trust museums! They are thieves of the dead."

Rosa scratched some of the black muck from the bear with her thumbnail. "I know somebody," she said quietly. "Somebody who may be able to tell you if it's authentic or not. He would be discreet."

"Who is it?"

"An old friend. He's in Novgorod. He's a . . . researcher." She avoided the word *historian*, malign as they were in Vasily's view. She couldn't remember Daniel's specific job appellation anyway. All she knew was that he was working for a major British television company, that they were making a documentary, and that he had left his phone number on her answering machine two weeks ago when he had arrived in Russia. She had written it down, never intending to use it but too superstitious to release the numbers into silence.

Vasily paced, peered through the blinds, returned to the table and sat. He spread his hands before him. "I trust you, Rosa. If you think he is a good man—"

"Oh, he's a good man. There is no doubt."

Vasily nodded. "Do what is right, Roshka."

"I'll see if he can come to St. Petersburg."

"You think he might?"

Rosa hid a smile. "Yes, I do. Don't you worry about a thing, Uncle Vasily."

Daniel closed out the afternoon cold and fished his room key from his pocket. The guesthouse smelled of cabbage and warm spices and he wondered what artery-clogging delights Crazy Adelina was cooking for dinner that night. He hadn't yet witnessed anything proving that Adelina was crazy, but four of the crew, who had been on the receiving end of a tirade about smoking in their rooms, assured him it was only a matter of time.

The note had been slipped under his door. It was flipped over on its face between the scarred writing desk and the dreary checked bedspread. Daniel stooped to pick it up, his heart taking an unexpected jump to see her name written there in Russian letters.

Rosa Kovalenka called.

Rosa called? Daniel had resigned himself to the certainty that she would never call. He sat on the bed and studied the note as though it might provide more details. What was she feeling and thinking?

The door to his room was still open, and he heard footsteps on the narrow landing. Em Hayward, the writer and presenter of the series. Daniel was supposed to work closely with her, editing the scripts, but despite her dark prettiness and her polite smile he felt inexplicably intimidated by her. Something wasn't quite right about her, as though the soft facade masked a steely intensity.

"Hello, Em," he called.

"Hello, Daniel," she called back, and closed her door.

He did the same, then turned to the telephone. He picked out Rosa's number nervously, each digit acquiring new significance: 8, the number of times they had made love during their brief affair; 1, how often he'd said "I love you" before she disappeared; 2, the presents he had given her—a silver bracelet and a deep blue scarf the precise color of her eyes. The other things he couldn't count in single figures. Train trips between Cambridge and London to see her; desperate phone calls that went unanswered; gin and tonics consumed to obliterate the pain. But Rosa hadn't stayed. Rosa had escaped to her uncle's place in St. Petersburg, and Daniel hadn't heard her voice in more than six months.

Still, he knew it when he heard it.

"Hello," she said. The soft curves of a Canadian accent—that was, after all, where she had grown up—but always lingering underneath that, the kiss of the exotic place from which she drew her heritage.

"Rosa?"

"Daniel," she said cautiously, and her caution iced his fantasies of reconciliation before they could grow too hot. "Thank you for calling me back."

"It's been such a long time. How are you?"

"I'm doing okay," she said. "I'm doing fine. And you?"

Did he mistake the tender note in her voice? Probably. He took a breath and calmed himself. "I'm well. I'm busy. I'm still having trouble with my Russian possessive partitives."

She laughed. "I'm sure you're underestimating yourself. You were my star pupil."

"The teacher who replaced you was very dreary. I didn't bother going back to lessons once you were gone." He winced, realizing he had said too much.

She left a beat of silence before saying, "Daniel, we found an interesting object bricked up in a wall at Uncle Vasily's latest development site. I have a feeling that it's very old."

"How old is the building?"

"Mid-nineteenth century. But this object . . . It looks much older, almost primitive. It's a gold bear about eight inches high, has an interesting design across its stomach. I've never seen anything like it."

Daniel tried to picture it. He picked up the phone and took it to the bed to sit down. "Is it solid? Full-round or relief?"

"It's bear-shaped, round. It's heavy and smooth."

"You say it looks primitive."

"Almost . . . pagan." Her self-conscious laugh echoed down the line. "But I know nothing about art or history."

"No, no. The Scythians did a lot of animal figures, but usually reliefs, not full-round sculptures. The early Slavs were very fond of bears."

"It looks almost human in the face. Odd eyes. They're closed and she's smiling, like she's thinking about something she likes."

"It could even be ancient Altai. They believed spirits could slip between humans and animals, and they used an eye motif . . . But it sounds too large. I don't know, Rosa, it's impossible to say without seeing it. You could take it to a museum."

"Uncle Vasily won't hear of it."

Daniel hesitated. "Do you want me to come and look at it?"

She surprised him by answering quickly and enthusiastically. "Would you? It would mean a lot to Uncle Vasily if he could find out what it is. Who knows, maybe it's just a piece of junk."

He took a second to catch his breath. Talking to her was one thing but seeing her in the flesh was entirely another. It occurred to him, urgently and brightly, that he hadn't made any progress at all in getting over her.

"Of course I'll come," he said. "I'd love to see you."

"Daniel, it's just the bear, you understand." Her voice grew soft. "If we hadn't found it, I might not have called."

It stung, but he was grateful for her honesty. "Yes, I understand," he said, trying to sound nonchalant. "I'll call you when I know which day I'm coming. All right?"

"Okay. I look forward to it."

Daniel replaced the phone in its cradle, feeling flat and disappointed. He knew the feeling well, and didn't want to descend into the melancholy haze that ordinarily followed it. Voices drifted up through the window, and he snatched up his room key and let himself out. Downstairs, behind the guesthouse, lay a tiny courtyard where his co-workers gathered to drink and share cigarettes.

"Here's Daniel!" called Richard, the chief sound operator, already half-drunk and in shoulder-slapping mode. Daniel slid onto the bench beside him and looked at the shiny new leaves on the birch spreading above them. "Isn't it supposed to be summer soon? When will it warm up?"

"Have a vodka, that will warm you up." This was Aaron, the producer, who had worked with Daniel on another project four years ago. Was that the last television job he had done? No wonder he had trouble making the rent. Aaron thrust a drink into Daniel's hand. Five other men sat on the bench or on the flagstones under the tree, and their voices echoed around the walls of the buildings that bordered the courtyard.

"Thanks." He sipped the drink and tried to let Rosa go. "Does anybody know what times the trains run to St. Petersburg from here?"

There was a loud snort of laughter. Aaron raised his eyebrows with a smile. "You're asking us? You're the train expert."

Daniel bit his tongue. He had refused to fly from London with everybody else. He didn't like to think of his aversion to airplanes as a phobia, but had to admit after five consecutive days on English, French, German and, finally, Russian trains only something as severe as a phobia could have led to such extreme measures.

"Why are you going to St. Pete?" asked Richard, reaching for a cigarette and offering one to Daniel.

Daniel shrugged and took the cigarette. He wouldn't call himself a smoker, but was taking alarming numbers from the crew at the moment. "To see an old friend."

"You should drive," Richard said. "Frank would let you take the hire car."

Frank was the executive producer, stuck back in London in urgent meetings with the accountants. Richard meant that Frank would never know where the hire car ended up.

"No, I prefer not to drive," Daniel muttered, hoping for a quick subject change.

"Afraid of driving too?"

"Wrong side of the road," Aaron offered. "That's it, isn't it?"

Before Daniel had to admit he was right, Aaron said, "Ask Em. She's going up tomorrow afternoon. And she's a Yank. They all drive on the wrong side."

"I'll just catch the train," Daniel said, blowing a long stream of smoke into the afternoon air. "I wouldn't know what to say to Em on a three-hour car trip."

"She's easy enough to get along with," Aaron said, puzzled.

"Nah, I'm with Daniel," Richard said. "She's frozen solid under there, I'd bet money on it."

"I can't stand the silence," Declan, one of the cameramen, said.

"The silence?"

'When you talk to her. She's perfectly silent. No nodding, no 'uh-huh,' no encouraging smile. Like she's watching an actor perform."

A laugh went around. Daniel joined in. It was a perfect description.

"I've heard that she had a man sacked for answering his mobile phone between shots," George, the production assistant, said.

Declan threw his cigarette into the gutter. "I've heard she has a kid, back in America. She abandoned him when he was a baby."

"I've heard she doesn't just abandon babies, she eats them," Richard said, finding this so funny that he doubled over with laughter.

Daniel smiled but didn't offer any speculations about Em, concentrating instead on his cigarette and his vodka. Maybe if he was more like these men, he'd be able to get over Rosa easier. Laugh her off as crazy, as a good time gone bad.

Aaron shook his head. "Em's not so bad. Sure, she's a little odd, but who in television isn't? Especially the really successful ones." He turned to Daniel. "Really, Em would probably enjoy the company."

Daniel finished his cigarette and his drink simultaneously. He couldn't ask Em to drive him to St. Petersburg; he couldn't even work with her on editing. He made excuses and took her scripts away and brought them back unmarked. What could he possibly have to say to her? He was a boy in a thirty-year-old man's body. These men around him had wives and children at home, self-assured swaggers and easy masculine friendships. They could probably fix cars and predict football wins and ask charming but cold women for lifts. Daniel stood and mashed his cigarette between two flagstones with his toe. "I've got some work to do," he said.

Upstairs, he paused outside Em's door. The walls were thin and he could hear her talking to somebody.

"Yes . . . well, I'll send one over. I think there are three different types. Would you like one of each?"

Daniel reached into his pocket for his key. Was this the abandoned child in America?

"Absolutely," she was saying. "Check with your father, but I'm sure he won't mind."

Her voice bore no trace of tenderness. She could have been talking to a business colleague. He got the key in the lock. Em's door opened as his was closing.

"Did you want something?" she said.

"Sorry?" He opened his door wider.

"I heard your footsteps pause outside my door."

He cursed the thin walls. "Oh, yes. I was wondering if . . . I need to go to St. Petersburg and Aaron said . . ."

"You're going to St. Pete? So am I. We could share the drive."

"I . . . uh . . ." Daniel forced his shoulders to relax. "I'm not used to driving on the wrong side of the road."

"Yeah, okay. I'll drive. Tomorrow good for you? I have some time off."

Daniel shrugged, surprised by her willingness. "Fine."

"I'll drop you off and spend some time in the shops. We'll organize it in the morning, over breakfast." She was already backing into her room, leaving Daniel in the hallway dreading a long car drive with a frosty woman he barely knew.

Rosa sat on the windowsill of her bedroom in Uncle Vasily's apartment, gazing down at the night-time streetscape: grimy footpaths drenched with the afternoon's rain, slats of wood covering potholes, groups of people moving past on their way to nightclubs and late-night restaurants, and the untidy tangle of tram cables spread above them. She could see it all but experienced it at a remove.

The door to her room opened slowly, the accompanying knock a few moments too late . . . the assumed intimacy of family.

"Rosa? Are you still awake?"

"Yes, Uncle Vasily," she said, turning from the window and lowering herself from the sill. "I'm not sleepy."

"I'm going to bed now."

"Good night, then."

He gave her a cautionary look and backed away, closing the door behind him. He would lie awake for twenty minutes, but eventually the stress of the day would claim him and he'd disappear under the layers of sleep, leaving her free to do as she pleased.

Rosa leaned her forehead on the window. The glass was cool. A lone figure waited across the road; an old woman with a faded blue headscarf, her hand extended to beg a few kopecks from passers-by. She had been standing there since nightfall. Rosa had watched her for hours, and the woman had not once looked up at the apartment block; yet, somehow, she knew the woman was waiting for her.

She pulled on her boots and red overcoat, untied her long black hair and sat on her bed to wait. By eleven o'clock she was certain that Vasily was asleep. She crept from her room and across to the front door.

It wasn't that Uncle Vasily was a tyrant who wouldn't let her out. She was twenty-seven, not seventeen; but to him she was a baby, the last memory of his sister, her mother. He would worry if he knew she was gone. She didn't want him to worry.

The chill of the street jolted her. The amber glow of streetlights in puddles was thin and cold in the dark. A muddy Fiat drove past belching exhaust and techno bass. The figure across the road hadn't moved. The scarf covered her face; her hand was extended like a collection plate. Behind her, a tall wrought-iron fence restrained a wild garden and an old cemetery. A dirty stone arch framed her. The sour smell of the street hung heavy.

Rosa pulled out a cigarette and lit it, taking a quick, unsure drag. She stayed on her side of the street, watching traffic go past, watching the *babooshka* as though the old woman were a statue.

Rosa finished her cigarette and threw the butt into the gutter. She crossed the road and the old woman looked up and smiled.

"Hey, grandma," Rosa said in Russian, "have you any advice for me?"

The babooshka held out her hand. Rosa saw a collection of bent kopecks and a couple of rusted washers. "Silver," she croaked. "I'll tell you your fortune."

Rosa reached into the pocket of her coat and fished out ten roubles. "I only have paper—" But the woman had snatched the note and stuffed it in her apron before Rosa could finish.

"You ought not smoke," the babooshka said. "It could kill you."

"With a bit of luck," Rosa sniffed, shrugging. "Is that my fortune?"

"No," she said. "Let me see your hand, beautiful girl."

Rosa offered her palm, and the old woman's callused fingers moved over it carefully.

"Oh, oh, I see a great love. I see many children."

Rosa snatched her hand away. "That's nonsense. Tell me what you really see."

The babooshka turned her wizened face up. Rosa saw for the first time the deep crevices of age scarring the elderly woman's cheeks. Rosa touched her own cheek and wanted to wail for the violent brevity of beauty.

"What did you dream about last night, beautiful girl?"

Rosa thought hard. Dreams tended to disappear the moment they had played out. Something about Vasily, and a thudding noise . . .

"A horse," she said at last. "A black horse." The dream returned to her afresh. "I dreamed of a black horse beating at the door of his stable, but then I knew I was dreaming and I woke up into another dream where my uncle was sitting in the dark crying and wouldn't tell me why."

The babooshka clicked her tongue, and Rosa felt a crushing sense of déjà vu. Echo upon echo. Her fingers itched to reach for another cigarette. "What does it mean, grandma?" she said.

"A black horse is wild and bad and you cannot control it. To dream within a dream is the worst misfortune: chaos, confusion, darkness descending." The old woman's hand crept out again. "If you give me more money, I will tell you what to do."

Rosa found another note and pressed it into the woman's hand. "Take this, but I don't need you to tell me what to do. I know that nothing can be done."

"God bless you, beautiful girl," the babooshka said, baring a mouthful of stained and rotted teeth.

"Eat well, grandma," Rosa said, leaving her behind and heading for the bright lights of Nevsky Prospekt.

She began the long walk past the glittering shopfronts, the crumbling buildings, the endless ice-cream carts, the beggars, the bitter-scented metro stations, the Western tourists in bars, and the fast-food restaurants, their cheerful logos rendered alien by Cyrillic letters. She soaked up the atmosphere of the damp city, longing for something that she couldn't put into words, some thrill or jolt that would remind her she was alive *now*.

Daniel was coming tomorrow. She wished she could say that she hadn't thought of him in the six months since their affair imploded. But she had thought of him a lot. She had thought about his hot, trembling caresses and his uncertainty-smudged dark eyes, and she had thought of another life that might have been. But then the thoughts made her sad; the angry-sad she had felt since the day her mother got sick.

Rosa crossed the bridge over Fontanka Canal and took a right turn down a less well-lit street, then right again, then paused on the corner.

Dark. The noise of the main street echoed in the distance, muffled by stone buildings. The bitter-earth wet-metal scent of the city was acute here, and puddles gathered on the uneven flagstones. A drainpipe dripped and sputtered. She saw the glow of a cigarette and heard voices. Focused her sight down a long alley between two buildings. Two men stood smoking in the dark; shadows clung to their faces. No light reached the alley. No crowds of people or zooming cars belching exhaust traversed it. It was perfectly dangerous. Rosa could taste it.

She turned and ambled toward the two men. They murmured. She was certain they had noticed her. The kick of adrenalin was mild, but she relished it. They paused in their conversation as she approached.

"May I have a cigarette?" she said.

The larger man reached for his packet, the other for his lighter. Within seconds she was inhaling.

"Thanks," she said, smiling, then continued down the alley, vulnerable and alone.

They did nothing. Rosa emerged at the other end in a public garden where lovers pressed their bodies against each other and rubbish gathered around picnic benches. She crossed between the trees and joined the traffic and bright lights again, feeling strangely deflated.

She slumped on the stone windowsill of a closed bakery, thinking about what the babooshka had said to her. *Chaos, confusion, darkness descending.* It was the truth, and Rosa already knew it.

But nobody else did. Not yet.

Two

At mealtimes, it was apparent how comprehensively Crazy Adelina's guesthouse had been colonized by the English. Apart from a hapless family of German tourists, every other body in the room wore a *Great Medieval Cities* T-shirt. They queued at the buffet for blinis and fried eggs, complained loudly in English about the lack of good food in Russia, and sat muttering together at the tiny round tables about the weather and the football. Twenty-one men and two women, Megan and Lesley, clinging to each other at a table in the corner. Em was nowhere in sight. Daniel loaded up his plate and sat at the spare corner of a long wooden table.

Daniel glanced around the room while he ate. At his table, a group of five men were heads-together in conversation, organizing the work for the day at the archaeology site. He didn't join in. The series had been in production for years, and the company had been filming at other locations for nearly eighteen months, but Daniel was only employed for research on the episode about Novgorod. While the rest of the crew knew each other well and would continue their friendships after Russia, he knew he would remain an outsider, soon forgotten.

Aaron slid into the seat next to him and reached across for the salt. "Glad I got you on your own," he said. "Frank phoned last night. I need to talk to you."

Daniel tensed, immediately assuming he'd done something wrong.

"Hey, relax," Aaron said, laughing. "It's good news. A colleague of his is putting together some travel-based language videos. They're starting with French and Russian. You do both, don't you?"

Daniel shrugged. "My French is rusty."

"They're keen as mustard to have you on board," Aaron said through a mouthful of fried egg. "I put in a good word. Could be an ongoing position as research coordinator if you impress them. How's that? A permanent job? Ever had one of those?"

Daniel felt a moment of alarm. "No, I haven't." So what had he done with his twenties? He scratched at a piece of dried food stuck

to the red-and-white plastic tablecloth. A half-finished Masters in
Russian history, two half-finished novels and a half-finished screenplay, a backpacking tour around Australia, three well-paid but casual
television jobs, countless bar jobs, and that was pretty much it.

"You do want a permanent job, don't you?"

The men at the table were getting rowdy. Somebody was telling
a joke about an archaeologist and a mummy. Daniel tried to focus
on his conversation with Aaron. "I don't know. I like to leave my
options open."

Aaron raised his eyebrows. "So what do you want me to tell
Frank?"

"Don't tell him anything yet. I'll think about it."

A moment later, Em was there at his shoulder. "Daniel? Can I
interrupt?" She crouched, resting her small pale hands on the table.

"Morning, Em," said Aaron. "Day off today?"

"Yes, Daniel and I are driving up to St. Petersburg. I'll need you
to sign off on the car for me."

"That's fine."

"Daniel, I'd like to leave just after one o'clock. That's not too
late for you?"

"No, no," Daniel said, though last night he'd spent the hours
until he fell asleep fantasizing about meeting Rosa for a long, lan-
guid lunch that ended with sex.

"Good. I'll drop by your room." She stood and delicately plucked
a roll from the bread basket before withdrawing.

"Does she ever join the rest of them for breakfast?" Daniel asked
Aaron.

Aaron watched her go. "Not really. Same with other meals. She's
not a people person." He turned his attention to Daniel. "But you
needn't be so afraid of her."

"I'm not afraid of her," Daniel said dismissively.

"Well, I don't see you having too many script meetings
with her."

"She doesn't need my help."

"Everyone can use a bit of help." Aaron refilled his mug from
the teapot on the table.

"Maybe I am a little intimidated," Daniel admitted. "She's famous, she's attractive, she's clever . . . and she's a bit cold."

"No, not cold. Just professional. And she'd probably appreciate some help with her Russian." Aaron laughed. "Though not for long."

"What do you mean?"

"Every shoot we've been on for this series, she's picked up the local language in a couple of weeks."

"Maybe she already knew them."

"No. Czech, Turkish . . . she was speaking Italian in six days."

"How well?"

"Well enough. Language is no barrier."

Daniel shook his head. "If she's a genius, she definitely doesn't need my help on the scripts."

"Humor me," Aaron said, taking his mug and readying to leave. "Do what you're paid to do. We're old mates. Don't make me have to get heavy with you."

Aaron left and Daniel poked at his blini, feeling like an ineffectual fool. Was it any wonder Rosa hadn't stayed?

'Why so glum, Daniel?" This was Richard, breaking away from the group and turning his chair to Daniel. "Work troubles? Or girl troubles?"

"Both. Neither," Daniel said. "I think the problem is me."

Richard shrugged. "You can't escape yourself," he said.

' Yeah," said Daniel. "I'd better get sorted."

Rosa found the bear uppermost in her thoughts and wondered about its enchantment. Its odd human-like face—Slavic eyes above the bear snout, a knowing smile on full lips—waited just behind the veil of her perception, ready to peek out as she fell asleep or when she gave her imagination over to idle thoughts. What did it want?

"What's that dirty piece of rubbish?" said Larissa, Vasily's lady friend, bustling into the office as though she owned it. Maybe she thought one day she would.

"The men found it at the building site," Rosa said.

"It needs a good scrub," Larissa sniffed, rubbing a well-manicured thumb over the bear's moldy belly. She strode through to Vasily's room, purple scarves and French perfume streaming in her wake.

"Maybe you do need a good scrub," Rosa said to the bear, picking it up and taking it into the kitchenette with her. She cleared a space between empty coffee cups and searched for a soft cloth, pausing for a moment to consider the bear.

Rosa's second sight was untrained, but she had learned over the years how to open it up and close it down at will; now she took a breath and opened it, feeling the rush of magic upon her eyes and ears. Pale vaporous ribbons snaked around the bear, and Rosa couldn't deny there was something sinister about them. She closed her second sight and used the cloth to gently rub away the dark stain of centuries. The bear was yellow-bright underneath. Rosa took it to the table.

Vasily came in as she sat down.

"It's a pretty thing," he said, falling into the chair opposite.

"That's a long face, Uncle Vasily."

"I broke it off with Larissa."

Rosa raised an eyebrow, feigning surprise. "Any reason?"

"It simply didn't feel right."

Rosa nodded. Vasily had never married, and Larissa was the latest in a long string of lady friends who seemed to last two months at most. Rosa's suspicion was that Vasily preferred the company of men, but he was the kind of man who would never admit such an inclination. It made Rosa sad to know the passing years might leave him lonely.

"When it feels right, Uncle Vasily, will you ask one to stay, no matter who it is?" she said.

"What a strange thing to say, Rosa. Of course I will." He smiled at her. For everyone else he had terrifying mood swings, but for her he always had smiles. "It was better to finish it now, before I go away."

"You're probably right, Uncle Vasily." Vasily was leaving for Moscow that afternoon for a business conference.

He touched her cheek. "You are so much like Ellena," he said softly.

Rosa couldn't meet his eye.

"Rosa, why won't you talk about your mother?"

"I can't, Vasily. It was so awful at the end."

"Then talk about the beginning, or the middle."

Tears brimmed and she swallowed hard. "You talk about her. What was she like when she was twenty-seven, like I am?"

"She was beautiful and clever, like you are. Her own mother had just died, and she met a handsome man named Petr Kovalenko. He had red hair and blue eyes."

Rosa smiled and looked up. "Go on," she said, although she knew the story.

"He was an architect and he dreamed of the West. We hated him for it, because he took our beautiful Ellena away, and their tiny girl named Rosa. They escaped to Prince Edward Island and lived in a misty valley and they were happy for a time. But all times pass."

Rosa nodded, thinking of her father's death when she was only eight. "They do."

"Now that tiny girl is here with me, and I worry about her."

"You don't need to worry about me, Uncle Vasily."

"When you find a nice young man to settle down with, I'll stop worrying."

"I found one, I let him go," she said. "I haven't much hope of finding another."

Vasily snorted. "All those boys you see. You have a new one every week! So many to choose from."

She dropped her head, not comfortable. "It's not serious, Uncle Vasily. They're just for fun."

"Fun?" Vasily's voice grew dark. "Not too much fun, I hope."

"I don't do anything you'd be ashamed of," she lied, "but they're not people to stay in my life, Uncle Vasily. They're not people to fall in love with."

He reached across and touched her hair. "You'll find somebody wonderful, Rosa," he said. "A girl as special as you need not worry."

At that moment, one of the draftsmen gingerly knocked at the door. Vasily turned with a snarl on his lips. "Is it important?"

"Vasily, we need you to approve these plans."

Vasily rose and took the plans from him, running a practiced eye over them. "Pah! These are not the right ones. Must I do everything myself?" Then he was gone in a thundercloud.

Rosa tapped her fingernails on the table in a rhythm. She sang a song under her breath and drove out thoughts of her mother. The bear smiled at her.

"You are a strange thing," she said, reaching for it and opening her second sight again. "Tell me something about you."

A chill prickle on her fingertips warned her to pull away, but she didn't.

"Go on," she said, "I'm not afraid of you."

Ice shot up her arm. The smell of blood and gunsmoke and visions of red splattered in dark places overwhelmed her. A series of agonizing jolts beat against her chest. Then, just as quickly, the feelings subsided. Yet something was left behind: a dark stain on her memory.

"Perhaps I am afraid of you after all," she murmured, and took the bear to hide it in her desk.

Rain sheeted across the road and the taillights of the car in front reflected off the slick asphalt. Em sighed for the fourteenth time and Daniel felt himself growing tense.

"Em?" he said.

A pale hand shot out in exasperation. "Look at this traffic! It would be quicker to walk."

Half an hour out of Novgorod and they'd come to a standstill.

"I'm sorry," he said.

She turned to him, a puzzled smile on her lips. "Daniel, it's not your fault."

Of course it wasn't, so why did he feel guilty? Because he was making her drive? Because he'd caused them to leave twenty minutes late by printing out pictures of nineteenth-century Russian artwork off the Internet to take with him? Or was it just because a dark-eyed woman with a cool smile was bound to make him uncomfortable? He determined to be rational and said, "I wonder what's causing this traffic jam?"

"It's probably an accident. Something must be blocking all the lanes. Here, pass me that map in the glove box."

Daniel did as she asked and gazed out the window. A car raced up beside them on the gravel shoulder and disappeared down a dirt side road.

"I think there's another way around," Em said. "I think that's where he's going."

"I'm sure the traffic will clear eventually."

She peered at him over the top of the map and raised an eyebrow. "Trust me, okay?"

She threw the map into his lap and, with a quick check behind her, wrenched the car onto the shoulder and down the dirt road. "This way we'll come out near Ljuban. It's further, but I'm sure it will be quicker."

Within a few minutes, they were traveling on a poorly maintained road dotted with potholes and crumbling at the edges. Stands of birch and larch whizzed past as the rain continued to fall, and the wipers on the big blue Ford kept a steady rhythm.

"See," she said, "the open road."

He laughed softly. "Sorry. I guess I'm a nervous driver."

"Nervous drivers are dangerous drivers," she replied, "and they always arrive late."

"Perhaps you're right."

"So, why are you going to St. Petersburg? What have you got planned?"

"I'm meeting with an old friend."

"Russian?"

"She is, yes. But she lived most of her life in Canada."

"And what does she do in St. Petersburg?"

"She works for her uncle, a developer. They found an old object while knocking down a wall, and she wants me to look at it for her. See if it's worth anything."

Em flicked the radio on and was silent for a long time. Daniel stared out the window and wished Em was chatty like Megan or Lesley, the other girls on the shoot.

They listened through two '80s rock ballads and then Em said, "She's an old flame, isn't she?"

Daniel looked around in surprise. "I'm sorry?"

"The woman you're seeing today. She's an old flame."

Daniel had to smile. "Yes, she is. How did you know?"

"I overheard some of the crew talking about you on the site this morning. Robert said you'd complained of girl troubles."

"They were talking about me?"

She waved a dismissive hand. "They talk about everybody. Those guys are worse than teenage girls."

"Rosa and I . . . knew each other, when she was living in London."

"Rosa. That's a pretty name. I always wanted a pretty name."

"Em's a pretty enough name," he said boldly. "What's it short for? Emily?"

She shook her head. "Nothing. It's just Em. No middle name, either. My mother used to tell me that they couldn't afford more than two letters."

Daniel laughed.

Em continued, "The worst part is, I was twenty-five before I found out that it wasn't true. I spent most of my life thinking you had to pay for the number of letters you used in a child's name."

"How did you find out differently?"

"I had a child of my own," she said guardedly.

"I didn't know you had a child," Daniel replied.

"Yes you did. Those gossips back in Novgorod must surely have mentioned it."

"Well, okay, they did. But I didn't know whether to believe them."

"I can imagine what else they told you. Yes, Daniel, I have a twelve-year-old son named Rubin. No, I don't live with him. He has a perfectly nice stepmom whom he adores, and his father is a professor of classics at Boston University."

"You must miss him."

She chose her answer carefully. "As long as he's well and safe, I'm comfortable."

Daniel didn't press the point. The rain came down heavier and he forced his hands to relax so they wouldn't ball up and reveal to Em how nervous he was about the speed she was using around corners.

"What did they say?" she asked. "Did they say I abandoned him?"

"I don't think anyone used that word."

"Some men don't live with their children, and nobody raises an eyebrow," she huffed. "For a woman, it's considered unnatural."

Daniel didn't know what to say, so said nothing.

"Maybe it *is* unnatural," she muttered, but he almost couldn't hear her over the windscreen wipers and, besides, he had no idea how to respond.

The trees flew past outside. Daniel sighed and tried to relax into his seat, turning his eyes to the road in front. The car rounded a sharp bend and, just a few hundred feet ahead of them in the gray mist, a truck had stalled in the middle of making a turn.

"Shit! Em!"

But she had already seen it, jamming on the brakes. The car began to slide. Daniel shouted and threw his hands over his eyes. The car spun. There was a dull thud, but no clash of metal on metal. His body jolted in the seat, but a moment later they were still. Daniel peered out from behind his hands to see they had come to rest in a ditch on the side of the road.

"Jesus!" he gasped.

"Always turn into a slide," Em said casually, putting the car into reverse. "Now, how are we going to get out of here?"

The truck driver had pulled his rig off the road and was running over to help them. Em wound down the window. The truck driver started speaking urgently in Russian, and Daniel found he couldn't focus through the pounding of his pulse to make sense of his words. Em, however, was managing fine. She discussed the situation with the truck driver confidently, if not grammatically precisely. Daniel gathered a few moments later, after some attempts to reverse the car out of the ditch, that their back wheels had become mired in the mud.

"I have some wood in the back of the truck," the driver said in Russian, and went off to fetch it.

Em turned to him. "Are you okay? You look pale."

Daniel assessed himself. His heart still thundered and his hands shook. The adrenalin was only now retreating through his veins, dragging its hot feet reluctantly.

Em peered closer. "Daniel?"

"I thought we were going to die," he managed.

She smiled, the puzzled expression returning. "But we didn't."

"We could have."

She clasped his fingers in her cool hands. He could feel her pulse in her wrists. Regular and calm.

"But, Daniel," she said, "we didn't. We're okay. We're just stuck in a ditch."

The truck driver was back. Em got out of the car in the rain and helped him to slant the planks of wood under the back tires. It took Daniel two minutes to realize that this was probably a man's job. He got out of the car to offer help.

"I'll do that, Em," he said, realizing he didn't sound convincingly masculine.

She looked up, her hair dripping. "I'm already wet, Daniel. You stay in the car. No use in both of us being uncomfortable."

But he couldn't arrive in St. Petersburg with Em soaked through and himself dry and warm, so he hovered nearby and offered help and translated difficult phrases for Em. She jumped in and out of the car, reversing in stages out of the mud. Fifteen minutes later they were on their way, both muddy and wet.

"Are you feeling better now?" Em asked as they pulled back onto the road. She switched the heater to high, and a blast of hot air fried his eyeballs.

"I guess so. I got a shock, that's all."

"Yes, you're right to feel shocked. I suppose we could have died."

"But we didn't," he said, echoing her words from earlier as a reassurance to himself.

"No, we didn't. There's nothing to be afraid of right now, so you don't have to look so pale." Em turned up the radio, and was lost in her thoughts all the way to St. Petersburg.

Three

Rosa was on the phone when Daniel and Em walked into her office late that afternoon. Daniel's clothes had partly dried, but clung to him uncomfortably. His pants, and Em's shoes and skirt, were splattered in mud. He couldn't have felt more unsightly in Rosa's presence, especially as she was as beautiful as ever. Her long black hair was loose about her shoulders, her ocean-blue eyes and white skin luminous. She gestured to them to sit in the overstuffed armchairs near the door. He sat down, but Em pushed her short dark hair behind her ears and remained standing while Rosa spoke in rapid Russian down the phone. Although she had been raised in Canada, she had spoken Russian at home right up until the day her mother died. Daniel found Russian the most beautiful of all languages to speak, gliding as it did between the back of the throat and the front of the mouth. To hear Rosa speak it was divine.

Finally, she hung up.

"Oh my God, what happened to you?" she said, emerging from behind her desk. She wore a black lace dress, red-and-black-striped tights, and a pair of lace-up stiletto boots: how Mary Poppins might dress were she in a porn flick.

Daniel rose and introduced Em. "Rosa, this is Em Hayward."

"Pleased to meet you."

"Likewise."

"We got bogged in the mud on the side of the road," Daniel explained.

"In the pouring rain," Em added.

Rosa went to her desk and began scribbling on a piece of paper. "You both need a warm shower and clean clothes. Here." She handed Daniel the piece of paper and a set of keys she found in a drawer. "This is the address for my uncle Vasily's place, where I'm staying at the moment. There's no one there. He's away in Moscow. Let yourselves in, make yourselves comfortable, borrow any clothes that fit."

"That's very kind of you," said Em.

"I'll join you shortly. I have to pack up the bear and organize somebody to answer the phones for me."

Then she was bustling them out the door, before he'd even had a chance to say, "You look wonderful. I'm so pleased to see you. Why did you leave me, anyway?"

Vasily's apartment was huge and immaculately clean. The sharp lines of blinds and angular furniture contrasted with the muted coffee and mulberry colors. Daniel closed the door behind them and placed the keys on the marble bench that ran between the kitchen and the living area.

"Which way to the bathroom?" Em asked.

"Don't know. I've never been here before," Daniel replied, tentatively peering behind doors. "This looks like Rosa's room."

Em pushed the door open and, without hesitation, crossed to the wardrobe and began selecting clothes.

Daniel was still opening doors. "Here's the bathroom."

Em edged ahead of him with an armful of Rosa's clothes. "Excuse me."

She closed the bathroom door behind her and Daniel hesitated near the door to Rosa's room. The wardrobe was still open, and he could see the sleeve of the red dress she had worn on their first date. He approached, gingerly pushing clothes on hangers aside to see if he could find the blue scarf he had bought her.

The door to the bathroom opened again, and Daniel jumped and backed away. Em stood in the doorway, still in her wet clothes. The hot water was running in the bathroom behind her, filling the room with steam.

"Have you found the towels?" she asked.

"No." He moved past her and tried another door. Vasily's room. The next one was the linen cupboard. He handed Em a towel and she disappeared. He grabbed one for himself then quickly showered in Vasily's ensuite. Expensive shampoos and body-scrubs were lined up on the windowsill, but he was too timid to use any. He agonized for a full two minutes about underwear—his own boxers were wet and it didn't feel right to borrow somebody else's—then decided to go without beneath an oversize pair of track pants and a blue buttoned shirt.

Rosa was knocking softly at the door to the apartment when he came out. He let her in.

"Hi," she said. "You found everything."

"You look wonderful," he said, unable to hold his tongue.

"So do you," she replied with an amused smile, "but I think you raided the fat end of Vasily's wardrobe. He has a thin end which he uses when he's off the vatrushki and vodka."

"I didn't want to go nosing around," he muttered, hoping she would never discover that he was free-balling under her uncle's clothes.

"Where's your friend?"

"Em? She's just a work colleague." Then he realized he hadn't answered the question and hooked a thumb in the direction of the bathroom. "She's in the shower. I found some clothes for her in your room. I hope you don't mind."

"Of course I don't mind. I asked you to come here and help yourselves, didn't I?" She dropped her car keys on the coffee table and went to the kitchen, carefully setting an old shopping bag on the bench. "Coffee?"

"Yes, please."

"Cigarette?"

"I'm trying to give up."

"It's for the best. Uncle Vasily doesn't like it when I smoke inside, anyway."

As she clattered about, Daniel leaned on the bench and admired her with sideways glances. He was amazed by the way she could arouse in him both devotion akin to worship, and desire akin to animalism: as though he wanted to build her a marble and gold altar and then fuck her senseless upon it.

She caught him looking at her and said, "What?"

"Are you happy here in St. Petersburg, then?" he asked.

She shrugged. "It's nice being with Uncle Vasily."

"You said, when you were leaving, that you hoped to find an adventure here."

"Did I?" she replied, laughing lightly. "That's a little dramatic, isn't it? I think I'd just spent too long in England."

"One year is too long?"

She smiled. "In England it is."

He took the joke with good humor. "So what kind of work are you doing with Vasily?"

"I'm a receptionist," she said, spooning coffee into the filter. "Nothing special."

"You're not teaching English, then?"

She shook her head; pointedly didn't meet his eyes. "No. Last time I taught, it ended badly."

Daniel bit his lip. She had lost her job teaching Russian when another student complained about her relationship with Daniel. He fell silent and she put the milk back in the stainless steel fridge, then he decided not to be silent.

"Rosa, I still don't really know why—"

Her hand shot out and her finger pressed against his lip. "No, Daniel. Let's just keep it light."

"I don't *feel* light."

Rosa opened her mouth to say something, but Em emerged from the bathroom wearing a loose blue dress, which was completely different from the well-fitted browns and grays she usually wore. Her feet were bare and she held her mud-stained shoes in her left hand.

"Sorry," she said, "am I interrupting something?"

Rosa came around the counter and greeted Em. "That suits you. You should keep it. I don't wear it anymore."

"That's kind of you," Em said, "but no."

"Would you like coffee?"

"I'm in need of retail therapy," Em said. "I won't stay."

"Your shoes . . ."

"It's fine. None of yours fit me. I have very small feet. I'll wear these and buy some new ones." She moved to the tiled area near the entrance and pulled her shoes on. "Thanks again. Is there a coat I can borrow for outside?"

"Take the one hanging there," Rosa said, pointing to her red coat on the rack. "I'll get your clothes washed and dried this afternoon."

"I'd appreciate that. And of course I'll pay you for your trouble."

"There's no need."

"I insist," Em said with a tight smile. "Daniel, I'll meet you back here in two or three hours. Is that okay with you?"

"Fine," said Daniel. "Enjoy your shopping."

The door clunked shut behind her and Daniel turned his attention back to Rosa. She finished making the coffees and slid one across the counter to him.

"What's wrong with Em?" she said.

"I don't think there's anything wrong with her."

"She's odd."

"Oh, you mean the silence. Like she's not really listening to you."

"No, there's something else." Rosa frowned as she sat on the stool opposite him. "Nothing sinister, don't misunderstand me. Perhaps it's unhappiness. Does she have a reason to be unhappy?"

Daniel shrugged. "I don't know. I don't know much about her. She's not with her kid, but she gives the impression that it doesn't bother her."

"Ah, well, never mind," said Rosa. "We're here to talk about the bear anyway." She reached for the plastic shopping bag. "I want you to give me your first impressions, okay? First impressions are important."

Daniel nodded, wondering what she meant. "Okay."

Rosa carefully unwrapped the bear and sat it on the bench in front of Daniel. It had the strangest expression on its face: a knowing smile that was almost unnerving, eyes closed as though it was thinking about a malicious pleasure.

"Well, it's not nineteenth-century," he said firmly. "Nothing about it, stylistically, suggests modern times. Or even medieval, given that Russian art has notoriously steered away from sculpture."

She tilted her head to consider him. "Is there a chance it's tourist junk?"

Daniel shook his head, reaching for the bear. "I don't think so—" As he touched the bear, a sharp buzz jumped onto his finger. He jerked his hand back, then felt like a fool; a baby frightened by a camera flash. He continued as if nothing had happened. "It's almost certainly gold. You see these scratches, this dent . . ." This time, no electricity. "Old gold is soft. And I can't see any machine marks which would suggest recent manufacture."

"How old?"

"It's hard to say. Bears were very popular with the early Slavs, though not usually this large or in this material. You see this design of arabesques . . . it's almost Byzantine, but the pattern within it . . ." he indicated with his finger, "that's a stylized antler pattern, which is definitely pagan. I don't know if I can give you a decisive answer."

"Go on, pretend you can. If you *had* to say something about it . . ."

"If I *had* to, I'd say this is southern, pre-Christian. Maybe something that came out of Kiev around the ninth or tenth century." Daniel's heart sped, afraid that he was overstating his certainty. "But I'm really not that sure. It's odd, Rosa. It's not typical of any time or place. So I could be out by hundreds of years."

She was quiet for a few moments as she sipped her coffee. "So how did it end up in a wall in a bathhouse?"

"I'd guess somebody hid it there. Bathhouses are supposed to be places of magic, and there was a brisk trade in grave antiquities in the nineteenth century."

"And what do you think the electricity was?"

He looked up. Her blue eyes met his steadily.

"Electricity?" he said.

"Daniel, I saw you pull your hand away. Did she give you a shock?"

"Perhaps static electricity," he said.

She huffed. "Of course it wasn't static electricity. I felt it too, the first time I touched her."

Daniel considered Rosa in the muted downlights of the apartment. He knew that Rosa believed in wild things, so he answered carefully. "What do you think it is?"

Rosa broke the gaze and slid off her seat. "I need a cigarette. Leave the bear here. Join me on the balcony."

Em crossed the road and was heading past the cemetery toward Nevsky Prospekt when a sly-looking old woman detached herself from the fence. A wide band of sunlight broke from the clouds and flushed through the new leaves on the birches behind the wrought iron. A spring breeze rattled branches. The woman approached Em purposefully, her pale eyes fixed on Rosa's red coat.

"I'll tell your fortune," she said in halting English.

"Do I look like a tourist?" Em replied.

"You look like the girl I met last night. She wore that coat," the woman said, slipping back into Russian.

"It's not my coat."

"But they are your shoes."

Em raised an eyebrow. "Nicely observed."

"Let me tell your fortune."

"I don't have time." Em brushed her aside and kept walking.

"What did you dream last night?" the woman called after her.

Em felt herself compelled to stop. There *had* been a dream. A strange dream, and now she remembered it she felt vulnerable and superstitious. She turned back, reached into her purse for a rouble, and handed it over. "Last night I dreamed of black wool," Em said. "Tangled, impossible to make straight."

"A dangerous and unpleasant journey awaits," the old woman said. The breeze intensified, flapping the corner of the woman's scarf. "You should beware of anything made of gold."

Em touched her gold watch unconsciously. "Thank you, now I must keep going."

The woman grasped Em's hand to make her stay, then pulled away quickly. "Oh my," the old woman said, her eyebrows shooting up and sending a thousand wrinkles charging toward her patchy hairline. "Oh, my. You're empty inside." She quickly spat three times and crossed herself.

Em grew irritated. "That which we are, we are," she said firmly, and strode off toward the expensive emporiums of the main street, relishing the thought of new shoes.

"There are rules," said Rosa, offering Daniel a cigarette. He took it tentatively and she turned to survey the view from Uncle Vasily's small square balcony. The shadowy groves of the cemetery, the domed necropolis and the River Neva slithering silver behind it, Aleksandr Nevsky Bridge pale in the haze. The morning's rain had ceased and a sticky humidity had set in. The kiss of spring took the chill edge off the air. Even here, eleven stories up, Rosa could smell the exhaust fumes of the traffic below.

"So what are the rules?" Daniel said after the silence had drawn out two minutes or more.

She turned to him, putting her back to the view. "We don't talk about *us*. We talk about you and we talk about me, and we talk about everything but *us* because *us* is six months ago. Okay?"

Daniel feigned a nonchalance she knew he didn't feel. "Okay."

"Good," she said, exhaling a stream of smoke. She jammed her cigarette between her lips, put her hands behind her and heaved herself up on the balcony railing.

"God, Rosa, don't do that," he said, jumping out of his seat.

She sat very still, getting her balance, then took her hands off the railing and waved them about.

"Come down," he said.

"You wouldn't be worried if we were on the ground floor." Giddiness flooded in as she imagined the drop behind her; a thrill of danger that was almost sexual slipped up her spine.

Daniel sat down again, putting his hands over his eyes. "I'm not watching."

"I'm leaning back," she teased.

"I'm not watching."

Foiled, she jumped down. "Okay, you win."

Daniel peeked between his fingers then removed his hands. "I forgot about your stunts."

"I didn't do many stunts in London."

"Climbing that tree in Hyde Park?"

"I was perfectly safe."

"You shimmied out on that tiny branch. I thought it was going to break and you were up twelve or fifteen feet."

"Fifteen," she said. "At least."

His voice softened. "You ruined what was meant to be a romantic evening."

Rosa turned away from him, gazing down toward the street. In amongst the bustling stream of people, she spotted a couple, arms around each other as though closing out the world. Love as a shield against chaos. That could have been her and Daniel, if she'd had a mind to allow it.

Rosa's first impression of Daniel was straightforward: a soft-spoken pretty boy with charcoal eyes and smooth skin. She watched him, he watched her, and if the rest of the class was aware of the smoldering tension between them, nobody mentioned it. Slowly, he began to distinguish himself in other ways. He was brilliant, he was passionate about Russian, which he spoke with glorious ease, he was funny with his self-deprecating humor. She found herself thinking a lot about him when he wasn't around. Little things would get caught on repeat play in her mind's eye: the way he rubbed his knuckles gently across his bottom lip while thinking, the almost-girlish tilt of his head when he was taking notes. She realized she was falling for him, and had thought the best way to get him out of her system was to date him, sleep with him, then discard him.

Things hadn't gone quite according to plan.

Once alone together, with time to talk, she had been pulled further into the vortex of feelings. He was clever, wise, but most appealing of all, damaged. He had been bullied relentlessly by his father and brothers, but somehow he had a strong-enough moral compass to remain a compassionate person. Rosa was fascinated by this, aroused on a level far, far more profound than the flesh, and soon realized that this one-off date was a very dangerous prospect: she was in too deep. Sleeping with him had compounded the problem, intensified the connection. Before she knew what was happening to her, she had succumbed to mad love, the kind that teenagers feel, the kind that poets try to capture in fourteen lines. But love was not for her, forever was not for her, it couldn't be. To preserve them both, she had broken it off after only a few weeks.

Rosa butted her cigarette and dropped it over the balcony railing. He had contravened the talking about "us" rule, so she ignored him.

The butt spun away toward earth. "Oh, yeah, it is a long way down. I wonder what it would feel like to fall that far."

"You've been skydiving. You know what it feels like."

"To fall that far without a parachute," she said. "I wonder what it feels like to hit the ground."

He was quiet and she let the quiet draw out between them. Buses roared, car alarms squealed, trains thundered underground. The clouds moved back in and began to spit lightly. She sat next to Daniel under the awning and picked up her coffee. It was cold.

"How's work?" she asked.

"It's okay," he said, nodding slowly. "It's a job."

"What's the program called?"

"*Great Medieval Cities.*"

"Interesting. What other cities are you doing?"

"I'm only working on Novgorod. They've done Istanbul and Rome and . . . some other places, I've forgotten. They wind up in London in winter, I think. But I won't be around then."

"What are you going to do instead?"

He leaned back in his chair and wouldn't meet her eye. "I've been offered a job researching for language videos. There's travel involved, and it could be ongoing."

"That sounds good."

"Do you think so?"

"Don't you?"

"It would take up a lot of time. I wouldn't be able to finish my thesis. Or my other projects."

Rosa considered him as the rain grew heavier and bounced off the awning. His dark unruly curls, his serious eyebrows, his bitten fingernails pressed against his soft lips. She knew how warm those lips were and reminded herself to stay cool. He turned his gaze to her and she smiled. "Daniel, you aren't finishing those things anyway."

"But I might."

"Might you?"

"Well, not if I take the job." Then he sighed and shook his head.

"You're right, you're right. I haven't worked on my thesis in a year and as for the novels and the screenplay . . ."

She recognized the tone of self-irritation in his voice. "Be nice, Daniel."

"I'm so—"

"Kind," she offered quickly. "Patient, passionate."

"Indecisive," he said. "Dithering, a non-starter."

Rosa shook her head.

"It's true," he said.

"Well, decide on something then," she said. "Take the job."

"I don't know . . ."

She sighed theatrically and spread her hands out. "Then I can't help you. But, you know, Uncle Vasily has a collection of gorgeous red wines. You want some? We could put on a load of laundry and drink out here in the rain until Em returns."

"That sounds great."

For the next hour they drank wine and filled each other in on the last six months: he carefully weighing his questions to probe her about her sex life, she carefully hiding all evidence of its vigor and frequency: tinkers, tailors, soldiers, builders, wait staff, pastry chefs, three ballet academy graduates on an end-of-term drinking binge, and a couple of adventurous American college girls in the park late one Sunday. Rosa gathered Daniel hadn't seen anyone else since they split, which was a pity. The quicker he was over her, the easier she would find it to let him go. As matters stood, the temptation always existed that she could tell him everything, reveal all those hidden truths, and be vulnerable to his conviction that any obstacle could be overcome.

When the day's light had bled from the sky and all the street-lights below had flickered into life and the rain had set in heavily once again, they moved inside to put the clothes in the dryer, then returned their attention to the bear.

"So what should I tell Vasily?" she asked, positioning the bear directly in the beam of a downlight over the kitchen bench. It took on a haze that looked almost holy.

"I don't know, Rosa. I'm not the expert you want me to be. Tell him to take it to a museum."

"He won't." She slumped forward on the bench, her head resting on her arm as she considered the bear.

"You can tell him it's gold."

"Yeah, and he'll want to melt it down and make cufflinks."

"Don't let him do that."

She ran a finger over the curved belly of the bear. "I feel drawn to her," she said softly. "I feel she's important."

"Because she zapped you?"

"Maybe. Or maybe because I feel sorry for her. Poor thing, shoved in a hole with her butt in the air for a hundred and fifty years. It isn't very dignified."

A knock at the door. "That will be your ride home," Rosa said in what she hoped was a light tone. "Can you let her in?"

Daniel opened the door for Em, who clutched at least a dozen bags in her hands.

"Wow," said Rosa. "You're serious about your shopping."

"And I'm wet again," Em said, dropping her bags. "The rain got heavy just as I started back."

Rosa helped her with her coat. "You want another shower?"

"No, just a towel this time. Your coat kept most of it out." She shrugged out of the coat and Rosa hung it by the door.

Em nodded at the bear on the bench. "Is that it? This mysterious artifact Daniel spoke of?"

"That's it," Rosa said from the hallway where she was fetching a towel.

"Ouch."

Rosa hurried back. Em was sucking her middle finger and Daniel was gazing at her, astonished.

"It zapped you," Rosa said.

"It certainly did."

Rosa paused to think. First herself, then Daniel, then Em. But not Vasily; not Larissa; not, to her knowledge, any of the men at the site. "Why you?" she said under her breath, but Em caught it.

"What do you mean?"

"She's marked all three of us."

"Marked us?" Em was beginning to look skeptical and Daniel embarrassed, so Rosa shrugged it off.

"I'm full of silly old wives' tales. Ask Daniel," she said, handing Em the towel.

"No, no. Don't be dismissive. Is there another explanation for the electricity? Daniel?"

Daniel turned his palms up. "I've no idea."

Em smiled. "Perhaps she has marked us then. Thank you for the towel, Rosa. Did Daniel manage to deduce where and when your bear was created?"

"Not really," said Daniel. "I have a ballpark figure, but I'm not particularly confident about it. It really needs to go to a museum."

"But my uncle won't hear of it," Rosa added quickly.

"A museum would have the right experts and the right equipment," Daniel said.

"Vasily's afraid the government will take it from him, and it might be worth a lot of money."

"How about a compromise," suggested Em. "Daniel, what's the name of that professor we're going to see at the end of the month?"

"Professor Gergiev, at Pomor University in Arkhangelsk." Daniel turned to Rosa. "He was my Masters supervisor for a little while, back in England."

"He'd know, wouldn't he?" Em said. "And he's at a university . . . they might have equipment to analyze the metal. If there are traces of other materials in it, they might suggest a provenance. Might also suggest the reason for the zap. It would make good television."

"Wait, wait," said Rosa. "Uncle Vasily won't let you take this to Arkhangelsk."

"It's for an English television show. It'll probably never be screened in Russia. He won't know."

"He'll know if the bear isn't around."

"How long is he away for?"

"Ten days."

"What if we can get it there and back within ten days?" Em

asked, picking up the bear and examining the pattern around its belly closely.

Rosa was puzzled by this woman. She was charming and affable on the surface, but there was an unyielding quality to her. As though she hadn't heard any of Rosa's protests.

"Sorry," Em said, after the silence had drawn out a few moments too long, "am I being pushy?"

Rosa laughed. "Yes. You are."

Em tilted her head on the side and met Rosa's eyes directly. "You just said she marked us. The three of us. Perhaps that's why."

Daniel found his tongue. "Come on, let's not be superstitious."

Rosa was struck by Em's logic. "No, no. Em is right, Daniel. Perhaps the bear wants to go to Arkhangelsk. Perhaps she wants us, at least one of us. If that's so, we should honor her feelings." She held up a finger. "But she must be back before Vasily returns. He has a temper like a storm at sea."

"You have my word," Em said. "I'll get on the phone to the producer tonight, I'll organize everything. We'll fly up—"

"I don't fly," Daniel murmured, almost inaudibly.

Em fought with her exasperation. "Then you can stay here."

"Em, I'm sorry. I barely know you, you can't take her alone," Rosa said.

"It's two days' drive," Em said. "Can't *you* come instead?"

"I have work here. Uncle Vasily is away. I must stay."

"Okay, then we'll drive. Daniel, *I'll* drive. I'll organize the crew to meet us up there. Does that satisfy everyone?"

Daniel nodded, Rosa nodded.

"Does it satisfy you, Em?" Rosa asked.

Em placed the bear gently on the bench. "Oh yes," she said. "I'm easily satisfied."

"Take her then," Rosa said, and she felt as though she had waded into a current tugging her onto some new and mysterious bearing. "But God help us all if Vasily finds out."

Four

Em woke in a dark and unfamiliar place. A few seconds passed before she remembered that she was still in St. Petersburg, in Rosa's uncle's apartment. She and Daniel had decided to stay to avoid the round trip back to Novgorod. The crew were sending their bags up to Arkhangelsk. Em rolled over and turned on the lamp to check her watch. Three A.M. What had woken her so deep in the night? She sat up and listened as far as she could into the dark, but everything was perfectly quiet. Then she realized it had been a dream that woke her. That same dream she had told the fortune-teller about: suffocating black wool, snarled impossibly. She could feel the texture of the wool tangled at her fingertips still, and it made her shiver.

Em switched off the light but didn't want to go back to sleep. Like anyone, she had her share of nightmares, and some were far more awful than this, but this dream stayed with her. She tossed back the covers and went to open the window. Fresh cold air poured in. Em liked few things better than fresh cold air.

She took a deep breath and gazed down at the sleeping city. The rain had withdrawn and a young couple out walking had paused at the gate of the cemetery for a quick grope. Em watched them with a detached sadness. Seeing young lovers always aroused in her a feeling that something to which she was entitled had been given to somebody else. The cold air was making her nose run, so she closed the window and went to her shopping bags. Working by the dim pool of lamplight, she organized her purchases into shoes, underwear, accessories and dresses, then folded them on the end of the bed.

Soft footsteps in the hall alerted her that somebody else was awake. She cracked open her door and peered out. Rosa, in a thick blue dressing gown, had switched on the kitchen lights. The bear gleamed yellow-gold on the bench. Em could hear the coffee machine spring to life.

Coffee.

Em found herself slipping down the hallway into the living area. "Hi," she said softly.

Rosa jumped, and turned, hand over her heart. "Oh! Hi, Em."

"Didn't mean to give you a fright."

"It's okay. Couldn't you sleep?"

Em shook her head. She could always sleep. She'd never had a moment of insomnia in her life. "Something woke me, and then I heard the coffee machine."

"I couldn't sleep, and this won't help." She held up the coffee cup. "Do you want one?"

"I'd love one." She eased herself onto a stool at the bench, yawning.

Rosa made coffee wordlessly. The living room was dark and the coffee machine was loud in the night-time silence. Em checked her watch again. Nearly four. She wouldn't be going back to sleep, she had too much to organize before they started the drive to Arkhangelsk. She still held hopes that Aaron could persuade Professor Gergiev to come to Novgorod early instead. Two days was a long time to spend in a rented car, especially when the steering had been soft since she'd driven out of the ditch on the way from Novgorod. Not that she'd tell Daniel; he was already afraid of his own shadow.

Rosa handed Em a steaming cup of coffee and she took a grateful sip.

"Wow," she said to Rosa, who was settling opposite her, "you make good coffee."

"I think you can always be good at something you care about," Rosa said.

Em reached for the bear and ran her fingers over the arabesque design. "So, why couldn't you sleep?" she asked.

"I was worrying."

"About the bear?"

"Yes."

Em touched the bear's closed eyes. "She's sleeping soundly, though."

"Is she sleeping? Or is she thinking about something?"

"I don't know." Em considered the bear's face. "What would she think about?"

"Something that makes her smile. Her trip to Arkhangelsk maybe."

"The bear will be perfectly safe, I promise," Em said.

Rosa hesitated, seemed about to say something, then stopped herself.

"Go on," Em said. "Say what you want to say."

"Yesterday afternoon, we talked about the psychic zap that all three of us felt from the bear."

"Yes."

"You didn't question me on it. You weren't surprised or cynical. You even said it was a good reason for me to allow you to go to Arkhangelsk with her."

"That's right."

"Were you serious? Do you really believe that? Or did you think it was a good way to get me to agree?"

Em was taken aback, and had to remind herself that people often read her completely differently than her intentions. "No, no. I wasn't using your beliefs to manipulate you," she said.

"So do you believe?"

"Believe in what?" Em said carefully.

"In enchantment."

"You think the bear is enchanted?"

"I'm certain she is," Rosa said, her voice dropping to a whisper. "Perfectly certain."

"I neither believe nor disbelieve," Em said. "But I do want to take the bear to Arkhangelsk."

"Why?"

"Because it would make good television. I'm very serious about what I do, Rosa. I assure you I have no sinister intentions."

Rosa raised a carefully shaped eyebrow and directed a glance toward the bear. "*She* might."

"Might she?"

"I'm not altogether sure that she's benign. Daniel thinks I'm full of superstition, but his dismissiveness makes him vulnerable."

Em watched Rosa for a few long moments, trying to assess her.

Rosa laughed. "You've been quiet a long time," she said. "You make me want to talk to fill the silence."

"It's not deliberate. I'm sorry."

"Em, if you believe, even a little bit, that the bear is enchanted . . ."

"I do believe a little bit," Em allowed. "Many unusual things happen. Many things aren't as they seem."

"Then you have to take care, for both yourself and Daniel. Do you understand?"

Em nodded. It was a reasonable request. "Is there anything I should do?"

"Just . . . be aware. That's all." Rosa shifted in her seat and brushed a strand of black hair off her face. "A bear is a powerful and dangerous creature. We don't have a real word for it in Russian. To say its true name is taboo. Instead we use *medved*, which means honey-eater. A figurative word."

Em nodded. "I'll take good care of the bear." She smiled. "And the boy."

"Ah. The boy." Rosa shook her head. "I don't want to talk about the boy."

Em took her at her word and said nothing further.

"Tell me, Em," Rosa said. "What woke you?"

Em sipped her coffee thoughtfully. "I had a nightmare."

"Did it frighten you?"

Frightened. Em pondered the word. The ticking of the clock seemed to slow, as though it was as early-morning tired as she was. "It made me feel very uncomfortable," she said carefully, "but not frightened. It was only a dream after all."

Rosa drained her coffee cup and stood. "Are you going back to bed?"

"No. I might do some work." She indicated her briefcase, which leaned against the coffee table. "I wanted to be up by six anyway."

"I'll see you when the sun rises then."

The builders were arriving when Rosa let herself into the bathhouse early in the morning. Jamie, the American foreman, looked up from his paperwork.

"Miss Kovalenka, we weren't expecting you."

"I wanted to speak to the builders," Rosa said, finding herself idly admiring Jamie's strong, tanned wrists. How had it escaped her notice that he was so good-looking? She found his eyes and a spark of interest jumped from her to him. She shook herself, told herself to concentrate, and said, "I wanted to know if anybody touched the bear before I arrived."

Jamie looked puzzled, but Rosa didn't know if it was her sexual attention or her question about the bear that had confused him. "I did," he said, "and two of the Russians, Leon and Kolya."

"Nobody else?"

"No."

Rosa bit her lip, deciding how to word her next question. The spotlights flared into life, sending shadows cowering into corners. "Jamie, did you feel anything odd when you touched her?"

"Anything . . . odd?"

"In your fingers. Like electricity, or a shiver."

He shook his head slowly. "No."

"Are you certain? It might have felt like she was very cold, or very hot."

"I'm absolutely certain," he said. "Why?"

She waved him away. "Oh, it's nothing. Just a silly theory I have. I'll ask the others," she said.

She found Leon and Kolya and put the same question to them. They both said no, but Rosa noticed that Kolya wouldn't meet her eye. As the building site came to life, she took him aside into a dark corner at the back of the bathhouse. Here the tiles were moldy and the smell of damp centuries was heavy. She sat on the old wooden bench still attached to the wall and invited him to do the same. He was a heavy man with dirty brown hair, and Rosa suspected he might be superstitious.

"You promise me to tell the truth?" she said.

He shrugged, still not meeting her eye. "Of course."

"The bear, Kolya. Did she mark you?"

"I don't like the way you talk, Rosa Petrovna."

"Are you afraid of enchantments?"

"This is a bad place, and anything found here cannot be good."

"Did you feel something when you touched her?" Rosa asked again. "Honestly now, tell me the truth."

He sighed, jiggled his feet nervously, then finally lifted his gaze to hers. "Honestly, no, I felt nothing. I didn't know what I was touching at first. Then I saw it was a bear and I was afraid. When you came along and said she was enchanted, I knew it was very bad magic."

Rosa fought an uneasy feeling. "Why so?"

Kolya gestured around him. "A bathhouse is where sorcerers practice."

"Not anymore."

"Their magic stays in the walls." He dropped his voice to a whisper. "Some of the men say the devil himself practiced here."

"The devil?"

"The mad monk."

"Grigory Rasputin?"

Kolya nodded quickly, superstitious about the name of the famous mystic being spoken.

"He was a man, Kolya, not a devil."

"They had some trouble killing him as I understand."

"But in the end they did kill him." Rosa infused her voice with a kind tone. "If you aren't happy working in this place—"

"No, no, I am happy to work," Kolya said, and the desperation in his voice almost pained her. Vasily was rich, but so many were poor; despite his fears, Kolya came to work in the bathhouse every day. Rosa supposed that the alternative was letting his children go without new shoes for their growing feet this winter.

"You're a good man, Kolya," Rosa said gently, pulling two hundred roubles from her purse and pressing it into his hand. "Vasily rewards you for your honesty."

"Thank you, Rosa Petrovna," he said, his pride stopping him from meeting her eyes as he jammed the money into his pockets. "Beware of enchantments."

"I will." But what about Daniel and Em? Could she trust Em to take her warnings seriously? Perhaps she should forbid them from going.

And yet, the bear wanted to go. It was clear that not a single other person had felt the mark of enchantment. Rosa didn't know how the three of them figured in the bear's plans, but they all belonged in the puzzle somehow. Maybe Kolya's superstitions about bad magic were unfounded. Maybe the bear dealt in blessings, not curses. Maybe an adventure awaited them all.

An adventure to burn bright in her memory.

She was outside walking up the street on her way to the office when Jamie caught up with her.

"Miss Kovalenka. Rosa," he said, carefully taking her wrist. His fingers lingered seconds too long, and Rosa felt the promise to return in their withdrawal.

"Yes, Jamie?" she said, trying to be cool but knowing it was too late. The familiar hot signals were already passing between them.

"Did you find out what you needed to know?"

"Yes, thank you. I did."

"If there's any way I can be of service . . ."

Her moment of interest had made him bold. The flutter of adrenalin had started within her and she knew that, if she allowed it, within a week she'd be fucking him in the bathhouse after hours. The thought inflamed her imagination, and a tide of warm blood washed into her.

Then she stopped herself. Was this really about Jamie, to whom she had paid scant attention in the six months he'd been working for Vasily? Or was this about Daniel and the feelings seeing him had awoken in her: desire, regret, despair, anger? Jamie was Vasily's employee; she had to be more cautious.

"Best not to offer me your service," she said softly. "I wouldn't treat you kindly."

He smiled uncertainly. "I don't believe that."

She wanted to explain to him. She wanted to say, "I'm a collector, Jamie. I collect vivid memories. I collect intense sensations.

Often it's selfish, sometimes it's cruel." But any explanation would bind her tighter into his imagination. Instead, she stepped away from him, hands up. "Sorry," she said, and she walked to the office without looking back.

Daniel kept telling himself that all this social anxiety would be character-building. He sat uselessly on Vasily's couch while Em made phone call after phone call. She was trying to avoid a two-day car trip to Arkhangelsk, but Professor Gergiev was in no mood to leave the university.

"That's it," she said with a sigh, hanging up the phone. "Gergiev says he can't take time out this close to the end of term to travel to Novgorod. So the mountain has to go to Mohammed."

He jumped up to follow her as she bustled down the hallway. "Aaron's okay with this?"

"Not as okay as I'd like him to be, and we're only getting a mini-crew." She flicked them off on her fingers. "Two cameras, one sound, no lights . . . pray for fine weather so we can do our interviews outside."

"What if we need to film in the archaeology lab?"

"Aaron says we can hire lights if we have to." She was packing her newly purchased clothes into a suitcase Rosa had loaned her.

Daniel paused at the door to the room. "So we're off to Arkhangelsk today then?"

Em nodded. "Timing's everything, right? We can't have your Russian princess getting eaten by the ogre she calls Uncle Vasily." She stopped what she was doing for a moment and fixed her gaze on him. "Daniel, one last time . . . are you sure you won't fly?"

Daniel felt like a beetle on a pin. His stomach twitched with embarrassment and self-loathing. Two days trapped in a car with Em, who was obviously annoyed with him for making her drive that far. The thought of letting Rosa down was worse. But neither of these things could persuade him to fly.

"Don't answer," Em said. "Your face says it all. I'm sorry, I should leave you alone. I don't understand, but I won't judge."

"I'm really sorry, Em."

"It's okay." She returned to her packing. "If it weren't for you, we wouldn't have this fabulous lead to follow in the first place."

"So the others are flying up?"

"Yes, this morning. They've got a suitcase for me and a suitcase for you. We're overnighting in Vologda tonight, so borrow some more of Vasily's clothes, and see if he has an overcoat. We might have to go out for food."

"Okay," Daniel said. "You've thought of everything."

"We'll get going around ten. I'll take you past Rosa's office on the way and you can drop in her keys and say good-bye."

"Thanks." *Good-bye.* He supposed he'd see her again when they returned the bear and all the borrowed clothes, but he had to accept that Rosa would be out of his life again soon. An empty dimness crowded in on him.

Em paused in her packing. "She's really nice."

"Yes."

"You still love her?"

He felt himself blush. "I don't know."

"Why did you break up?"

He had to laugh at himself. "I don't know. She's never told me."

Em returned to zipping up her suitcase. "Sometimes people change," she said. "Sometimes they don't feel the same things as each other."

Daniel had once been certain that Rosa felt the same for him as he did for her, and her tenderness and kindness toward him since he'd arrived in St. Petersburg suggested she still felt the same way. So why had she left him? If she could look him in the eye and tell him she didn't love him, then he might have a chance of moving on. But she was mysterious and refused to talk about it. That was why it was so painful. That was why it was impossible to give her up.

Now, intimidated and bossed around by Em, about to take off on a round trip of more than a thousand miles for Rosa, Daniel grew angry. He was doing so much for her; the least she could do for him was answer him directly.

Daniel had long since given up wishing that he could be a different kind of man. He had been born with a feeling heart, and his father's tyranny had not been able to change him, it had only been able to frighten him. But sometimes he wished he could at least *pretend* to be all those things that men were meant to be: strong, brave, ruled by thought instead of emotion. Surely then he would be able to make Rosa come back to him. Even as he had this thought, as the memory of her soft skin and fierce eyes rocketed through his senses, he could feel his own damnable weakness again.

As he packed his things and got in the car with Em, through traffic and right up to the door of Rosa's office where he left Em waiting outside, he rehearsed the demand over and over in his head: "No excuses, no deferrals, Rosa. Tell me why you left me." In his imagination, he sounded forthright and commanding. In reality, with her dewdrop beauty there to unnerve him, the question sounded petulant and shrill.

"Daniel," she said, as she pocketed the keys. "I've said I won't discuss it. Now have a safe trip and—"

"That isn't fair!" he said. "You know it isn't fair."

Rosa held a finger to her lips. "Everyone can hear you."

"I don't care if they can hear me," he said, dropping his voice to a whisper because he actually cared very much. "You can't keep fobbing me off like this. If you just said that you didn't love me—"

"Come on, let's go to Vasily's office," she said quickly, ushering him ahead of her.

When the door was safely shut behind them, she turned to him and said, "Daniel, why are you doing this? I thought we agreed to keep it light, not to talk about the past."

"No, I never agreed to it. Those were your rules, not mine."

Her face flushed and he wondered if she was angry or embarrassed. "We split up more than six months ago, Daniel. You have to let it go."

"I can't. And the reason I can't is that you've never told me why."

"It wasn't working. I told you that."

Daniel paused. She sounded so matter-of-fact, so reasonable. Perhaps it hadn't been working; perhaps he had missed important signals and the whole love affair had taken place in his head. "I thought it *was* working," he said hesitantly.

Her body softened and she fixed him with her expressive blue eyes. "I don't want to make you doubt yourself, Daniel. Not any more than you already do."

"Then swear on your life that you don't love me, and I'll let it go."

She gave a derisive laugh and looked away. "Swear on my life? That's hardly valuable enough to swear on."

Daniel took a deep breath. "Swear on the golden bear. You think she's enchanted. Swear on all her enchantments, on all her blessings and curses, that you don't love me."

Rosa grew irritated and Daniel saw her hands involuntarily make a little cross. "*Ne sglazi*, Daniel. It's dangerous to say such things."

"Not if you tell the truth."

"I won't play this game."

"Tell me and I'll let you go."

"You have to let me go anyway. You have no choice." She strode to the door and held it open for him. "I won't talk about it another moment. Just go."

"Rosa, this isn't fair. I'm like a prisoner."

"It's a prison of your own making. It's over between us and has been for some time."

"Just tell me why."

A man in a hard hat holding a set of plans peered around the corner, alerted by the raised voices.

"Miss Kovalenka? Is everything all right?"

"Yes, Jamie. Daniel was just leaving."

"Do you want me to show him out?" Jamie said, his booming American voice infused with a male competitive tone so acute that Daniel was reminded of bulls in a paddock bellowing at each other over a prize cow. Daniel looked from Rosa to Jamie and wondered if they'd slept together. A bolt of intense jealousy speared into him. He calmed his breath and put his hands in the air.

"I'm going," he said. "Good-bye." He left without another glance, blood rushing past his ears, the back of his neck tingling with angry electricity.

Em was waiting. She started the car as he got in.

"You took your time," she said impatiently.

Daniel slumped into his seat, no energy left for conflict. "I'm sorry."

She had put the indicator on and was about to pull out when Rosa appeared and hammered on the window.

"Wait," Daniel said to Em.

Em sighed and knocked the car back out of gear. Daniel wound the window down.

"Daniel," Rosa said, and her eyes were glassy but she wasn't crying. "Did you mean it? Will you let me go if I tell you?"

"Yes. Yes I will."

"Do you swear? No matter what I tell you, do you swear not to pursue me? Swear on your life? Swear on *my* life?"

A sensation of dread crept over him. He had unwittingly waded into something darker and deeper than he imagined existed. His heart began to pound. A crowded tram rattled past.

"I'm sorry," Em interrupted, "but we really don't have time for this."

"She's right," Rosa said. "It's a long story, Daniel, and I want everything to be right when I tell you. But if you promise to stand by your oath, I'll tell you everything when you get back."

Daniel was at once excited and bereft. "Yes, all right. If that's how you want to play the game."

"It's not a game," Rosa said, her face serious. "It's never been a game." She kissed her palm and held it up. "Good-bye. Keep each other safe. Mind the bear." She indicated the backseat where Daniel, as a joke, had tucked the bear into a seatbelt like a passenger.

Em put the car into gear. "We'll see you at the end of next week, Rosa," she said. "If you need us in Arkhangelsk, we're staying at Hotel Pamyat near the university."

The car pulled out, cold air rushed through the open window, and Daniel watched Rosa in the rearview mirror until she disappeared from sight.

Five

Five hours out of St. Petersburg, Em was concerned about the car. The steering had felt loose and wobbly since their near-miss with the truck on the way from Novgorod, but the problem was worsening. Speeding around a tight bend, the steering dropped out altogether momentarily, threatening to send them into nearby trees. Then it engaged again, and she was back on track. The adrenalin burst was over as quickly as it had come.

Daniel snapped his attention to her. He must have noticed. "Is everything okay?" he said.

"Yeah," she replied. "Just took the corner too quickly." She deliberately slowed, aware of how the car steered around the next bend. Soft, but still there. Given they had hundreds of miles yet to travel, Em decided they would be better off changing cars in Vologda. In the meantime, two things were important: drive carefully, and don't let Daniel know how carefully.

"Sorry I'm such a nervous passenger," he was saying. "I hope it doesn't put you off."

"Not at all. In fact, it's quite rational to be afraid of driving. Many people die in cars." Em wondered if this might be the wrong thing to say, and tried to fix it with a light teasing tone. "Much less safe than airplanes."

Daniel mumbled something about fear of flying being very common. Em couldn't hear him clearly over the radio. They had been listening to it for hours, chasing stations across the dial as distance made them drop out and drop in. Now they were on a local news channel, which was helping Em build her Russian vocabulary. Words found their way into her head, lodged there and began to resonate with meaning. A few she asked Daniel about, but many she could deduce from context. The grammatical aspects were becoming clearer now too. The language was seeping into her consciousness: not a word at a time as teachers taught it, but rather like a symphony, where all the elements made sense only in relation to each other.

Em turned the radio down and said, "What did you say? I couldn't hear you over the radio."

"I said that fear of flying is extremely common, but people always treat me as though I'm really odd for being afraid."

"It's common, but most people fly anyway," Em said. The trees racing past in turn obscured and revealed the sun, casting flickering shadows in the car.

"Then they're not really afraid."

"I expect it's all about probability. Plane crashes are rare."

"But they do happen. You can't deny that people do die in plane crashes."

Em shrugged. "I suppose so. So you've never flown?"

"Oh, yes, I've flown."

"You weren't always afraid to?"

"It's a long story."

Em indicated the road ahead of her, the miles of coniferous woodland around them. "It's a long trip."

"I used to get on planes, the same as anybody. I loved to travel. My family was . . . it wasn't ever a pleasant situation. . . . I loved to get away." He took on the serious countenance of an old storyteller, working through some trauma by telling it over and over again. "A few years ago, I was backpacking around southeast Asia. I'd heard about a job in Los Angeles, so I booked a fare in Taipei. I got to the airport way too early, the rain blew in. Never seen so much of it, a deluge." He smiled grimly. "Everyone was uneasy getting on the plane. It wasn't just me." He lifted his hands apart, make-believe wings that landed in his lap a second later. "Anyway, we're taxiing along the runway, the wind is buffeting the wings, everyone's getting more and more nervous. There was an elderly woman sitting next to me, by the window. She told me she hated flying, and I . . . I told her everything would be okay." He shook his head. "The flight attendants were still chatting in low voices, strapping themselves in for takeoff. Then the plane left the ground and twenty seconds later—" He paused, his breath caught in his throat.

"What happened?"

"I don't know. There was a tremendous noise . . . I remember that. But there's a black space in my memory then. When the memories start again, it's all fire and smoke and screaming. Hysteria. Chaos. I glanced over to the woman next to me, I still don't know if she was alive or dead. I unbuckled my seatbelt and just ran. Madly, bumping into things, pushing at people. Some were running in the other direction. Everybody operating on instinct, nobody thinking straight. The heat, the sound of the flames . . . then I was outside. Only a handful of us got out."

She took some time to process this. "A lucky escape."

"It was a nightmare."

"But you're all right now."

"I don't think I am. If I have to go to an airport, even to drop somebody off, I get wound up. The smells and sounds, the hum of the air-conditioning." His voice became constricted and his words fell over each other. "It's a torture. The idea of getting back on a plane, that weightless feeling on takeoff . . . it makes me ill." He laughed self-consciously. "I'm getting edgy just talking about it."

"I can hear that. But you know, fear's not very productive," she said. "It makes people unnecessarily vulnerable."

"You act like it's something I should be ashamed of."

"Not at all," Em said, reminding herself to choose her words more carefully. "People always take things I say the wrong way."

"What are you afraid of then?"

As if on cue, the steering wheel wobbled under her hands. "Nothing," she answered.

"Nothing? Nothing at all?"

"Nothing I can think of."

"Spiders? Snakes?"

"It would depend on if they were poisonous, or likely to bite me."

"Heights? Being trapped in a lift?"

"No. Although, again, if I were likely to fall or to suffocate, I wouldn't just accept it blithely. I have a survival instinct, like anyone. But I tend to think that whatever gets you in the end will probably be the thing you least expect. You know, you could spend your whole life avoiding planes and end up getting hit by a bus crossing the road for a coffee."

"Thanks," Daniel murmured. "That's heartening."

Em's stomach growled conspicuously. "Speaking of survival instincts, should we stop soon for lunch? What's the time?"

Daniel checked his watch. "Nearly three."

"No wonder I'm hungry. Check the map. Any little towns nearby that we can detour through for food and gas?"

Within half an hour, they had found a tiny spot on the map that consisted of a convenience store, a petrol station, two streets and a car park surrounded by tall pines. They pulled into the car park next to a bent telegraph pole and Em gratefully opened the door and stretched out her legs.

"Are you going to fill up?" Daniel asked.

"On the way out. I need to eat first. But there's something I want you to do for me, Daniel."

He turned to her, his dark eyes puzzled. "What is it?"

"Your Russian's much better than mine." She reached over to the glove box and pulled out the rental papers for the car. "Can you phone the car rental company back in St. Pete and ask them if they have a service outlet in Vologda?"

Daniel took the papers. "Certainly. But why?"

She tried to sound light, almost dismissive. "It's probably nothing, but the steering has felt a bit soft since we had our little incident in the ditch. I'd prefer to exchange the car if we could."

Daniel nodded vigorously. "Yes, that would be safer. What do you mean, soft? It's not going to fail, is it? You just mean it feels wobbly? It's still working though?"

"Oh, yes, of course. Nothing to worry about." She pointed to the phone booth outside the convenience store. "Tell them we'll want to change cars tomorrow morning, around eight. If we can get away from Vologda before nine, we can be in Arkhangelsk at a reasonable hour. We're due to start shooting first thing the following morning."

Em locked the car and walked across the car park to the toilet block. The washrooms were filthy, but it would be hours before they reached Vologda and the comfort of a clean hotel room. So she endured it, and also accepted that the convenience store only made two kinds of sandwiches, both with meat that was obviously not fresh. She took her sandwiches and juice back to the car and watched Daniel at the phone booth in his gray pullover and slightly-too-large jeans. His dark curls caught the sunlight that was spearing between the spruce peaks. She couldn't hear what he was saying, but the length of time the call was taking indicated that he was being bounced between one operator and another, explaining his story over and over. Bureaucracy was generally an inconvenience; Russian bureaucracy was a nightmare.

A breeze moved gently in the treetops, and there was no traffic around to break the lazy quiet. Em finished her lunch and rested her head on the back of the seat to close her eyes for a few moments. Sunlight made patterns on her eyelids. She felt calm and positive.

"Em!"

She opened her eyes. Daniel was calling to her from across the car park. He'd finished his phone call.

"What's up?" she shouted back, leaning out of the car.

"I'm just going to buy something to eat."

"Take your time." Em was growing used to Daniel and his nervous nature, even growing to like him. She leaned back, her eyes flicking to the rearview mirror which, at this angle, reflected the backseat.

The bear was staring at her.

A liquid jolt to her heart. She turned.

The bear sat tucked into the seatbelt, eyes closed as they always were.

Em tried the rearview mirror again. One golden bear, eyes closed. Of course. She had just imagined that hot moment when the eyes seemed open.

For the next few minutes, Em watched the bear, trying to work out what trick of the light had fooled her. If Rosa had never spoken to her about enchantments, she would have dismissed the incident already. But Rosa had been clear about it: *be aware*.

Daniel climbed into the car, opening a bottle of Coke. He had a carton of cigarettes under one arm. "They have a service agent in Vologda, but it's just a garage and workshop. They might not have another car for us, but they said they'll look at this one and track down a replacement if they can't fix it in the morning."

Em grew irritated. "Fix it in the morning? But then we'd be leaving Vologda after lunch. We won't get into Arkhangelsk until midnight."

"I'm sorry, that's the best he could do."

"Never mind." She nodded toward the cigarettes. "You're not going to smoke those in the car, are you?"

"No, no," he said, opening the carton and pocketing a single packet. "I owe the film crew."

"Daniel," she said, "I think we should probably pack the bear away properly. It's not safe to have her just sitting there on the backseat."

Daniel turned to look at the bear and smiled. "She has her seatbelt on."

"Why do we call her, 'she' anyway?"

"Because Rosa does, I suppose."

"It's a distraction. Really, I think she'd be better off packed away in a bag." Em was already out of the seat, snatching up the bear to nestle it safely in a shopping bag. "There, that's better."

Daniel had opened his lunch and was busy eating. Em started the car and put the radio back on. "Okay, let's get going."

"Poor bear. She was probably enjoying the drive."

"She's been stuck in a wall for over a hundred years. I'm sure the shopping bag won't bother her." Em shook her head. "And let's stop talking about her as if she's real."

"Not afraid of her, are you?"

Em laughed. "No. Of course not."

The rattle and click of keys at the front door made Rosa look up from the television. It was late at night, and she was alone. Was somebody trying to break in? Or was it another resident of the apartment block, too drunk to find their own door? She hurried over and slid the chain across.

"Who's there?" she said.

The door opened, caught on the chain.

"Rosa, it's Vasily."

Vasily? What was he doing home? Rosa quickly unhooked the chain and let him in. He had someone with him, a pale thin man dressed in a dark suit. Finding her manners, she offered the stranger a smile before turning her attention to Vasily.

"I hadn't expected you home until late next week," she said, trying to sound bright and not at all guilty.

"Pah! The conference was a shambles, full of nobodies and no-hopers, and the hotel rooms were icy. When I complained they tried to charge me another ten thousand roubles a night! I walked out." He dropped his keys on the bench and turned to smile at her. "My pretty girl. You've kept the apartment so tidy."

"You were only gone a day." She pointedly turned her gaze to his friend.

"Forgive me," Vasily said. "Rosa, this is Yuri Fedorov. Yuri, this is my niece Rosa."

"It's a pleasure," he said.

Vasily touched her chin gently. "Rosa, will you make us some coffee?"

Rosa scurried into the kitchen, hoping until it hurt that Vasily wouldn't ask about the bear. What could she do? Daniel was probably already halfway to Arkhangelsk by now.

"It was my good fortune to meet Yuri tonight, Rosa," Vasily said as he settled on the sofa and invited Yuri to do the same. "We were next to each other on the plane and we got talking and do you know what Yuri does for a living?"

"No. What?" said Rosa, spooning coffee into the espresso filter and filling the machine with water.

"I'm a jeweler," Yuri offered.

Rosa forced her hands to be still. "Is that so?"

"Not just a jeweler," Vasily said, "but a valuations expert for an insurance company. I told him of my . . . find, and he graciously offered to come back here with me and tell me what it's worth."

"On the proviso that I get first refusal if he decides to sell it," Yuri said, with a smile that wasn't altogether pleasant.

Rosa winced. "Ah, the bear."

"Yes, the bear, Rosa. Where is she? Yuri can look at her while you make coffee."

Rosa carefully set out three cups and put her back to the coffee machine. "Vasily, I'm sorry. The bear isn't here."

A twitch of annoyance crossed his brow, and Rosa realized that for the first time she would be on the receiving end of one of his infamous tirades. She braced herself.

"Not here, Roshka? Where else could she be?"

"My friend came up from Novgorod. He says it's definitely gold, but couldn't date the object himself. So I let him take it—"

"You let him take it!" Vasily roared. Then, remembering himself, he turned to Yuri with his charming smile. "I'm sorry, Yuri. I've brought you out of your way needlessly."

Yuri stood and handed Vasily a business card. "I understand. When the bear returns, I'm happy to look at it."

Vasily showed Yuri out, insisting on giving him money for a taxi, full of polite apologies and expansive laughs about silly girls not knowing the value of priceless objects. Rosa gritted her teeth and finished making coffee, then hovered in the doorway to the kitchen to await the onslaught. The television still muttered softly in the background.

The door closed. Vasily turned, his black eyebrows drawn down hard.

"I'm sorry, Uncle Vasily—," she started.

"Foolish girl. You should never have let the bear out of your sight."

"I trust Daniel, Uncle Vasily. I know how important that bear is to you."

"Do you really? Yuri spoke in terms of hundreds of thousands of American dollars. He also spoke of selling it quickly. It would be out of the country before the government takes it from me and puts it in a museum."

Rosa felt her blood chill. She was a foolish girl. Vasily was right. "I'm sorry, I'm sorry. But I know that Daniel will keep it safe."

"Where is the bear? Be honest with me now."

"She's on her way to Arkhangelsk."

"Arkhangelsk!" he shrieked. "What does he intend to do with her there? Put her on a boat to England?"

"No, there's a professor at the university—"

"Universities are worse than museums!"

"Uncle Vasily, I—"

He took a step toward her and drilled his index finger into her shoulder. It was so startlingly different to his usual delicate touch that she gasped.

"You will go to Arkhangelsk and you will bring it back before any professor can look at it."

"Yes, yes, of course," she muttered nervously.

He softened. "Rosa, don't be afraid of me."

"I'm not afraid of you hurting me, Uncle Vasily. I'm afraid of you hating me." Her eyes brimmed and she had to swallow back tears.

Instantly, he grabbed her in a bear hug. He squeezed her once, hard, then set her free. His voice regained its hard edge. "Go to bed, Rosa. We'll speak again in the morning."

"Should I ring an airline? Book a flight for tomorrow?"

"I'll take care of it. I know someone. You go to bed."

Rosa knew that he wanted her out of sight, afraid of his own anger. She dutifully turned and went to her room.

Arkhangelsk. Even if she flew tomorrow afternoon, she would probably still beat Daniel there. He and Em would have arrived in Vologda by now. She wished she had thought to ask where they were staying in Vologda; it would save a lot of trouble if she could simply phone them. Em would be upset. After all the bother of driving to Arkhangelsk, not getting her story would certainly irritate her, but it couldn't be helped. Vasily's will was inexorable.

Rosa turned off her light and climbed into bed. Her curtain was still open and she could see a bright quarter of the moon in the corner of the window. She watched it for a long time before she closed her eyes.

What about Daniel? She had promised to tell him the truth. He would expect to hear it in Arkhangelsk. Could she really go through with it? She supposed she must, if she could be certain he would keep his promise never to contact her again afterward. She reminded herself to take the silver bracelet and the blue scarf he had given her, to return them. Gifts were like knots between people, which had to be unpicked. Her stomach ached and she flipped over and pressed a pillow against her belly and cried because she loved Vasily and had let him down, because she loved Daniel and had let him down.

But mostly just because she was selfish and hated that life was so unfair.

Rosa ventured out of her room warily the next morning, and found Vasily dressed in his singlet and trousers, smelling of talcum powder and with his hair freshly greased. He whistled as he fried eggs in the kitchen.

"Good morning," she said.

He turned and his eyes were soft. "Ah, my girl. Have you forgiven me?"

"Have you forgiven me?"

"Dear little Roshka. Of course."

"Have you booked my flight to Arkhangelsk?"

"Yes, this afternoon at three. I'll take you out to the airport myself as I have business in the area." He indicated the pan. "Eggs?"

She shrugged and perched on a stool at the bench. "Yes, but not too greasy."

He served her breakfast—fried eggs, too greasy, with thin pancakes—and sat opposite her.

"Uncle Vasily, I think I need to explain something to you," she said, not touching her food.

"What is it?"

"I didn't give your priceless bear away on a whim."

He put down his knife and fork and swallowed a mouthful. "Then why, Rosa?"

She took a deep breath, dreading invoking the spirit of her dead mother. "Uncle Vasily, I have the second sight, like Mama."

His eyebrows twitched. "You do?"

"Mama told me you don't believe in it."

"It was a long time since Ellena and I spoke of it. As I grow older, I'm more able to believe strange things."

"The bear . . . she gave off a shock of energy. To me. To Daniel." Rosa wisely didn't mention Em. "But not to anyone else. Not to you, or Larissa, or anyone who touched her at the bathhouse. Do you see?"

"I think so."

"I let her go with Daniel because I thought she wanted to go."

Vasily drew his lips into a pensive line and was lost in thought for an age. Rosa ate a few mouthfuls dispiritedly. Finally, Vasily said, "Rosa, I didn't know you had the sight."

"I don't tell anyone."

He stood up, pushing his breakfast aside. His mood was urgent, decisive. "Come with me. There's something I need to show you."

Puzzled, Rosa followed Vasily to his bedroom. He knelt in front of his oak dresser and pulled out the bottom drawer. There was a smell of old wood and sandalwood drawer liners.

"Come, sit by me," he said, patting the floor next to him.

Rosa joined him, shrugging out of her dressing gown; Vasily always had the heating in his bedroom on high. The pale carpet was soft beneath her knees.

From the drawer, he pulled out a flat wooden box, which he opened.

"Do you see this, Rosa?" he said, withdrawing a dirty silver bracelet that rattled and tinkled with charms.

"What is it?" Rosa said, extending her hand.

He dropped it onto her palm. "It was your mother's. She gave it to me when they left Russia." He chuckled. "She said Petr had insisted; that in the West she would have no need of good luck."

Rosa felt the tickle of magic from the bracelet. "These charms . . ."

He pulled the bracelet into a straight line on her palm. "Rosa, it's an amulet. Ellena started it when she was fourteen. She made a lot of these herself; others she found." He pointed them out one by one. "Here, a ruby she engraved with an 'E' for Ellena. A silver knife, a silver key and a silver swallow. I don't know what any of these mean. Maybe you could look them up in a book. Here, these are two of your baby teeth. Do you remember? When you were four, you fell off your bicycle and knocked them out."

"I remember," Rosa said softly, reverent in the presence of such a wonderful, magical object.

"These little bells she stole from a gypsy. The knots are just silver thread, but she told me these were the most important. Each of them tied her to someone she loved: so there is one for you, one for Petr, one for me. This miniature mirror is from her childhood dollhouse. This one . . ." He flipped open the last charm, a tiny locket. A piece of dried grass was glued inside. "She told me that this is grass she found growing through the eyehole of a horse's skull. It was supposed to be a very potent charm."

"Mama knew about enchantments."

"She did. I once laughed at her for it."

"She hardly mentioned magic. Papa didn't like it. When I was thirteen, she taught me a few protection spells and told me to be wary of my power." Rosa dangled the bracelet in front of her and it spun slowly. "Apart from that, she honored Papa's wishes and didn't speak of it." Until close to the end, when information had gushed out of her, careless and jumbled. Rosa offered the bracelet back to Vasily. "Thank you for showing me this."

"No, Rosa. You keep it. I have had a lifetime of good luck."

"Are you certain?" Rosa said, her fingers already closing possessively around the charms.

"Of course I am certain. Wear it, and have good fortune always."

"Are you sure we haven't come too far?" Em said.

Daniel looked up from the local map of Vologda he had taken from the hotel foyer that morning. "Absolutely sure." They were searching for the service agent of their rental company, and had driven a long way north of the river into an industrial area that looked as though it had been uninhabited since the collapse of the Soviet Union. "It should be down that road."

"Road?" Em said. "That's a dirt track."

"Then it should be down that dirt track." He was growing more comfortable around Em. Her odd habits—the quiet detachment, the momentary irritations, the aloof coolness—were becoming familiar to him, and he no longer inferred from them any special dislike. She treated everyone the same way.

Em turned the car and Daniel tensed, always alert in case the steering failed. They bumped down the dirt road and came to a dilapidated garage with a bent metal sign out front.

"That's it."

Em laughed. "God help us." She pulled into the dirt parking area. "Now, do you have the spare car key I gave you back in Novgorod?"

"Yep," said Daniel, reaching into the inside pocket of his jacket. Empty. An embarrassed realization. "Oh, no. I think I gave it to Rosa."

"You gave it to Rosa?"

"My room key back at the guesthouse too. I put them all on the same keyring, and I was so . . . distracted when I gave Rosa her keys . . ."

"It's okay," Em said. "We'll sweet-talk him. That is, if he has another car for us." They left the car and went to the garage in search of the owner.

A short man with big ears, a dirty beret and greasy overalls emerged from the front door as they approached. "Hello," he called in heavily accented English. "You tourists? Phone me yesterday?"

Daniel switched into Russian and said, "The car's steering is soft. We'd prefer a replacement car if one is available."

"I have no replacement cars," he said, gesturing around him. "You see. But I will fix this one."

"We don't have a lot of time," Daniel said. "Could you look at it straightaway?"

"I'll look at it soon. Should be ready around four."

Em's ears pricked up at the word "four" and she grabbed Daniel's shirt. "Four this afternoon," she spat. "Can't he do it sooner?"

The mechanic shook his head and returned to English. "Busy, busy, busy."

Daniel peered into the dark garage and could see only one other car up on the ramp. "Are you sure?"

The mechanic stroked his chin and his face took on a petulant expression. "Maybe if you don't believe me, it will take until five."

Daniel shrugged. "Em, we have no choice."

She sighed. "Okay. But ask him if he'll drive us back to the city center."

The mechanic enthusiastically agreed to drive them, and it was only when he was dropping them off on Prospekt Pobedy that Daniel realized he expected payment. Em pressed a note into his hand, retrieved the bag with the golden bear in it, and he drove off. The bustling market was alive behind them, redolent with the smell of food, spices and flowers.

"So shall we go back to the hotel?" Daniel asked.

"We've already checked out," Em said.

"But we're checking back in, aren't we? I mean, we'll have to stay an extra night."

"Why?"

"Isn't it an eleven- or twelve-hour drive to Arkhangelsk?"

"I don't mind driving at night."

"Is it safe?"

"It's probably safer. No traffic. Daniel, we just don't have that much time. Professor Gergiev is expecting us tomorrow morning at eight. If we have to reschedule, it might be days before he's available again. We have to leave for Arkhangelsk today, even if it means driving until four in the morning. Aaron and the others will be there too." A trio of teenagers jostled past them, wearing clothes printed with English slogans that they probably didn't understand. She indicated a dreary coffee house across the road, wilting flowers in its window boxes. "For now, we need somewhere to sit and pass the next seven hours."

Daniel groaned. "Shouldn't we do some sightseeing or something?"

"I find work always passes the time, and we need to get together a script for tomorrow. I was going to do it tonight, but I'll be driving." She gave him a meaningful lift of the eyebrows. "Remember, it's your job too."

The time passed in working on the script, in a walk around the city center, in a long lunch, in repeatedly and unsuccessfully trying to phone Aaron to let him know they were running late, and in sitting for a while on a park bench. There was no denying that it was a long and boring wait, and the stress of boredom was made worse for Daniel by his growing feeling of dread about traveling so many hours late at night. What if Em fell asleep at the wheel? Or a late-night long-distance truck driver plowed into them? Or a wild nocturnal animal crossed their path and caused an accident?

Damn it, if he'd just been able to fly like a normal person. Presumably the rest of the crew were in Arkhangelsk—having caught a perfectly safe flight that had landed on time—and were already relaxing at the hotel.

At four o'clock, after a taxi ride with a surly driver, Daniel and Em finally arrived back at the garage where they waited for ten minutes for the mechanic to get off the phone from his wife. Their car was parked nearby, and Em went over to check that nothing had been stolen from their suitcases.

"Hello again," the mechanic said to Daniel when he had finally hung up the phone.

"Is the car ready?"

The mechanic smiled and shook his head. "No."

"No?"

Em joined them. "What's going on?"

"The car's not ready," Daniel said, forgetting to switch back into English. This didn't faze Em at all, and Daniel found himself admiring her astonishing ability to pick up the new language.

"I need a part," the mechanic said. "It will be in tomorrow."

Em held out her hand and clicked her fingers. "The keys."

"Em, what are you doing?"

"It isn't safe to drive," the mechanic said.

"It got us this far," she said.

"Em, no," Daniel said, galvanized by the mechanic's warning. "We can't drive it if it's not safe."

Em switched into English. "He's just saying that so he can charge us more to fix it."

"But what if—"

"The keys," Em said again. "Now."

The mechanic shrugged and withdrew the keys from his dirty overalls. Em snatched them from him and stalked back to the car.

Daniel ran after her. "Em, come on. It's a long drive in a car that's not safe."

"It will be fine," she said. "Get in."

Even though he hated her domineering tone, he did as she asked. She was leaning over to the glove box to retrieve the map. "We'll take a quiet route," she said. "We'll stay off the main roads, away from any traffic. I'll drive slowly and carefully." She started the car.

"I've got a bad feeling about this, Em," he said.

She turned to him and met his gaze fully with her own. "Daniel, think of all those flights you refused to take because you had a bad feeling. Have any of them ever crashed?"

Daniel was taken aback, couldn't find an answer on his tongue.

"Maybe your bad feelings are just *feelings*. Common or garden variety. Not presentiments." She put the car in gear and pulled out. "From what Rosa told me, you don't even believe in presentiments."

"The mechanic said—"

"Forget what the mechanic said," Em replied as they bumped back down the dirt road. "Never trust a mechanic. Trust me instead."

Daniel fastened his seatbelt and took a deep breath. "Okay, I'll trust you."

Six

Hotel Pamyat in Arkhangelsk was a Soviet-era tourist hotel, poorly lit and drab. In the cold foyer, some touches had been added by the new owners—bright paintings and track lighting—but nothing could hide the building's innate austerity.

Rosa waited at the reception desk for five minutes, drumming her fingers on the scarred wood while the receptionist casually finished some paperwork.

"How can I help?" she said eventually.

"I'm looking for two of your guests. Daniel St. Clare and Em Hayward."

The receptionist punched a few keys. "No, nobody here under that name."

Of course, it was only four o'clock. They were probably still a few hours away by road. Rosa booked herself a room then asked, "Do you have a group booking for a television crew? *Great Medieval Cities.*"

Again the receptionist turned to her computer. "I have a booking for Spartacus Television Productions."

"Which rooms are they in?"

"Three-twenty to three-twenty-four."

"Thanks."

Rosa scooped up her room key and took the lift to the third floor. She knocked on the door to three-twenty and a man of about forty-five, with long blond hair in a ponytail, opened it.

"I don't speak Russian," he said, in extremely poor Russian.

"It's okay. I'm Rosa. I'm a friend of Daniel's."

The man's eyebrows shot up. "Oh. Are you the girl troubles?"

"What?" she said, confused and wondering if she should be insulted.

He shook his head. "Never mind. Daniel's not here yet."

"What time are you expecting him?"

"Around eight tonight. I'm Richard. Do you want me to give him a message?"

"Which room will he be in?"

"Well, given that Em will take the corner room because it's bigger," he said with a smirk, "that will leave Daniel three-twenty-three."

Rosa eyed the door.

"Do you want me to give him a message?" Richard said again.

"Yes, let him know I'm staying in the hotel. I'm in five-nineteen."

"Is he expecting you?"

"No." Rosa shook her head. "No, he's not."

"You'll be a nice surprise then."

"No, I won't," she said. She considered telling this man that their trip to Arkhangelsk was going to be wasted, that she had to take the bear and send them all back to Novgorod. But she couldn't do it. She would break the news to Daniel and Em first. "Good-bye."

"My mates and I are going out for dinner at seven," he called after her. "You're welcome to join us."

"Thank you, but no," she said, and the lift doors closed on his next question.

Rosa settled herself into her room and lay back on the bed. The paint on the ceiling was peeling, but the mattress was firm and the linen smelled like lavender. She sighed and closed her eyes, a weary anxiety seeping into her bones. Vasily's early return had thrown matters into chaos. She hoped that Daniel wouldn't get into serious trouble for dragging a film crew up here. Really it was Em's fault, and Rosa surmised that Em was more than capable of dealing with the censure of her colleagues.

Daniel was so much more vulnerable: the third son of the tyrannical principal of an elite school; motherless since two years of age and raised by a succession of foreign nannies; the only St. Clare in three generations not to achieve a doctorate; two older brothers who barely spoke to him except to express their disdain. Despite the nest of vipers he had grown up amongst, Daniel was gentle and kind, passionate and funny.

Rosa sat up, determined not to allow her imagination to travel those well-worn paths of what might have been. She had a few hours to pass and it was best to keep herself busy.

At eight o'clock, after a long walk by the gray sea in the gray afternoon, an early dinner, and a half-hearted visit to the tourist shop behind the hotel foyer, she passed Daniel's room again. Nobody there. Richard's room was empty as well. She decided to leave a note under Daniel's door, in case his colleagues didn't return until late or forgot to pass on her message.

At nine o'clock, the corner of the note was still peeking from the door where she had left it.

At ten o'clock, Richard told her that Daniel and Em were probably just running late and not to worry.

"We're filming at eight in the morning," he told her. He was drunk, and his lecherous interest was more carelessly displayed. "They'll be here. Em wouldn't miss the start of a shoot for anything."

"They haven't called?"

"They're probably out of range. Don't worry." He smiled at her meaningfully. "You want to come in for a drink?"

"No, I think I'll go to bed."

She lay in the dark for a long time, fingering the charms on her mother's bracelet. Unlike Vasily, she knew what they all meant: a swallow brought good fortune and luck on travels, unless it flew through a window, which augured a death in the house; a knife was protection against bad magicians; a spoon ensured a child's good health. She felt her way along the bracelet, considering herself both blessed by her mother and cursed by her. Eventually, she dropped into a light sleep.

She woke just before midnight and sat up, confused. Daniel hadn't arrived yet. Or perhaps he had, but hadn't wanted to wake her. She pulled her dressing gown on over her clothes and went down the hall to the lift.

In the dim light of the corridor she could see the corner of the note, exactly where she had left it. Moments ticked by unknowing, and even the silence in the corridor seemed pensive.

Rosa returned to her room and sat at the window. Her breath

fogged the glass, streetlights outside spilled light onto her hands as they rested on the cold sill. A prickle walked leisurely up her spine, a knot of knowing tightened in her stomach. Something had gone wrong, something bad had happened.

Where was Daniel?

Daniel was sleeping. At last. Em had thought he would stay awake, tensely watching the road, all night. But now the tension had evaporated, his sleeping face was soft against the headrest and Em felt free to press the accelerator a little harder to make up some of the time they were losing in this convoluted route up to Arkhangelsk.

She felt as though she had been driving forever. The light had long ago fled the land; it was nearly midnight. The road had become narrow and unmarked, the dirt shoulders broader and more pitted with holes. The monstrous conifer woodland closed around the carriageway, and only the occasional village or farm punctuated the dense growth. The last vehicle they had passed was a dirty truck, laden with precariously loaded logs, steaming into the night. That had been two hours ago.

Em yawned. She would have liked to get some sleep, but she wasn't turning the wheel over to Daniel. Not because he was unused to the car's left-hand drive—which side of the road they drove on was hardly an issue out here—but because he would feel how the steering had deteriorated into a spongy, unresponsive mess. She had been growing used to it, but they wouldn't be driving it back to Novgorod, that was for certain.

The dark closed in, the road kept disappearing under her, the hum of the engine seemed to be beating an inaudible rhythm; she stretched her mind to listen . . .

Time slowed. Em's eyelids flickered . . .

Her eyes flew open, her heart jolted. The car had drifted to the left. She must have nodded off for a half-second. But something had woken her, some shimmer of rainbow light from the backseat, reflected in the rearview mirror. She checked the mirror. Nothing. Risked a peek over her shoulder. Nothing.

A dream, then. The kind that intervenes upon the moment of sleep. She shook herself and wound the window down a few inches. The cold air woke Daniel.

"Em?" he said dozily.

"It's getting stuffy in here. Sorry. Are you cold?"

Daniel reached into the backseat for the big overcoat he had borrowed from Vasily. "I'm fine, I'll put this over me." He yawned. "How long was I asleep?"

"Not long. About forty-five minutes."

"This road's rough, isn't it?"

"Yes, but we should pick up an exit in about ten miles. Maybe we can stop for a cup of coffee. Help keep us awake."

He eyed her suspiciously. "You're not getting sleepy, are you?"

"Not at all."

"Because I can drive for a while if you need a rest."

"No, it's fine, Daniel. I'm fine." She switched the radio on. Snow on every channel.

"We must be a long way from anywhere," Daniel said, and something about his words gave her a chill.

Em snapped the radio off. "How did you meet Rosa?" she asked. She didn't really care to know, but conversation was a good barrier to sleep.

"I enrolled in an advanced Russian course and she was my teacher," he said, yawning again.

Em suppressed a sympathy yawn. "So you'd learned Russian before?"

"I had a Russian nanny for six years when I was a little boy."

"A nanny?"

"Yeah. My mother died of cancer when I was two." Daniel went on, filling in his family history, responding to her carefully placed questions to keep him talking as the road wore her down.

Finally, he said, "Shouldn't we have reached that turn-off by now?"

"Perhaps I underestimated." She smiled at him. "Optimistic. I'm thinking about a warm bed."

They traveled another half hour in silence, and Em started to worry that she'd missed the turn-off. What if they'd passed it in that moment she'd dozed?

"Is that it?" Daniel said, pointing to a long dirt road. Two bent posts, once the pillars of a street sign, stood at the corner. Em pulled into the road and stopped the car, knocking it into park.

"I'm sure it's a paved road we want," she said, leaning over Daniel to pull the map out of the glove box. "Let me see."

By the yellow light of the overhead bulb she ran her finger down the map. By her estimation, they should have passed the turn-off twenty minutes ago. And this road wasn't even marked.

"Maybe the map's misprinted," she said.

"Do you know where we are?"

"I know where we're supposed to be."

She studied the map a few moments longer, while the car hummed and Daniel looked on nervously. Finally, she folded it away. "You know, I think we'll just keep driving the way we've been going, and see what happens. I mean, we're heading in the right direction, there will be a turn-off somewhere."

"If you're sure."

"Nothing else we can do. We have to be in Arkhangelsk by morning."

She switched off the overhead light and put the car back into drive. It stalled. The engine went dead, light and sound sucked into nothing.

"What the hell?"

"What happened?" said Daniel.

Em tried to start the car. Nothing. The dark outside, now the headlights were off, was absolute.

"What happened?" Daniel repeated.

"Maybe the battery's gone flat."

"But the car was running."

Em turned the key again and again. Not even a click or a wheeze rewarded her.

"It must have been more damaged than we thought on the way up to St. Pete," Daniel was saying. "Shit, what do we do?"

Em pounded the steering wheel. "This is so irritating. We're stuck out here in the middle of nowhere, we have a shoot in Arkhangelsk in about eight hours, and my cell phone has been out of range virtually since I left St. Petersburg."

Daniel sighed and leaned his head against the window. "It's all my fault."

Em looked at him. "Daniel, that's not helpful." Something caught her eye in the distance. She leaned closer and peered into the dark beyond Daniel. "You know, I think I can see a light."

Daniel turned. "I can't."

Em nodded confidently. "I can. Between those trees. Maybe it's a service station." She was already pulling her coat off the backseat.

"Wait. What are you doing?"

"I'm going to walk up there and see if somebody will come take a look at the car. Or maybe let us use their phone."

"You can't go alone."

"That's right. Pull your coat on."

"Shouldn't we just wait here for somebody to come by?"

"They might not."

Daniel reluctantly pulled his coat on. "Em, I don't know if this is wise. There could be wolves out there."

"It's not far. And there's safety in numbers. We can't just sit here and do nothing."

Em could see Daniel struggling with her decision and fought down a burst of impatience. "Come on, Daniel. We've done this on your terms so far—"

"My terms? Driving at night in a car considered mechanically unsafe?"

"We could have flown," she said irritably. "We would have been there twelve hours ago."

He buttoned his coat in silence. "Okay, let's go then."

They were two steps beyond the car when they realized how cold it was and came back for hats, scarves and extra layers. Daniel also grabbed the bag with the bear in it.

"We should bring her," he said. "Just in case somebody breaks into the car while we're gone."

"Fine," Em said, locking the car and pocketing the keys. "Let's go."

They walked off the road, down a shallow gully, and into the trees. The undergrowth was tough and moist, the trees very close together. Em led the way, ducking spiderwebs and hoping they wouldn't tumble off the top of a ridge.

"Shit," Em said, kicking her toe on a jutting rock.

"You okay?"

"Yeah, just kicked my toe." She carefully made her way forward, eyes on the woodland floor for other hazards. Not that she could see much in the dark. If only the sky wasn't clouded over. Even the palest wash of starlight would help her see. All around was the tang of pine and a slightly sour smell of old puddles and rotting layers.

When they had been walking for a few minutes, she lifted her eyes to look for the light. It had been extinguished.

"Oh no," she groaned. "It's gone out."

Daniel looked up. "Oh no," he echoed.

Em leaned against a tree. "What do we do now?"

"I think we should go back to the car."

"But the light . . . I mean, presumably there's somebody home still . . ."

"Em," Daniel said forcefully, and she found herself paying attention. "This is nuts. We're not sure where the light was, or what it was. We could get lost and wander all night. We could wander off a drop, or into a bear, or any number of things. What we know for sure is that the car is five hundred feet that way." He jerked a thumb over his shoulder. "It may not start, but it's warm and we can lock it until daylight comes."

"But the interview."

"Em, we're not going to make the interview," he said, and she knew he was right.

Em sighed. "All right, back to the car. You lead the way."

She followed him in the dark, nearly kicked her toe on the same rock again, and told herself that Professor Gergiev could be rescheduled. They broke from the trees, trudged up the gully to the road.

The car was gone.

Daniel spun in a slow circle. "Have we come out somewhere else?"

Em was momentarily so confused that she couldn't speak.

"Em?"

"Where's the fucking car?"

"We must have come out in a different spot."

She pointed to the two posts. "This is where we left it. This turn-off. That old sign."

Daniel dropped the bag with the bear in it and lowered himself to the ground. He put his head in his hands. "I can't believe this. Our car's been stolen."

"How could someone steal it? It wasn't even running."

"This is a nightmare."

Em put her hand out and pulled him to his feet. "Come on."

"I'm not going anywhere," Daniel said. "I'm waiting here until daylight."

"Yeah, I know. Let's get closer to the road though, so we can flag someone down if they pass."

Daniel picked up the bag and they walked out to the main road, found a tree to shelter against, and tried to make themselves comfortable.

"Thank God we have all our warm gear on," Daniel said.

"Small mercies," Em replied, lost in thought. It was impossible that they should be out here in the middle of cold nowhere, their car stolen, utterly lost. The unbroken darkness added a surreal cast to events, as though it were a strange dream. Nor could she shake a vague guilty feeling.

"Are you okay?" Daniel asked.

She sighed. "None of this is okay, Daniel. But I expect we'll work it out once the sun comes up." She patted his knee. "Try not to worry too much. All right?"

Daniel pulled Vasily's coat tighter around himself. "All right." He reached into his pocket and peeled open the packet of cigarettes. "Do you want one?"

She shook her head. His lighter flickered in the dark. Overhead,

the clouds parted on a moonless sky, and Daniel and Em sat close
together and waited for dawn.

Rosa watched as the first light struggled through the crack between
the curtains. Had she slept at all? Perhaps she had dozed briefly, but
her body felt tight and poised, as though she might need to make a
mad dash any second.

She rose, still dressed in the previous day's clothes, and went
back to Daniel's door. He wasn't there.

Richard, roused by her knocking, peered out.

"Not there, eh?"

"You haven't heard from them?"

He shook his head and yawned without covering his mouth.
Rosa flinched.

"Don't worry," he said, covertly glancing at her crumpled clothes.
"He can look after himself. And if he can't, then Em certainly can."

Yes, Rosa thought as she returned to her room. If the problem
was a flat tire or a wrong turn, sure they could look after themselves.
But in her memory now she saw the bear's smile as malevolent, taking pleasure in evil thoughts. She slammed the door of her room
behind her and paced the floral carpet. She should never have let
them take the bear.

Then she stopped. All three of them had been marked, not just
Daniel and Em. Rosa still had something to do with this.

She rummaged in her bag for the silver bracelet Daniel had
given her. She had intended to give it back, but now she wove it
tightly around her mother's charm bracelet, making three knots.
One for her, one for Daniel, one for Em.

"Please, please," she muttered, not really knowing what she was
doing, operating on instinct. "Let this work."

Rosa sat by the window and allowed the dawn light to fall on
her. The sills were painted with white enamel, layer upon layer
that flaked at the touch of her fingernail. She found the tiny mirror
charm on the bracelet. It was no bigger than the upper joint of her
pinky finger, but she rubbed the surface gently. "Let me see him,"
she said. "Where is he?"

At first, only the reflection of her own eye looked back at her, but then there was a shift. Her second sight opened up. She saw the magic working, invisible movements, like heat waves on a dry road.

"Where is Daniel?" she said again.

The mirror shimmered, her eye disappeared, and the surface clouded with fog. She focused harder, her stomach churning with anxiety. Was this a trick of her imagination? Or was the mirror telling her that Daniel lay beyond a veil of fog? Beyond death? She began to panic.

Rosa's head hurt so she snapped her second sight closed. The fog cleared, her eye appeared in the mirror once again. She glanced away, out the window and onto the dirty street. A battered red car tried once, twice, three times to reverse park in a tiny space against the curb, then drove off in embarrassment, its exhaust a gray cloud in the cold air.

There had to be another way to find him.

She turned once again to the bracelet, considering the charms one by one. The swallow gleamed in the half-light. She had the answer.

Rosa dressed in clean clothes then ran downstairs to the reception desk. The receptionist, a good-looking young man, whom ordinarily Rosa might have set her sights on to conquer, sat behind the desk with his chin in his hands.

"Do you have a road directory for this area?" she said.

"Arkhangelsk region?" he said.

"The route between here and Vologda."

He pulled out a drawer and flicked officiously between files. "In Russian or English?" he said.

"It doesn't matter."

He handed her a map. "Ten roubles, thanks."

"I only need to borrow it."

"It's ten roubles."

"Charge it to my room. Five-nineteen." She snatched up the map and went to one of the worn leather sofas in the foyer. Outside, a tour group was arriving, being herded off the bus in their overcoats, their breath fogging in the morning air. The sliding glass doors opened and a blast of cold air made Rosa shiver. She smoothed out the map and took off the charm bracelet, still knotted to Daniel's silver one. She held it so that the swallow dipped downward. The foyer was filling up now with noise and movement. Rosa opened her second sight and shut it all out.

"Which way did he go?" she said and held the bracelet very still.

The swallow spun once, twice, then settled on a direction, its beak dipping almost imperceptibly to a point on the map. Rosa marked the place with her fingernail and went directly to the reception desk, pushing through a crowd of bleary-eyed American tourists. Somebody shouted at her, but she wasn't listening.

"I need a hire car, and quickly," she said to the man behind the desk.

He drew his eyebrows down in irritation. "I can't help you now," he said. "I'm busy."

"Look . . . ," she started, then stopped herself. In a time like this, there was only one person who could make things happen.

From the privacy of her room, she phoned Vasily.

"Rosa, it's very early," he said.

"Uncle Vasily, you must listen to me, and you must try not to be angry."

"I don't like the sound of this, Roshka."

"The bear hasn't arrived, Uncle Vasily, and I know . . . deep in my bones, I know that it's because something bad has happened."

"What, Rosa? An accident? A burglary?"

She sighed and sank into the chair next to the dresser. "Worse, Uncle Vasily. I fear worse. I fear curses, and spells, and bad magic."

A long silence ensued, and Rosa let it beat out. Vasily needed time to digest her words.

"Rosa?" he said finally. "I can trust you?"

"I love you, Uncle Vasily. I'm not crazy, or stupid. Daniel has disappeared behind a veil. I can't find him in this world. I have to find the place he disappeared, I have to know if he's—"

"You fear that he is dead?"

"I don't know where he is," she said, and her voice cracked over the words, "and I feel like it's my fault."

Vasily's voice was tender. "Is this the boy, Rosa? The one you loved?"

"Please, Uncle Vasily, will you help me?"

"What do you need?"

"A car and a driver."

"Pack your things and wait outside the hotel. I'll have somebody there within half an hour."

Vasily was true to his word, and the surly-looking Ukrainian driver showed no surprise at her insistence that he should take her to a point on the map decided upon by a silver swallow, and no irritation with her chain-smoking the entire five-hour drive.

They left the highway and drove through smaller and smaller settlements, out onto a pitted road. Rosa's stomach grumbled and her eyes were gritty. But she spotted it, long before the driver had.

"There!" she called out, slipping out of her seatbelt and leaning forward to thump the dash. "The blue car on the side of the road."

The driver slowed, indicated, then turned onto the side road to pull in beside Daniel and Em's hire car. She hoped to find them both inside, sleeping, wondering why she had bothered to come here looking for them.

"Wait here," she said to the driver, opening the door and letting herself out into the warm morning. The sky was clear, and the sun dazzled off the windscreen. She put her hand up to shield her eyes, but could already see there was nobody in the car. The bear was no longer on the backseat with the suitcases. She tried the door; it was locked. She peered through the window. No sign of anyone: no note, no hint at all of what had happened.

Rosa stood back, glanced toward the immense woodlands, then to the road. Her second sight twitched, as though something nearby was signaling her. A chill ran over her skin. Her heart was in her throat. There was no sign of Daniel and Em.

Where in the world had they gone?

Seven

Ah, Rosa Kovalenka. Perhaps they are not in the world at all.

What do you think, reader? Do you have your suspicions? No doubt as you read further, some things may become clear. And then, some things may become less clear, and you will say, "Papa Grigory! You make the tale too difficult to follow!" Sometimes Totchka says that to me, when night is come and I draw up a chair beside her warm bed to tell her stories. I forget I am talking to such a little girl, and I confuse her with too many characters and times. She is only young after all, and the passing years bring her no more sense, nor understanding. I don't mind, for nor do her coughs and wheezes worsen, nor her hands grow colder.

It is warm today, and I have all the wooden shutters opened to the light. Totchka's little fingers struggle with wool as she wraps it tight around a peg, making a doll. She sits near the window on a worn rug. The sun falls on her dark hair and illuminates the velvet softness of her cheek. I could never look so perfect in such unfiltered sunshine. The years have worn me down. My beard is flecked with gray, my skin is ruddy and my soul is black, but I am good to Totchka. Believe what you will of the rest of my tales. I am good to Totchka because I love her.

You will be tired by now of my domestic affairs. I would like to tell you about my little painted house, and the fields that surround it. But you will arrive here soon enough, and I promised to tell a tale of the bear.

So I must transport you back in time to the tenth century, to Kiev, from where the Rus first ruled. We shall go to Olga's palace, but do not imagine a palace of gold and fine objects. Imagine pale bricks and unpainted wood, and narrow sunless windows. Imagine unevenly tiled floors and rugs imported from the south, and pagan frescoes high on the walls. Imagine the smell of pine and rain and woodsmoke, mixed with the salty smell of unwashed human bodies. And imagine, most of all, Olga herself. Her husband died in battle nine years ago. Her son is too young to take the throne. So she rules the Rus in his stead. She is a woman with a hard face and a soft belly; and somebody has her turned over on her belly right now. Bearded men look ridiculous naked, so we shall give him some clothes from the waist up, one of those blousy shirts fastened with a row of buttons up the spine. The bed lies on top of the big stove that keeps Olga's chamber warm on rainy afternoons such as this.

Cast into a corner of the bed lies the Golden Bear. She is newly minted, and her eyes are wide and innocent. Yes, of course they are open: she only ever closes them to sleep, and we all know that bears can sleep a long time. The bear watches Olga and the Secret Ambassador, and she learns about things.

The bear thinks that humans are very odd indeed, and at no time more so than now: half-naked and grunting and rubbing themselves all over each other. She is only new to the world, cast in gold three weeks past, and brought from the misted lands with the Secret Ambassador. She remembers little about her birth; it is taking her a while to adjust to sentience. A flash of shadowy woodlands, of magical colors, of strong hands on her head. But since she arrived in Olga's palace this morning, events seem clearer and make sense in chains.

At length, the grunting and rubbing stops and the Secret Ambassador collapses onto the dense mattress. Olga turns over to look at the ceiling and is lost in thought a while.

"Do you like my gift?" the Secret Ambassador asks.

"You know that I do. It's very fine, but it is not a gift for me. I made that clear when I asked for it."

The Secret Ambassador kisses Olga's collarbone, accidentally gathering a mouthful of tawny hair. Olga's narrow eyes do not leave the ceiling. The rain thrums on the roof and windows and, from somewhere deeper in the palace, a steady dripping has started. The Secret Ambassador reaches for the bear and lays her gently between Olga's softly sagging breasts.

"You should keep it," he says. "I carved the mold with all the love I feel for you."

"I need a suitable gift to impress Konstantin the Purple-Born. I'm taking furs and honey and wax and slave girls, but I want him to see that the Rus are not just barbarians eking a living out of the woods."

"Konstantin has many gold objects."

"None so fine as this, surely," Olga says. The bear can hear uncertainty in her voice. Olga is stroking the bear's belly. The pleasure is tainted by sadness: Olga intends to pass her on to somebody else.

Olga lays the bear aside and climbs down, naked, from the stove. The Secret Ambassador finds his clothes and follows her. Olga whistles low and melodiously. A thump and a scuttle sound from under the stove and a little domestic servant scurries out. This is no surprise for magic is common in the world; though it will not long be this way.

"My clothes," Olga says.

The *domovoi* runs about, finding Olga's shift and blouse and skirt and colored vest, then begins to dress her, pulling her to a seat and crawling over the arms of it to fasten her buttons. The little magical being works quickly but inexactly, and Olga is forced to straighten her seams and rebutton her sleeves, affectionately complaining and calling him "grandfather." While she is being dressed, the Secret Ambassador sits opposite her and puts his bare feet on a low table.

"When do you leave for Constantinople?" he asks. The bear surmises that this is her next destination, and thinks that Constantinople is not so beautiful a name as Kiev.

"Two days hence," Olga says, dismissing the domovoi and casting a glance toward the opaque glass of the window. "Truth be told, I'm a little frightened."

"I've heard the way is hazardous."

"We must take a river craft so that it can be carried beyond the rapids across country. But then it is too light for the winds and waves of the Black Sea."

"Take offerings for Perun and Veles."

"We have fifty cocks to kill."

"Then you will be safe. Our gods will watch over you, and you will return to me." He smiles at her, and the bear sees Olga smile for the first time. It gives her hard face a cruel cast.

"I have to return, Secret Ambassador. My son is too young to take the throne by himself."

"He was old enough to go into battle against the Derevlians."

"They killed his father!" she exclaims. "He had to partake in our revenge."

"As I hear it, the child was barely big enough to throw a spear."

"He could throw a spear. He just couldn't throw it above the horse's head." Olga laughs and runs a fingernail over the carved wood of her chair. "He will be a good prince one day. I love the boy."

"Is he the only one you love?"

"You know it's true."

"But I love you, Olga."

She lifts her shoulders and glances away. "Mothers only really love their sons and no one else."

"He is a lucky boy."

"I want everything for him, Secret Ambassador. That is why my visit with Konstantin the Purple-Born must go well. I need to persuade him to lift the winter fishing bans, and to allow the Rus greater access to the silk trade. I hear of the immense wealth of the Byzantines, and I want some of that wealth for myself, for my son." Her voice becomes infused with a ruthless tone. "If others have it, why shouldn't we?"

"You have so much more here in your own lands."

Olga sniffs derisively. "The Byzantines think we are barbarians. That we live in treehouses."

"They don't know of the richness of your secret world. They don't know of the misted lands where your stories grow."

"Stories don't command coin."

"Coin doesn't command happiness."

Olga laughs darkly. "Nothing commands happiness. Happiness comes willingly to some, and avoids others as she pleases. I have rarely met her."

Olga stands and returns to the bed, where she nurses the Golden Bear against her bosom. "You have a sweet face," she says to the bear.

The Secret Ambassador smiles. The face is Olga's own, although she hasn't recognized it. "Perhaps you should keep her," he says.

"No, no," Olga says. "Though I am glad to have her as my traveling companion." The rain eases outside and Olga swings her legs over the edge of the bed so that her bare feet can press against the stove. "You should go now, Secret Ambassador. But I hope to see you on my return."

"You do?"

She waves him away. "Don't ask for promises of love. I won't give them."

The Secret Ambassador leaves, and the bear finds herself happily tucked in the bed of her new mistress.

The Golden Bear is sad to discover that she will be packed away for the long journey to Constantinople. She has enjoyed seeing things and learning things. But she soon realizes that being packed away is no impediment; she can still see and hear things, just by closing her eyes. The grand sweep of the Dnieper River, which rolls and tumbles the boat beneath her, is as visible as though she were a crow flying above it. If she thinks hard, she can feel what Olga is feeling, or sometimes hear her thoughts. In fact, as the journey progresses, the bear finds that any mind is open to her and she delights in popping in and out of people's heads: the merchants, the lesser princesses, the slaves shackled at the ankles.

I can know anything, she thinks, and she knows why the Secret Ambassador carved her mold with a smile. To know anything is a wonderful enchantment.

Olga comes for her on the evening before they are due to leave the boat, finally in safer waters.

"Come, little bear," Olga says, unwrapping the bear and tucking her under her arm. "Tomorrow you will meet your new master, the Emperor Konstantin."

Olga sleeps poorly that night, tossing and turning in her narrow bed. She is cold, she is worried. She dreams of little Sviatoslav, home in Kiev, and imagines a monster shaped of attenuated bones and cold shadows slithering across the floor to his bed. Poverty, hunger, helplessness surround her.

On waking, Olga dresses in her finest robes. A roll of gold silk constrains her wild hair. A flame-colored chiton over a rich green tunic. Shoes of gilded kid. Her rarest fur, shimmering dark brown.

The lesser princesses dance attendance, cooing about her beauty and her grace. She narrows her eyes and draws her lips down in disdain. Any one of these little whores would steal her son from her; she would like to put them all to the sword. She wishes she could have brought her trusted domovoi, but it would be ill luck indeed to take the magic from the fireplace. The gangplank is lowered and the thump shudders through the boat.

Olga emerges from her dark chamber into a perfect warm morning. The sun is far away and high, the blue sky makes her eyes ache. Seabirds circle and a mist of insects catch the sun on their wings. Below her is the golden gate of Byzantium. Two tall pillars of marble support the magnificent arch. A delegation from the emperor awaits them. She takes a deep breath and strides toward land.

The Golden Bear rests in a carved box, but in her magical eyes she can see the narrow paved streets of Constantinople, the mighty sea walls, the monuments and columns. The bear sees a building, three times as tall as Olga's palace, and knows that Olga is feeling more and more like the barbarian princess she loathes to imagine. The city is simply splendid. Wealth oozes from every intricately sculpted structure, from every merchant who passes in colorful silks, from the women with expensively perfumed hair who stare Olga down, expressing distaste for the stale smell of the fur she wears.

But more embarrassment awaits Olga. The small guard have stopped and now their commander (even he is dressed better than Olga's interpreters) is ushering Olga and her forty-three traveling companions into a building he calls the Magnaura, just north of the Great Palace.

Up to the terrace they walk, then through the arch into the huge apsed hall.

Olga's eyes grow as big as the moon.

The hall itself is marbled and tiled with mosaics in colors Olga has only imagined. Gold streaks every surface and one entire wall is decorated with silver dirhams. In Kiev, men would kill each other for a handful of these coins.

Still more. The hall is dotted with gilded trees and in each tree mechanical birds with rare gems for eyes sing perfect tunes. Olga glances around her. Every member of her retinue is agog; the display of grandeur overwhelms them. And Olga knows she must keep her head.

She is led to another arch. Olga takes a deep breath and strides into the reception room.

This room is bright, lit by a window in the ceiling. The walls are bare, to draw attention to the throne in the center. Up six steps, the throne is guarded by gilded mechanical lions. Konstantin sits, like a god, clothed in dazzling robes. Olga refuses to allow the display of gold and precious gems to crush her. The lesser princesses have already prostrated themselves on the cold floor, along with the merchants, the interpreters, the men of state.

But Olga stands firm, and offers Konstantin only a proud nod. In painstakingly practiced Greek, she says, "It is my pleasure to meet you, Emperor."

A lesser princess hurriedly rises and tries to hand the box with the Golden Bear to Olga. But Olga knocks her back, mutters, "Not now." She knows she can't present Konstantin with an odd, uneven bear molded by magicians.

Konstantin the Purple-Born catches Olga's gaze. The bear knows that he thinks Olga is, indeed, a barbarian princess. But he is intrigued by her dignity and her hard beauty.

"The pleasure is mine, Princess of the Rus," he responds. He climbs to his feet, and everybody in the room throws themselves once again on the floor. Except for Olga.

Konstantin smiles at her. Olga smiles back.

By the second day, Olga is invited to dine at Konstantin's table and to stay in the Grand Palace, a dazzling dream of marble and riches. Olga wonders if she will ever grow used to the wealth that weighs down every surface, every cup and plate. Even the food is rich, leaving Olga night after night with stomach cramps and foul gas.

Olga does not grow fond of Konstantin, though he is clearly growing fond of her. He is a cold man, with fingers like fish fillets and an overly wet mouth. His robes are so stiff that he can barely move, and much of his time and energy is taken up with the religious observances and state duties that have made him boring.

Still, Olga is fascinated by the churches in this city. They are almost as rich as the Grand Palace, with gold cupolas and towering turrets. Most of her mental energy is spent on trying to estimate Konstantin's wealth, and how she most easily may access it.

At dessert on the fourth night, Konstantin dismisses his ministers and Olga hers. Behind their shoulders sits only one interpreter. The dining hall echoes with the sound of their solitary plates and the unvoiced questions that Konstantin intends to put to her. Food smells hang moist in the air, and Olga cannot bring herself to take even a bite of the layered pastry in front of her.

"What troubles you, Princess Olga?" Konstantin asks, wetting his lips with the tip of his tongue. "Are you unwell?"

"I am well enough," she says, "but I think the dessert has defeated me."

"Are you so easily defeated?"

Olga carefully withdraws all heat and irritation from her voice. "No, of course not."

"We have spent days now in negotiation, but I feel I haven't had a moment to talk with you alone."

Olga glances around at the interpreter and has to smile. "This is alone?"

"You can be trusted to keep secrets, can't you?" Konstantin says to the interpreter, a slight man with a patchy beard. He nods. "You see," Konstantin says, returning his attention to Olga. "We are alone."

Olga gazes toward the kitchen.

"We could talk about something other than trade," Konstantin suggests. "Is there anything you would like to know about me? About my empire?"

Olga considers this carefully, and decides that this intimate moment he has fashioned allows her some informality. "Yes, there is," she says. "I would like to know why you are so wealthy and I am not."

Konstantin laughs. "That is simple. We worship Christ, and you worship barbarian demons."

Olga is startled. She has never thought to make this connection. "You mean your gods provide you with all these riches?"

"Our God. There is only one."

The world stops for a moment as Olga is engulfed in this thought. What had the Secret Ambassador ever given her but a bent bear and a thorough plumbing? No jewels, no gilded birds, no necklaces of silver coins. It is only a little thing to change allegiance, surely. The benefit to her people would be immeasurable. Especially to her son. Those dreamed monsters would finally be driven away.

"Olga," Konstantin says, his voice dropping to an intimate murmur as he slips into her own language. "Olga, you are beautiful."

She is distracted. Almost doesn't hear.

"Olga, I have something important to ask of you," he says.

Olga fixes him with her hard eyes. "The answer is yes," she says.

"Yes?"

"Yes, I will convert to Christ."

Within two weeks, Konstantin baptizes Olga himself and proclaims himself her godfather. Until the moment that she is plunged under the water at the mouth of the river, she refuses to talk to Konstantin at all, calling herself unclean and unworthy of his compliments. It is, of course, a strategy. Olga can read Konstantin's hot passion for her, and wants to hold him off as long as possible. After the baptism, as she sits still wet and shivering on the riverbank in the late afternoon sun, Konstantin outlines to her all of her responsibilities as a Christian woman. She is only half-listening, wondering when the gold and gems will start to be provided by her new god.

"Princess Olga," he says, at the very last, "there is one more thing that must be finalized between us."

Olga swallows hard. Konstantin dismisses the richly robed attendants and takes her hand. In faltering tones, in Olga's tongue, he says, "I would like you to marry me."

Marry him? And be Empress of Byzantium? Wealth without measure, and she but a chattel at his disposal. Once Christ started pouring the wealth onto her in Kiev, she wouldn't need him. She could rule in her own right, at least until Sviatoslav came to the throne. And then her son would be a powerful prince of Kiev, not a half-brother to the next emperor, his own land swallowed into the insatiable gullet of Byzantium.

Olga smiles shyly and gestures for her interpreter to come forward. She watches Konstantin's face fall as the interpreter delivers her answer. "You have just baptized me and proclaimed yourself my godfather. A Christian woman cannot marry her own father."

Konstantin's eyebrows shoot up, and for a moment Olga feels sorry for him. Then she flicks her wet hair over her shoulder and says, "I am cold. I will return to my chamber, and tomorrow we will sail home to Kiev."

The bear does not yet understand how all these events will impact on her, but finds herself growing afraid while resting in her still-unopened box. The journey home is harsh. The boat nearly sinks in the Black Sea, and the portage route around the rapids is muddy and claims the lives of two men. Olga sits gloomily in her cabin, repressing the urge to perform the sacrifices she would ordinarily have ordered to make their way safe. Instead, she prays to Christ for safety, and for some gold to make into a throne, and for a marble palace. She occasionally peers out of her cabin to swear at the crew for making the journey so miserable and hazardous.

Perhaps this is what the bear is afraid of: Olga has changed. Olga once loved her and thought she had a sweet face, but Olga hasn't thought of the bear once since her conversion, and the bear worries that she is to become discarded junk with no warm room to sit in.

On Olga's return, she sleeps a troubled sleep for three nights. On the fourth day, the Secret Ambassador arrives. Olga is not in her chamber when he comes knocking. He finds her instead in the cold state room, sitting on a long bench under the window. The room's plain timbered walls are dark and high, and the princess's face is drawn and shadowed.

"Olga?" he says, approaching her.

Olga turns her face away from his offered kiss, and dismisses her guards with a wave. When they are alone, Olga offers him the box.

The Secret Ambassador's eyebrows twitch, but he shows no other sign of the unease he feels. He opens the box, the bear is inside.

"Take it back," she says. "Everything has changed."

"What do you mean?"

"I have a new god now. His name is Christ."

A wave of frightened heat washes through the Secret Ambassador's body. "You cannot have Christ as your god. You are tied to the native magic of your land."

"I have clear instructions," Olga responds, her voice cold. "I am to banish all the unclean demons." She stands, thrusts the box into his hands and begins to pace.

"Who gave such instructions?"

"The Emperor Konstantin. My godfather."

"Why do you let him command you?"

Olga stops and turns, her eyes blazing. "I command myself," she shouts, "and I command you. You and your unholy host are a supplement to this land, not its rulers. Men rule here."

"Olga, you are not a man," he says, adopting a gentle chiding tone.

"I am as much a man as my husband ever was. As much a man as my son needs for his future to be secure." Olga comes to rest near the window, and pushes open the shutter. A cold breeze licks in, making the flames in the hearth jump. Her voice remains steely. "Secret Ambassador, you know that I speak the truth. If I tell you to withdraw, you must withdraw."

"And also the domovoi who keeps your fire burning? And the leshii who helps you fell trees to build houses? And the magic of Mother Moist Earth herself, who makes your crops grow?"

Olga is quiet a long time. The Secret Ambassador waits in the dim room. Finally, he places the box gently on the floor and approaches Olga, tries to slip his fingers over hers on the windowsill.

"Don't," she says roughly, pulling her hand away. "My new god will give me better than trees and dirt. He will give me gold and sapphires."

Irritation overcomes his good sense. "You are a fool," he spits, seizing her wrists roughly and shaking her.

"You are my servant!" she shouts. "Do as I say. Withdraw all your unclean magic from this land and never again cross this palace threshold."

"And you will command this even though it may not be the wish of all the Rus. You believe they will stop making sacrifices and performing their native rituals?"

She stares him down. "The Rus are my people to rule."

The Secret Ambassador takes a step away from her, lifting his hands in surrender. "So be it, Olga," he says, and the cold note in his voice touches her spine and makes her tremble, "but you cannot banish us entirely. We are of this land as much as you. We will linger behind the veil of men's thoughts. We will always be there."

"I don't care where you are, as long as you aren't here."

He raises a finger to hold in front of her eyes. "Tonight, then, in the cold before dawn. If you are awake, you will feel it, like a wave retreating on the sand. And remember, the further out the wave draws the mightier the crash when it returns."

Olga does not answer as the Secret Ambassador strides toward the door.

"Take your filthy idol with you," she says, indicating the bear in the box.

"No, it is yours, Olga. A reminder of what you have lost." Then he is gone, and his footsteps echo down the wood and stone hall.

Olga's body relaxes forward, and she crouches on the floor next to the bear. The bear sees tears spill from Olga's eyes as her shaking fingers come down to touch the bear gently on the belly.

"I loved him," she says quietly, then takes a breath and glances toward the window. "Christ save us all," she murmurs, and her voice is lost in the empty room.

Night falls and a cold hush mists across the land. Midnight follows on its heels and everything at the palace grows still. Olga can hear the whoosh and thud of the stove and nothing more. She does not sleep. She draws the furs close around her and stares into the dark room. The smell of pine and woodsmoke hangs in the stagnant air. The hours draw out: one, two, three . . .

And then it comes, a feeling like the waves withdrawing. If she listens closely, she can hear their whispered roar in her heart. Every pore on her skin shrinks, and a shiver runs across her. Something is moving, reluctant feet are leaving, a buzz of energy is dimming. She closes her eyes and the tide pulls out, tugging on her sinews and veins. The roar intensifies, rushing into her ears. She covers them with her hands, but the sound is in her head, not in the world.

At once, it stops. An emptiness infuses her, and all the muscles in her body are tensed against the tide's return.

It does not come.

Olga waits a day, two, three. A week. Her body grows more and more tense.

The leshii is not at his cottage. The domovoi is not beneath the stove. But she still hears them sometimes: invisible footsteps in the woods, scuttling noises from her chamber.

Still she waits for the wave to crash back over her.

The world has lost some of its brightness and color. Only children dream in the old colors. The people feel an emptiness, but it is an emptiness that may soon be filled by the new God.

Olga waits and always remains empty.

How does this tale end? It doesn't. It hasn't. Few people live forever, and Olga certainly didn't. She was followed by her son, and his son, and so on. Christianity found eager hearts to inhabit; believers in the old magic lived alongside them.

The bear was carted about from household to household, a treasured chattel of the princely family. She was wise and formed no further attachments, recognizing that she was fated to outlive all whom she met. The Rus flourished for hundreds of years, and then the Mongols came, and with them blood and ash and the crushing of bones. Whole cities were put to the sword, and the bear saw it all and her heart grew colder. We cannot remain forever in the dreamy innocence of childhood. Knowledge comes to us. Indeed, we seek it out.

And knowledge changes us.

The Golden Bear saw many things, and books could be filled with her experiences. But a good storyteller always knows to select only the tales that are important to his ending. Let it be known simply that the Golden Bear survived the Mongol onslaught by the devices of a wily slave who hid her in his shack in the cold northern woods, and whose family treasured her until she was taken as tribute by Vsevolod of the Large Nest, ruler of Moscow. And there she remained for many centuries, and witnessed many things, including the rise of a prince named Ivan, surnamed the Terrible.

But that is a story for another time.

So you see how one world became two, and I will tell you now the traditional names for these two worlds.

Mir. The world where Uncle Vasily lives, where cars and trams stalk roads of tar, where giant machines can fly and rulers govern from staterooms rather than armed on horseback.

And *Skazki.* The world of stories. It is believed that all our magical demons—the leshii, the russalki, Morozko the frost demon, and the child-eating witch Baba Yaga—only exist in stories. Skazki is a cruel and bitter place. It is also a place where your own death cannot find you; only a death not-your-own. Have I confused you? I'm sorry, I do not mean to.

But surely, by now, you know where Rosa's lover is.

PART TWO

You withdraw into crimson twilight,
In endless circles.
I hear a tiny echo: distant footsteps.
Are you near or far, or vanished into the sky? . . .
Do you draw close, burning,
In endless circles?

—ALEKSANDR BLOK

Eight

Rosa's body was stiff with indecision; she didn't know which way to turn her head, which path to set her feet upon.

"Rosa Petrovna?" The Ukrainian leaned against his car, his eyes hidden behind sunglasses.

Rosa turned. "I don't know what to do," she said.

"Have you lost someone?"

She considered Daniel and Em's car, so empty and so indifferent. "I have lost him more than once," she said under her breath, then turned to the driver. "Wait for me a few minutes."

"As you wish."

Rosa opened her small leather backpack and rummaged in it for her keys. Daniel had accidentally given her the spare key for the hire car. A cursory check of the car's tires told her they were all intact. She let herself in and searched the backseat, unzipping the suitcases and plowing through the borrowed clothes. She popped the boot and searched that too. The bear wasn't here. Daniel and Em had taken the bear with them.

Or the bear had taken Daniel and Em with her.

Rosa slotted the key into the ignition. It started on her first try. She put the car into gear and drove it a little way up the dirt road. The brakes were fine; the gears were fine; the steering was fine. There was absolutely nothing wrong with this car. So why had they abandoned it? They had packed up the bear and locked the car before they left, so Rosa presumed they weren't forced out by thieves or murderers.

She backed up again, and got out, leaned on a crooked pole.

"You can go," she said to the Ukrainian driver. "I'll be fine from here."

"Vasily said you'd need a lift back to St. Petersburg."

"Tell Vasily I'll call him soon."

The Ukrainian driver shrugged and pulled her suitcase from the car. He slid back into the driver's seat and, within moments, he had disappeared down the narrow rutted road.

She packed the car and started it again, driving for a few minutes over muddy potholes until she reached the end of the road, marked by a rusted dead-end sign. Beyond were untidy spruce and birch, their long branches crowding out the daylight. Rosa parked the car and got out. Again she was unable to decide what to do next. Search the woods for hours? She already knew Daniel wasn't here. The fog in the mirror had told her that. She felt helpless and tiny, an insubstantial speck in the enormous reach of Russia. And beyond.

Her second sight twitched, and she locked the car and tried to discern from which direction it came. The day was very still. Clouds had moved over the sun, and Rosa could hear birdsong, faint and far away. Somewhere to the west and north, a tickle in the atmosphere. She ducked around the sign and started walking.

Bracken crunched beneath her feet. She followed her second sight into the woods, then down a rocky gully. The sky dimmed. A plane went by, high overhead, the drone of its engines making tuneless but strangely hypnotic music as it disappeared into the east. She walked the gully a little way, then came back up a rise and into slightly sparser trees. Beyond them, the woods opened out into a rolling field.

Rosa caught her breath, squinting toward the sky. She felt strange and frightened, standing on the edge of this field. The beckoning sensation, an itch behind her forehead, originated here. Her raw ability was not enough to pin it down, nor to cast her mind beyond it to find Daniel. She leaned against a tree and tried to focus, letting her second sight open. Out there . . . colors and sounds, indistinct from one another. Smoky blue and violet, the faintest whisper of voices. A veil, lighter than a summer breeze.

Rosa left the cover of the trees. A cold sensation shivered over her. The veil was just a few feet ahead. She held her breath and strode toward it, through it, but nothing happened. She was still in the same field on the same summer morning.

Puzzled, she reached out her fingers to touch the veil. Her second sight opened, but the shimmers were pale. The morning sun fractured the magic. Daniel and Em must have crossed at night, when unseen forces were stronger.

Midnight would be her friend. At midnight, the veil was thinnest. She could wait in the car until then.

Rosa sighed, turning on her heel.

The hulking figure of a man stood directly behind her.

She screamed, he seized her arm, wrenched at her wrist, then dashed for the trees.

Rosa looked down to see that he had torn her mother's charm bracelet from her wrist.

"Hey, give that back!" she shouted, and took off after him.

The man had the advantage. While Rosa had to keep an eye on sudden drops and rocky ground, he flew over it with an ease that demonstrated he knew the area well. But she was light and young, reckless and determined. The clouds blackened and threatened rain, but still she ran, thrilling to the thundering of her heart. The dark figure was always just ahead of her. Then, abruptly, the ground sloped away ahead and he disappeared over the edge. Rosa skidded to a halt at the top of the ridge.

The man stood at the verge of a still lake, which was about a hundred feet across. Tangled weeds and skinny flowers grabbed at his boots. He held the bracelet in his right hand, over the water.

"That was my mother's," she said. "It's worth nothing to you. Give it back."

He smiled and shook his head. She made her way down the slope. Gravel slid beneath her feet and she wondered how he had managed to get over the ridge so quickly and easily. She picked her way down, and he stood motionless, waiting for her. Her heart was frightened, but she was not.

Finally she stood on flat ground, ten feet away from him.

"Don't come any closer," he said in a quiet, yet resonant voice. He was easily sixty, with dirty gray-streaked hair, a shaggy beard and stained clothes. His eyes were hooded and dark.

"I just want my bracelet back."

"I'll be keeping it."

She took a step and he dangled it over the water again. "Stay where you are or I'll throw it in the lake. You'll never find it."

"Give it back."

"I will. Eventually. Not now."

"It's worthless to you."

"You don't know that." He shook it gently, and the charms chimed against each other. "I'll keep it safe for as long as you stay with me, but when you leave I'll give it back."

Rosa was puzzled. "Stay with you?"

"At my home."

"I'm not coming to your home. I'm not staying with you."

"You are, because I have what you want."

"Only because you stole it."

"Not the bracelet," he said, smiling. "I have knowledge."

Rosa felt her skin shrink from him. Her body wanted to run, but she wouldn't let it. "I don't know what you mean."

"Come home with me."

"No thanks, granddad. You're not my type."

He raised his eyes to the sky and, as if he had directed it, the sun broke from the clouds, bathing him in light. Rosa was momentarily startled by the sunlight, almost didn't notice the strange sight before her.

Then her eyes, perceiving something unnatural, were drawn to the ground at his feet.

He cast two shadows.

"You're a *volkhv*?" she gasped.

"I can't let you wear this bracelet at my home," he said.

Rosa was wary and puzzled, but recognized that her resistance was already faltering. She had read about powerful magicians like this man and, although she had always believed in them, had never thought she would be lucky enough to meet one.

"What makes you think I'm coming to your home?" she said.

"My daughter Elizavetta is sick. We need an employee to help with the family business."

Rosa shook her head. "What are you talking about?"

He ambled toward her. She stood her ground, despite her trepidation and amazement.

"Come," he said, "you will have your own lodgings. You will be warm and comfortable."

She shrugged off his insistent fingers. "No. Explain what you mean. Explain who you are."

"I am Anatoly Dimitrov Chenchikov and, yes, I am a volkhv. You are a silly girl with a foreign accent and a pitifully weak magic bracelet. You hope to cross the veil. You cannot."

"How do you know I can't? My friend did."

He smiled. "Ah, so now the mystery deepens. Someone you love has crossed the veil. How?"

Rosa didn't tell him about the bear. "I don't know."

"We shall find out together. You have a piddling trickle of second sight. I will show you how to use it." He nodded. "There are twenty-seven crossings in all of Russia, and twenty-seven guardians nearby. You were lucky to find me. Don't let this opportunity slip through your fingers."

Rosa's heart leapt with excitement, but still she hesitated. "Why can't I have my bracelet back?"

Anatoly chuckled. "For the same reason you aren't allowed to use your mobile phone on an airplane. You'll get it back eventually. After the journey." He extended his hand, a fatherly gesture. "Come, girl. It will be an adventure."

An adventure. Rosa knew she had to stay nearby until midnight anyway. In the meantime she may as well see where the volkhv lived. She took a deep breath and reached out. His palm was rough and dirty, and now she was close to him she could smell stale sweat. "I'm Rosa Petrovna Kovalenka," she said.

"I know. It was written on the suitcase you left in the blue car. My son-in-law, Ilya, has already taken your things to our home." He led her firmly around the lake and back up a gentle slope into the dark woods. "Come, Rosa. You have much to learn."

Anatoly kept hold of her hand as they moved through the woods. Rosa remained silent, memorizing the route through the trees so she could make the return journey later. Maybe Anatoly could teach her something, maybe he couldn't. He was certainly a power-ful magician and she might need his assistance. Finding Daniel was uppermost in her mind; to see the place he wandered and to bring him home safely.

"There is our farm," he said in a quiet voice as a brick fence, painted white, came into view. There was a gate in the fence, also white, high and arched with iron doors. The paint was peeling and discolored, the grass grew long, giving the impression that nobody had lived here for a long time. Anatoly finally dropped her hand, and felt in his pocket for keys. "We are careful always to lock the gate, so remember that if you leave. There are precious things within."

"What kind of things?" Rosa asked.

"Bees," he said with a smile, jingling the keys merrily. "We're honey farmers."

Rosa was struck by the practicality of this. She had had a roman-ticized notion that a volkhv and his family might live isolated from the world, conjuring bread and wine from rocks and water but, of course, they had to survive the same as anyone else. They had to have money for the markets and for schoolbooks.

When they arrived at the gate, Anatoly turned her to face him. "Rosa, I could feel you nearby since you arrived this morning, and I came for you quickly. My family think you are a new employee, here to help with the business until Elizavetta recovers. There is no rea-son for them to believe otherwise. Do you understand?"

"Okay," she said indifferently, shrugging. She had no intention of staying beyond midnight. "Let me ask you some important ques-tions first."

"You may ask only three questions."

"Is my friend . . . is Daniel in danger?"

His hooded eyes lifted to the sky. "It's hard to say. He may be. Is he clever?"

"Yes."

"Then he will probably be safe for a while."

"How long before I learn how to cross the veil?"

"As long as it takes, Rosa. It would be dangerous to go unpre-pared."

"A day?"

He laughed. "No. Longer."

Rosa grew frustrated. "A week?"

"No more questions."

"What's beyond the veil?"

His voice became hard. "No more questions. You are here to give my son Makhar his daily lessons, and in spare moments you will help my wife with the bottles and labels. You understand?"

Rosa bit back a retort. She was nobody's nanny or housekeeper. But she sensed that Anatoly would only give her what she needed if she went along with him. "I understand," she said. "When can I be alone with you again?"

He took her hand and caressed her fingers gently. Rosa felt a cold shiver of mixed revulsion and anticipation. "No . . . more . . . questions."

Anatoly released her, ran his hand once over his beard, and opened the gate. Rosa followed him into a neatly maintained, shady garden. The family home was an old timber cottage painted pale blue, with tidy beds of herbs and flowers lined up along the path. Anatoly indicated off to the right. "Behind the house are the hives, down toward the stream is the old outbuilding. We've made it into a guesthouse. That is where you will stay."

They walked up the front path. Rosa noted the sun symbol above the door, the bunches of stinging nettle hanging over the windows, the cross painted on the jamb: wards against magic. She felt a prickle of excitement. To be immersed in this world, where enchantments were real and not dismissed as superstitions . . .

Anatoly pushed the door open, calling out that he was home. Rosa stood in a large room. A kitchen and a dining table took up one half; the other half was decorated as a living room with bright curtains, a faded sofa, and an aging television set stacked with magazines. The welcoming smells of honey and baking bread overlaid a less pleasant smell—damp, or rottenness. The floor felt slightly tacky under her shoes. A narrow hallway led off toward other rooms. All the timber was unpainted, making it feel as if she stood inside a treehouse. A woman at least twenty years younger than Anatoly came gliding down the hall toward them. Rosa assumed it was his daughter, until Anatoly introduced her as his wife.

"Who's this?" she said suspiciously, her nose wrinkling as though she had smelled something bad.

"This is the young woman I mentioned before I went out. She has come to help until Elizavetta is recovered."

"And I told you that I didn't want any help." The woman had a wide face, with prominent cheekbones and flared nostrils. Her hair was very fair, but her eyes were dark and sharp.

"Ah, pish! You can't manage everything on your own, and you don't speak English and this young woman does. Makhar must keep up with his lessons."

The woman moved forward and extended her hand for a limp shake. "I'm Ludmilla," she said.

"Rosa," Rosa replied.

"I don't want you here, but my husband does."

"I won't give you any trouble."

"Is that a promise?"

Rosa opened her mouth to promise, then remembered she was in a volkhv's house, and that promises were more than just empty things people said to fill silences. Instead she changed the subject. "What illness does Elizavetta suffer from?"

Ludmilla and Anatoly exchanged a look, but Rosa couldn't read what it meant.

"She'll be well soon enough," said Anatoly. "I'll go and find Makhar." The door banged shut behind him.

Ludmilla moved to the stove—a huge cast-iron mechanism that looked as ancient as the trees shadowing the kitchen window—and pulled the bread out. "Well, you're in time for lunch, Rosa."

"Thank you, I haven't eaten yet today."

"You can help me set the table." She nodded toward a crooked sideboard, and in it Rosa found table linen and cutlery. She had to force her arms and hands to work at such mundane tasks: laying the cloth, arranging the knives and forks. Her stomach itched, but midnight was hours away. She blocked Daniel from her mind, and Uncle

Vasily too. He would be worried about her, but she didn't want to call him in case his worry convinced her to come back to St. Petersburg empty-handed.

"How many for lunch?" she asked, as she paused over the last place setting.

"Five. You, me, Anatoly, my son and Elizavetta's husband. I'll take Elizavetta's to her room."

"How old is Elizavetta?" Rosa asked cautiously. Ludmilla seemed far too young to have a married daughter.

"She's nineteen. I'm thirty-four and you're right, my husband is much older. I see your mind working, Rosa. Be careful your curiosity doesn't make you rude."

Rosa set the table in silence, wondering how a fifteen-year-old Ludmilla had ever paired off with Anatoly, who must have been at least forty at the time. Ludmilla placed the bread on the table, along with butter, honey, cold meats and cheeses in plastic tubs, and Rosa helped her lay it all out on plates.

While Rosa was at the sink washing her hands, Ludmilla glanced at her irritably. "Anatoly takes too long. Will you go and find him?"

Rosa wiped her hands on her skirt. "Which way?"

"Around the back toward the hives. Follow your ears."

Rosa ducked out the front door and around the side. Tall spruce trees shaded the house, and although the grass was overgrown it was not out of control. She could hear buzzing, and did as Ludmilla had advised, following her ears.

Down a gentle slope she found them. Two dozen hives dotted the garden, which led to a stream. A cloud of bees surrounded each hive. Anatoly had stopped about thirty feet from the hives to talk, in an intense and authoritative tone, to a young man. A little boy of about nine years hung onto Anatoly's hand, kicking his toe impatiently.

"Anatoly!" Rosa called.

Anatoly broke off mid-sentence and looked up as Rosa approached. "What is it?" he asked.

Rosa stopped before them. "Ludmilla sent me to tell you lunch is waiting."

"She is an impatient woman." He roughed up the little boy's snowy hair. "Makhar is just like her, aren't you?"

Rosa considered the man with Anatoly, presumably Elizavetta's husband. He was about twenty, with yellow-gold hair, strong shoulders, warm tanned skin, a long straight nose and determined mouth. Oddly, though, his eyes were different colors: one brown and one green.

He offered Rosa a strained smile. "I'm Ilya," he said.

"Nice to meet you," she replied, offering her hand. "I'm Rosa."

Anatoly chimed in quickly. "Ilya is Elizavetta's husband," he said. "My son-in-law."

Rosa turned to the little boy. "And you are Makhar? I'm going to teach you English."

Makhar switched to English and said, "Nobody else here speaks a word of it, except Elizavetta, and we use it to pass secret messages."

Rosa laughed, sticking with Russian out of politeness to her host. "Well, that sounds like fun, but right now your mama wants you to come home for lunch."

"Are you American?" he said.

"Canadian," she replied, "but I was born here."

"That's boring. Never mind," he said, and he wrested himself from Anatoly's firm grasp and ran back toward the house.

Anatoly took Rosa's shoulder and gently turned her to follow Makhar. "Tell Luda we'll be right behind you," he said. "I have one last thing to discuss with Ilya."

Rosa made her way back to the house. Her ears told her that Anatoly waited until she was a safe distance before resuming his conversation with Ilya. In the kitchen, Makhar waited at the table alone, drumming his feet impatiently against the underside of the table.

"Where's your mother?"

"She takes food to my sister."

Rosa glanced toward the hallway. Quiet voices.

"How long has your sister been ill?"

Makhar shrugged. "She's been in bed for a month, but she was ill before that. Ever since Nikita died."

"Nikita? Who is Nikita?"

"Her husband. I mean, her husband before Ilya."

The door burst open and Anatoly came in, stopping Rosa from asking the million new questions that sprang to her tongue.

"Where is Ilya?" asked Makhar. "He promised to teach me a song at lunchtime."

"He'll have his lunch later. He has to clean up the guesthouse for Rosa's stay."

Makhar turned on her with an expression of unabashed jealousy and excitement. "Hey! She gets to stay in the magic place."

Rosa hid her surprise.

"It's not magic, Makhar. It's just a guesthouse." Anatoly touched his hair fondly.

Makhar began to pick at his food when the voices from down the hallway grew impassioned.

"But, Elizavetta, you must eat something."

"I won't! Leave me be!"

A second later Ludmilla was retreating along the hallway, a tray of food still in her hands. She caught Rosa's eye with a cold warning stare, and Rosa looked away.

"Let's have lunch," Ludmilla said, rattling the tray onto the kitchen bench. "Otherwise we'll never get any work done."

Anatoly avoided Rosa for the rest of the afternoon, forcing her to sit with Ludmilla at the table sticking labels on honey jars. She worked impatiently, glancing at the door at every slight noise, her mind swirling with thoughts of Daniel, of what lay beyond the veil, so that she worked haphazardly and slowly. Ludmilla was tight-lipped but polite. Rosa's only glimpse of the rest of the Chenchikovs' home was on a trip to the bathroom, where she quickly surveyed each of the cramped, dusty rooms—except Elizavetta's; her door was shut—before being recalled firmly by Ludmilla. A request for a cigarette break was met with an icy admonition that nobody *ever* smoked within the house, or garden, or guesthouse, and certainly not ever around the bees.

Finally, after dinner, Anatoly instructed Ilya to take her to the guesthouse. Makhar was in his pajamas on the sofa, watching a dubbed American comedy. The fire was low in the grate. Nobody hurried to stoke it, as the warmth of the day still hadn't withdrawn completely.

"Can't you take me, Anatoly?" Rosa said.

This request drew a suspicious scowl from Ludmilla.

"Ilya knows the way as well as I do," Anatoly said, his eyes not leaving the television screen.

"But I thought you were going to . . . outline the terms of my employment," she said, careful to keep her real purpose here a secret.

Anatoly smiled up at her. "Tomorrow will do just as well."

Rosa swallowed down her annoyance. She'd worked for him all day and he'd given her nothing in return. If he thought she would be washing his dishes again tomorrow, then he was mad. By then, hopefully, she'd be across the veil again and away, chasing after Daniel.

"We'll speak at length tomorrow," he said to Rosa. "Ilya, come straight back. I need you to help me load some crates into the car for the morning."

Then the door was closed behind them, and Ilya offered her a tentative smile. "This way," he said, leading her through the garden and hives. "Anatoly said you were from St. Petersburg."

"That's right. Just looking for a change of scene, some fresh air."

"It's good that you could come. Ludmilla's been trying to do everything by herself."

"I'm sorry that Elizavetta is sick," Rosa said. "Has she seen a doctor?"

"Anatoly's taking good care of her at present," Ilya said, feeling in his pockets for a key and deliberately not meeting her eye.

"Is Anatoly a doctor?"

"No, but her malady is nothing Anatoly can't treat. Besides, summer is here and soon she will be able to take some air and sunshine in the garden." Ilya stopped at a crooked wooden structure with a sloping roof, perched on the bank above the stream. "Here's the guesthouse."

She surveyed it with a lift of her eyebrows. "It's a bathhouse."

"It used to be. All the inside has been rebuilt."

This is why Makhar had called it a magic place. She wondered where Anatoly practiced his magic now this building had been turned into guest accommodation, but dared not ask Ilya.

He urged her forward. "Anatoly had me fetch your bags from the car earlier today."

"How did you get in?" she said. "It was locked."

"Nothing is locked to Anatoly," he said, smiling. "I noticed some men's clothes. Are you expecting someone else?"

Daniel's clothes. Or, at least, the clothes that Vasily had loaned him. Another pang. Was he wandering, cold and bewildered, in a strange land? "No," she said. "Just me."

They walked up the four steps to the front door of the guesthouse, and Ilya unlocked it. "How long do you think you'll stay?" he asked, and Rosa began to understand that Ilya was as curious about her as she was about him.

She turned to him. "Not long."

"Is there more to it?"

She smiled. "I don't know what you mean."

"Are you here for more than just a job?"

Rosa pushed open the door. "Is there a bathroom in here?"

Ilya reached above her head and switched on the light, closing the door behind him. "No, there isn't. You have to use the one at the house. But Ludmilla locks the door when she goes to bed, so if you need—"

"Do I get a key to the house?" she said.

Ilya shook his head. "I'm afraid there are no spares."

Rosa sighed. She had hoped to sneak up to the house after everyone was asleep and get her mother's bracelet back. It would have to stay here until she came back with Daniel. She looked around her.

The windows were high and narrow, the bed was covered in a faded patchwork quilt, the floorboards were softened by a thick rug; an old armchair sat in the corner under the lowest part of the roof, a battered wardrobe under the highest; a matching dresser stood next to the bed. A low buzzing noise came to her ears, and she wondered if the bees ever slept.

"There's no fire," Ilya was saying, "but there's an electric heater in the wardrobe if you need it."

Rosa's suitcase was on the bed, along with the cases she'd loaned to Daniel and Em. "What time do they go to bed up at the house?" she asked, unzipping her case and pulling out clothes.

"Everyone's locked in by midnight," he said, handing her a key to the guesthouse. "I suggest you do the same."

Rosa took the key and met his eye. "Are you serious?"

He nodded.

"Why?"

"It's safer. Really."

"Locks can't keep everybody out," she said lightly, flicking a strand of hair off her shoulder. "You said Anatoly can open any lock."

Ilya smiled, and Rosa was struck by how attractive he was. "You needn't be afraid of Anatoly."

Rosa leaned over and placed the key on the dresser. "Thanks for your help."

"There's a key to the front gate on there too. I expect you'll want to go home for a weekend, or go into town on your days off."

"How close is the nearest town?"

"About an hour's drive." He moved toward the door. "Good night, Rosa."

"Good night, Ilya."

He left her in the tiny guesthouse with the creaking floorboards and the insistent buzzing.

Rosa resumed unpacking, looking for a comfortable pair of pants and a warm shirt. Today's running after Anatoly in low heels and a lace skirt had been hard; tramping around the fields and woods, looking for the veil, she would need more practical clothing. She stripped to her underwear and changed, her thoughts preoccupied with remembering the route and worrying about Daniel. Did he even know where he was? His disbelieving nature was a liability to his safety: the longer he didn't acknowledge that he may be experiencing something magical, the more likely he was to wander into danger. At least Em had some sense; Rosa was glad she was with him.

So typical of Daniel, she thought, to need a woman to look after him.

She sat on her bed to go through her suitcase for a pair of socks, and the buzzing continued. For the first time since she had heard it start, she looked up. In the corner of the window above her bed, a bee was trapped inside.

"Oh, sorry," she said, standing on the bed to push the narrow window open, "I didn't realize you were in here with me."

The bee found the fresh air and slipped through, leaving Rosa standing with her hands on the sill, peering out into the dark. Night-time cold was beginning its creep across the land. She'd need a coat, too.

She finished dressing, slipped on her shoes then checked her watch. Only a few hours to wait. Anatoly could tie her up for days if she let him. As soon as midnight was upon her, she would be away across the fields, looking for the veil.

Nine

Em cast a hopeful glance down the long, empty road.

"Em!" Daniel called from the side of the road where he sat smoking a cigarette and picking the skin from around his nails. "There's nothing coming."

"There has to be something." Em had been watching the road since sunrise; hours of fruitless waiting. "A truck, a farmer's pickup, a lost tourist . . ." She shielded her eyes against the glare in the east. "It feels like we're the only people who have ever used this road."

"Just us. And car thieves."

Em turned, considering him in the mid-morning sunshine. He was hunched and anxious. She was starting to get anxious too. Not about the interview—she had let that go—but about the strangeness of the situation. How could it be that on this, the emptiest of roads in the universe, thieves were on hand to do their work at precisely the same time the car was unattended?

"Check your mobile again," Daniel said.

Em pulled her cell phone out of her pocket. No signal, and the battery was running low. "Nothing." Neither of them had slept last night, and her eyes were sore from tiredness and from the fine dust of the road. "How much longer are we going to wait here?"

Daniel rose and butted his cigarette under his toe. "Until one of us becomes convinced that no car is ever going to pass this way."

"I'm already convinced."

"Then we'd better start walking."

Em approached him, pushing her hair behind her ears. She longed for a shower and a change of clothes. "I think that's for the best. Toward that light I saw last night. If I can get my hands on a working telephone, I can make this all better." She hitched onto her shoulder the shopping bag with the bear in it and led the way into the woods. Daniel fell into step behind her. "If I can reschedule the interview for late this afternoon . . . even early tomorrow morning. Then we can still have the bear back before Rosa's uncle returns."

"Mm-hmm."

"I expect we'll have to report to the police about the car being stolen. I hope that won't hold us up too much. Maybe you can do that while I organize the professor and the film crew."

"Mm-hmm."

Em gave Daniel a smile. "Sorry, I'm thinking aloud."

"At least you're thinking about solutions," he said. "If I was thinking aloud, I'd be saying, 'Where the hell are we? Where the hell are we? Where the hell are we?'"

"Oh, I'm thinking that too. Of course I am," she said. "Daniel, do you think it's strange at all that the car should disappear so quickly on such a deserted road?"

"I guess thieves take advantage of any opportunity."

"The car wouldn't start."

"Maybe it was some temporary problem. The mechanic in Vologda said that it wasn't safe to drive."

Was that an accusatory tone? Em ignored it. "I'm concerned that thieves found it so quickly. I doubt that they were driving past. They might live in the area." She nodded in the direction they were walking. "They might live in the house we're trying to find."

Daniel fell silent. At length, Em said, "I'm sorry, have I made you worried?"

"Yes," he grumbled.

"I didn't mean to. Daniel, here's some advice. Today is going to be a day of uncertainties, I have no doubt about that. If you can't be calm, then take a breath and pretend to be calm. It's the next best thing. Okay?"

"I'll do my best."

"Maybe we'll find a whole village. A gas station, a car-hire company, a hotel, and lots of friendly people. Take heart."

They moved further into the trees. A ridge opened out in front of them, so they inched their way into the gully and followed it for a mile or so. Em grew warm and shrugged out of her overcoat. Her caramel wool suit and brown pumps were comfortable for driving, but not for hiking. She was sweaty, itchy, and tiring rapidly.

They came to the other end of the gully and back into trees. Em stopped to catch her breath.

"Well?" he said.

"We should have been there by now," she said, sitting down and taking off her left shoe to rub her foot. "I'm certain we've been tending toward the right direction."

"Are you certain you saw a light last night?"

"Yes."

"Because I didn't."

Em hesitated. She had seen other lights, strange colored lights in that moment between sleeping at the wheel and waking. "I'm sure, Daniel."

A cloud moved across the sun and Daniel peered upward anxiously. "I hope it doesn't rain."

"At least it's warm. Let's count our blessings this didn't happen to us in the dead of winter."

"We would never have got out of the car in the dead of winter."

Again the accusing tone, subtle but unmistakable. "Daniel, I know you didn't want to leave the car. But we did. We can't change that now."

"Sorry." Daniel crouched next to her. "I'm not angry. I'm guilty about not flying. It's not fair to blame you."

"Well, to be fair to you, you did say that you had a bad feeling about us leaving Vologda yesterday afternoon. Perhaps we should have trusted your intuition." She slipped her shoe back on. "Though Rosa seemed to think you don't believe in anything as mystical as intuition."

Daniel rose and gazed off into the distance. "Do you want to keep going? Or do you want a rest?"

"A quick rest. My feet are hurting. Your shoes are much more sensible."

"I'll scout ahead a few hundred feet," he said. "You wait here."

Em waited while Daniel moved off. She could hear his footsteps, the scuff and rattle of leaves, birds hopping between branches and chirping softly, but no other sounds that would indicate civilization was nearby: no planes, trains or cars. She hoped they hadn't wandered into an enormous uninhabited woodland. If so, they wouldn't last more than a few days. A jolt of survival instinct. She stood up and went after Daniel.

"You know, Daniel," she called, "maybe we should just go back to the road."

He turned, frowning. "Why?"

"We could get lost in the woods."

"I know my way back from here," he said. "Straight along the gully then west."

"But as we go further . . ."

Daniel pressed his lips together as he thought about this. "Okay, either we wait out on the road for a car that may never come along, or wander in the woods looking for a house which we may never find. If a car comes, it might not stop for us anyway. If we find a house, at least we have a chance to tell somebody what happened."

"So you want to keep walking?"

"You saw a light last night?"

"I think so. Yeah."

Daniel pulled off his scarf. "I have an idea," he said, picking at one of the decorative knots. "We'll mark our path. I'll tie a piece of wool to a tree branch every twenty feet or so. That way, if we haven't found anything in a few hours, we can follow the path back to the road and try our luck out there again."

"That's a great idea," she said, relieved.

He pulled out a long strand of wool and tied it to a branch. "Okay. Marker number one. We'll come back here if we haven't found anyone to help by . . . what time?"

Em checked her watch. Swore when she saw it had stopped. "I don't know. What time is it now?"

"The sun was directly overhead before the clouds moved in. It's probably around lunchtime."

"Which would explain why I'm so hungry. Look, Daniel, I have really uncomfortable shoes on. I'll only be able to walk another couple of hours before my toes start to bleed. Let's give it about an hour, then head back."

"Agreed."

They moved on, Daniel stopping every so often to tie a thread around a branch, carefully ensuring that the last thread was visible from the position of the new one. Em felt reassured by the sight of the bright crimson and purple markers among the trees. She tried to ignore her sore toes. They walked on together, long after they both tacitly agreed that there had probably been no light in the woods the previous night, long after her feet were beyond returning to the road, long after hunger and thirst had become the predominating discomforts. Rescheduling interviews and the possibility of ruining her wool suit had moved a long way down the list of priorities.

A loud electronic beep stopped them in their tracks, oddly out of place in this quiet woodland.

Em reached into her pocket. "A death rattle," she said, pulling out her cell phone. "The battery just ran out."

"Let's stop and rest a minute, and decide what to do next."

"I'm really tired."

"I'm not sure, but I think I can hear water."

"Oh, water would be good," she said, pocketing the cadaver of the cell phone. "I can walk as far as water."

They headed a little further north, tying wool threads to branches, until they found a narrow stream cutting through the forest.

"Do you think it will be safe to drink?" Daniel asked.

"I think it's more dangerous to be this dehydrated," Em said, picking her way down to the shallow edge of the stream. Brown mossy rocks were visible on the stream bed. The water bustled and gurgled. She bent to drink: cold and sweet.

"It tastes fine," she said to Daniel, who had joined her. "In fact, it tastes wonderful."

Daniel drank and then splashed his face, sitting back on his haunches and removing his shoes with a sigh. "Em, I think we're lost."

"I think you're right," she said. "How are you doing in there? I see you're pretending to be calm."

"I'm a mess, Em," he said with a self-conscious laugh. He ran a hand through his hair, which left a curl sticking up at the front. It made him look even more flustered. "I'm panicking."

"To be frank, I'm a little worried too. What next?"

"We could follow the stream. Much more likely to find a house or farm."

"We're not returning to the road then?"

"I don't know. I have this awful sense that we're making all the wrong decisions. I'm afraid to make any more." He wrapped his arms around his knees. "I'm so hungry I could eat bark."

"Me too."

"Is there anything in that shopping bag besides the bear? Chocolate bars? Day-old sandwiches?"

Em slid the bag off her shoulder. "I doubt it, but you're welcome to check." She lay the bag on the grass and pulled out a cashmere scarf she had bought in St. Petersburg, then the bear. "See, nothing," she said, showing the empty bag to Daniel.

Daniel was staring at the bear, ashen.

"Daniel?"

"Her eyes," he managed.

Em turned the bear to face her, already knowing what she would see. Although she had witnessed it before, it still sent a shock of adrenalin to her heart. "They're open," she said.

Daniel shrank back involuntarily. "They weren't before, were they?"

"Be calm, Daniel. Don't flip out."

"It's hunger. It's tiredness. I'm hallucinating."

"Then I'm hallucinating the same thing."

"My memory's faulty. She always had her eyes open."

"She didn't, Daniel. They were closed."

"You're wrong. You're wrong." He scrambled to his feet, then stood woozily. Em grabbed him and helped him to sit, telling him to put his head between his knees. His shoulders rose and fell too fast.

"Breathe normally," she said, stashing the bear. "Remember what I said. Pretend to be calm, pretend it's all okay."

"I can't, I can't. I saw . . ."

"I saw too. I can't explain it and I'm frightened." Yes, that was the feeling: a discomfort that she wanted to shrink from, a longing for somewhere warm and safe. Fear. "I'm afraid of it too, Daniel, but I've put her away now. Let's not look at her again."

He raised his head, and Em saw that his eyes were rimmed with red. She was reminded of her son when he was only small, crying about a bad dream, and was puzzled that Daniel could allow himself such freedom to express his childish emotions.

His breathing slowed and shuddered as he got himself under control. "What do we do?" he said, swallowing hard. She could tell he was trying to sound brave and capable. "I can't go any further."

"I can't either. We'll camp here tonight; follow the stream tomorrow."

"It was bad enough when I thought we might die here, but there's something else going on."

"Something neither of us can explain. I know. We'll keep busy. We'll build a fire and we'll try to find something in the woods to eat, and we'll play logic games and make alphabet lists. We'll keep the fear at bay, because it's no use to us." She stood and offered him her hand. "Come on, let's find some firewood."

Daniel's mind was a black, confused place. Though fear wanted to hold him immobile, Em wouldn't let it. She ordered him about: collecting firewood, building a fire before nightfall, then keeping his mind occupied with games. Alphabet lists: apple, banana, celery followed by Afghanistan, Brazil, Canada, followed by azure, brown, cyan . . . Then logic problems: if two trains are traveling toward each other on the same track at one hundred miles per hour . . . It stopped him from curling into a fetal position and gnawing his knuckles, but the logic problem that neither of them could solve was how the bear, a solid inanimate object, had changed form since the previous day.

He couldn't imagine a more hellish situation. Lost on the edges of a Russian wilderness with inexplicable enchantments around him, aching with roaring hunger. At least it took his mind off the social anxieties of being forced into the company of a brusque woman he barely knew. As night deepened, the clouds moved and the stars became visible. Daniel sat as close to the fire as he could. Em was further off, huddled into her coat with her back against a tree.

Stillness brought thoughtfulness. "Em, can I see the bear again?"

"Are you sure you want to?"

"Perhaps there's a mechanism in it, something we didn't notice before."

But Em was already shaking her head. "I've checked."

"Let me see for myself."

She sighed, and drew the shopping bag from her coat. Daniel felt his skin shrink over his muscles. She handed him the bear.

Daniel sat up, cradling the bear on his lap. Her eyes were open and staring back at him. It wasn't as bad as he'd thought, looking at the bear a second time. Perhaps he'd started to accept it. Rosa would have accepted it in an instant. Her disdain was reserved for skeptics: *Who are you, Daniel St. Clare, to suppose you know everything about anything?*

"Are you okay?" Em asked. She had left her position against the tree, and come to crouch next to him.

Daniel was touched by her concern. She certainly wasn't as cold as everybody had said, though he still found her lack of any visible reaction to the day's events unnerving. She was handling it like ordinary people might handle unexpected guests dropping in.

"You know the worst part?" Daniel said to her. "It's not just that she moved. It's because it's her eyes."

"I know. As though she was sleeping, but now she's awake."

"Why is she awake, I wonder?" Daniel said.

"Rosa said she wanted something from us."

"To get us lost in the woods?"

"Daniel, we've been two days without sleep, walking miles in woodland. I think we're both in danger of becoming hysterical."

Daniel shook his head, swallowing a laugh. "If this is you hysterical . . ."

"I handle things my own way. I'm puzzled and a little afraid. But I know that things often seem worse when I haven't slept. I suggest we put the bear away, pull close to the fire and try to sleep. Even if it's only for a few hours."

He handed her the bear. "You're right. Though I don't know how I'll ever get to sleep with so much on my mind."

"Let your body take over. Turn your mind off for a while." Em rolled onto her side, trying to pull her overcoat down over her knees.

"Easy to say."

"Easy to do, Daniel. If your body needs to rest, all you have to do is let it. Be quiet and still. You'll feel better in the morning."

Daniel lay down and closed his eyes. He was anything but comfortable—his legs ached, his stomach gnawed, the ground was hard beneath him—but he was exhausted. He focused on the noises around him. A night breeze in the treetops, the hoot of a distant owl, Em's sleeping breath, the rustle and pop of the fire, his own heartbeat warm in his ears.

It took time but, at length, he slept.

Em shook him awake some time later. He couldn't estimate how long precisely, but night had rolled back leaving dim morning light in its place.

"What is it?" he said, his mind still hazy.

Em's eyes were worried. "Something weird is going on."

But she didn't need to tell him, because it became apparent the instant he glanced around him.

"Shit!" He sat up, unable to trust what he saw. They sat in a wide, open field. The stream was gone, the trees were gone, their fire, the branches and all their markers.

"I woke up from the cold, twenty seconds ago," she said. "I'm as puzzled as you."

Daniel didn't point out that "puzzled" fell well short of describing his state of mind. "Could we have wandered in the night?"

"Both of us?" She arched a perfectly shaped eyebrow. "Daniel, Rosa tried to warn us. She said the bear was enchanted—"

"There's no such thing as enchantments!"

"Well, you explain where we are. You explain the color of the sky."

Daniel looked up. She was right, the sky was an odd silver-gray, although clear of clouds. The sun was distant and tinged with violet, lending an odd cast to the landscape.

"I've gone crazy, that's it," he said. "This is just some wild hallucination."

"Whatever you say," Em replied, "but we're stuck in this hallu-cination together, and I'm really hungry and I see a cottage in the distance."

Daniel's eyes followed where she was pointing. Backlit under the sky, a little cottage surrounded by silver birch puffed smoke from its chimney. Daniel's body froze. "We're not going up there, are we?"

"Food, warmth and explanations," she sniffed, pulling herself to her feet.

He clutched his knees to his chest. "We don't know what might be in there."

She yanked him to his feet. His legs were jelly beneath him.

"Get up," she hissed. "Get moving. This is a serious fuck-up and I have no idea what's going on, but I won't let you make it worse by falling to pieces. Move."

Her anger shocked him out of his pit. He gathered his coat and the bag with the bear in it, and followed her across the field to the mysterious cottage.

The grass was long in places and seeds clung to his jeans. The sky brightened, but he couldn't guess the time. The air was very still, only the faintest hint of a breeze up high. Em walked ahead of him, her hands out at her hips to touch the heads of the long stems. The surreal light gave a false familiarity to the scene, as though he'd seen it before in a painting or a dream. The cottage was small, little more than a square hut, with fancy carved shutters and a design of suns and moons painted over the lintel. It looked inviting, with its cornflower blues and dandelion yellows; but the garden around it gave quite a different impression, tangled and overgrown with briar and sedge. The silver birch trees draped their heavy branches over the roof and windows.

Em stopped on the doorstep and waited for him. "Are you okay?" she said.

"No."

"Nor am I. Take a deep breath and keep breathing."

She lifted her hand and rapped five times hard on the door. Daniel's body tensed. Moments passed.

"There's nobody home," Em said, then pushed the door with her toe. It inched inward. "But it's open."

Daniel looked at her silently.

"We're going in anyway, right?" she said. "We need food."

He shrugged, uncertain.

She sighed—exasperated—then turned to the door and gently pushed it open. "Hello? Is there anyone home?"

Daniel translated the sentence into Russian as they crossed the threshold. The cottage was neat and bright: just one large room with walls of unfinished pine. A large, square stove, decorated with ceramic tiles and heaped on top with blankets and pillows, dominated the space. Em was already going through cupboards.

"Bread, pancakes, jam," she said as she pulled the food out and crowded it onto the long wooden table, along with plates and knives.

Daniel hesitated near the other end of the table. "What if the owner of all this food comes back and finds we raided his cupboards?"

"Don't worry, we'll leave some money. We haven't eaten in a long time. Whatever we've got ahead of us, we'll need sustenance."

Daniel pulled out a chair and sat with her while she spread jam onto the bread and rolled the pancakes and began to eat. Hunger won out over fear, and he reached for the bread.

For a few minutes, the only sounds were the sounds of their greedy eating, and Daniel felt some of the tension leave his body. Yes, fear had made him jittery and shaky, but hunger had played its part as well.

"What's that noise?" Em said, stopping in mid-reach for another pancake.

Daniel pricked up his ears and listened to the distance. Far off, he caught a whooshing sound, as loud as industrial machinery, but one suburb over. Before he could place the sound, it raced toward them, whooshing and rattling, gathering intensity, barreling toward the cottage. "It's coming closer."

"It's wind."

The still air outside was being churned by a vast engine, roaring down on the branches above them, making them bend and snap. Quickly, precisely . . . a jet plane or a meteor bearing down on them.

Daniel moved to push himself out of his chair and run—anywhere—when the wind abruptly stopped. The door to the cottage blasted open, and the owner stepped in.

He was more than six and a half feet tall, with a wild beard and wild hair, rough skin that resembled bark and pale protuberant eyes. He was dressed in ragged green clothes. Daniel and Em were frozen like prey, with crumbs on their chins and jam on their fingers.

"Who are you?" he asked. The language he spoke was Russian, but a coarse, accented variety Daniel was unfamiliar with.

Em took over, smoothly rising from her chair and dusting herself off. "Forgive us, we thought nobody was home. I'm Em and this is Daniel."

He stared at her offered hand, paying keen attention to her watch. Then, without shaking her hand, he pulled out a chair to sit with them. "At least you haven't eaten it all," he said, spreading jam thickly on a pancake and shoving it in his mouth. "Where are you from?" he said through a giant mouthful. "Sounds like Mir. Am I right?"

Daniel noticed for the first time that the man's clothes were all on backward.

"Actually, I'm from Boston originally but I've lived in London a while," Em said. "Daniel's from Cambridge."

"Yes, yes. You're from Mir."

"So where are we now?" Daniel ventured, dreading the answer.

"Skazki." The man leaned back and smiled. A chunk of food hung in his beard. "Oh, you're lost, aren't you? You've never heard of Mir or Skazki?"

Daniel caught Em's eye, switched to English. "He's using the Russian words for *world* and *story*," Daniel said.

"None of your strange talk," the man said. "It's rude."

"I'm sorry, but we don't understand what you mean," Em said to him.

"You'll understand soon enough. Whether you believe it is another thing." He wiped his enormous hands on his trousers and folded them in front of him. "Sorry, I haven't introduced myself. You can call me Vikhor."

"Well, Vikhor," Em said, "I'm sorry that we came in uninvited, but we're lost and haven't eaten for a long time. I'll pay you for your trouble of course."

"Pay me? In Mir money? That would buy me nothing but a cowpat in this world. Do you have any gold?" Once again, his eyes flicked to her watch.

Em caught his inference. "I have this watch," she said, "but it's hardly a fair exchange. It's worth thousands, and we only had a bit of food."

"Oh, it's a fair exchange. You give me the gold, I won't eat you."

Em's cool practicality was stunned out of her. Her eyebrows shot up and her mouth formed a silent "O" of surprise.

"Your timepiece won't work over here, anyway." He clicked his fingers and held out his hand. "Come, girl. Give me the gold. I'm pleasant when I'm rich. I'm extremely unpleasant when I'm poor."

Daniel saw Em hesitating and panicked. "Just give it to him, Em," he said. "The guy's some kind of psycho."

Vikhor shook his head. "You Mir folk are such idiots. Do you think I'm a murderer? A thief? Yes, I murder, yes, I steal. But I am neither of those things. I am a leshii. Do you know what that is?"

Daniel felt his stomach turn over. Impossible conclusions were falling into place. Vikhor called this place the world of story, he looked like a cross between a man and a tree, and a leshii was a wood demon from Russian folklore.

"Where the hell are we?" he said, terror making his voice thin.

"You've crossed the veil, boy," Vikhor said, standing and forcibly removing Em's watch. He dangled it in front of his eyes, then pocketed it. "Welcome to the land of enchantments."

Ten

Rosa slipped out of the guesthouse at twenty minutes after midnight, careful to close the door quietly behind her. The sky was clear and the moon shone brightly above. A breeze had freshened and the tops of the trees rustled and shushed. Rosa pulled up the hood of her coat and shoved her hands firmly in her pockets. Head down, she made her way along the fence and past the hives. The bees still darted about and hummed their tuneless melodies. The windows of the Chenchikovs' house were all dark. Moonlight fell obliquely on the roof, illuminating a ghostly streak of smoke from the chimney. She didn't realize she was holding her breath until she was out the heavy front gate, locking it behind her.

Was she afraid of Anatoly Chenchikov? Perhaps. It was hard to be entirely comfortable around a man who cast two shadows, and whose eyes reflected the world upside-down.

She crossed the rutted driveway and stopped for a few seconds to look around. This tree? Or that one? Everything looked different by moonlight; the strange, inverse shadows made liars of the landscape. She headed into the woods and lit a cigarette.

Took a moment to enjoy the first drag.

"Aah," she said. Then coughed, checked behind her that nobody had heard, and kept walking.

"*Elizavetta!*"

Rosa stopped, turned sharply. The man's voice, an urgent whisper, had come from somewhere near the Chenchikovs' front gate. Careful to be quiet, she backed up a few steps and hid behind a tree to look.

Nobody there. The white brick fence was bathed in moonlight. She scanned left and right, but saw no one.

"*Elizavetta!*"

The voice was oddly disembodied, coming from everywhere at once. "I'm over here," Rosa said. Her voice was loud in the quiet dark. She waited a few moments. Nothing happened. He didn't speak again. She figured she mustn't sound like Elizavetta and continued on her way. Was this why Anatoly liked to lock up so tight? To stop young men from visiting his daughter? Elizavetta was nineteen and already onto husband number two, so Rosa couldn't argue with his logic.

She kicked her toe on a fallen branch and glanced down for a second, when a noise ahead caused her to look up. About a hundred yards away, leaning against a tree, was the figure of a man.

Rosa's heart jumped instinctively. He hadn't been there just three seconds ago. How had he got in front of her so quietly?

She stopped and tried to make out his features, but he was entirely in shadow, as still as the tree he leaned on.

"Are you looking for Elizavetta?" she said.

No answer.

"She's sick. I don't think she leaves the house."

Again no answer. He was motionless and dark, and Rosa wondered if he wasn't a man at all, but a statue out here in the woods. She advanced a little further, readying herself to laugh at her conversation with a wooden doll, when the shadow detached itself from the tree and streaked past her, toward the house. As though he hadn't seen her at all.

Rosa watched him go, then doubled back to follow him, stubbing out her cigarette on a large rock.

Voices ahead. She slipped behind a tree and peered out.

At the edge of the woods, the figure of a man and the figure of a woman. His face was still in shadow, though Rosa could now see his hair was dark. The woman, however, was lit by moonlight. Her hair was long and as pale as Makhar's, her skin almost ghostly, and she wore a long blue nightgown. They were embracing violently, like lovers who were forbidden to meet.

Rosa presumed the young woman was Elizavetta. "Maybe not that sick after all," she mumbled to herself as she turned to make her way through the woods toward the veil.

Two cigarettes later she found it. A hum lay on the air, and the vaporous colors were easily visible to her second sight in the dark. They fell in an undulating curtain, about ten feet high, in a long span that tapered off just at the edge of her sight. She walked toward it. The field dipped and fog had gathered in the low-lying areas. She spread her arms and took a breath, walking right into the veil.

The instant she touched it, the colors disappeared. Out the other side, still in the field, she turned. The colors had returned. She tried again. Once more the curtain disappeared the moment her body came into contact with it. Back and forth she went, growing warm and annoyed.

It was the bear, of course. She had been Daniel and Em's ticket to cross. Rosa had known all along that the bear was enchanted, and those enchantments had taken Daniel and Em across the veil. Rosa needed enchantments of her own. Her mother's bracelet? Even if she could get it back, Anatoly had said it was pitifully weak. No, she needed incantations, spells, the help of a strong magician. Somebody like Anatoly Chenchikov. She sat in the grass, leaving her second sight open so she could watch the colors move and hear their low, strange hum. Voices and music came to her, distant and faint. Nothing clear enough for her to understand or recognize.

She tried to imagine Daniel, what he was thinking. Had he realized the danger he was in yet? Or did he still think he was wandering some uncharted part of Russia? Rosa drove her fingernails into her palms. If he was dead already, it was all her fault. She should never have called him, involved him with the bear. She should have let him go home safely to England to forget about her. Deep down, had she wanted to see if he still loved her? Because when Daniel looked at her with love in his eyes, the most forbidden of fantasies wove their seductive spell: sunlight, picket fences, flowerbeds, children's voices.

Blood began to ooze from her hands and she uncurled them. The pain was a comfort to her, a way of sharing Daniel's distress. A sudden, clear memory of her mother sprang to mind. It was a week after her father's death and Rosa had woken in the night. A shaft of light had spilled from Ellena's half-open bedroom door. Rosa had crept out of bed to look, and watched her mother unseen. Elena sat on the floor, her legs crossed. There had been a glint of metal, a sharp intake of breath. Rosa had felt frightened and backed away. The next morning she had seen an interlinked design of tiny arcs scored into the flesh around Ellena's left ankle. One for each day that Rosa's father had been dead. In the weeks that followed, the design grew, a simple and beautiful pattern of guilt and loss.

Rosa climbed to her feet. She had to accept the inevitable. She wasn't crossing the veil tonight . . . perhaps she wasn't crossing it for a week or more. Instead, she was going to be a nanny and a housemaid. Anatoly Chenchikov was her best hope for the next step in the adventure.

A thunderous hammering at her door the next morning roused Rosa from a deep sleep. For a moment she was disoriented, sitting up and checking her watch. Ten minutes past nine. It was unusual for her to sleep so late.

"Just a second," she said, throwing back the covers and pulling on a skirt and blouse. She opened the door, still smoothing back her hair, to see Makhar standing on her doorstep.

"School starts at nine, Rosa Petrovna," he said.

"I'm sorry. I overslept." She rubbed her eyes. "So it's school this morning?"

He nodded. "School in the morning, honey jobs in the afternoon. I do half a day school, but I only get a short summer break. Papa and Ilya have gone to town," he said. He thrust a dog-eared exercise pad into her hands. "Can we do school down here in the magic house?"

Rosa drew the little boy inside and closed the door. "As long as you don't mind working on the floor."

"I made you some breakfast," he said, producing a sandwich from his schoolbag.

"What's on it?" she asked tentatively, taking it from him.

"Honey."

Rosa bit into it. She had never tasted raw honey, and was surprised by its thick, gritty texture. She could hear a light rain pattering outside. Makhar was already settling cross-legged on the floor next to her bed.

Rosa sat next to him, licking honey off her fingers. "Listen, Makhar, we'll do one lesson down here, but I'm going to need coffee and a bathroom pretty soon."

"Can we do maths? I love maths."

"We can do maths," she said, stretching her legs out in front of her.

Makhar frowned, peering at her ankle. "Did you scratch yourself, Rosa?"

Rosa tucked her foot away. "It's nothing," she said. "What's your favorite? Multiplication?"

"Long division," he said.

Rosa bent her brain backward, trying to remember long division. "Ah . . . long division."

"I'll show you," he said, taking the exercise pad from her and opening it up to a page full of maths.

She leaned over and looked at the sums. "Yes, I remember this one. Okay, let's do twenty-four into six thousand and six."

He was an eager student, his tanned fingers clutching his blunt pencil earnestly. He needed little help, and after four sums was bored.

"You want me to make it harder?" she said. "We could do ones with decimals."

"Elizavetta hasn't shown me decimals yet."

"Well, maybe I can show you." Rosa thought about the young woman she had seen outside the gate last night. "Makhar, what does Elizavetta look like? Is her hair the same color as yours?"

He wrinkled his nose. "She's not as pretty as you."

Rosa had to smile. "You only think that because she's your sister."

"You're really pretty. Mama said so last night to Papa after you were gone. She sounded really mad about it." Then with theatrical gaucheness, he clapped his hand over his mouth and said, "I'm not supposed to say anything."

"About what?"

"I'm not supposed to say anything about anything."

"Perhaps you should stop then," Rosa said. Obviously Ludmilla had warned him about family secrets. "We can just concentrate on learning decimals. I don't want to know any of your magical secrets. Though they must be just about bursting out of you."

He smiled with excitement, his imagination seizing on the idea of magical secrets. "Sometimes they are, like fireworks in my tummy."

"That sounds painful."

"It is." He put his hand around his belly and pretended to moan and groan. "Oh, oh, magical secrets! They burn!"

Rosa pounced on top of him and tickled him. He fell over backward, screaming with laughter. "Stop! Stop!" he squealed, his face growing pink. "Stop tickling!"

"I'm not tickling. I'm just trying to get the secrets out."

"I'll never tell! Never!"

"Not even one? One little secret?"

"If you stop tickling me, I'll tell you one," he laughed.

She abruptly stopped, and he lay beneath her gazing up with new adoration, his chest heaving with laughter.

"Okay," she said in English, just in case somebody was listening outside. "Tell what happened to Nikita."

Makhar swallowed his last mouthful of laughter and adopted a suitably sober expression. "He died."

"I know that much, but how did he die?"

"Elizavetta killed him."

Rosa narrowed her eyes. "Are you making that up?"

"No." His eyes were all innocence. "It was an accident."

"Tell me about it."

"Elizavetta and Nikita used to fight a lot. She never fights with Ilya. I like Ilya a lot better."

"He seems very nice. Go on. She and Nikita fought?"

"They had a big argument and Nikita went off into the woods, which he always did. But he didn't come home that night and Elizavetta and Papa got really worried and went out the next day to look for him. Papa found wolf tracks and went back to get the gun. They thought that a wolf had caught Nikita. I wasn't there so I don't really know what happened next. When they came back,

Nikita was dead with a hole in his head and Elizavetta was crying and went to bed and didn't get up until Papa brought Ilya home for her."

Rosa was so astounded by the story and so puzzled by its incompleteness that she didn't know which question to ask next.

Makhar bit his lip. "You won't tell Mama that I told you?"

"Of course not," she said, helping him sit up again. "But how did Elizavetta—"

"Makhar! Rosa!" Ludmilla's voice was directly outside.

"In here!" Makhar called, pulling his exercise book onto his lap.

The door swung inward, and Ludmilla peered in. "What are you doing?"

"Rosa Petrovna's showing me decimals," Makhar said.

Ludmilla turned her attention to Rosa. "Classes are in the house, at the kitchen table, from nine o'clock sharp," she said. "I thought I told you that."

"I overslept," Rosa said. "I haven't slept so well in ages. And then when Makhar came to wake me, he asked if we could do one class down here—"

"In all household matters, you should follow the advice of my husband or me. Not our nine-year-old son," Ludmilla said frostily. Rosa fought back the indignant reply that had sprung onto her tongue. Instead, she smiled sweetly and said, "I'm sorry."

"I have breakfast waiting for you," Ludmilla said.

"I already ate the sandwich Makhar made for me," Rosa replied, "but I'd love coffee."

"I think we have some coffee in the pantry." She held out her hand to Makhar. "Come, boy. We'll give Rosa Petrovna a chance to get ready for school properly, and we'll start at ten today."

They left and Rosa quickly pulled on some shoes and ran a brush through her hair. All she had to do was play nice and do what Anatoly wanted for a day or two. Surely that couldn't be too hard?

The coffee was instant and stale, and she longed for a cigarette. Makhar was a keen, bright pupil, especially of maths, and not at all perturbed by the constant interference of his mother, who hovered about and admonished him for everything from putting a decimal point in the wrong place to slinging his arm affectionately around Rosa's neck and calling her Roshka.

After an hour of maths, Rosa needed a break.

"Makhar, you are too clever for me," she said. "Let's take five minutes to relax and then work on English lessons."

"I've been writing a story in English," he said proudly.

"I'd love to read it."

"I'll get it," he said, racing off down the hallway.

Rosa went to the kitchen bench and put the kettle on the hob again. Ludmilla was mending clothes on the sofa.

"Can I make you something?" Rosa asked. "A coffee?"

"I don't drink coffee."

"I found it!" Makhar shouted from the other end of the house.

"I wish he wouldn't shout. He'll wake his sister," Ludmilla said, her mouth drawn into a stern line. "He's excitable, so try not to stimulate him too much."

Rosa went back to her stained coffee cup, adding an extra sugar to take the edge off the horrid taste of the coffee. This was tiresome. Ludmilla was treating her like a servant and Anatoly was nowhere to be seen. She began to wonder if the volkhv intended to teach her anything at all, or if he just thought she'd make good free labor.

Makhar bowled back down the hall and hurried to his chair. "Come on, Roshka," he said.

"Makhar," Ludmilla said sternly, "call Rosa by her real name."

"It's fine," said Rosa. "I don't mind."

Ludmilla sighed and returned to her sewing.

"All right," Rosa said to Makhar as she sat next to him. "Read it out to me."

"Once there was four pirates . . ."

"Once there *were* four pirates . . ."

"Yes, yes. There *were* four pirates, and their names *were* Johnny, Billy, Snap and Crazy Jack."

"Go on. I like the sound of Crazy Jack."

Makhar continued his tale, including a great deal of crazy shouting from Crazy Jack, which drew Ludmilla's repeated plea for quiet. Makhar couldn't control himself, however, as an epic gun battle at sea commenced. The thundering of the cannons was too much for his mother.

"Makhar!" she shouted. "I said *quietly*."

Too late. A door creaked open in the hallway.

Ludmilla was up in an instant, hurrying toward the hall, but Elizavetta emerged first, shuffling weakly toward the kitchen, using the wall for support. She wore an irritable expression on her face. Rosa knew immediately that it was the woman she had seen last night; her long, white hair was unmistakable. She was frighteningly thin, with pale blue eyes and a sad rosebud for a mouth.

"Who are you?" she asked Rosa.

"This is Rosa," Ludmilla interjected. "She's helping Makhar with his classes."

"You woke me up, you little monster," Elizavetta said to Makhar.

Rosa wanted to say, "Well, if you weren't out late with your secret boyfriend you might have been up an hour or so earlier." Instead she said, "I'm sorry, Elizavetta. Makhar got carried away with his pirate story."

Elizavetta rolled her pale blue eyes. "That piece of rubbish. Ha!"

Ludmilla had Elizavetta under the elbow. "You should rest."

"I feel very ill," Elizavetta said, leaning on her mother heavily. "Could you bring me water?"

"Let me help you back to bed first."

Rosa watched them go, noticing that Elizavetta could barely walk without assistance.

"Poor Elizavetta," Makhar said guiltily. "She's very sick."

"I'm sure she'll get better soon," Rosa said. "Keep reading. Quietly, this time."

Makhar continued reading, while Rosa turned the mystery over in her head. If Elizavetta was so sick and weak, how had she managed to leave the house alone last night? And how had she opened the heavy gate and walked the uneven ground to the edge of the woods to meet her lover?

Rosa lay on her bed with a book on Russian folklore she had borrowed from the Chenchikovs' meager bookshelf. The morning's lessons were over and, until Anatoly and Ilya returned from town, Rosa was at leisure. She wasn't particularly interested in the book itself—it was information she already knew—but Anatoly had made notes in the margins that she was attempting to decipher.

She heard voices outside, far off. Makhar calling, the sound of a car engine. She sat up and waited. Anatoly had promised to speak with her today.

Within minutes, Anatoly pushed open her door. "Are you ready?" he said. In his left hand, he held a pot of dirt.

"It's about time."

He checked outside then closed the door behind him. "It's better that Ludmilla thinks I'm busy with my bees."

"Why must you keep secrets from Ludmilla?" Rosa asked. "You're a volkhv. It's your business to dispense enchantments."

He leaned his back against the door. "If you had spent your youthful beauty on an old man, you might understand," he said. "Ludmilla is a jealous woman."

He ambled forward and sat heavily next to her on the bed, dropping the pot at his feet. His arm pressed casually against hers. Rosa could smell stale sweat and unwashed hair.

"I have something for you," he said.

"What is it?"

He reached into his shirt pocket, then held his fist in front of her. "It's the start of something," he said, his resonant voice adopting a portentous tone.

She stared down at his hairy knuckles, and watched a trickle of sweat squeeze out from his tightly closed palm. It paused in a fold of his skin, gathering to a drop. Rosa watched, expectant. A sense of possibility grasped her, and she felt her face grow warm with excitement. The drop fell, making a dark splotch on Anatoly's thigh.

"Let me see," she said, prizing open his fingers. On his palm was a flat papery disc with a seed at its center.

"It's a wych elm seed," he said. "You're going to use it in your first spell."

"I see. And how will this help me?"

He picked up the pot and handed it to her. "Go on, Rosa," he said. "Put the seed in the soil."

Puzzled, Rosa pushed the seed into the dirt.

"Good. What would you do next? If you wanted it to grow?"

"I'd water it and put it in the sun."

"Then I say leave it dry and put it in the cupboard where it's dark." When she didn't move, he said, "Go on."

She stood and put the pot in the cupboard, closing the door behind it firmly.

"You see," he said, "water and sun are not always necessary. How do you think we manage when winter clings to June and the bees have no flowers to visit? In 1993 every other honey grower in the region went out of business. Except for the Chenchikovs."

"How?" she asked.

"Zagovory."

Rosa found the word untranslatable and shook her head in puzzlement.

"Incantations, spells, magical stories." His chest puffed out. "I'm a powerful volkhv. You might have a tenth of my power one day, if you work hard."

"I really just want one spell. To get me across the veil."

He took a slow breath, and exhaled with a patronizing shake of his head. "Let me ask, Rosa, how far can you run?"

She shrugged. "What's that got to do with anything?"

"How far? Before you have to stop?"

"I don't know. Maybe two miles."

"So if you needed to run twenty miles, would you not prepare yourself? Running a little further every day? Or would you just start running and hope you made it?"

Rosa grew agitated. "Anatoly, how long will this take?"

"As long as it takes. You have magic in your smallest finger." He waved his own pinky finger in front of her face. "That's it. The rest grows with practice."

"If I don't get across soon, he might die."

"You cannot think of that. You must focus on what I teach you, on growing your power. Now . . ." He slapped her knee gently. "Zagovory are structured very simply. An invocation: for your seed, I suggest the sun. An appeal to the elements: try water. A tale to link your heart to your head to the magic in your body: in this case, a tale of Mother Moist Earth to show your respect. Then state what you wish, bind the spell, and repeat every day until you see the seed sprouting."

Rosa tried to remember all this. "Do you have that written down somewhere?"

"Of course not. It's dangerous to write zagovory in plain language. I have a few notes about, but only in *tarabarshchina*."

"Another Russian word I don't know," Rosa said, laughing. "I'm learning more from you than spells, Anatoly."

"The enchanted cipher of the volkhv through the centuries." He squeezed her hand once, then drew her to her feet. "Come, Rosa. Try it."

Rosa was uncertain but eager. She tried to remember Anatoly's instruction. "Sun, I beseech you. Tsar water, I invoke your aid." She took a deep breath. "Mother Moist Earth . . ." She turned to Anatoly. "I'm sorry, I don't know what to say."

"You must be creative," Anatoly said. "A magician's power can stand or fall on the strength of his stories. Let me show you." He stood directly behind her. Although he didn't touch her, his breath was close enough to tickle her ear. Electricity ran up her neck. His voice dropped to a hypnotic whisper. "Out in the great ocean there stands a white-hot rock. On the rock stand three brothers, and Mother Moist Earth gives each one a test.

" 'What can grow without rain or sunshine?' Mother asks.

"The first brother says, 'Nothing can grow without rain or sunshine.' And Mother pitches him into the ocean.

"The second brother considers a while and then says, 'Nothing can grow without rain or sunshine.' And Mother pitches him into the ocean."

Anatoly fell silent for long seconds, and Rosa's body tensed in anticipation. Her spine grew warm.

"Go on, Rosa," he said at last, "you finish the story."

Rosa cleared her throat. "The third brother says, 'I know what grows without rain or sunshine. It grows in the darkness, it grows in empty fields, it grows in the icy grip of winter. It is love.'"

Anatoly turned her to face him, smiling. "Ah, that is beautiful."

She took a step back, felt that her face was flushed. "As love grows, so does this tree grow without rain or sunshine. My word is firm, so it shall be."

"Good, very good," Anatoly said, clapping his hands together. "How do you feel?"

"Tired," she said. "And warm." She wanted to loosen her top button, but feared Anatoly might take the gesture the wrong way.

"That means you have done your work properly. So, you must keep the pot in the dark. Don't allow any light in unless you absolutely must. And you must repeat the incantation every day."

"I can't write it down?"

"Why? Is there something wrong with your memory?"

Rosa bristled. "No. I'll remember it."

"And the one I teach you next week? The one after that?"

"It's going to take more than a week?" she exclaimed, horrified.

Anatoly nodded, tugging his beard gently. "You love him, don't you? The boy who has crossed the veil?"

"Well, I . . ."

"Now, now. Speak the truth. You will never cross the veil if you can't speak the truth."

"Yes, yes, of course I do," Rosa snapped, "but we're not meant to be together."

"And how does Rosa Kovalenka know what is *meant to be*?"

"I just do. I don't remember agreeing to tell you all my secrets anyway, Anatoly." She folded her arms. "Why is it so hot in here?"

"Magic is hot," he said. "I do my best work naked."

She hid a shudder. "When can I have another lesson?"

"When the seed sprouts."

"It could take days!"

Anatoly shook his head. "That will depend on how strong your magic is. I predict I'll be back tomorrow." He turned and opened the door.

"What about my bracelet? Wait. Don't go yet," she said. "I have so much to ask you."

"Forget your silly bracelet. A worthless trinket. Luda expects me. She will grow suspicious."

"Just tell me what's over there. What is on the other side of the veil?"

"I don't know, Rosa. I've never been." He smiled. "You can tell me when you return."

That evening, after dinner with the family and a hot shower, Rosa returned to her guesthouse. Her penknife lay open next to the armchair. Tonight, she would sleep in a warm bed, Daniel would wander in cold shadows. She released a trapped bee from her window, and wondered how far around her ankle the design would stretch before she saw Daniel again.

Before crawling into bed, she went to the cupboard to check on the pot of dirt.

A shoot, already three inches long, poked out of the soil.

"So," she said. "It won't be long."

Eleven

True to his word, the leshii was pleasant after he'd been paid, but had an ever-growing list of demands. He refused to answer any of Em's questions until she agreed to cook him a week's worth of pancakes and bread. A pale and trembling Daniel had been dispatched to the chicken coop to collect eggs. Em was relieved to have him out of her sight for a little while. His fear was so electric it threatened to charge Em's heart too. Amazing, unexpected, impossible things were happening to her.

She knew she had to keep her head.

As she kneaded dough, Vikhor sat at the table picking his teeth with his toenails.

"I'll need at least three loaves of bread," he said, stretching back and crossing his arms over his head. Em noticed that all his clothes were on backward. "I'll be away for a week."

"Where are you going?"

"To work."

"Where do you work?"

"In the woods."

"What do you do?"

"You don't want to know." He smiled. "Anything else you want to ask?"

Em didn't know where to start.

It was very warm in the gloomy wooden house. The pale brick stove in the center of the room was stoked and roaring. She put the kneaded loaf aside and began another, pulling the sticky dough from the wooden bowl and thumping it into the kneading trough. She hadn't made bread since she was a child, but she rarely forgot anything.

"There are a lot of things I want to ask," Em said. "I'm completely mystified by everything I've seen and heard since I woke up this morning."

"Mir folk are often like that. You're not adaptable." Vikhor drummed his long fingers on the scarred table. "You know, I've heard that in Mir you have tiny glowing boxes with numbers on them, and with them you can talk and send pictures to people for a million miles. Is that right?"

Em thought about her cell phone, dead in her pocket. "Yes."

"I don't quiver with fright when I hear about such wonders. My face wouldn't drain of blood were I to see such a thing." He pulled his face into an exaggerated impression of Daniel which, under other circumstances, might have been hilarious.

Em allowed herself only a guarded smile.

"You could tell me any wonder of your world, and I would accept it." He nodded decisively. "I can adapt to anything because I can believe in anything. Mir folk can't do that and it makes them weak."

"Is that so?"

He rose and leaned on the bench in front of her, glancing left and right before dropping his voice to a whisper and saying, "Fear is treacherous, it clouds judgment. I warn you, your friend is a danger to you in Skazki. You should abandon him if you want to survive."

Em wiped her hands on her pants and scratched her eyebrow. "Mir folk can't do that," she said, adopting his phrase. In fact, she did worry that Daniel was going to become a liability if they wanted to get out of here quickly and safely. She patted the second loaf and put it aside. "I need to pin down some clear facts. Will you help?"

"Of course. You bought my help."

"First, how did we get here?"

"You crossed a veil. Don't you remember?"

"Not really. I remember some strange lights . . . Look, has it got anything to do with this bear?" She fetched the bear from her hiding place and sat her on the bench. Daniel would never have let Em tell Vikhor about the bear, but she figured he needed all the facts if he was going to help her.

"Aha," said Vikhor, his index finger touching the bear's nose. "She belongs to this world, certainly. I think I even know who owns her. I've heard stories of this bear whispered on the wind."

"So you think she helped us cross over?"

"Of course. She brought you home with her."

"Then how do we get back to Mir?" Em said.

"You don't."

"Well, we got here, we must be able to get back."

"You can't."

Em didn't miss a beat. "I'm sorry, but that makes no sense. There's a veil, you've made that clear. We crossed it, so we can cross back."

The leshii considered her across the bench, straightening his back and folding his arms. "You could ask the Snow Witch. She'd know how to get you home."

"And who is the Snow Witch?"

"She owns the bear."

Em sank her hands into the bowl and chased the last of the dough onto the bench. "Fine. Where could we find the Snow Witch?"

"East and east and north a-ways."

She held her dough-smeared hands out, palms up. "That's it? Nothing more specific than that?"

"I've never met her. I've never been to her palace. But you're bound to meet somebody else who can help, if you don't get eaten first." He nodded toward the bear. "Where did you find her?"

"In St. Petersburg."

"Hidden?"

She blew a strand of hair out of her face and started kneading. "Yes."

"Be careful then. Somebody put her there for a reason. Somebody didn't want her to come home." The leshii's big, dirty fingers were probing the bear in every crevice, leaving smudges on the bright gold. "I'd buy her from you, if you want to get rid of her."

Em shook her head. "She's not ours," she said. "We're minding her for a friend."

He shrugged. "Have it your way. I was going to offer you this lovely gold watch in exchange." He dangled her watch before her. "You might need it to buy your way out of a tight spot."

Em wasn't certain if this was meant as a joke, but didn't feel much like laughing in any case. Vikhor returned to his chair to wait, humming an absent melody. Pale sunlight struggled through the window, making patterns with the vines. Em digested all this information, irritated with herself for not knowing what to ask next. There would be a solution: she knew that. Locating it was going to prove difficult and, according to Vikhor's warnings, they were a long way from home in very hostile territory.

"What else?" Vikhor asked.

"I don't know what else to ask," she said. "What do you think I need to know?"

"Hmm, let me think. When did you arrive in Skazki?" he asked.

"I'm not certain. When we woke this morning, we were in the bottom of your field. But we may have actually crossed the veil the previous morning. There were strange lights while I was driving. I'd nodded off for a moment."

"Ah, dangerous," he said. "To be moved while you aren't aware of it. Who knows where you could end up next? Did you do it to her?"

"I'm sorry?" Em said, puzzled.

"Did you move the bear around while she slept?"

"I . . . well, yes we did, I suppose."

"She's paying you back. Be careful not to sleep at the same time as your companion. You could wake up on the ice floes."

Em braced herself against the bench. "There are ice floes around here?"

"No, not around here. But you could wake up anywhere in Skazki, and there are some treacherous places, and all my treacherous cousins inhabit them. You're lucky you found me first. Any of them would have finished you off by now."

"How many cousins do you have?" she asked, determined to keep her voice even.

"We're everywhere. We're all over this land. Wood demons, fire demons, water and wind demons, witches, shape-shifters, magicians and hunters and the unclean spirits of the dead. You'll find Skazki is infested with magic, mostly bad magic." He tapped his pocket. "We're all happiest when we've got some gold in our pockets."

"You're not going to ask for more, are you?" Em said.

"No, no. Fair is fair, and we made a deal. Skazki folk are cruel, but not unpredictable. You're safe as long as you stay here."

"But as long as we stay here we can't get back home?"

"That's right. You'll need to return the bear to the Snow Witch."

"And Daniel and I can never sleep at the same time?"

"I wouldn't advise it. Not if you want to be certain where you'll wake up."

Em took strange comfort in this: there were rules and they were simple. No sleeping at the same time; gold would bribe demons; the Snow Witch could get them home. "Do you know anyone else who can help us find the Snow Witch?"

He pondered this, his bushy eyebrows drawn down hard. Minutes ticked past and Em wondered if he ever intended to answer her question, but finally he said, "There are those who know. And there are those who know where to find those who know."

Em took a second to untangle this logic. "I see. So we just keep asking as we travel?"

"If you don't get eaten first."

Em was growing irritated by all this talk of getting eaten. "And gold will buy us goodwill?" she asked, making a mental inventory of every gold item she wore. Now that her watch was gone, she was left with a ring and a pair of earrings. Perhaps Daniel had more.

"Oh, yes. We don't have any gold of our own in Skazki, so we're very fond of it." He laughed. "You just don't want to run out of gold before you run out of questions."

Em opened the stove door to check the fire. A whoosh of bright heat flared out, making carbon streaks on the surrounding mosaic. She slammed it closed and oiled three bread tins, wondering for the first time what was taking Daniel so long. She hoped he hadn't wandered off in his hysterical state.

"Anything else?" he said.

She smiled. "Why are your clothes on backward?"

"Maybe yours are," he replied with a nonchalant pout.

"My friend is taking a long time with the eggs," she said. "I might go and hurry him up while the bread is rising."

"As long as you come back to make my pancakes."

"Of course."

He caught her gently by the wrist, his odd green eyes connecting with hers. "I still think you should abandon him. He'll weigh you down on your journey."

"I'll think about it," Em said, and wondered if she meant it.

The empty basket rested at Daniel's feet and the chickens pecked and clucked around him as he sat, chin in hands, on the dirt floor of the coop.

His strongest urge was to cry, but he refused to submit to it. Em was in there, cool and practical, finding information and making plans. Daniel's fear, however, had paralyzed him. He was capable of nothing more than sitting here among the cobwebs, surrounded by the smell of chicken droppings, staring into hopeless middle distance.

Anger bubbled in his blood. Anger with himself, for not being able to cope. With the situation, for being so incredible that it made his brain hot. With Em, who was so even-headed it made him want to rattle her bony shoulders until her teeth popped out. What was she? Some kind of alien who felt nothing?

A chicken ran over his toe, and he kicked out at it savagely. Missed. Felt guilty.

"Daniel?" Em's voice from the house.

Daniel leapt to his feet and began searching the crudely built boxes for eggs. They were warm in his hand.

"Are you okay?" Em asked, peering into the dark.

"As well as can be expected," he huffed. "You're fine, I see."

She raised a perfectly arched eyebrow. "Stuck in another dimension full of people-eating goblins? Yes, absolutely fine."

He turned, felt his body sag. "Damn it, Em, I feel so helpless and overwhelmed."

She snapped her fingers, a schoolteacher's gesture. "Don't assume that I don't feel those things," she said. "Just gather the eggs and bring them inside. Vikhor is leaving as soon as I've made him twenty-seven pancakes. He was very specific about how many he wanted."

Daniel reached into the next box, came out with a handful of chicken poo. "Thrice-nine," Daniel said, wiping his hand on his pants. "In Russian folklore it's a lucky number."

"Is that right?" Em said.

A short silence ensued, and Daniel supposed that Em had left noiselessly. He turned and she was still there; her dark eyes had grown thoughtful.

"How do you know that?" she asked.

"Know what?"

"The thrice-nine thing?"

"My Russian nanny, Rima," he said. "The one who taught me the language. She told me all the old stories."

"So why are the leshii's clothes on backward?"

"To confuse his enemies."

Daniel continued collecting eggs, and Em didn't ask any more until he had finished. He put the full basket on the ground.

Em tilted her head. "How much more do you know?"

"About what?"

"About these fairytale creatures?"

Daniel thought about Nanny Rima's tales; they seemed both magical and unnerving, like half-forgotten dreams. He'd never imagined that any of it could be true. "A lot, I guess."

"Daniel, do you see? You have information which could keep us safe until we get out of here." She touched his shoulder. "I'm glad you're here with me."

The first beam of light cut through the fog of his fear. Em was right: he knew about this world. This hopeful realization was immediately chased by a new fear, a more specific fear: if the leshii was real, then what other horrors out of Nanny Rima's stories lay waiting for them?

"We stick together, okay?" Em said firmly.

"Of course."

The door of the cottage opened and Vikhor stepped out, frowning and waving his arms. "Pancakes!" he shouted. "What's taking so long?"

Em took Daniel's basket. "He'll be gone by nightfall, then we have a lot to talk about."

By sunset, Vikhor was ready to leave.

"I'll be back in a week. You're welcome to stay or go as you please, use my bed, take clothes and food. Just let the chickens into the garden in the mornings, and if anyone comes selling milk or honey, get as much as you can. Use eggs for payment. And don't tell them you're from Mir. It's best that word doesn't get around."

Daniel watched Em as she bustled around the leshii, handing him wrapped packages of food and straightening his green cloak as though they were an old married couple.

"Thank you for your help," she said. "Any last piece of advice?"

"Gold helps with everything," Vikhor said. "Don't be too foolish with that bear. If you need to barter with her for your life, do so. I wish you luck on your journey."

Journey? Daniel took a deep breath. Of course they couldn't stay here forever, but he'd thought he had a few days' grace.

The leshii left, closing the door behind him.

Em turned to Daniel. "You'd better sit down."

"Do we have to leave the cottage right now?" he said, finding himself a chair.

"Who's the Snow Witch?" she said.

"I've never heard of her."

"Nanny Rima's stories?"

Daniel thought hard. "No. No recollection."

"Damn." Em chewed her lip a few moments. "Okay, I'll tell you what I know, and we'll work out what to do next."

She filled him in about the bear, the Snow Witch, the gold, and the fact that they could never be asleep at the same time. As he listened, he knew she was right, that they had to find the Snow Witch. But the thought of going outside made him cold with fear.

"But, Em, we could die out there," he said. "If we just wait here . . ."

"What, Daniel? What happens if we wait here? We live with Vikhor happily ever after?"

Daniel thought hard. Outside, night was closing in and a breeze freshened from the north. Tree branches rubbed and scraped on the roof and eaves. "Rosa," he said at last. "Rosa will come for us."

Em paused. "I hadn't thought of that."

"She'll figure it out. She believes in enchantments, she knows we have the bear." Daniel felt a twinge of embarrassment for himself: what kind of man relied on women—Em and Rosa—to rescue him? He could just imagine what his brothers would say: *weakling, puppy, limp-wrist*.

Em laid her hands on the table calmly. "Okay, Daniel. But what if she doesn't?"

Daniel pressed his fingers to his forehead. "We'll have to go, I suppose."

He heard her chair scrape back, and when he looked up she was pulling bread and honey out of the pantry. "What are you doing?" he said.

"Making dinner. We haven't eaten since we got here."

Of course. Making dinner. Like everything was normal. "You amaze me," he said, and he heard that his irritation was poorly concealed. "How can you be so calm?"

She narrowed her eyes. "Daniel, I would have thought, under the current circumstances, you could find more to be amazed about than me."

"Sorry," he said, finding the ragged edge of a fingernail with his teeth.

"I'm sorry too," she replied, then came to sit next to him. "We're in this together. We can't snipe at each other. It's dumb."

"I know that," he said. "I know that, it's just . . ."

"We'll stay here, but only for a week. If Rosa doesn't come, we have to move."

Dread swirled in his stomach.

"I know you hate it, Daniel. I know that fear is strangling you and all I can promise you is more uncertainty," Em said. "But whatever happens, just breathe, and keep breathing. As long as you're breathing, you're alive; as long as you're alive, there's nothing to worry about."

They flipped a coin to decide who would sleep first and Daniel won. Em was glad, because he looked exhausted and pale, and the oblivion of sleep would give him a chance to escape. She was glad for her own sake too; he was wearing her out.

She sat with her back to the stove, staring out the window into the dark overgrown garden, breathing deep and regular. Daniel was awake for a while: she heard him tossing and turning. Eventually, an empty stillness in the room told her that he had dropped off. For light, she had one candle. When it burned down it was time to wake Daniel, and give him a fresh candle to last until dawn.

And so, in the dim cottage, she waited.

Outside, the wind grew fierce, the tiny panes in the windows rattled.

She hoped that Daniel was right, and that Rosa would come for them. Rosa seemed capable and intelligent, and she clearly knew more about enchantments than either Em or Daniel, but Em would not rely on her.

She eyed the bear, who sat wide awake on the table. The candlelight flickered gold and amber on her bright surface.

"You started this," Em whispered. "Are you going to help us get home?"

There was no answer of course and, anyway, Em knew that the bear didn't care if she and Daniel made it home or not. They were expendable.

Outside, in the distance, there was a crash and a thud—like a tree being pulled over. Em glanced over her shoulder at Daniel. He stirred but didn't wake. Em crept to the window, pressed her face against the glass. Her breath made fog, which obscured any view through, into the thick foliage.

Another crash and thud. Curious, she went to the door and

stepped out into the dark. She pulled the door behind her, but kept the handle firmly in her palm. Sounds drifted toward her on the wind.

A scream. A crash. The howling of a sucking whirlwind that rattled off into the icy reaches of space.

Then, a baby crying.

She paused on the doorstep and listened. Another tree came down, somewhere miles into the woods. The crying continued, louder or softer depending on the strength of the wind. Rattling and howling and trees shaking and falling.

Abruptly, the crying stopped.

Em let herself back into the cottage. Daniel hadn't woken. She took up her position next to the stove, resumed her deep, even breathing. Best that Daniel hadn't heard the noises, especially not the crying and its sudden cessation. Daniel's imagination was a slave to uncertainty. Em's was not.

Vikhor had been right, when she'd asked him what work he did in the woods . . . she didn't want to know.

Rosa didn't come.

Dawn followed dawn, and Daniel saw them all while Em slept. No light footsteps approached the cottage, no soft voice called him from the fields, no raven-haired beauty in a lace dress appeared, ready to take him home.

The possibility of her coming grew more remote with each sunset in the leshii's cottage. Even if she crossed the veil, how would she find them? They could be a thousand miles from where they first entered this strange land.

Em kept him busy with tasks around the cottage, her mouth a firmly drawn line of determination. Cooking bread and pancakes, sewing together cloaks and backpacks from the pile of furs and skins they found at the back of a cupboard, repairing hats and gloves. If they did speak to each other, it was about anything but the impending journey. Em loved to play logic games, she was a phenomenally bright student of Russian, and her memory for things she had seen and done was astonishing in its detail and scope. She could recite almost all the words from every documentary she had ever narrated, and was happy to fill the time by telling Daniel everything she knew about the Crusades, or the lives of puffins on the Faroe Islands, or the latest advances in genetic technology.

Once six nights had passed, though, she dropped all pretense of diverting him from the topic uppermost in his mind.

"We'll have to head off tomorrow, Daniel," she said baldly, as he pulled up the blankets and lay down to sleep.

"I know," he said, pressing his toes against the chimney. He closed his eyes and prayed that Rosa would arrive some time in the night, but she didn't.

Morning light bathed the kitchen as they organized their packs. Daniel's held the food; Em's was lighter, holding only the moleskin and the bear. Daniel wore a rough woollen shirt and pants, many sizes too large, which he had found in the leshii's wardrobe. Em had sewn herself a similar outfit, and had made shoes from bark and fur with the remnants of her old shoes and leftover squares of material.

Daniel's heart fluttered and he tried to focus on small things to keep his imagination from panicking. He packed bread and pancakes into the plastic shopping bag the bear had traveled in. It was only then that it occurred to him he hadn't seen the bear all morning.

"Em," he said, quickly checking under the bedcovers and in the back of the wardrobe, "where's the bear?"

Em dusted off her hands and came to stand with him at the table. "Pick up the loaves of bread again. You'll feel the difference."

"What?"

"Go on."

He did as she said, unpacking the bread. The second loaf he reached for was obviously heavier than normal. He'd been so preoccupied that he hadn't noticed.

"She's made of gold," Em said. "We don't want anyone to know we have her. She's our ticket home. If we don't have her when we get to the Snow Witch, then we have nothing to bargain with."

Daniel smiled. "She won't be happy, packed away in a loaf of bread."

"No worse than a plastic bag." Em sniffed. "Although I think we should keep her separate from our food. Somewhere she can't get lost or stolen. Here." She handed him a sling made of her cashmere scarf. "Tie this around your body, under your cloak. Guard her with your life."

Daniel did as he was told, sliding the loaf into the sling and tucking it under his arm.

"Now sit down," Em said. "One last important thing." She began taking off the ring on her right hand. "Do you have any gold on you? Anything at all? Vikhor didn't seem to think it mattered how big or small a piece it was."

Daniel sat down as she pulled out her earrings and laid them on the table next to the ring. "I'm sorry, Em," he said. "I have nothing."

"Nothing at all?"

He held out his hands, showing her a plain silver ring on his right pinky finger, and a tatty woven band on his left wrist. He didn't even like to wear a watch, in case it increased expectations that he would turn up on time. "I've never been able to afford gold."

Em glanced at their meager stockpile. "We have three items. That's three questions."

Daniel shook his head. "Perhaps we should just stay here."

"You know we can't. You know we have to leave. We have to find the Snow Witch. She'll get us home." Em scooped the jewelry into her palm and hid it in the bottom of her pack. "Are you ready?"

Daniel stood, taking a deep breath. "I guess so."

They opened the door onto the cool, sunny morning, and headed into the east.

Twelve

Rosa stood at the top of the stairs in the guesthouse doorway, staring out into the garden. A breeze from the west turned the undersides of leaves to the afternoon sun. Bees buzzed around Anatoly's head near the hives, catching light on their wings then dropping it again as they descended. All day, Rosa had waited and still Anatoly hadn't found time to come and speak with her.

Three times now he had said, "When the time is right, Rosa." But "right" for Anatoly was not right for her.

In his white bee-proof suit, the veil over his head made him look like an alien's bride. He slid the frames in and out of the boxes. The alternate drawing and clunking chipped at her nerves. She tapped her foot, she chewed the inside of her cheek, she longed for a cigarette.

"Fuck him," she said, turning and pulling open the door to the cupboard. The wych elm shoot was now six inches long: she needed to know if this meant she had enough magic to cross the veil yet. If not, she needed more spells, more exercises, more information.

Rosa grabbed the pot and thundered down the stairs, striding across to the hives. A fine cloud of bees swarmed and separated around his head. He turned to watch her approach.

"What is it?" he asked irritably.

Heedless of the bees that spiraled around it, she dropped the pot onto the top of a hive. "Don't ignore me."

"I'm not ignoring you, I'm busy," he said. "You should go back to your guesthouse. You'll get stung."

Rosa could feel a bee had settled on her hair, another on her upper arm. "I don't care about getting stung. I care that you still haven't spoken to me, and I have this to show you." She indicated the shoot.

Anatoly lifted the edge of his veil and peered at it. "What is it?"

"It's the seed that you gave me yesterday afternoon."

A number of emotions chased each other across his face in a moment. Surprise, disbelief, puzzlement. Then he adopted his usual somber expression. "You've done well. Keep going with the spell."

"I need new spells. I don't care to grow trees, Anatoly. I will be satisfied with nothing less than crossing to the other world, and that won't happen while I'm teaching Makhar decimals."

She had raised her voice, and Anatoly glanced around nervously. He used the back of his glove to brush the bee out of her hair. "Come with me," he said, dropping his equipment.

Back at the guesthouse, the door safely closed behind them, he removed his veil and gloves and fixed her with a steely glare.

"Why aren't you afraid of me, Rosa?" he asked.

"Should I be?"

"Everyone else is."

"We had an agreement. I've been here three days and I've taught your son and stuck labels on jars and washed dishes every night. You've taught me one spell that I didn't care to know."

Anatoly's top lip twitched, and Rosa braced herself: she didn't know if he was repressing a laugh or a snarl.

He smiled, shook his head and chuckled. "Will one spell a day satisfy you?"

"Yes. I suppose."

He nodded, his fingers on the end of his beard. "You are much stronger than I thought, Rosa. I'm sorry. Don't come to me again out in the open. Ilya may have arrived at any moment." He squeezed her hand. "Meet me at the front gate in ten minutes. There is something we must do together before we can proceed any further."

Anatoly kept her waiting for twenty. Divested of his bee-protection suit, he now wore a stained pair of overalls and a musty flannel shirt. He handed Rosa a button.

"Here," he said, "keep this safe a little while."

While he unlocked the gate she turned the button over in her fingers. It was shaped like a bow, and most of the yellow paint had come off to reveal brown plastic beneath. "Whose is it?"

"It's Luda's. I pulled it off one of her shirts." He ushered her out and locked up behind him. "Rosa, her jealousy is an impediment to us getting any work done. I love my wife, but she isn't reasonable." He smiled. "Perhaps I love her *because* she isn't reasonable."

"So what are we going to do?"

"A simple hiding spell. One can use it for specific things—hiding an object, for example—but it's also possible to use it to create a blindness in another individual. Not just to an object, but to an activity. Provided you have something they treasure to bury."

Rosa looked at the button again. "She treasures this?"

"She treasures the shirt. Her mother sewed it for her as a wedding present. It is long since too threadbare to wear. Now, keep your eyes open for an ant hill."

They trudged into the woods. Each ant hill she pointed out was dismissed by Anatoly as not being the right one.

"So what kind of ant hill is the right one?" she said finally, when they had been searching for forty minutes.

"One with nine paths leading up to it." Anatoly had stooped over another little mound, peering at it. "You see. This one has five." He pointed out the streams in which the ants were leaving and returning.

Rosa bent to count them, then straightened her back. The low sun hit her eyes. Anatoly's two shadows forked out from his feet. At the tip of the first shadow, she spotted another ant hill.

"There," she said, hurrying over. "One, two . . . Yes, there are nine."

"Good work," he said. "Now where is the button?"

"Here."

"You remember the structure of the zagovor?"

"Yes."

"So, tell the button your spell and then bury it."

Rosa sat on the ground, holding the button over the ant hill. "Spirits of the wood, I beseech you. Mother Moist Earth, I seek your aid." Rosa thought for a moment. "In a city on the gulf, there was a girl who would keep a secret hidden. Her uncle didn't know, her lover didn't know, her mother and father were dead and knew nothing. She angered her uncle and still did not tell. She lost her lover and still did not tell." Rosa's body grew warm, and she knew the magic was working. "She dishonored the blessings of her dead parents and still did not tell. As her secret remains hidden, so will my dealings with this volkhv remain hidden from Luda Chenchikova." She pushed the button into the opening of the ant hill with sweaty fingers. "My word is firm, so it shall be."

Rosa turned to Anatoly, who met her gaze with a serious expression. He was silent for a few moments, then said in a measured tone, "Very well done, Rosa."

She stood, brushing off her hands and trying not to smile. "What can we expect will happen now? Will she not see us?"

"She'll still see us and hear us, of course, so we have to be careful not to be too open in our dealings. But she'll not notice little clues, she'll not read anything into our time spent together." He rose and glanced back toward the farm.

"What about Ilya and Makhar? What if they put ideas into her head?"

"The ideas won't take hold. She doesn't like you, Rosa, and she still won't like you. However, she won't notice if we are missing at the same time, she won't come looking for us at the bathhouse."

Rosa noted that he'd used the word "bathhouse" instead of guesthouse, but didn't question him.

Anatoly took a step closer, gazing down at her. "Rosa, we could do whatever we wanted. Luda won't know."

Rosa felt her body shrink from him, but held her ground. "All I want to do is learn magic," she said firmly.

"Are you sure?"

"What are you suggesting, exactly?"

"I should very much like to get inside you, Rosa."

"I should very much like you to stay right where you are."

He chuckled softly. "You know, I have had lovers before. You wouldn't be the first, nor the last. And a volkhv knows things about a woman's pleasure that no other man knows."

Rosa hated her stupid body for betraying her with a quick rush of curious excitement. She felt herself blush. "No," she said. "Thanks, but no."

He held his hands out. "The offer remains, should you change your mind. I won't insist, and I won't ask again."

The spell was strong and effective. Ludmilla didn't notice Rosa and Anatoly returning together from the woods, nor did she think anything of the way he visited her each afternoon while dinner was cooking inside.

Rosa found that now she was using her magic every day, she could endure more readily the tedium and indignity of her work at the farm. On Wednesday, Anatoly taught Rosa how to cure his toothache. On Thursday, Ludmilla reported a mouse leaving the fireplace: a fire omen. Anatoly made a magic square to hang on the mantel while Rosa prepared an enchanted egg to burn in the hearth. On Friday, Anatoly showed Rosa his spell for controlling the bees without the aid of smoke, but Ilya interrupted them before she could try it. Each night, she said a little blessing for Daniel and drew a little blood in his name. Each day, she could feel the magic growing in her muscles and sinews; the joints of her fingers were tight with it. She put off phoning Uncle Vasily—what would she say to him?—because she knew, she *knew*, that by the end of the week she would be strong enough to cross the veil.

On Friday night Rosa slipped out the gate with midnight at her back. She waited until she was well into the woods before fumbling for her cigarettes. The trees were quiet and calm, the clouded sky still and mute. She picked her way through the trees, more certain of her route this time, rehearsing in her head the zagovor she would use. An owl sat blinking on a nearby branch, and she hooted to it softly. It spread its wings and flapped away. Under the flapping, Rosa could hear something else. A distant shushing. She turned her eyes upward. The air was still . . . no, the tips of trees on the dark horizon were moving. A shiver crossed her body. Cold from the approaching wind, but also anticipation. Bad magic stirred the air.

She hesitated. Should she run back to the guesthouse? The speed the wind was approaching wouldn't allow her even to make it back to the gate in time. She glanced around for a place to hide, but how would she hide from an enchanted creature? They were cunning, they knew the woods and were not confused by the dark. She froze as the wind bore down, making branches creak and lifting fallen leaves.

The shadow slid past two hundred feet to her right. A sizzle of adrenalin. Only the corner of her vision caught it and she turned her head to follow it with her eyes. It had already disappeared into the trees.

Rosa paused. Then followed.

The woods were alive with creaking and thudding and rustling. The shadow slipped between trees ahead of her, always too far ahead for her to see it clearly. Was it a leshii? A demon of frost or fire? This close to a crossing, it could be any kind of creature. Rosa both longed to see it, and was so terrified that her heart jumped in her chest.

Somewhere in the darkness, she lost sight of it. She stopped, panting, gazing around her. Turned in a slow circle.

It hit her from behind. A thud in the center of her back that sent her flying to the ground. She cried out, quickly scrambling to her feet. It kicked her feet from under her and she landed again, this time on her back. It loomed above her.

Not a leshii or a demon. A young man with his face in shadows.

"Hey," she said. "Who are you?"

He shook his head mutely then turned to run. Rosa stood, pressing her hand into her back. "Wait," she called, but her voice was carried backward on the wind.

He had disappeared.

Rosa brushed leaves off her clothes. Was it the same young man she had seen before, with Elizavetta? She was so angry at being knocked over by him that she considered heading back to the guesthouse and telling Ilya that his wife had a secret lover.

But that wasn't why she had come out tonight.

The wind was dying down now. Just a random night breeze, not an omen of bad magic after all. She turned back the way she had come, finding her way to the field.

The veil waited. Her second sight revealed the bright colors and distant music. She walked right up to it, her palms brushing the space just outside the soft gold and violet waves. Her fingers tingled, her scalp prickled.

With a deep breath, she said, "Sister moon, I beseech you. Tsar air, I beg your aid." Eyes turned to the clouds, she told her tale. "On a small green island in the cold sea, the youngest of three sons was born. His name was Daniel, and he fell in love with a rose who offered him only her thorns." Rosa bowed her head, waiting until the pang of guilt and loss had passed sufficiently for her to continue. "She led him far and far away from his home and comfort, until he crossed the veil from this world to the next. As he has crossed, so may I cross this veil. My word is firm, so it shall be."

Rosa stepped forward. This time, instead of the veil disappearing, it held. She felt resistance against her body, elastic. But she couldn't push through it.

She stepped back and said the spell again. Tried the veil once more. The elastic gave a fraction, began to separate and dissolve into stars, but then sprang back stronger than before.

Half an hour passed, an hour. Over and over she said the spell and tried to step through the veil, until her body was sore from beating itself against the resistance, and sweat ran in rivers under her clothes and hair.

"Damn it!" she said at last, collapsing to her knees. She picked up a rock and threw it at the veil, watched it hurtle through to the other side and land in the field.

She took a moment to catch her breath, closing down her second sight so the colors couldn't taunt her. She swore at the veil in every language she knew and lit a cigarette.

It was simply taking too long. Already Daniel had been gone more than a week. What if it took weeks or months to grow her magic? She felt a twinge of the raw panic she had been suppressing all week.

"Okay, patience, patience," she said, pulling herself to her feet and making her way back through the woods. She thought of her mother's bracelet. Anatoly had called it a worthless trinket, but if it was so useless, why did he have to keep it from her? And if it was more powerful than he said, then could it help her cross the veil? Maybe if she could find it without Anatoly knowing . . .

Footsteps in the forest had her withdrawing behind the trunk of a tree. She heard the footsteps pause too, as though wary of her. She waited, listening.

"I know you're there!" a man called, and he sounded desperate and angry. "Leave her alone! She's mine!"

Rosa recognized the voice as Ilya's, and stepped out of hiding. "Ilya? It's me, Rosa." She could see him in the distance, near the edge of the wood. She waved and he waved back slowly. She hurried over to join him.

"Hi," she said, catching her breath.

"What are you doing out here?"

She looked around and shrugged. "Oh, forbidden things."

He frowned. "What forbidden things?"

"Smoking cigarettes, mainly." She pulled out her packet and offered him one.

"I don't smoke." He narrowed his eyes. "You've come a long way from the front gate for a cigarette."

She lit one and took a long, slow drag. "I guess I have." She tilted her head to the side, pouted and expelled the smoke in a lazy stream directly over his head. "Who did you think I was, Ilya?"

"What do you mean?"

"You said, 'leave her alone.' Who were you talking to?"

"It's a private matter. A family matter."

"Who did you want him to leave alone? Elizavetta?"

"I must get back to the farm," he mumbled, turning his shoulder to her. "It's cold. It's late."

"Not that late. You look like you don't sleep until dawn anyway. Worrying about your wife?"

"Of course I'm worried. She's sick."

Rosa took his arm, crushing her unfinished cigarette under her shoe. "Ilya, come back to the guesthouse with me. I've got a jar of stale coffee and an old kettle down there. We can talk."

"We have nothing to talk about," he said softly.

"How do you know that? Perhaps we do. Come on." She led him

away firmly, through the gate and around the garden. He didn't resist. Gray shadows collected around the house, and a night bird called far off. In the guesthouse, she stripped off her coat and plugged in the electric heater. Ilya took the armchair while she made coffee.

"I can't offer you sugar or milk," she said.

"I don't mind."

She handed him a cup and perched on the edge of her bed. "Anatoly has a possession of mine, a silver charm bracelet, and I'd like to get it back. Do you have any idea where he might have hidden it?"

"Perhaps you should ask Anatoly."

"He doesn't want me to have it."

"Then you'll never find it. He can hide things so you'll never see them again."

Rosa thought about the button in the ant hill and knew this was right.

"There's more to you, isn't there?" Ilya said, nursing his cup between his strong fingers. "I knew it when I met you."

Rosa eased off her shoes and folded her legs under her. "There's no point in denying it, but Anatoly thinks it's a secret," she said. "I need to learn magic, and quickly. Anatoly's helping me."

"Is that why you were in the woods?"

"Yes. There is a veil out there, between this world and the next. Someone I love has slipped through, and I intend to go after him." She lifted her cup to her lips, watching Ilya over the rim. His oddly matched eyes were turned down, and she took the opportunity to admire his smooth olive skin and his wide mouth. He was very still, and Rosa sensed a great unhappiness in him. "What about you? Is there more to you? What part do you play in Anatoly's secret world?"

A smile broke through the serious expression. "I play no part in secrets."

"Nothing mysterious about you, then?"

He shook his head. "No. I do what I can to help with the bees, but I don't feel or see anything extraordinary."

"You can see Anatoly's two shadows, though?"

"Oh, yes, anyone can. When we're in town together, I have to walk next to him to block the light. It requires some pretty fancy footwork."

They laughed, and Rosa felt him soften toward her. She pushed her advantage. "So, Ilya, who were you looking for out there in the woods?"

The goodwill evaporated. "It's private."

"I've seen someone out there, you know. A dark-haired man. I saw him just this evening."

"Then you should be careful, because he is dangerous."

"Not to me," she said. "I think he was looking for someone else."

Ilya stood and handed her his untouched coffee. "Good night, Rosa," he said.

"Yes, you'd better get to bed," she said, still digging for information. "Elizavetta will notice you're gone."

"I share a room with Makhar," he said. "Elizavetta's sleep is too easily disturbed."

She saw him to the door, his mournful expression stilling her next question. "I'm sorry. Sleep well," she said.

He took a breath as though to say something, then thought better of it and merely nodded once before disappearing into the dark garden.

Buzzing woke her. Late-morning sunshine was slanting through the high window. That, combined with the electric heater she had left on, and the layers of blankets, made her uncomfortably sticky.

Still, it took her a moment to move. She sat up and rubbed her eyes. Weariness weighed down her arms. She checked her watch. Nine hours' sleep and she had woken up tired. It probably had something to do with the intense mental and physical effort at the veil the previous night.

Her eyes went up. A bee was knocking itself against the timber boards of the ceiling. She stood on the bed and opened the window, hoping the bee would find its way out. Then she lay down on her back, and watched it for a while.

Bees were such clever creatures: they built colonies, made wax and honey, were masters of teamwork. But a bee's only defense was her sting, which pulled her guts out with it. Rosa yawned and stretched her arms over her head. She hadn't had a chance to try Anatoly's bee-control incantation; perhaps she could persuade this bee to leave with magic.

"Summer breeze, I call on you; Tsar air, hear me." She launched into Anatoly's zagovor, felt the warmth of magic in her elbows and fingers, then demanded that the bee leave.

Nothing happened.

Rosa frowned. Had she forgotten some aspect of the spell?

She was too tired to think about it. There was no doubt her magic was growing, but it would take time. She picked up a book and shooed the bee out the window, closing it firmly and wondering where the insects were finding their way in.

Rosa went up to the house to shower and dress, then asked Ludmilla for directions to town.

Ludmilla drew her a map, then said, "Why are you going to town?"

"I have to phone my Uncle Vasily back in St. Petersburg," she said.

"You can use the phone here."

Rosa shook her head. She had things to ask Vasily that she didn't want Anatoly to overhear. "I'd like to get out, see the town, look in the shops."

"Good luck," Ludmilla sniffed. "There's a petrol station, a tavern and a general store. You'll find a phone box in the car park." She picked Anatoly's wallet up off the kitchen bench and handed Rosa a few notes. "I need some groceries. Will you pick them up for me? It will save me a trip."

"Sure."

The phone started ringing, and Ludmilla tossed the wallet on the bench. "I must get that. Check the day book for the shopping list. Make sure you staple the receipt in when you get home." She pointed to a household diary in the hutch, where all the daily tasks had to be enumerated and checked off. This was how the Chenchikovs kept their farm running on such short staff.

Ludmilla dashed off and Rosa found the right date. The list was in Ludmilla's neat hand: two dozen eggs, a pound of butter, a jar of instant coffee. Rosa smiled, thinking that maybe Anatoly's wife didn't hate her after all. At the top of the page were some scribbled notes, a different handwriting. Anatoly, maybe? Rosa tried to read it, but couldn't. The language was foreign to her, even though it was written in Russian letters.

Rosa pocketed the money and Ludmilla's hastily drawn map. "See you this afternoon," she called.

As the sun moved overhead, the day grew warmer and Rosa shed her light jacket and rolled up her sleeves. The air was humid, and the sun felt good on her bare arms. The blue Ford was where she had left it, and she wondered if the police were looking for it by now. It started the first time and she backed out and turned the car around, pointing it toward the main road.

The drive was longer than she'd expected—a little over an hour—and the town much smaller. She pulled into a potholed car park behind the tavern and saw the phone box Ludmilla had spoken of. A scrappily handwritten sign across the front read "broken."

Rosa sighed, picked up her bag and let herself out of the car. She would have to try her luck in the tavern.

Inside, the ceilings were low and the lights were dim. The echoing cool was a pleasant contrast to the sunny warmth outside. The decor was at least fifty years old, but the picture of Stalin over the bar was too prominent and too dust-free to be a relic of another time. The smell of cooking reminded her that she'd skipped breakfast and it was already lunchtime. Two wiry drunkards held up the bar, the clink of their glasses loud in the emptiness. The long orange towels arranged across it were soaked and stank of vodka. Rosa approached the bartender, a fortyish man with a defeated expression.

"I need to use your phone," she said.

"Long-distance or local?"

"Long-distance. St. Petersburg."

"Five hundred roubles for ten minutes only," he said.

Rosa shook her head. "That's too much. Did you break the phone box yourself?"

"You could always drive to the next town."

Rosa found the money in her purse and gave it to him. "I'll have a bowl of pelmeny also. Some rye bread on the side."

He reached behind himself and handed her the telephone, still anchored to the back wall.

"You don't have something more private?"

The bartender glanced at the two men on the other end of the bar. "They aren't listening and I don't care."

Rosa shrugged, and dialed Vasily's number.

It rang four times before he answered, giving her time to brace herself against the hysterics that she suspected might ensue.

"Hello, Vasily Beletsky."

"Uncle Vasily. It's me."

"Roshka?" His voice was immediately frantic. "Where are you? What has happened?"

"I'm fine, I'm fine. I'm staying with a family about a hundred miles northwest of Oksovsky."

"I thought you were in Arkhangelsk! Where's the bear?"

"I'm still trying to find it."

His voice grew soft. "Ah, Roshka, I don't care about the bear. Just come home. I've been so worried."

"You're not to worry, I'm perfectly well."

"Do you have anything to do with the missing American woman?"

"Which woman?"

"It's been on the news. A television reporter and her assistant. They went missing on the way to Arkhangelsk. They were booked into the same hotel as you, and there was talk that they'd come with a strange artifact. Did you give the bear to television people?"

"I don't know who you mean," she lied. Better that Vasily knew nothing, just in case investigators came to ask him questions. She would certainly have to rid herself of the car very soon. "Look, I can't expect you to believe anything that has happened to me, so it's best if I don't tell you."

"But, Rosa—"

"Is there anything else of Mama's at your place? Any of her magical things?"

Vasily was silent for a few moments, and Rosa knew he was suppressing a thousand questions. "I think there are some old books," he said at last, "but they aren't here, they're in storage."

"Can you send them up for me?"

"I can. It may take a day or two."

"As soon as you can, Uncle Vasily." She gave him the address and the phone number at the Chenchikovs' farm, and warned him against speaking of her mother to whoever answered the phone if he called.

"I'm hardly going to unburden my heart to strangers," he said.

"Sorry, Uncle Vasily. Just in case, don't mention the books you're sending me. Anatoly Chenchikov is a volkhv." Rosa was aware that the bartender had just glanced up, and cursed herself for not speaking more quietly. She turned her back. "He doesn't want me to bring any of Mama's magic into the house, but I need it."

"Rosa, forget the bear—"

"It's not the bear I care about," she said. "It's the boy who went with it."

"You're breaking my heart, Rosa."

"I'm not responsible for your heart, Uncle Vasily. I'm sorry."

"When will you be home?"

"I don't know. A few weeks maybe. You're not to worry. You managed perfectly well without me before I arrived in St. Petersburg, and I wouldn't have stayed forever anyway." Her meal landed at her elbow, and she surveyed it warily. Pale meat dumplings floating in broth with a chunk of antiquated sour cream on top. The yellow cast of the cream and the overripe smell of the meat told her that she'd regret eating it. "I have to go, Vasily," she said, even though her ten minutes weren't up. "Someone's waiting for the phone."

"I love you, Roshka," he said.

"I love you too. Good-bye."

"Thank you," she said to the bartender, hanging up and turning to leave.

"You didn't eat your lunch."

Rosa shook her head. "I wasn't hungry once I saw it."

"Are you staying with Anatoly Chenchikov?" he asked.

"Does it matter to you?"

"It matters to me if a pretty girl gets herself in trouble with a devil."

"I'll be fine."

"Will you?"

Rosa didn't answer, pulling open the door and walking out into the bright sunshine.

Dying for a cigarette at eleven P.M., Rosa kicked off the blankets. She had been trying to sleep for an hour and she was tired enough, despite her late morning sleep-in. But her mind was full of thoughts that would not lie down and be quiet, so neither could she.

Ludmilla's rule about not smoking inside the walls of the farm was starting to annoy her. Rosa pulled on her coat and shoes, leaving her warm pajamas underneath, and shoved a packet of cigarettes and lighter in her pocket. She braced herself against the cold clear night, and left the guesthouse.

One light on at the cottage, deep inside. The kitchen was dark, no flicker from the television.

She followed the stone fence around and approached the gate, slowed and hung back when she heard Anatoly outside. She pressed her back against the cool stone and inched along to listen. It sounded as though he was at the edge of the woods; the wind picked up his voice and carried it back to her.

"I beseech the moon and all the stars . . ."

Rosa realized he was performing magic and moved closer to the gate to peek around the pillar. He turned in each direction, begging assistance of all the shadows from the north, the south, the east and west. He broke a glass at his feet and cut his palm on the shards as the zagovor grew more and more complex. Rosa focused on his voice, which was passionate, almost desperate. What was the spell for?

Finally, he crumpled to his knees and threw back his head. Clearly and loudly, he announced his intention. "As this blood soaks the earth and is absorbed within it, so may Nikita Kirygin's revenant spirit be absorbed into the night sky and leave my girl alone." He let his head fall forward, his voice dropping. "My word is firm, so it shall be."

Rosa moved back into the shadow of the fence and closed her eyes a second. Now she understood what poison infected the heart of the Chenchikov family.

They were being haunted by Elizavetta's dead husband.

Thirteen

As the sun rose full on the first day of the journey, the clouds on the horizon burned off and the sky dazzled Daniel's eyes. It was silver-blue at first glance, but he had the sense that if he looked deep—behind dense layers of air and light—there lurked swells of green and aches of violet. He was so preoccupied with trying to define how these impressions of color were created that he lost his fear for a while in wonder.

The leshii's well-worn path from the cottage to the woods was wide enough for them to walk side by side. New growth sprouted everywhere, the sun and shadows playing on the sticky new leaves. Under his feet, remnants of the previous year's autumn were scuffed and displaced. Daniel glanced at Em. Without make-up, in an un-forgiving shaft of summer light, her skin was sallow around her eyes giving her a tired appearance. The roughly sewn traveling outfit was bulky and ill-fitting on her slender frame, and her hair was tucked under a dirty woollen cap. Despite all this, she still had a glamour about her, the spell of her resolute determination and un-canny mental abilities. She was pretty too, of course, but "pretty" seemed almost a ridiculous word to apply to such a serious, shrewd creature.

"What are you looking at, Daniel?" she asked, without glancing in his direction.

He averted his eyes. "Sorry, I was . . . admiring the stitching on your . . . coat. You're full of hidden skills, aren't you?"

She didn't respond and Daniel fell two or three steps behind her to nurse his embarrassment. The path widened in front of them. The woods grew thinner, giving way to maple and elm, and silver-leaf birch that shimmered against the soft breeze. The light moved differently on the leaves here, illuminating sinuous and unexpected colors: a touch of blue-green in the darker leaves, a shiver of gold in the pale maples. Daniel had to admit, despite his longing to be back home in his own world, that this place was beautiful.

"How long do you think we should walk before taking a break?" Em called.

Daniel caught up to her. "What do you think?"

'We don't want to walk until we drop. We'll get further if we take regular rests. Perhaps every hour?"

"All right. Yes."

"We'll camp around sunset. Are you still happy to take the early sleep?"

"Are you still happy to take the late one?"

She stopped and turned to him, a patient smile on her lips. "You decide. It will be character-building."

"Okay, I'll take the early sleep."

"Good." She resumed her pace. "The days are getting longer, and we can't expect eight hours each a night. Three or four should do us. I'm certain it will only be in the short-term. A few days and we'll be home in our own beds."

Daniel allowed himself to be persuaded by her positive tone.

The path widened again, and a slope dropped away on their right. Daniel could see now that they walked the ridge of a hill. From up here, he viewed a rolling landscape of golden-green light and blue-violet shadows. The sky was an enormous clear vault above them. The sight took his breath away.

"Wow," said Em, her eyes as wide as a child's.

"It's—"

"Beautiful," she finished for him. "Though that word feels very mundane."

Two black birds took off from a tree nearby, skimming off into the distance. Daniel watched them disappear. "So do you really think it will only take a few days to find the Snow Witch?"

"Maybe. Maybe a week."

Daniel tried to discern whether she really believed this but she was, as ever, impenetrable.

"Fork in the road," she said, indicating ahead where the path turned back into woodland.

"East and east and north a-ways," Daniel said.

"North it is, then," she said.

They moved back into the shade, and Daniel thought he heard a rustle and a clunk off the path. "What if we don't find her that soon?" he said. "What if we wander for weeks or—"

"Let's play a game," she said. "List every animal you can think of starting with an 'a.'"

"I'm sick of lists."

"What then?"

He regarded her in the dappled light of the woods. "Have you ever done anything really dumb?"

"Of course."

"Okay, then. Tell me the dumbest thing you've ever done. Then I'll tell you."

Em shrugged. "I was at university, in a sociology exam. The question called for a two-page answer, but I misread it as a two-paragraph answer."

"Did you fail the exam?"

She shook her head. "No."

Daniel repressed a laugh. "I think you've misunderstood what I meant by dumb," he said. "I guess I meant embarrassing, funny, ridiculous."

"Oh."

"For example," Daniel said, warming to the topic and keen to shut out the sound of unknown things moving amongst the trees. "About a year ago, I went for a job interview. I'm not good at interviews, so I was very tense and it was for quite a high-paid job as a research coordinator with the BBC. The interview panel was three men, all dressed in gray suits and very somber-looking. One was a human resources officer, a plump florid chap with a bowl haircut. We were in his office, grouped under a window. I referred to him respectfully as 'sir' throughout, but as the interview wore on he became more and more icy toward me. I couldn't figure out what I was saying or doing wrong, and became really nervous and desperate to impress him. The other two seemed anxious about the tension between us. Everything was falling apart, and in my desperation I started toadying to him, saying things like, 'a man of your great standing' and so on . . . other embarrassing things."

They were walking up a gentle incline now, and Daniel took a minute to catch his breath. "The final straw came when I was leaving, and I caught a glimpse of a photograph on his desk. A very attractive young woman. I picked it up and said, 'Is this your beautiful wife?'

"He replied, 'No, that's my daughter.'

"I was mortified, of course, and made to cover my loss quickly by saying, 'You must be a very proud father.'

"He couldn't stand it a moment longer. He snatched the photo from me and said, 'In fact, I'm a very proud *mother*.'"

Em began to chuckle.

"I immediately reassessed the situation, realized that despite her mannish suit and haircut she was, indeed, a woman. I had no idea what to say, realized nothing could fix it, but still found my tongue galloping away with me.

"'I thought you were a man,' I said, then instantly regretting this, I added, 'I expect I won't get this job.'

"They agreed and saw me out."

Em smiled. "Okay, yes. That's pretty dumb."

"Your turn."

She pursed her lips, thinking. "Back home, my first break was reading the traffic report live on the radio during drivetime. One morning, there had been an accident on the corner of Hoob Road, but I read it as an accident 'on the corner of Boob Road.' My colleagues thought that was pretty funny."

"It is funny," Daniel said. "Were you embarrassed?"

"No. It was just a mistake, and a fairly easy one to make, don't you think?"

"Um . . . yes."

Em gave him a bright smile. "Go on, ask another question."

"All right, then. Your most disastrous date."

"Hmm," she said, brushing a bug off her wrist. "I'd have to think about that. They've all been pretty awful."

"I hadn't picked you for unlucky in love," Daniel said.

"Why not?" she asked sharply.

"I . . . just . . . you're so sure of yourself in every other aspect . . . I'm sorry."

"Oh, don't apologize. I'm very unlucky in love, Daniel."

Daniel's curiosity had been aroused. "You must have had a few good dates. I mean, you were married, weren't you?"

"Yes, briefly."

"Long enough to have a child."

She sighed. They walked in silence for a few moments, then she said, "I'd rather not talk about it. You tell me your worst date story. I'm better at listening."

The mood had become too serious now. "They've all been pretty bad, I guess."

"Even with Rosa?"

"Especially with Rosa." Daniel realized that he had forgotten Rosa's promise for next time they met: to tell him the reason they couldn't be together. Out here, in this strange place infested with bad magic, he began to doubt that he would ever know.

The trees opened up again on another wide view of the land.

"And it looked like such a perfect day at first," Em said.

"What do you mean?"

She indicated gray clouds building in the south. "Let's hope the weather holds."

Em woke just before dawn. Something had troubled her out of sleep. She lay still for a moment, cracking her eyes open a fraction. Was it the aches and pains of her body? Her feet were sore; her calf muscles were tight from a full day of walking. Daniel's back was turned to her, in silhouette from the fire. He'd confessed his apprehension about his first night watch out here in the open spaces of Skazki, but Em had noticed he was more and more in control of his fear.

Drip.

That's what had woken her. A raindrop.

She noticed that Daniel's face was turned to the sky. The stars were cloaked in rainclouds. Em sat up.

"Is it raining?"

"Not yet," he said, turning to her. "Just spitting. Maybe it will blow over."

She reached her hands out for the low flames of the fire.

"You're awake early," he said. "Do you want to eat something?"

"Just one pancake."

"Have two. We need the energy for all the walking." He opened the backpack of food, and they ate silently.

"Everything went well on your shift?" she asked.

"I heard noises . . . but a long way off."

Em turned her glance into the dense woods. They were camped under a towering birch tree. "What do you think is in there?"

Daniel didn't answer. The rain grew heavier, dripping off the branches above them and sizzling in the fire.

"I was just sitting here thinking about home," Daniel said quietly. "About soft blankets, and electricity, and instant noodles. All those ordinary things we take for granted."

Em heard the sad longing in his voice. She examined her own feelings. Yes, she would very much like to be home. She would very much like to be dressed in a fine woollen suit, with Italian boots, cruising the shops at Knightsbridge. But the situation was different and, for now, all her energy had to be directed at resolving the problem. She didn't like it, but it didn't make her sad.

"I'm sure we'll be home very soon," she said. "Perhaps today we'll meet somebody who can help us and be on our way."

"Yes, but that somebody might prefer to eat us than help us."

"We have gold. We'll be safe." She looked up. In the glow of the firelight, the illuminated raindrops were spinning down toward them. "We should gather a bundle of dry firewood while we can. We're going to get wet."

"We have a moleskin."

"One moleskin. Two people."

"We'll have to share it," Daniel said, and Em could tell this embarrassed him. In his imagination, perhaps it was the fateful moment in a movie where the male lead and the female love interest are forced into proximity.

She pulled out the moleskin and unfolded it. "Never mind. I'm sure the rain won't last long."

That was the last of the positive talk she forced on Daniel, for not only did the rain last, it set in and looked like it might stay for weeks. Day broke weakly, the sky was the purple-gray of bruises, and the rain thundered down. They stayed close under the moleskin, shuffling slowly on the sodden path, as rainwater filled their shoes. The woods were drowning, the ground turning to mud. Birds sat mournfully on their perches, immobile and ruffled as they waited out the deluge.

Em and Daniel traveled wordlessly. All their concentration was focused simply on putting one foot in front of the other without slipping. They stopped after two hours. Drank a little water. Continued wordlessly. The woods were changing now, becoming flatter and sparser. The path was less well-trodden, sometimes just an overgrown muddy strip. Still they walked and still it rained. Finally, when Em spied an elm with low-hanging branches, she declared a stop to the day's misery.

"We can hang the moleskin here," she said, raising her hands to run along the low bough. "Then we can light a fire under it."

"The ground's wet," said Daniel.

"Everything's wet, and getting wetter. We might have to wait out this rain."

Daniel agreed, and they set up camp. A spare fur went on the wet grass, the moleskin was affixed to the tree, and a fire was lit with the dry wood they had collected earlier. Em wasn't comfortable, but nor was she freezing and soaked. She settled close to the fire and Daniel did the same, his chin in his hands, gazing at the flames.

"This is unbearable," he said.

"We have to bear it."

"We're lost, we're wet, we're surrounded by supernatural dangers—"

"We've been walking for two days and haven't seen anything dangerous at all."

"Believe me, if the leshii is real, then so are the others."

"Go on, then," Em said, experiencing a delicate lick of fear. "I should know what we might be up against."

"Demons who can turn your blood to ice. Water spirits who drown children to keep them company. Witches and wizards who travel on the wind, or who hunger for human flesh . . ." His voice grew thin.

"But nothing so far," Em reminded him. "So far, we've been safe, and we're safe right now, if a little wet." She patted his knee. "Come on, let's play more games."

"No more lists."

"No, no more lists." She had worked out by now that Daniel was best distracted in talking about people and feelings. "Tell me your earliest memory."

Daniel dropped his hands and clasped them around his knees. "You go first this time."

"Okay." She tucked her hands under her cloak. "My dad was a housepainter, and one day my mother was sick so I went to work with him. He was painting this enormous house with a tall white fence. I remember it very clearly. I crawled up to it before the paint was dry, and touched it. My palm was white, and I smeared it all over my clothes."

"You say you crawled up to it?"

"Yes."

"How old were you?"

She shrugged. "About seven or eight months, I suppose."

"And you really do remember it?"

"Oh, yeah."

"I think that's really unusual. Remembering something from that far back."

"Perhaps it stood out because I got in so much trouble from my father." She brushed a raindrop off her nose and huddled closer under the moleskin. "Your turn."

"I remember the night when I was moved from a cot to a bed," he said. "The bed was directly under a window and the tip of a tree branch brushed the pane. It scraped on the glass all night, and I was terrified, but my nanny would come in and say I was just to go to sleep and to stop crying. I couldn't express what was wrong, I was only two."

"Why do you think you were afraid?" she asked.

"Because it sounded like the branch was knocking, trying to get in."

"But trees are inanimate objects."

"I know that. Now. Kids have all kinds of crazy ideas."

Em was about to say, "I didn't," but stopped herself.

Daniel filled the silence. "You'd know that. You have a little boy. Wasn't he ever afraid of anything irrational?"

Em kept her tone carefully guarded. "I didn't stay long enough to know that," she said, and was aware that it sounded cold. "He was only a few months old when I left."

"Oh."

"I know that makes me sound like a bad mother."

"I'm sure you had your reasons."

So many reasons. Impossible for anyone else to understand. "Yes, I did."

"What were they?" he asked bravely.

She considered him. The firelight reflected amber on his skin. He hadn't met her eye and she was struck by the softness of his face, the boyishness. Should she answer his question? And if yes, how? Could one actually start an explanation with "I'm not like everybody else"?

"I'm sorry," Daniel said. "Where are my manners?"

"I don't think we need to worry about manners under the circumstances," she said. "There are plenty of other things to worry about."

"Still, it was rude—"

"I'd like to try to explain," she said. "Do you have any nieces or nephews?"

"I have one nephew. My oldest brother's son."

"Do you see him often?"

Daniel shrugged. "Christmas. Maybe once or twice during the year."

"How old is he?"

"I think he's eight now. Maybe seven."

"You love him?"

"I . . . well, I suppose so. He's a nice little kid."

"Of course. You'd be really upset if something bad happened to him. Like if he got sick, or if he died, or even if his parents split up. You wouldn't like that."

"No."

"But you don't feel any burning desire to see him. You never sit there and feel an ache in your heart that makes you want to put your arms around him and hold him tight."

"No. I can't say I do."

"That's how I feel about my son." And that was the best she could do, because to explain why she had even had the boy in the first place was too complicated.

Daniel was nodding in sympathy, but she could tell he didn't really understand.

"So, when this little baby came along, and I liked him well enough but that was all, and he was so dependent on me, and took up every second of my day and most of my nights . . . I got quite resentful. I thought it was best for both of us if I got out."

"I suppose that was very brave of you."

Em stared at the fire for a few moments, thinking about this. "Not brave. Just practical." She shifted uncomfortably on the damp fur, determined to change the subject. "I really hope this rain eases overnight."

"At least we'll sleep well," Daniel said. "The walking tires me out. I feel jetlagged."

"How would you know? You don't fly," she teased.

He slumped forward gently. "If I did, we wouldn't be here."

"If I wasn't so bossy we wouldn't be here either," she said, "but it's too late for all that now."

Daniel slept, and then Em, despite the rain that continued all through the night. In the gray morning, their spirits low, they decided to move on.

"The rain could last a week," said Daniel. "We could have found the Snow Witch and been home by then."

So they packed up and moved again, limbs leaden with weariness and misery. The clouds hung low and darkened to a cruel blue-black, a wind whipped up and the path became obscured. Following their instincts, they kept heading northeast, into another thick wood that was dank and muddy and as dark as night-time. It wasn't possible to tell when the sun had set, as they hadn't even seen it rise. They battled with rough ground, ridges and falls. When exhaustion overcame them, they stopped and camped again, took turns catching a few hours' sleep and prepared to do it all again on the equally dismal next day.

As she trudged up a rocky slope in the woods, the rain thundering on the canopy of leaves above her, Em realized that the weather was a far greater threat to them than any supernatural monsters. The moleskin barely kept the moisture off their clothes, and they had used the last of their dry firewood the previous night. Tonight, unless the rain stopped or they found good shelter, they would start to freeze. Already her feet were numb with cold, which was useful as they didn't register the pain of continued walking.

She wasn't afraid of dying, but she was afraid of dying horribly. Wandering, cold and starving in sodden woods far from home, was about as horrible as she could imagine.

"We have to find shelter today," Em said.

"I know," Daniel replied. He had already grown used to the proximity that sharing the moleskin forced upon them. Their elbows and forearms bumped and he no longer shrank back into himself and muttered apologies. "If we don't—"

"Let's not think about it."

On they went, finding another path and following it despite the fact that it was loose and muddy. They didn't stop for a break; they were already moving so slowly it didn't seem prudent. The path wound upward, and Em's thighs ached from pushing herself up the incline. Then downward, and her calves ached from the effort of clenching her feet to the ground so she didn't slip. Up and down the path went, steep and sudden, and Em felt like a zombie, shuffling desperately along in the deluge, dead-eyed and lost.

Until her right foot missed its place on a steep decline, and she felt herself falling.

Down, slamming into the ground and mud.

"Em!" Daniel called behind her.

The slippery ground carried her, turning her and rolling her down the slope. Her hands went out to find purchase anywhere, but everything was sodden. She kept sliding, rain drenched her, rocks thumped her arms and back.

And finally she landed, feet in some stinking mess off the side of the path.

Daniel's footsteps behind her, cautious but quick. She took a breath, wondered if she'd broken a rib.

"Are you all right?" he called.

The stupid questions people asked! "Of course not," she snapped. "At the very least I'll be covered in bruises." She sat up, peered at the blackened mess her feet had found, and recoiled with a horrified gasp.

"What is it?"

"Body."

Daniel was with her then, helping her to her feet. He glanced at the body and then quickly turned his head. "What is it? Human or animal?"

Em leaned over it, holding her breath against the smell, which even two days of rain hadn't erased. "Human. As to male, female, black or white, impossible to tell. It's been skinned."

Daniel held his stomach and bent over.

"Don't throw up," she said. "We don't have much food."

But he threw up anyway, and Em waited patiently, poking at sore spots on her arms and ribs to see if they were bruises or fractures. She was pleased to note that she was still intact.

Daniel turned to her, wiping his mouth with the back of his hand. Rain poured down.

"Where's the moleskin?" she asked.

"I dropped it back on the slope in my hurry to get down here."

"You go back and get it."

"We're going to keep walking?"

"What's the option?"

"Sitting here and waiting to die."

"I sincerely hope you're joking," she said. "Go and get the mole-skin."

He left her in the shadowy dip in the path, and she picked up a stick and bent close to examine the body. The flesh was black, and bones poked through here and there. Wolves had been at its feet and ribs. Em reassessed her earlier opinion about horrible deaths. Being skinned alive was certainly worse than dying of exposure.

"I really don't want this to happen to us," she said to Daniel when he returned with the moleskin. "We must get out of these woods by nightfall."

Daniel wiped rain out of his eyes. "I keep hoping I'll wake up and find this is a dream."

She pinched his arm. "Let's move."

The path dipped down a little further, then rose again.

"Why would somebody want human skin?" she asked. "Why leave the body?"

"Dead candles," Daniel said. "Very powerful magic. Tallow candles made with human fat."

"Well, then, a couple more days on rationed food and hard labor, and we won't be worth hunting," Em said darkly.

The path narrowed onto the top of a ridge and they were silent as they walked up the slope. Then Em looked to her right and, through the trees, could see a grassy valley below.

"Daniel," she said urgently.

"I see it."

A dozen little wooden houses, huddled together. Not pretty painted cottages, but raw wood huts with long sloping roofs.

"Shelter," Daniel said, cautiously.

"Yes," said Em. "We're saved."

Fourteen

They cut from the path and headed directly for the valley. The trees had been cleared, and long grass had grown up. It was apparent immediately that the tiny village had long been abandoned. Most of the roofs had fallen in, the walls were sagging and eaten by the elements. The furthest hut was little more than a log skeleton, with grass growing where its floor should have been.

"We just need to find one that's dry inside," Em said, cracking open a door and peering in.

Daniel joined her. He could see daylight through the roof. "Not this one."

Em turned to him. She was drenched, muddy and pale. "You look in the ones on this side of the path, I'll check out the others."

So they split up across the village and began poking in the houses. The first three Daniel looked in were awash and muddy. The fourth one, however, was dark and enclosed. A quiet *drip drip* indicated that rain still made its way in, but the floor was intact and the stove was dry.

"Em!" he called. "I found one."

He stepped into the dark to wait for Em. There was a dank, rotted smell. At least the huts exposed to the sky had light and air in them. This one felt like years of shadows had gathered in its corners and been trapped. Two old chairs and a table sat in the middle of the room. He tested one for strength. It shattered beneath his hands.

Good. Firewood.

He gathered some dried leaves that had blown in the door, opened the stove, chased out two spiders, and began packing wood into it. He was so relieved it made him want to laugh hysterically. Camped out in an abandoned, cobweb-infested hut in a Russian otherworld, and he was as excited as a child on Christmas Day. Em joined him, her face hopeful.

"Oh, Daniel. This is great."

"There's a leak by the window."

"We'll just stay on this side of the room." She indicated the lighter he was using to start the fire. "Still plenty of gas left?"

"I think so. I bought it new outside Vologda. How long ago was that?"

"It feels like a long time, but I think it was less than two weeks ago."

"A time when we were dry. I can't even remember it," Daniel said, and began stripping off his coat and shoes. "I'm going to hold my feet to the flames until I can feel them again."

"Me too." She peeled off her sodden layers, down to the brown suit she had been wearing when they left Vologda. "God, I would love a strong macchiato right now."

"Tea," Daniel said. "Hot and sweet."

They lay on the floor in front of the open stove, their feet resting on the ceramic tiles surrounding its mouth. Smoke crept out, settling in their hair and prickling their eyes before escaping through cracks in the boards.

"There's another hut," Em said, when their contented silence had run its course. "The roof has fallen in, but the stove is under cover. I think we should light it, too, and hang our clothes in front of it. With a bit of luck, they'll dry overnight."

"Will we leave tomorrow?"

"Not if it's still raining. We're in danger of dying out there, Daniel, and not from murderous candle makers."

"I know." Fear crashed back over him. He reminded himself of Em's advice . . . *keep breathing. As long as you're breathing you're alive.* "For now, we've got shelter and fire, and loads of food still."

"If you're not sick of pancakes and bread." She propped herself up on her elbows and lowered her feet. "What would you like to eat right now?"

Daniel closed his eyes. "Some kind of pasta, with cream and basil."

"Oh, yeah. Or Mexican food, a mountain of it, beans and salsa and melted cheese and beer. The kind of meal that you eat so much you have to loosen your clothes afterward."

"Stop. You're making me hungry. For more than toast and jam."

She sat up. "I wrapped two eggs in the side of my pack," she said. "Just in case. I could boil them up as a treat."

Daniel's mouth watered. "Yes. Yes, yes."

"That's if they didn't break during my fall," she said, plowing through her pack. "Ah, here they are." She pulled out a metal mug and leapt to her feet. "I'll gather some water and get on with cooking dinner. Could you go to the hut just across the path from this one and hang our clothes in front of the stove?"

"Sure."

He was halfway out the door when Em said, "Daniel, wait. I should warn you, there's something you won't like in there."

Still in a light-hearted mood, he thought she was teasing. "What's that? Spiders? Rats?"

"Bones," she said, humorlessly. "Human bones."

Human bones, stacked up and surrounded by a ring of skulls, dry and dusty as they waited by the stove. Daniel tried not to look at them, and wondered at Em's ability to see them and then act perfectly normally.

He lit the fire and hung their clothes from the roof beams. All the while, the blind skulls watched him and he wondered who they had belonged to and why they were all piled up in here.

Em had cooked a feast of boiled egg, toast and pancakes with jam, and Daniel took his sleep first. Em woke him after six or seven hours and they swapped places on top of the stove, in the dank and mildewed bed linen.

Daniel sat for a long time, watching the fire while Em slept. He was warm and rested and his belly was full. Outside, the rain had finally eased. Em would want to be on her way in the morning. He remembered their furs, hung in front of the fire in the other hut. They needed turning, and the fire needed stoking. He gathered some wood and left the warm room behind.

The wind had picked up, blowing the clouds apart. Narrow strips of night sky appeared. The other hut was not quite as warm, and the presence of the bones made him nervous. Better to get this done quickly and head back to Em. He fed the fire and turned the skins.

His back was to the stove when he heard the knocking. He glanced over his shoulder, expecting to see a rat. But nothing moved.

The knocking continued, however, and it was coming from the cinder tray.

Daniel turned, waited.

"Who's there? Who's there?" A little voice from the cinder tray. "Grandfather is trapped in here, let me out?"

Daniel felt his skin creep.

"I know you're there," the voice said. "You lit the fire, it's woken me up. I'm trapped in here."

Daniel knew that "grandfather" was the name applied to a household spirit, a domovoi. They were usually friendly, if mischievous. But, importantly, *not real.*

"Come on, come on," the voice said. "Don't delay. Grandfather wants to thank you for bringing fire back to the hearth."

Daniel took a deep breath. He had seen a leshii, he knew he was in the land of enchantments, there was no need to be afraid of a tiny domovoi. He kneeled in front of the stove and pulled the cinder tray. It stuck, grated, then came free.

The domovoi popped out. Twelve inches high, a beard down to his knees, in ragged clothes. Not nearly as sweet-faced as a garden gnome—far too grizzled and snaggle-toothed for that—but sharing a similar stature.

"Who are you?" he demanded.

"Daniel."

"Daniel, you may call me Grandfather." He looked up at the furs. "Are they yours?"

"I'm drying them off. We've been wandering three days in the rain." Daniel noticed his ears were ringing faintly.

"We?"

"My friend and I. She's in the hut over the path. I should get back to her—"

"Don't be in such a hurry. She'll sleep well. No domovoi in that house anymore. I'm the last one left in the village. Surviving on my wits."

"You were stuck in a cinder tray."

"At least I was alive. A trick I learned from a bear in the woods. Slow down your breathing and heart, and you can sleep for centuries."

Daniel indicated the bones next to the stove. "What happened to them?"

"Those folk used to live here," Grandfather said. "A nasty end they came to."

"I think I'd better get back to my friend."

"Nonsense, sit down. Eat something with me."

"I'm not hungry."

"There must be something you'd really like . . . think hard."

Daniel considered the domovoi by the firelight. "Unless you have a cup of hot tea in that cinder tray—"

"Cup of hot tea. Here you are." He swept his little arms in front of him, and a tin mug appeared.

Daniel suppressed a laugh. It was like a trick in a movie. The ringing in his ears was worse, and he shook his head to see if it would clear it.

"Go on, have it," said Grandfather. "You'll find it just as tasty as the real thing."

Daniel sat on the floor and lifted the cup to his lips. It smelled wonderful. The first sip was divine, the second not quite so much. There was an aftertaste of sawdust. He put it aside.

"Anything else you want?" Grandfather asked.

"No. I really should be going." He made to get to his feet.

"Going where?"

"Back to—"

"You're from Mir, aren't you?"

"Yes."

The domovoi adopted a sober expression and indicated all the bones. "So were they."

Daniel paused.

"You want to know what happened to them?"

He sat down again, swallowed hard. His ears were quieting now, as though finding their balance in all this madness. "All right. You'd better tell me."

The rain had ceased, but the wind grew stronger. Daniel could hear it gusting through the woods and rattling over the rotted eaves. The moldy smell of damp and memories was heavy in the room.

The domovoi crossed his legs and sat, his back leaning against the warm mug of magic tea.

"We get a lot of Mir folk here in Skazki," he said. "Some, the leshii bring across to eat. Some, they wander in here and get lost and die. But the folk who lived in this village, they came across deliberately."

"Why?"

"It was about eighty years ago. Russia was under the rule of the Red Tsar, a tyrant to surpass all the tyrants they had known."

"You mean Stalin?"

"I don't remember his name. But the family, they knew a volkhv and he helped them all escape into Skazki. They thought to set up a village here, keep each other safe." The little man shook his head, his pale eyes growing sad. "Oh, what a terrible mistake, for they lasted only a few short months before Vedmak came out of the woods."

"Who's Vedmak?"

"A cruel wizard. His arms are skinny and folded like a mantis, his head too big for his neck to hold upright. He lives up there, in the woods."

"And he killed these people?"

"I was here. I saw it with my own eyes peeping out of the cinder tray. The wind came roaring down on the village, clattering over the roofs and slamming all the doors open. The folk of the village ran in here, because it's the biggest of the houses. They huddled together and said their spells and hoped for the best, but Vedmak was at the threshold a few minutes later, all dressed in white and waving his bony arms to make magic. He froze them all inside their bodies, so they were still alive when he began to skin them."

Daniel felt his flesh prickle with fear.

The domovoi continued. "When Vedmak had stripped their bones, he piled them up neatly, as you see now. They've been all my company this long, long time."

"And this wizard, Vedmak? He lives nearby?"

"Right up on that ridge." The domovoi waved his arms to indicate the direction Daniel and Em had traveled from that day.

"Then we're not safe here."

The domovoi smiled, and Daniel saw a glint of malice in his eyes that made him shiver. "Safe from Vedmak? Probably. He doesn't trouble himself too much with this place anymore. But—"

"But what?"

"There are other things." Grandfather cast his eyes around the room. "They might not trouble you, but there are no guarantees."

"Who? What are you talking about?"

"All those folk, they died a death not-their-own. You know what that means?"

Daniel nodded. "So their souls are doomed to wander revenant until the day of their own death comes. But surely if they died nearly eighty years ago, they must all be at rest by now."

"You don't understand Skazki, my boy. Here, your own death can never find you. All their spirits still haunt this place, and would certainly love to meet some warm human bodies to possess and destroy."

Daniel began to panic. "What can we do?"

"Give me gold."

The sudden change of mood made Daniel hesitate too long.

"I said give me gold. Now. For I would only have to shout 'blood' and they would all wake and come for you."

"The gold is in the other house," Daniel said. "My friend has it. I'll go and get it straightaway."

"I don't believe you."

"Then come with me."

"I can't leave this hearth, it's my own."

"Honestly, just give me a few seconds—"

"Blood!" he yelled, and his voice echoed around the empty room. He smiled a crooked smile.

Daniel froze with shock.

"They didn't hear me, I think," said Grandfather.

"I'll get the gold. I'll come right back. Don't call again." Daniel raced out the door and across to the other hut. He began plowing through Em's pack for her stash of gold.

"What's going on?" she asked sleepily from the bed.

"Gold. I need gold. The domovoi next door is threatening to wake the revenants if—"

"Slow down, Daniel. I can't understand you."

"BLOOD!" came the cry across the night sky.

Daniel was already on his feet, the pack still clenched in his fist. "Stop it," he shouted. "I'm coming."

He dashed back and threw a gold earring at the domovoi. "Here," he said. "Now call them off."

A creak from the wall behind him. He tensed.

"Too late," said Grandfather, admiring the gold by the firelight. "They're already coming."

"But—"

A thud and a shout from next door. Em didn't know what was going on. He had to get back and warn her. But he'd just wasted a piece of gold and couldn't leave without asking.

"The Snow Witch," he said, as he pulled the cloaks from the roof beam. "Do you know where she lives?"

"Oh, east and east and north a-ways," the domovoi said. "Look out behind you."

Daniel spun. A dark shape was heaving out of the wall, long fingers stretching toward him. He yelped and ran. Em was at the door of the other hut already.

"What the hell is—?"

"Just run," Daniel shouted, pulling her onto the path. And when she turned in the direction they had come from that morning, he said, "No, too dangerous. Go south, just for now."

They ran across the sodden field, an army of shadows pouring from the village to chase them. Daniel's heart pounded like a jackhammer in his chest. His feet skidded on the muddy ground, but he clung tight with his toes and kept running, Em two feet behind him shouting for explanations.

The woods beckoned, towering trees that bent in the wind and showered hours-ago raindrops on them. He glanced over his shoulder. The horde of revenants slowed when they saw the woods, frightened by dull remembrances of life and the enemy who had stolen from the woods to end it.

"Straight into the trees, Em," he called. "They're too scared to follow us in there."

"Should we be scared too?"

"Probably." His feet pounded across the field, until finally he reached the sanctuary of the woods. Em was a half-second behind him. They kept running, disappearing into the trees, until finally Daniel felt they had lost their pursuers. He bent over, holding his knees, panting.

"What . . . the hell . . . just happened?" asked Em between gasps of breath.

Daniel waited until his breath returned to him. "Revenants," he said.

"Explain revenants."

"Like a cross between a ghost and a vampire," Daniel said. "They don't steal blood, they steal life. They possess you and drain you."

"And how did we come to have an army of revenants on our tails?"

"The domovoi. The house spirit where I was hanging out the cloaks. He demanded gold and thought I wasn't going to pay. He called them."

"So you've used one of our pieces of gold. Did you get anything useful out of him? About the Snow Witch."

Daniel smiled weakly. "East and east and north a-ways."

Em groaned. "Shit!" She kicked a log, then sat on it. "At least it's stopped raining."

Daniel leaned his back against a tree. "The domovoi said something else, Em. It's really troubling me."

"Go on."

"In Russian folklore, everyone has their own death. They are fated to die a certain way: illness or old age usually, or unavoidable accidents. When someone dies very unexpectedly, through a series of awful coincidences, say, or because they were in the wrong place at the wrong time, they are said to have died a death not-their-own. You follow?"

"Yes. Why is this bothering you now?"

"If you die a death not-your-own, you're doomed to wander revenant until the date of your own death. But here in Skazki, your own death can never find you. So you won't die of old age. I guess you could even live forever if you could avoid the hostile creatures. But if you do die, there's no rest-in-peace . . ." Daniel trailed off, so horrified by the idea that he couldn't give words to it.

"I see," Em said. "What you're saying is that this is a place where 'a fate worse than death' is more than a B-movie cliché."

"That's right."

She was quiet for a long time, and Daniel turned his face up to the sky to watch clouds blow away and the distant stars shine through.

"Daniel?" she said, and he didn't like the note of panic in her voice.

He turned to see that she was searching around them with frantic eyes.

"What is it?"

"Did you bring the food?"

"The food was with you."

"I thought you had it. You had the packs."

"I had one, yours." He braced himself. "You didn't bring the other? It was at the end of the bed."

"I didn't see it," she said, softly. "I left it behind."

"We have no food?"

"We've lost it all."

Fifteen

Rosa looked at Anatoly and Ludmilla differently now. Over dinner, as Anatoly carved the chicken, Rosa read the lines on his face as signs of anxiety, not sourness. Helping Ludmilla fold clothes in the dank little laundry at the back of the house, she saw the older woman's bony shoulders as those of a mother who has too great a burden to bear. The revenant spirit of a man killed too soon, through some unpredictable circumstance, was a dangerous thing to his young wife. He would blight her life, sap her energy, have her join him. This was the cause of Elizavetta's sickness.

But why could Anatoly not cure it? Why could a volkhv of such power and energy fail to banish a single revenant spirit? He was clearly desperate to do so.

As much as she was puzzled and, although she hated to admit it, concerned about the family's problems, she simply had to focus if she was ever going to get Daniel back. She allowed a respectful twenty-four hours to feel sorry for Anatoly, but began pestering him for more spells directly after school on Monday.

"Come then," he said. "We'll go out to the grove, away from the farm. I'll show you a magic knot so powerful that you can take it with you to the other world and keep yourself wholly safe."

This time, they didn't leave by the front gate. Anatoly took her down to the stream and showed her a narrow strip of mud and two stepping stones that led around the side of the brick wall encircling the farm. Once on the other side of the wall, he led her up the muddy bank and past an enormous spruce tree that had twelve knives embedded in its trunk.

"What are these for?" she asked.

"Not important. I'll tell you another time," he said, taking her hand and pulling her smoothly behind him. "Today, protection knots."

They entered a shaded grove. The stream trickled gently beside them, the ground was soft and grass grew only sparsely. Rosa gazed around her. "Is this where you come to do your magic?"

"Sometimes, yes. Not at night." He glanced around. "It's not safe here at night."

Rosa knew he referred to Nikita's visits.

"Do you ever do magic in the bathhouse?"

He smiled. "It's a guesthouse."

"You never use it for magic?"

"Well, perhaps I do now and again," he said, "but we have seasonal workers who come to stay in the summer harvest, so we need space for them."

"Is there still magic in the walls?"

"I pulled it all out before you moved in."

"I see."

"Elizavetta was born in there, and Makhar. My father died there, and I hope to die there too, but even a volkhv must be practical, and we have no money for a new building." He gestured around. "A shaded grove can work just as well, though the magic tends to escape into the treetops."

Rosa looked up. Weak sun struggled through the thick branches. She almost imagined she could see it, violet smoke circling the tips of the trees and then diving inside to be absorbed into the sap.

"Why here today?"

Anatoly pulled out a length of black wool. "Because this is not just ordinary magic. This is difficult magic; this goes beyond a yammering zagovor." He handed her the wool. "This knot will be your shield in the other world."

Rosa wound the wool over her fingers. "Okay, tell me what to do."

"Seven double knots," he said. "With each one, we name the places you will be safe." He coached her through the process, and she did one practice run without tying the knots. Then, summoning up the magic in her fingers and wrists, she worked the spell.

"As I travel on the road," she said, tying a double knot. "In the field." Another knot. "Through the crossroads ... between the houses ... across the seas ... into the woods ... over the trembling marshes ..." She threw the knotted yarn on the ground. "None shall come near me. My word is firm. So shall it be."

Anatoly lifted his eyebrows. "Shall we see if it works?"

"Go on."

He took a step toward her, his foot hovered above the yarn and crossed it. His other foot did the same.

Hollow disappointment. "It didn't work."

' No," Anatoly said. "It didn't. It's a good thing you don't have to protect yourself from me."

Something about the cool delivery of these words made her prickle. "I don't?"

"Of course not, Rosa, you know that." Now he was warm again, his arm hooked around her shoulders. "Let me try the knots. Perhaps we have the wrong wording."

Rosa watched as his grubby fingers unpicked all her knots. The wool was beginning to fray. "You made these very tight, Rosa." He straightened the yarn in his fingers and cleared his throat. "As I travel on the road . . ." He went through exactly the same process as Rosa had, casting the knotted yarn on the ground.

"Now," he said, beckoning her from his side of the yarn. "Try to cross."

She lifted her toes, tried to step over the knots. An invisible blow to the bottom of her foot sent her pitching backward. She landed hard on her backside.

"Ow!"

Anatoly helped her up. "It worked."

She rubbed her lower back. "Yes, obviously," she said irritably. "Why for you and not me?"

"I'm much more powerful."

"But my magic is growing."

"Not as quickly as we thought."

She remembered the bee in her window on Saturday morning, how it hadn't responded to her. "It feels like I'm going backward."

"Have you checked on your sapling? Is it still well?"

"I haven't looked since the weekend."

"Then let us see."

Anatoly pocketed the magic knot, and they returned to the guesthouse. Rosa opened the cupboard door, and was appalled to see that the wych elm had withered. The green shoot on the end was spotted and dull.

"It's dying." Hollow panic crept into her stomach.

"You've been saying the spell?"

"Every morning when I wake." Was she stuck here forever?

Anatoly stroked his beard, pulling on its wispy ends. He made a noise, somewhere between a hum of consideration and a sigh of unhappiness. Rosa grew uneasy.

"What do you think is wrong?" she asked, dreading the answer.

"It does appear that your magic is diminishing."

"But it shouldn't be."

"No. But nor is it unheard of. We did a lot of work in the first week. I have said before it's like training for a long run. If you do too much too soon, you can set back your cause."

"Are you saying I've had some kind of training injury?"

"Ha!" He offered her a reassuring smile. "Yes. That's how I'd see it. The only thing that would fix it . . ."

"A rest," she said, closing the cupboard door and sagging back on it. "That's what you're going to suggest."

"Yes, it is."

"How long?"

"Until you're better."

"A day? Two?"

"I'd leave it a week."

Impatience galvanized her body. She launched herself forward and grabbed Anatoly around the wrists. "I can't bear to wait that long. He could be dead by then. I must get across to find him."

"You have no choice."

"There must be something. You're a strong volkhv, couldn't you send me across?"

"And be left without my own magic? I have things to do here, very important things."

Rosa remembered his trouble with Elizavetta and bit her tongue. "It's not just the veil I need magic for," she said. "I have to hide that hire car. The police will be looking for it."

"I know you are frustrated, Rosa," he said, his voice growing gentle as he peeled her from his wrists. "You may still accompany me all this week and watch the magic I perform. You will learn, but passively."

"But the car—," she said, dropping onto the bed.

"Don't worry about the car. Nobody will find it. We're beyond the edge of nowhere out here." He sat next to her and stroked her hair. The gesture was fatherly but proprietary. "Leave it a week and don't worry, Rosa. A week will make all the difference."

The days crawled by. She was tired all the time, and this was the only thing that kept her from lying awake at night cursing that she was stuck here, not moving, while Daniel battled on without her. If he had been alone, she would have given him up for dead already. She still hoped that Em could keep them alive until she got there.

She dragged herself out of bed and dressed for the day, hearing voices in the garden while she brushed her hair.

"I don't feel well."

"Just sit in the sun for half an hour. It will do you good."

"I want to go back to bed."

Rosa opened the door of her guesthouse. Ludmilla had Elizavetta by the hand, and was leading her out to a moldy deckchair she had set up in full sun by the herb beds.

"The sunshine will help, Elizavetta," Ludmilla was saying. "The fresh air is good for your lungs."

The girl grumbled but allowed herself to be dropped into the seat. Rosa crossed the garden quickly, offering them both a quick wave, and found Makhar sitting at the kitchen table waiting for her.

"History this morning, Roshka," he said. "You promised to tell me about Ivan the Terrible."

Rosa could have wept. History lessons with a nine-year-old. How was it possible that she was stuck in this mundane cycle? "Let me use the bathroom and make some breakfast. It's only a quarter to nine."

"Hurry, then."

"Start reading ahead. I want you to read three pages before I sit down."

"Ivan the Terrible came to the throne in 1547, aged only seventeen . . ." His little voice followed her down the hallway, earnestly reading out of his history book. On the way back from the bathroom, she noticed Elizavetta's door was ajar.

Makhar read on. "In 1553, he gave the order to build St. Basil's Cathedral in Moscow, to celebrate victory over the Tatar Mongols . . ."

Rosa hesitated half a second, then went in.

The stale air was thick with the smell of sleep and dust. The bed, an old timber four-poster, had curtains hung around it. An ancient dresser, stained dark brown, provided the space for nearly a dozen photographs in frames. Rosa bent to study them.

Elizavetta, plump-cheeked and smiling—almost unrecognizable—in the arms of Nikita. He was in his late teens, with the easy smile of a man who has never wanted for female attention; thick dark hair growing over his collar and falling into his eyes, a navy T-shirt and blue jeans. The next photo featured him in a serious pose, staring straight into the lens with a full-lipped pout. Then a photo of Elizavetta and Makhar with Nikita leaning in behind them. Rosa quickly scanned the rest. Nikita riding a horse. Nikita drinking from a beer can. Nikita and Elizavetta in wedding apparel. Every photo featured Nikita. There were none of Ilya.

"In 1560 his wife died, and he went mad with grief . . ." Makhar diligently continued reading, his voice muffled down the hallway.

Rosa turned, assessed the bed. Nobody would know. She parted the curtains and knelt on the mattress, flipping up the pillow. The place every superstitious teenage girl keeps her most precious things. A lace handkerchief: inside, a lock of dark brown hair and a gold wedding band. The inscription inside the ring read ELIZAVETTA AND NIKITA, ETERNAL LOVE.

Rosa hid the items again and moved to the window. She peered around the edge of the curtain, and could see past the laundry and out to the hives. Anatoly and Ilya, in their bee-protection suits, were busy scraping wax from frames. What did Ilya think of this room? It was little more than a shrine to Elizavetta's first husband.

Footsteps in the hall. Rosa turned. Makhar was standing in the doorway.

"Roshka?"

"I thought I saw a rat."

"We don't have rats. Papa scares them away with magic."

"Just a shadow then." She had her arm around his shoulders. "Don't tell Luda. We don't want her to worry about rats."

"I don't want her to worry about anything," Makhar said, and Rosa knew he understood she had been snooping. "I'll close Elizavetta's door so nothing else gets in."

It was Ilya's job to collect the mail from town every Monday. Makhar found this occasion profoundly exciting, although none of the letters were ever addressed to him. He and Rosa were taking a science lesson in the woods—a thin excuse for Rosa to smoke a cigarette—and he had already acquired a healthy collection of grasshoppers when the sound of the car echoed down the long dirt road nearby.

"That's Ilya," Makhar said, ready to discard his jar of grasshoppers with careless haste.

"Wait, wait," Rosa said. She had only just lit a cigarette. "Why are you so excited? Are you expecting something?"

"Sometimes my aunt in Moscow sends me a comic book."

"How often?"

He shrugged, time being immaterial. "Sometimes."

"Okay, we'll go back. But slowly. I want to finish this cigarette."

"Smoking's bad for you, Roshka," he said, running ahead. He tapped the trees with his palm, muttering a song under his breath.

Rosa took a last quick drag and butted her cigarette. "I'll race you," she called, and they dashed back to the house.

They arrived at the same moment as Ilya dropped a packet of letters on the kitchen bench. She thought of her request to Vasily, and tried not to look too hopefully toward the pile.

"So, Makhar," she said, settling with the little boy at the table. "Shall we go on with long division in decimals tomorrow?"

Anatoly descended on the mail, began flipping through the envelopes casually. One caught his eye and he pulled it open to read.

"I'm sick of long division," Makhar said. "Can we do something else?"

"If you like. Percentages?"

"Elizavetta makes a pie if we do percentages. Then we cut up little percentages to eat."

"Then we'll make a pie."

Anatoly sniffed, and threw the letter in front of Rosa. "For you," he said tersely. "Are you careful who you give our address to?"

Rosa was momentarily stunned. "Did you open my mail?"

"It's from somebody named Vasily."

"My uncle in St. Petersburg. It's private. You shouldn't have opened it."

"No secrets here, Rosa," he said.

Rosa's blood was burning. She quickly glanced over the letter: a few stern words about his hopes for her return, but mostly chat about golf and business. No mention of her mother's things. She wondered if he still intended to send them. "I have a right to private correspondence," she said, biting back her anger for Makhar's sake.

Anatoly didn't respond. He continued leafing through the mail. Ludmilla arrived with an empty laundry basket under her arm, and Ilya gave Rosa a sympathetic smile. She tucked Vasily's letter into her waistband and touched Makhar's snowy hair.

"All done for the day," she said.

"Time for lunch," he said.

"Set the table, Rosa," Ludmilla said.

Rosa's lungs filled with frustration. "I won't be having lunch today," she said, rising and going to the door. "I'm going to have some time to myself." She resisted slamming the door as she left.

Shortly after dinner, when the sun was still low in the sky to the west but night had already come to the east, there was a hesitant knocking at the door of Rosa's guesthouse.

"Ilya," she said, surprised to see him there on her top step.

He glanced around nervously. "Can I come in?"

"Of course."

He had something under his coat, which he had folded both his arms over. She showed him in and closed the door.

"Would you like coffee?"

Ilya shook his head. "No, no. I shouldn't stay. Anatoly thinks I'm washing out the honey drums." He pulled open his coat and handed Rosa a package, wrapped in brown paper. "This came for you in the mail today."

Rosa took it gently. "It's from Vasily. Why did you . . . ?"

"I know what he's like. I knew that if he saw it he would open it. I'm sorry I didn't find your letter before he did, or I would have set that aside too."

Rosa eyed the package. "Thank you so much, Ilya. I'm in your debt."

"You can repay me by not saying anything to Anatoly."

"I certainly wouldn't tell." She took his hand firmly. "You must stay and drink coffee with me. I have sugar and milk now, and fresh coffee."

He hesitated, watching her fingers. She withdrew them. "Please."

"Yes . . . all right."

"Sit down," she said, throwing the package onto her bed. "I need to talk to you about something."

As she boiled the kettle, the breeze freshened overhead making the trees whisper and hiss. From the corner of her eye, Rosa saw Ilya stiffen. "Don't worry," she said. "I'm sure it's just an evening breeze."

"I don't know what you're talking about."

She turned to him. "I'm talking about Nikita. You know that."

He looked down and away, picking at the worn upholstery on the arm of the chair. "Nikita is dead."

"How did he die?"

"An accident in the woods."

"A death not-his-own," she said, then finished making the coffee in silence. She handed him a mug and sat on the end of the bed, her legs pulled up underneath her. "Ilya, I know. His spirit is still out there, isn't it? Anatoly can't banish him."

Ilya was very still. He closed his eyes and drew a deep breath, speaking almost inaudibly. "He will though."

"Nikita is making Elizavetta sick."

Ilya opened his eyes, and Rosa was struck again by the oddness of them. One was dark, and seemed warm and soft; the other was light, and seemed flinty and cool. As if he could not decide to be either open or closed to her. "Some nights, Nikita pulls Elizavetta's spirit from her body—"

"I know, I saw."

"The separation of spirit and flesh weakens her. We haven't been able to stop it yet. I sometimes think we never will. I sometimes think she'll die."

Rosa thought about all the photos of Nikita in Elizavetta's room, and wondered what Ilya made of them. "How long have you been married?"

"Nearly a year." He was staring into his coffee cup. Rosa sensed he left much unsaid, but she reminded herself to be patient, that intense curiosity would have him running out the door in twenty seconds.

"Ilya!" Anatoly's voice, outside, near the hives.

Ilya jumped from his chair. "I have to go."

Rosa pushed him back down. "Don't be silly. He'll see you if you leave now." She climbed onto the bed and opened the window. Anatoly was in a long overcoat, calling for Ilya by the hives. The evening had deepened, and he was nearly all in shadow.

"Anatoly!" she called. "Have you lost something?"

He turned, peered toward her. "Some*one*, Rosa. Have you seen Ilya?"

"No," she said guilelessly. "Maybe he's gone for a walk in the woods."

Anatoly hesitated a moment, and she could feel the needling pressure of his mind seeking out hers, scouring it for the truth. But nobody kept secrets better than Rosa. "You're right," he said. "He likes to walk in the woods on windy nights."

He turned and set off around the garden. Rosa closed the window.

Ilya smiled at her nervously. "You're not afraid of him."

Rosa thought about Anatoly as she'd just seen him outside, all in black, a bear of a man with shadowy eyes and a grizzled beard. "No. Not really."

"It's good for me to see somebody who isn't afraid of him. Luda is afraid of him. Makhar is afraid of him. I see that you are not and it gives me heart."

"He hasn't done anything to frighten me." She settled on the bed, arranging her pillow behind her back and stretching out her legs, and wondered if this was true. Today, when he'd opened her mail, that had frightened her. The ease, the confidence with which he violated her simple right to privacy. Such a small act, really, but so telling. "What has he done to frighten you?"

Ilya shrugged and didn't say anything further. Although he seemed uncomfortable, he wasn't hurrying to run away. He stared into the middle distance, occasionally sipping his coffee. Rosa found herself admiring his profile, imagining her fingers slipping around the back of his warm neck and up into his hair. What beautiful hands he had: long, tanned fingers, strong and square.

"We can look after each other," she said. "You and me."

"That would be nice," he said. "This family is . . . claustrophobic. I'm glad you came." He wouldn't meet her eye, and she felt a keen stab of desire for him. She wanted to climb across his lap and crush his mouth with hers.

"How did you meet Elizavetta?" she asked instead, crossing her ankles demurely.

"I met Anatoly first. He knew my father. He needed somebody to help with the last summer harvest and my father owed him money. A deal was struck. If I came to work for three months, Anatoly would cancel my father's debt." The wind rattled over the roof and Ilya's eyes went up, his shoulders tensed.

"It's okay," she said. "It's just wind. Go on."

"The moment I saw Elizavetta I knew I didn't want to return to my own family," he said. Then he chuckled. "It was already getting very crowded. I have six brothers."

"Are you the eldest?"

"The youngest. None of them have left home. I blame my mother's cooking."

Rosa leaned forward. "You're the seventh son?"

"Of a seventh son, actually," he said, smiling self-consciously. "I know. I'm supposed to be—"

"Overflowing with magic," she finished for him. "Yet you say you've never felt anything?"

"No."

"It may be latent. You may need to grow it."

"Anatoly expressed the same astonishment, but he tested me and said there's definitely nothing there." He waved a dismissive hand. "I don't mind. I don't want such a burden."

Rosa turned this over in her head.

"Anyway," he said, "I met Elizavetta and we fell madly in love and were married very soon after."

"Madly in love," Rosa said, keeping the skepticism out of her voice. "That's nice. You're still madly in love?"

"Yes," he said quickly, then, "I mean . . ."

Rosa let the silence sit for a moment, then said, "What do you mean?"

"Her illness has taken its toll. We aren't close. We haven't . . . we don't share a marital bed."

"And she has eleven pictures of Nikita on her dresser," Rosa added. "Don't forget that."

"I never expected to replace Nikita," he said with a downward turn of his mouth. "She feels a lot of guilt over his death."

"Then it was her fault?"

A long pause. Rosa waited it out. If he answered, then a new intimacy would have been forged between them.

It was worth waiting for. "She shot him accidentally," he said. "Nikita was hiding in the woods—sulking by all accounts—and

Anatoly handed her the gun while he tied his shoelace. The safety catch was off, she bumped her elbow, the bullet left the barrel. Sixteen feet away, Nikita was sitting behind a tree. The bullet passed through a knothole, cracked through the other side and lodged in his brain. He died on the way back to the farm."

Ilya knotted his right hand into his left and sent his gaze toward the window. Did he regret telling her the family secret? It was impossible to tell.

Rosa slid off the bed. "I might put the heater on," she said. "Will you stay for another coffee?"

"I haven't finished this one."

She found the heater and plugged it in. "It's because I can't smoke. I drink coffee instead. Nine or ten cups a day."

"How do you sleep at night?"

"That certainly hasn't been a problem," she said, switching the kettle on again. "I sleep like the dead. I wake up tired."

"I do too," he said. "I think maybe it's the quiet out here, so far from the traffic."

Rosa finished making her coffee then sat on the floor in front of the heater, her feet stretched toward the bars. "I don't know if I trust Anatoly," she said.

"I think he's worth trusting."

"Do you think he liked Nikita?"

"I know he didn't. Elizavetta told me that they fought all the time."

"I don't trust him," she muttered again, but Ilya didn't respond.

The wind picked up outside, and Ilya pulled himself to his feet. "I'm going out to the woods."

"It will do you no good. If Anatoly can't get rid of him—"

"I feel better if I do something. Besides, Anatoly is looking for me."

She saw him to the door, taking his arm gently just before he left. "Ilya," she said, dropping her voice to a whisper, "you say you've been married to Elizavetta a year. How long since you've shared a bed?"

His eyes met hers, and he looked bewildered and ashamed.

"I've . . . we haven't . . ." He shook his head and peeled her hand from his arm. "That's not a question to ask me, Rosa," he said. "I have to go."

She closed the door after him regretfully. She had rather hoped to peel all his clothes off him and tumble him into her bed. Her desire for him grew stronger the more annoyed she became with Anatoly. A few hot bouts of lovemaking would certainly make being stuck at the farm more bearable. Instead, she returned to the heater, picking up her package. It was long and flat and silent, where she had been expecting a rattling box of objects. She tore off the paper and found inside three exercise books and a note from Vasily.

Rosa, this is all I could find. I hope it holds what you're looking for, but I can't understand a word of it. V.

Rosa put the letter aside and opened the first book, immediately seeing what Vasily meant. The letters were familiar, but it was another language. Not a single word jumped out at her as being recognizable.

"Damn," she said, quickly flicking through the other books. They were all equally useless to her. Her mother had written everything in a secret code.

Rosa had the car keys in her pocket as she left her guesthouse later that night, but still didn't know whether she intended to use them. Her nerves and thoughts were ringing and jangling against each other, and she didn't yet want to succumb to sleep. Ilya's visit had made her feel many things, mostly desire and suspicion. So, as she left to have a cigarette in the woods, she still wasn't sure why she was going to the car. Perhaps to hide it, to try her magic once again. Perhaps to drive it, to leave the Chenchikovs behind.

Two steps outside the gate, and a shadow on the edge of her vision caught her attention. Anatoly himself. He sat with his back against the brick wall, gazing into the woods. He hadn't seen Rosa yet, and in this unguarded instant, she saw all the weight of his despair sitting heavily on his shoulders.

She shrank back into the shadows, watching him for a few

moments. It wasn't possible for her to pass without him seeing her, yet she didn't want to return to her guesthouse. Anatoly was unaware of her presence. Rosa's gaze divested him of his usual power. Here was a sad fat man, with a bulbous nose and a straggly beard. Not the spark-eyed magic creature she normally saw.

Boldly, she approached him. "Anatoly," she called.

He started, then when he recognized Rosa in the dark, he gathered himself, ran a hand through his beard, but made no move to stand up. "What are you doing out here?" he said sternly. "You should stay in your guesthouse, you should—"

"I'm having a cigarette and, anyway, there are no secrets now." She crouched next to him and lifted his left hand, which was lacerated and still bleeding from the zagovor. "I know what you're doing out here. I've already seen what you don't want me to see." Gently, she traced her fingertip through the blood. A man never seemed more alive than when he bled, when it was made evident that he was not a machine of molded parts.

The wind rose in the trees and whipped her hair across her face. He sucked in his breath in response to her touch. "I would do anything to make my daughter well again," he said softly.

She dropped his hand, and sucked the blood off her fingers. It fizzed like sherbet on her tongue. "I know that," she said. "I believe it."

Long seconds passed as they gazed at each other. Shadows crawled across his skin as the trees moved around them.

"I need a cigarette," she said, rising.

"Rosa, don't be out too late. It isn't safe. You have lessons with Makhar in the morning."

"Don't worry about me," she called. Her lighter flared into life and she exhaled into the sky. "I'm the least of your problems."

As she headed into the woods, she thought about Anatoly. A man of power and magic, a man with the ability to fulfill his will through force. How little trouble it would be for such a man to hand his daughter a loaded gun, then make certain the trigger jumped. How little trouble to find another, more suitable, son-in-law and then drain him of his precious latent magic. More than that: how little trouble for him to convince Rosa he was helping her, and then siphon off her magic to help only himself.

Days were turning to weeks, and soon it would be a month. Rosa knew he was never going to let her cross the veil.

So, was she going to run away? Back to St. Petersburg, to Uncle Vasily? She wouldn't give up on Daniel, of course. She would find somebody else to help, somebody who danced obediently to the tune of Vasily's money. But how long to find that person? Anatoly had said there were only twenty-seven like him left in Russia. And how long, if ever, before Rosa could feel magic in her joints again?

Her cigarette was a tiny orange beacon in the dark. The keys rattled in her pocket and she had nearly decided by the time she arrived in the section of the woods where she had left the car. Then the decision was taken from her hands.

The car was nowhere to be seen.

"Ah, Anatoly," she said under her breath. Now she understood his casualness with her about hiding the vehicle. He had wanted to come out here and do it himself, so that Rosa couldn't find it. So that Rosa couldn't leave.

She turned. The wind whipped her hair and sent her scarf flapping behind, and a clutching sensation possessed her lungs, as though a trap was being closed on her.

Sixteen

Are we not all trapped, though, Rosa? Is not every sentient being, from the meanest beetle to the humblest child, to the wealthiest Mir folk, to the most powerful of Skazki magicians—me, Papa Grigory, who can roam freely in the minds of others and cannot die—are we not all caught in a trap of our own making? All of us desire. Desire drives us to satisfy ourselves. And our satisfaction is often found in a snare of conditions and obligations.

Rosa will come. Spend no moment of your concern on her. She will come. I expect her in little more than a week. I look forward to her arrival very much. I still have some hope that her friends will lose themselves and the bear without her assistance, but they have been shrewd and fortunate so far. Leaving their fate to chance would be foolish. I need Rosa, and Rosa needs me. I will tell you something you may not have guessed: since the moment that bear re-entered our world, I have not rested easy.

Of course, I would never let Totchka sense my concerns. I like her world to be made of sunlight and smiles. She sleeps now. It is late at night and I find I don't need as much sleep as I grow older. We share a lovely bedtime ritual: when she grows sleepy, I lie next to her on the bed and stroke her dark hair and sing to her. She watches me and watches me, holding her eyes open as long as she can, holding on to wakefulness and togetherness as though they are the only two things in all existence that matter. Then sleep catches her, her eyelids flutter, and she slips away.

Should I glance over at her now, I would see her soft cheek and the fall of her dark hair. They are the only things exposed to the firelight. The rest is safely under blankets, burrowed among pillows. Her breathing is slow and soft; the fire crackles gently and I rub my tired knuckles. The moon is hiding behind clouds tonight. It has rained for days out there, but we are warm and dry in here. I am almost perfectly content. The bear is the only thing that troubles me.

Are you surprised? Did you think I felt fondly toward the bear because of our long association?

Then you must understand: it is not the bear I fear. It is what's inside her. Does that puzzle you? Good. Tales should be full of puzzles.

I promised you more of her stories. The Golden Bear has seen all the intrigues of history, ours and Mir's, and how those histories have knotted and slipped and knotted again.

Imagine for a moment that you share some of her memories. What moments would burn brightest? It is hard to say because images and music, scents and sensations, wash over her constantly, entwined with the endless noise of human voices as they love, argue, grieve and plot against each other. The years come and go. She sits and she watches the to and fro of time, and sometimes she sleeps for long years because the frantic procession of Mir folk tires her.

Then, one day, she wakes and wonders why she has woken.

It's the bells.

Ringing out into the cold sky, the clang and chime of bells, some warm and resonant, others sharp and musical. Intricate patterns and rhythms pealing over the snow-laden Cathedral Square and, even further beyond the Kremlin, out over the timbered streets of Moscow and down the hill to the river.

The bear listens and knows that something wonderful must be happening. From her shadowy corner in the Terem Palace's Cross Chamber she ranges out in her mind's eye and follows the bells all the way to the Cathedral of the Assumption. Solemn men sing as the bells ring in a cacophony of importance and the crisp frosty sky shivers. Inside, the dark spaces are lit by dazzling wheels of candles strung up high that glint off the gilded doors and illuminate the painted saints on the columns and walls. Deep mullioned windows let in a little of the gray daylight. On a carved wooden throne at the center of it all, wearing a fur-and-gold cap encrusted with gems, is Russia's new Tsar, Ivan the Fourth.

Despite the solemnity of the ritual, the mood in the crowded cathedral is one of joy and relief. The grand-duke's son, now seventeen, is old enough to be crowned and take over the rule of Russia in his own right. The bear surveys the crowd, sees the bearded faces of the noblemen—the boyars—who surround the throne. Two faces command the bear's attention.

The new Tsar, Ivan, who is tall and spare, with long hands and a thin pointed beard, brows arched like a bat's wings, and a long hooked nose. He is very young, but has the bearing of a man much older. The bear has seen him before, of course. They live together at the palace. Today, dressed in his official robes and wearing the Crown of Monomakh, Ivan looks every inch the grand Tsar, the autocrat, the man who will lead his people with a hard hand and will one day be called Ivan the Terrible, Ivan the Awesome, Ivan the Purifying Storm. The bear wonders if Ivan will now relinquish his childhood pleasures, and stop throwing dogs from his third-floor window or unleashing his ungovernable temper on his servants.

The other face that is conspicuous to the bear is one that she has not seen for many years, but one she is not surprised to recognize. The Secret Ambassador, dressed like the other boyars in his stiff brocade kaftan, watches proceedings with a passive gaze. He is thinking about the separation of the worlds, and how the two might be once again tied.

Since Olga ordered Skazki to withdraw, things have changed. The Church has a clawhold in the minds of Russian people and many of the old ways have been diluted or abolished. Yet life in this harsh land is more suited to pagan thought, so most folk still hold on to scraps of the old rituals and beliefs. The Secret Ambassador is anxious to ensure that the old ways don't slip from their minds completely. Some of the boyars have been talking about Ivan's intention to marry very soon. He has called for every virgin of marriageable age in Moscow to be brought before him for consideration. The Secret Ambassador sees in this an opportunity to reunite Mir and Skazki, for Skazki blood to be intertwined with the rulers of Russia.

He needs only to make Mokosha agree.

Mokosha is the most powerful woman in Skazki. Of the six old gods, Mokosha is the only female, an immortal and ever-beautiful deity. For centuries, women of Mir shed the blood of animals to appeal for her help in conception and childbirth. Since the separation of the lands, more and more turn to the Christian deity in prayer and Mokosha finds herself bored. She lives in a dark stone house by a river in one of the thrice-nine lands of Skazki, where she watches out the window in hope of something more than the swinging of branches to catch her eye. Like all of the old gods, she is content to stay in Skazki. It is only the hunting creatures—the witches and demons of place—who cross between the worlds for prey.

When the Secret Ambassador arrives, she is already waiting at the door for him. "Come in," she says, grasping his hand and pulling him inside. Little bells tinkle; charms hanging over the threshold. Mokosha is dressed in flowing robes of black, decorated with fur and snakeskin. A necklace of bird skulls is wound twice around her long pale throat. Her coal-black hair is unbound and falls around her sharp face and broad shoulders. "Sit with me, Koschey," she says, offering him a chair. "Tell me of life beyond these windows."

The Secret Ambassador brushes snow off his coat and takes a seat. The room is cluttered and dark, filled with collections of twigs and stones and skulls. The fire is high and hot, sending shadows fluttering around the room. Surrounding him are smells he cannot distinguish one from another: herbs and dried flowers and female smells and moist earth and other things, things that remind him of long-ago pleasures and willing lovers whose arms have long since crumbled to dust.

"In Mir, a young man has come to the throne of Russia."

"Will he ask us to return?"

"I fear not. His father and his grandfather would not hear of it. The Church has them all in thrall, but I know a way we can insinuate ourselves without anything so obvious as an invitation to return."

Mokosha sits on a wooden stool by the fire and leans forward eagerly. Her icy gray eyes are wide. "How?"

"A marriage."

The Secret Ambassador knows that Mokosha has already guessed the rest of the plan. She tilts her head to one side, eyes narrowed. "I will not do it."

"You are the only one."

Her voice is indignant. "I am an immortal being."

"And so you will outlive him. You need only marry him, bear his children, then return to Skazki upon his death."

"Human children?" She shudders with revulsion. "No, no. You must ask somebody else."

"There is nobody else to ask."

"Take a russalka, any one of them would do."

"The russalki are all under ice until spring. He intends to marry within weeks. Besides, they are unpredictable and foolish. They will drown their own children. They will disappear on moonlit nights, and pine for the water until they go mad."

"Someone else then."

"Mokosha, the blood of men and magic barely mix. It is you alone of all of us, magical creature of fertility and birth, who would be able to bear children in Mir." He inclines his head in deference. "And it must be somebody beautiful. Somebody who we can be certain he will choose from a crowd of virgins."

Mokosha stands and paces, and the Secret Ambassador is put in mind of a caged wolf.

"I am to be paraded like a milking cow then?" she says. "Should I allow my teats to be unbound so he may inspect them more carefully?"

"I know it is so far beneath you. I know it is an insult. It could almost be a joke. But it isn't." He imbues his voice with all the gravity he can muster. "It is our hope for the future."

She turns, wrapping her arms around herself. "I am a god," she says softly. "How am I to submit to life in Mir as a woman? Women are ranked so low. Those that defy their husbands are buried alive. The ones who live are beleaguered with trivial tasks. How am I to concern myself with whether a jar and a spoon should be stored upside-down or right-side-up?"

"It is only for a brief time. And then your blood will be mixed with the blood of Russia's ruling family. As long as the blood passes along, parent to child, we have a knot which binds us to Mir, and we cannot slip away completely."

Her mouth turns down in an expression both miserable and angry. "There is nobody else?"

"Nobody, Mokosha. You know that." He pulls her to her seat, folding her hands in his. "Our world rests upon your shoulders."

"Don't. That isn't a fair thing to say."

"It is the truth."

A minute ticks past, and her breath is troubled. She sighs and shifts, then says, "How would it be done?"

The Secret Ambassador feels the wall of resistance give. Relief makes the words stumble too fast from his mouth. "A boyar family in Moscow lost their daughter last year. They are willing to have you pose as her, so long as the marriage proceeds. Neighbors and friends who knew the dead girl will be rewarded for their silence. All will enjoy new standing with the Tsar. Her name was Stasya and this will be your new name. Stasya Romanovna."

"And the children?"

"Bear as many as you can. Let your blood flow far and wide in the important families of Russia. When Ivan dies, you may return to Skazki and continue as you always have."

Mokosha, nervous energy tingling in her legs, stands again and goes to the window. Hushed snow is falling on her roof, and over all the woods and streams for miles. The land is frozen as it is every year at this time, but it always thaws. The years always swing in and out, decades always pass. Time is not a thing to be feared when one is immortal; it is the enemy only of those whose death rushes toward them with every stuttered tick. Mokosha breathes and ponders while the Secret Ambassador waits in hope.

"I see I have little choice," she says at last.

"No, Mokosha. It is still your choice."

She turns from the window. "Don't call me Mokosha," she says. "You may call me Stasya."

Mokosha, now Stasya, has changed more than her name by the time she arrives at the Kremlin to meet Ivan. Using a mixture of herbs and magic, she has dyed her hair ash-white, and has adopted the colored silk robes of a noblewoman rather than the rough natural fabrics of a pagan goddess. She wears a sarafan decorated in stars and moons, and an elaborate covering upon her head, its long veil of blue damask skimming behind her. In the Cross Chamber, Ivan's reception room up high in the Terem Palace, she queues with more than a hundred other girls.

This competition brings her so low that she feels she could scream. The idiot girls around her are full of giggles and false compliments, but Stasya refuses to talk to any of them. She is a god, for all that she pretends to be an ordinary young woman; nor is there anything ordinary about her beauty. She is otherworldly, pale and noble, with haunting eyes, but even this won't be enough to ensure Ivan selects her for his wife, because love is notoriously ill-sighted.

No, the Secret Ambassador has been very careful not to leave Ivan's choice to fate. Instead, he has cloaked Stasya—crown to toes—in magical glamour. There is no chance of the young Tsar choosing another.

Though Stasya secretly hopes he might.

The ceiling in the Cross Chamber is low, and the deeply recessed windows mean that no light illuminates the decorated corners. The arches are painted, the portals are intricately carved, the dark timber furniture merges into the shadows. Candles in the alcoves provide the flickering light, and fill the air with a warm wax smell. Here is where the bear sits, on a chest of ebony. The bear recognizes Stasya as a visitor from the land of her birth, and is excited that Ivan might choose Stasya for his bride.

Face after beautiful face passes before Ivan, who feigns boredom even though he doesn't feel it; he has the vanity of a young man. He is surrounded by boyars in their long hats and richly embroidered kaftans urging him to pick this one or that one, to heed this family or another. Ivan wants to marry the most beautiful, the most noble, the most able to bear his sons and establish his dynasty.

His hands on the edges of his carved chair, he extends his neck and shoulders forward, and the bear is put in mind of a vulture. His hooded black eyes flick left and right, scanning the face and body of a boyar's daughter, then dismissing her with a flip of his right index finger.

"Not this one," he says.

Her family gather around her as she weeps. The bear knows she is weeping with relief.

And on down the line. "Not this one." "Not that one." "Not her."

Until finally Stasya steps before Ivan. She is unsure what she should do. A number of the other girls have smiled at him, or asked after his health. She remains silent and stone-faced as she ponders on the correct way to address him.

"Your majesty," his aide says to him, "this is Stasya, daughter of Roman Yurievich Zakharin."

Stasya meets his eye. She parts her lips to greet him, then sees the sudden transformation of his expression: love and desire have seized him. "It is all my joy to meet you, Stasya Romanovna," he says.

Stasya feels something inside her shift. She is falling, she has lost control of her fate. She holds on to her breath, as though it may be the last one breathed as a free woman.

"Have you anything you would like to say to me, child?" Ivan says.

Stasya wants to shout at this boy, "I am not a child." She does not. Instead, she says, "How long do you think you will live, Ivan Vasilevich?"

Ivan blinks slowly, then a smile comes to his face. "I shall live at least another fifty years, maybe sixty."

"I have sixty years to spare you, then," she says, "if you'd care to marry me."

A murmur runs about the room, a number of the boyars are frowning their disapproval. Ivan turns to his aide and nods decisively.

"This one," he says.

On her wedding night, Stasya takes the Golden Bear into the cavernous royal bedchamber as a reminder of the world she has left behind. From among the cushions and furs of the canopied bed it gives her comfort to gaze upon the oddly decorated creature, and the bear feels the pleasure of being loved for the first time in many centuries.

The bear sits atop an ivory casket and watches as time passes, as Stasya's belly grows and expels a human child, a little girl named Anna. Of course, Stasya has borne many children before. Most of the witches and wizards of Skazki grew in her womb and came screeching from her body on windy nights. They suckled roughly at her breasts for one evening then, grown to full size, ran from her cottage into the wide dawn to make their mischief. Stasya felt nothing for any of those creatures, and expects to feel nothing for the human spawn. In fact, she expects to feel revulsion. It is only natural to fear difference in such a way.

Surrounded by silent nurses and bloodied sheets, Stasya holds the little child in her arms. It is pink and helpless, with Ivan's heavy brow and Stasya's long fingers. Stasya counts the fingers, each tiny digit as soft and light as moonbeams. She is overwhelmed by feelings of vulnerability, as though the child's helplessness is contagious. In an instant, Stasya falls in love with her daughter, and this act, this terrifying weakness, changes something in her fibers and sinews. The bear can sense it. Stasya is becoming human.

What woe, what grief and horror, when the child dies before its first birthday. And then another, Maria, only a year later. And then a third, Dmetri, dropped by a careless nurse into the river. The constant cycle of elation and grief wears Stasya like rapid water wears a stone. She becomes smaller and harder, she loses her texture.

Ivan loves Stasya dearly, and thinks more children will cure her melancholy. "We have lost three," he says, "but perhaps the next three will live long and be happy. We must try again."

So her belly swells for a fourth time, but now the boyars talk in whispers about Stasya. They suspect she is a witch.

"She poisons her children through witchcraft."

"My wife says she spoiled and tangled the wool when she came visiting."

"She has an unearthly gleam in her eye."

"The Metropolitan says she shows no interest in prayers."

"She hangs nettles in her bedchamber."

"Ravens gather at her window."

So it goes on, until opinion of her is tainted like good soup with bad meat. She confines herself for the entire pregnancy in the bedchamber. Long shadows in the dusty sunshine are all the sights to see from her bed, where she sleeps and waits and waits and sleeps.

Her sleep is often punctuated with awful dreams of dead babies: sometimes the infants are pink and slick with birth blood, but deafeningly silent; sometimes they are pale and blue and cold, dusted with the soil of the grave; sometimes it is simply a dream of a heartbeat fading to awful stillness, and she wakes with a start and pounds her own heart to make sure it still beats. The life inside her stretches and kicks blithely. There are no guarantees for this child, there is no comfort for Stasya in numerical probabilities. It may die, just like the others. She cannot endure not knowing its fate.

Although the rumors of magic endanger her, she turns to that forbidden craft in her moment of desperate uncertainty.

Stasya leaves the Kremlin as the sun rises on the melting snow. It has been a mild winter, and the markets are opening early for spring. She ignores the stares of those she passes, who are amazed to see the Tsar's pregnant wife trudging over the uneven ground in a brocade housecoat and furs, her long ash hair unbound. Down the hill and toward the river, the market becomes a melange of animal smells and noises. Peasants shudder in the cold and children curl in balls next to green fires while their mothers wash clothes on the river's edge. At the end of a long row of miserable goods proffered by miserable folk, eight miserable sheep in a pen bleat their wretchedness to the dawn cold.

"My child," she whispers, crossing her right hand over her belly, "which one of these beasts will tell me what will happen to you?"

"Are you going to buy one or not?" a grubby man in layers of brown rags asks her.

She turns to admonish him for speaking so to the Tsaritsa, then holds her tongue. A shivering child clings to his side, a girl of about eight with a thin, haunted expression. Neither this girl nor her ill-tempered father know who Stasya is. All noblewomen look the same to them: well-dressed, well-fed and warm. Other distinguishing features—eyes, lips or hair—are incidental.

"That one," she says, indicating a ram at the back of the pen. "I'll pay a good price for him." The child gasps as Stasya produces a handful of silver coins to pour into his palm.

Through the shivering dawn streets, Stasya leads the sheep back to the Terem Palace. Whispers follow her. *Why is such a noblewoman out buying a dirty sheep? Isn't that the Tsaritsa? I've heard she practices the old ways. This confirms it, for why would the Tsaritsa select her own sheep unless it is for augury? Augury with a ram's shoulder! Then she is as ungodly as rumor tells.*

Augury is a language learned in Stasya's infancy, embodied in her muscles and bones like ancient memory. She clears all the servants out of the hollow kitchen and secures the doors. It has been a long time now since she performed any magic, and many things have changed. She fears that the woman she once was—Mokosha, the goddess—is buried so deep in human suffering that she will never again be free. But the magic warms her fingers and expands up into her muscles, supple and strong as ever. She kills the ram and hacks bloody shoulders from its body, throws them on the hot coals and waits for the meat to soften and lift. Stasya's hands are covered in blood, her fine shoes are sticky with it. She crouches at the stove like a vulgar witch and pokes at the hunk of meat. It falls away, exposing the white bone. Stasya peers at the bone, looking for marks and notches. The charred meat smells bitter, mingling with the metallic stink of the blood on the floor. She focuses her eyes, hot and dry from the fire, and opens up that second sight with which she was infused in the moment she sprang from Mother Moist Earth.

On the ram's shoulder a long notch and a smaller beside it. Ivan and the child: a boy. She is not in the scene. Ivan holds something above his head—a staff? With the iron poker, she turns the other bone. Here, the next scene. The child lies upon the ground, his father crouched over him in a position of grief.

Dead, then? Killed by his own father?

"By all the stars, no!" Stasya sits on the floor and weeps helpless tears. The child inside her is already doomed. Blood seeps into her skirts, and a hesitant knock brings her back to reality. Stasya touches her belly and knows this tide of feeling has swept her away, too far. She grows more human every day, and with that, more mortal. She climbs to her feet and unbolts the heavy wooden door. Outside in the gloomy corridor, four servants wait for her.

Stasya gestures with bloody hands toward the ram's carcass.

"Use every part," she says. "The skin for a coat, the entrails for the table, the breast for soup. Stuff the kidneys, roast the ribs, boil the feet, and fry the liver with onion. Leave nothing for any to find."

One of the servants shrinks away from her. Another, her Church faith making her too bold, says, "And the shoulders, lady? Shall we stuff them with eggs?"

Stasya drills her index finger into the woman's collarbone and mutters, "You shall not tell a soul." With an icy stare that she hopes will frighten them into silence, Stasya leaves and winds up the dark, narrow stairs to wash away the blood.

The Secret Ambassador visits from time to time. Ivan is mistrustful of him, knowing by now where he is from. Although Ivan thinks the godless folk belong in godless country and not here at court, he loves his wife and knows that the Secret Ambassador cheers her bouts of melancholy. Over the years, Stasya confesses to the Secret Ambassador all her concerns. The Secret Ambassador listens, nods and hums in sympathy, but is unmoved. She must stay in Mir, she must keep bearing children.

And so she does, with a lump of lead in her heart. Stasya's fourth child, little Ivan, is doomed to be killed by his father. Her sixth child, Fedor, is half-witted. But the one between them, her only living daughter, Evdoxia, brings her great joy. She is healthy and bonny, and Stasya finds a measure of peace at last in her company. Long days are spent in the royal bedchamber, learning to read and write, singing songs, lining up the poppets as soldiers, or children or women at plow. Sometimes the four of them spill out into the palace for long hiding games, or to hear their voices echoing between the vast stone walls and up the narrow stairs. Always, always, Stasya is aware she must have more.

She miscarries and miscarries and miscarries again, and it becomes clear that these three children are the only ones left. Ivan is not concerned: he has two male heirs, even if the youngest is simple. Ivan does not listen to Stasya's warnings about little Ivan's death at his hands. He laughs and says, "What nonsense! As if I would lift my hand against my own son."

The Secret Ambassador is less confident.

"If you have seen the future, and little Ivan doesn't survive to become Tsar, then we have to rely on Fedor who is a fool and cannot govern."

"What about Evdoxia?" Stasya says. "She would be clever and fair."

"She is a girl. The Russian people aren't yet ready to see a woman rule them in her own right. No, you must have another."

Stasya is weary at the thought, too weary to pace the fifty feet of the bedchamber. She sits heavily. Her joints ache and she is troubled by constant stomach pains.

All of this from agreeing to spend sixty short years in Mir. Had she known what bearing human children would do to her, she would have refused the Secret Ambassador's request: that visit seems so long ago it may have belonged to someone else's life. "I cannot have another child. My womb won't quicken. I believe I am ill and I fear that I may die."

"You cannot die. You are a god."

"How certain of that are you?" she asks, standing and leaning against a pillar of the bed. A breeze creeps through the window, setting the tapestries dancing. "I suffer illness and pain. I grieve for all my dead babies . . ." She swallows a sob. "I am not invincible, Secret Ambassador. Another child would kill me. My husband no longer takes his pleasure with me for fear of it."

The Secret Ambassador shakes his head irritably. "Mokosha," he says, calling her by her old name, "you are formed for fertility, for childbirth, for bearing fruit endlessly. I cannot believe what I hear."

"Then believe what you see, Koschey," she snaps, turning her tired face up to him. "I have aged. I lose my beauty. Are these not signs enough that I am not now what I once was?"

The bear feels a twinge of sadness, knowing that Stasya is right. She will pass on, as every other man, woman and child.

Unmoved, however, the Secret Ambassador takes his leave. He is determined. There is one thing he knows about Mir society: if a wife won't comply, a husband may be appealed to.

Ivan is a roamer, often throwing on a workman's cloak and

disappearing into anonymous crowds away from the affairs of state. The Secret Ambassador suspects where he may find the Tsar today. A grand cathedral is being built across the square in celebration of his victory over the Tatars. Ivan is obsessed with it, and interferes with the painters and masons and architects until they despair of finishing anything unimpeded. The Secret Ambassador ducks under the low thresholds and arches, scanning the faces of the workmen who bustle in and out of shadow, in and out of hearing. Eventually, he finds Ivan standing at the bottom of a twisted staircase gazing at a half-finished fresco of saints. Around it, a byzantine floral pattern is painted on a white background. The smells of paint and earth are strong, and Ivan's cloak is musty.

"Ivan," says the Secret Ambassador.

Ivan turns. The angle of his neck has grown more pronounced with age, giving him a hunched, expectant look. "I should cut your throat for not addressing me as your Great Lord, Tsar and Grand Duke."

"I am not of your world. I am not your subject."

Ivan laughs. "My wife tells me you cannot die anyway. That you store your soul outside your body and make yourself invincible." Ivan's eyes are already returning to the fresco.

"Do you believe your wife?"

"She's probably full of lies, most women are. But I don't care what you are, for I am blessed by God and I know you cannot harm me." His voice drops to a malevolent whisper. "Those who are afraid of witches are always those who fear that God will forsake them."

The Secret Ambassador waits a few moments, then Ivan says, "What do you want?"

"I want to talk to you about Stasya."

Ivan takes his elbow in a sudden expansive mood. "Come with me. Let me show you how great God's love for me is. For all of this," he gestures around, "is my vision, and my doing."

The Secret Ambassador allows himself to be led up gloomy corridors that lead nowhere but to other corridors. The walls are close and the ceiling closer, for the Secret Ambassador is very tall. Somehow, this maze of passages divides and rejoins and sews all the towers and chambers together. The air is stale and the Secret Ambassador is put in mind of the kind of half-waking dream of enclosure that troubles him in the early mornings. Everywhere, masons and builders work in noisy groups, their tools and voices echoing, filling the chambers.

"Is it not beautiful?" Ivan says, running his fingertips over the wall as a child might.

"It is certainly very impressive."

"These corridors remind me of being born. Do you remember being born? Or are your kind hatched from opened graves?"

"I have no recollection of my birth."

"I do. A bloody affair it was, lots of yelling." Ivan stops in front of a deeply recessed window, flanked with decorated columns. A shaft of sun lights his hair, and the Secret Ambassador notices streaks of gray. "You know what I shall do the moment this cathedral is finished?"

The Secret Ambassador smiles, holding his hands apart in a puzzled gesture. "I have no idea."

"I will jab a burning poker in the eyes of the architect," Ivan says, feigning the action, "so he can never build another equal in magnificence."

The Secret Ambassador stifles a laugh, for he knows that Ivan is serious. "Your will is final. That is why I wish to speak to you."

"About Stasya?" Ivan says. "What is it?"

"You must resume your duties as a husband," the Secret Ambassador says, always mindful that Mir folk speak in coy euphemisms.

"Why? Why do you care if I stick her, or my cousin's cow?"

"She must bear more children."

Ivan shakes his head. "No, Secret Ambassador. The babies are making her sick. Another one may kill her."

"It can't. She isn't being honest with you. She was created to bear children."

"I'd believe her lies before yours." His voice dropped to a mutter, "Even if you are both sorcerers."

"She has foreseen little Ivan's death. Fedor is an imbecile. Who will rule Russia once you are gone?"

"Pah! Little Ivan is as robust as a summer pig. Her worries are only dreams fashioned from too much grieving. Even if he does die, my daughter Evdoxia may yet bear many fine children."

"Do you want all to rest on her shoulders?"

Ivan slaps the Secret Ambassador's arm with the back of his hand. "I won't listen a moment longer."

"You must listen—"

"Go! Go back to your land of violet mists. It is not your time any more. Leave us to be who we will become."

The Secret Ambassador withdraws through the maze. He has more reasons to worry than he has admitted to Ivan or Stasya. Among the boyars, at meetings and dinners and state gatherings where he insinuates himself, he hears talk of murder.

Suspicion of Stasya grows apace. Fedor's birth has thrown fuel on the flames, for who gives birth to an imbecile child but an unclean mother? The Secret Ambassador doesn't fear for Stasya: he still believes she is immortal and will withstand any poison they can give her. It is the children he fears for. Enemies at court who despise Stasya would see her children murdered. Every shred of his hopes to unite the worlds would perish with them.

The Secret Ambassador has not yet told this to Stasya. He may not fear for her life, but he fears for her heart. She is not the woman she was. She has become fettered by love and by her fear of loss. There is nothing for it, though. He must tell her. He must ensure that at least one of her children survives.

It is a warm July morning and Stasya plays with her three little ones, spread out in happy chaos across the pale hazelwood floor of the royal bedchamber. Their giggles and shouts continue as the Secret Ambassador takes their mother aside for his long explanation.

As she listens, fear runs in Stasya's veins because she knows he speaks the truth. She knows she has enemies who would see her dead, but she had never considered that they would wish her children dead too.

"What do you suggest?" she asks. Her throat is constricted and her skin tingles.

"Fedor is simple. Ivan would never let go little Ivan. But Evdoxia is healthy and may bear many children to carry on the line. We could send her away from the palace."

"Worse! Those who plot against me would perceive my reasons for the separation. They would know I suspected them. They would find her and kill her."

"We could change her name. Pretend she has perished like your other babies. The Zakharin family would take her in, just as they claimed you when you first crossed over to Mir."

Stasya gazes at her children on the other side of the room. The little girl lisps an admonition to her older brother; he has grasped one of her chubby arms too roughly. He drops her arm, laughing at her temper. Stasya shakes her head in wonder. "You cannot mean to take from me my only living daughter."

"You know she cannot stay here."

Stasya ponders this for days and weeks. All around her she sees enemies. Rumors and whispers about plots to poison her, to poison her children, her husband. She wants at least one of her babies to live, and not for the reasons the Secret Ambassador proffers. Stasya hardly cares anymore whether the schism between Skazki and Mir is irreversible. She knows now she can never go back: that she is doomed to die like a mortal woman. No, she wishes only that one of her children may live a long and happy life, bear children of her own and grow old in the company of those she loves.

So she agrees to the Secret Ambassador's plan.

There are many tears on the day the little girl is taken from her mother. Evdoxia, still too small to understand, is easily consoled when given the Golden Bear as a poppet. But as the Secret Ambassador throws on his cloak and prepares to leave with the child, Stasya closes an icy hand around his fingers.

"You see now what you have asked of me, Secret Ambassador? I have given my freedom. I have given my child. Do not presume I will also give my life to your cause."

"Why do you persist with this nonsense? You are immortal."

"I fear I am all too mortal," she replies, her hand slipping from his.

For the first time, the Secret Ambassador feels a twinge. He doesn't understand how it can be so, and yet Stasya does look frail.

He lays over her image another drawn from his memory: of a robust coal-haired goddess in snakeskin and fur, and sees that too much has changed.

"I will return," he says urgently. "Once I have the child settled with her new family, I will return for you. Tell everyone the little girl has died. It doesn't matter if they don't believe you. We can go back to Skazki. You'll be safe from their whispers and schemes."

Stasya takes a deep, shuddering breath. "Good-bye, little one," she says, touching her daughter's hair. "I will see you again soon. I presume I'm not forbidden to visit?" She raises an eyebrow at the Secret Ambassador.

"Of course you may visit. As soon as she has settled in."

Evdoxia is renamed Xenia and placed in the charge of the Zakharin family, where she becomes the intended for their son, Fedya Nikitich Romanov. When the Secret Ambassador attempts to return to the Terem Palace, however, he finds his way barred. The Tsar has forbidden him any further audience with Stasya. He is to return to his own lands and not come again.

The Secret Ambassador now fears for Stasya's life. It is within his power to remove her soul from her body and prevent her death, but he is frustrated in every attempt to see her. He hears of her death by poisoning just a few months later.

And so the Secret Ambassador learns a great lesson, but great lessons do not restore to us the ones we care about.

I expect that you wonder how long I will hold you up with stories of past times. Patience now. It all signifies. When the end comes, I want you to know enough that you may understand me. Perhaps even to forgive the things that I have done.

Let me summarize for you quickly.

The Golden Bear stayed with the Romanov family and watched as Stasya's daughter bore six children and lived to seventy-five years. One of those children, Mikhail, developed an obsessive fondness for the bear and toted it about with him everywhere, as though it whispered secrets to him that he could not live without.

After Stasya's death, Ivan became impossible: as though his wife had been a weight upon his temper. All his rages were set free, his suspicions became obsessions, and only cruel acts soothed his thundering madness. Within one generation, folk began to think fondly of Stasya and of her family. So when Ivan died, having killed one of his sons and leaving only a mindless fool behind, the boyars imagined the Romanovs as rightful heirs to the throne. Of course, the insistence of the Secret Ambassador, with his subtle magic and his wolfish eyes, played their part.

This is how Mikhail, veins replete with his grandmother's Skazki blood, became the father of a dynasty of Tsars who would rule in Mir for centuries. And thus the worlds became tied a little closer. Mir folk practiced a dual faith: praying to their God, and indulging the old ways. Was this enough for the Secret Ambassador? No, for he was stubborn and steely, and longed for life the way it had been lived before Olga. He would stop at nothing to unite Mir and Skazki, even if it meant taking on Petr the Great.

But that is a story for another time.

Ah, I have so many stories to tell. I have often wondered if my body and my mind are made of stories, that nothing about me is real: I consist only of tales told over and over until they have solidified, grown warm and started to breathe.

But, of course, stories are part of all of us, Skazki folk as well as Mir folk. Our tales are the very essence of self-knowledge; of how we remember ourselves. Rosa believes this, I am certain; she casts herself in a thousand vivid stories so that she doesn't fade to gray and slip into shadow. Shall we return, now, to her tale?

Or perhaps the tale of the man she loves? Yes, let us see how Daniel fares as he wanders among the folktales of his childhood, and sees no happy endings anywhere.

Seventeen

"At least we won't go thirsty."

Em scowled at Daniel. "Is that meant to be a joke?"

"Just trying to see the bright side."

Em scanned the area. For two and a half days they had wandered in and out of woods and fields in a vaguely northeasterly direction. Although the sky had now cleared to silver-violet, the rain had left the ground sodden. Since this morning, they had been wading ankle-deep in marshland. She was hungry and tired, and this misery was compounded by the clouds of midges and mosquitoes that hung about her, tickling her nose and stinging her cheeks and flying suicidally into her mouth whenever she attempted to speak.

Just a few days ago she had believed she might freeze to death. Now it was more certain that she would starve. Their bumbling attempts to catch a rabbit had resulted only in waking a tiny, owl-faced wood demon that chased them for two hours before giving up on them. He had probably decided they smelled too bad to eat. Their furs were moldy and rank, their bodies filmed in dried perspiration and mud.

She glanced at Daniel. More than two weeks since they had left civilization, and he'd only been able to grow a sparse beard. His cheeks and upper lip were still bare. Em found herself by turns irritated with him then overwhelmingly grateful he was here with her. At the moment she was irritated. His fear and despair had hardened into sarcastic cynicism.

"Look, mushrooms!" she said, spying a ring of mushrooms a hundred feet ahead of them.

"Or are they toadstools?" Daniel muttered.

"Let's look closer."

They approached the fairy ring and Em found herself thinking about mushrooms fried in butter, served next to fluffy scrambled eggs with crisp bacon. The mushrooms in front of her, however, were anemic white and covered in fine yellow powder.

"They look poisonous," Daniel said.

"Do you know for sure?"

"No, I'm not an expert on wild mushrooms. Looks like you got lost with the wrong guy. Lucky you—"

"Shh, Daniel. I liked your endless complaining better than this ridiculous sarcasm."

He drew down his eyebrows. "And I liked your poker face better than your bitch face."

Em turned to admonish him, but found herself giggling. "Did you just call me 'bitch face'?"

The corners of Daniel's mouth turned up and he repressed a laugh. "Yes, I did."

She snorted a laugh, which set Daniel off, bending over in belly-aching laughter. She joined him, not really enjoying the hot-faced hysteria, but unable to stop it.

When she'd calmed, Daniel was fiddling with the knot under his shirt that held the bear close to his body. "Something to eat, Em? Some moldy bread?"

"Is there much left?"

The sling fell free and Daniel withdrew the golden bear. She wore only a narrow skirt of bread now, covered in mold and spattered with mud. Slowly they had chipped away at her protective outer layer until protecting her seemed a ridiculous thing to do when they were so dizzy with hunger they could barely walk.

"We need to eat," Daniel said. He was already tearing the remaining bread from the bear and dividing it into two. Em noted he saved the smaller chunk for himself.

"No, Daniel, you're bigger than me. You should have the larger piece."

"That's very kind."

"It's just practical."

They sat down on a flat rock, munching on the lifeless bread. It tasted like the back of an old refrigerator, but Em chewed and swallowed and wondered when she might eat again. It would take weeks for them to starve, wouldn't it? By then, surely, they would have found something to eat. Perhaps they would have even found the Snow Witch, and she would have sent them home. Em sighed and pulled her feet up on the rock. She slipped off her sodden shoes and bared her toes to the weak sun. They were wrinkled and white. In all likelihood, she and Daniel would never meet the Snow Witch; they would meet their deaths first. Em didn't know what else they could do apart from moving forward, trying to catch a few hours of oblivion each night, then moving on the next day.

Daniel finished eating and started to stow the bear back under his shirt. "Why are you always so practical?" he said as he fastened the bear close to his body.

Em was confused. The question almost didn't make sense. "Because it makes life run better." A noise among the reeds caught her attention. A thud and a rustle.

Daniel's head snapped around, alert.

"Rabbit?" she whispered.

"Giant rabbit," Daniel said without a smile. "Don't want to see a rabbit that big."

The noise again, closer. Em was pulling on her shoes in an instant.

"Which way do we run?"

Daniel indicated a hundred yards ahead. "Toward those trees. Better chance of hiding."

"For him too."

"We're open targets out here. Come on."

They hit the ground and ran for the trees. Em caught a shape in the corner of her eye: hulking and black. She pushed herself forward, trying to keep up with Daniel, fighting down dizzying hunger.

In the trees they slowed, but didn't stop. Five minutes passed. Daniel grasped the trunk of a tree and paused. Em crouched next to him, catching her breath. The ground was sodden; bracken layered thick in the undergrowth. A chorus of insects buzzed and clicked around them, a perfect soundtrack to the itching physical discomfort and the ripe damp smell.

"Did we lose it?" she asked.

"I don't know if it even saw us."

"I saw it. Him. Big and black."

Daniel cocked his head, listening. "Can't hear anything." He helped Em to her feet. "You're okay?"

She nodded, swallowing a pant. "Yep. I'm good."

They turned, and in the same second a black shape stepped out from behind a tree trunk. He made a noise, like a cry of discovery. "Ah!"

Em screamed, Daniel turned to run. The black creature flung his hands out and a jet of salty, oily ink shot into their faces. Em couldn't see anything. She heard Daniel fall to the ground with a groan. She palmed her eyes, stumbled.

Then she was swept up, flung backward over the beast's shoulder. "No! Put me down!" she shouted. His arm was an iron grip around her knees. Daniel was conspicuously silent over the other shoulder as the creature began to run. Her sight resolved again, and she watched helplessly as the marshy woods disappeared behind her, upside-down.

Daniel felt himself coming up out of darkness. He tried to cling to it. The darkness, though cold and frighteningly blank, was predictable. Wherever consciousness was taking him, he was certain it was difficult and unpleasant.

My head hurts, he thought. And was surprised to hear the words out loud.

"Daniel?"

He opened his eyes. Em knelt a few feet away, stripped down to her Mir clothes. He looked at himself, and saw he was the same. His furs were gone; the pack with their moleskin was gone. With a quick feel, he discovered that the bear was still strapped against his body under his clothes.

"Where are we?" he said, sitting up uncertainly. "Is it a cave?" The air was stale and dank and . . . some other scent. Fishy. It smelled like fish.

"In a cave on the river's edge," Em said. "You must have got more of the ink in your eyes than I did. It knocked you out. I watched which way we came."

"Who brought us here?"

"I still haven't seen his face, but he's big, all dressed in black, with a bushy black beard. He took our furs to dry them, he said. The pack is somewhere back at the marsh, so thank God we moved our valuables when we did." She slapped the rock in front of her. "He put this here so we can't get out."

Daniel looked around. The ceiling of the cave was low, only three or four feet. It was dry but very cold. He heard a flapping sound, and turned to see a net full of fish dumped at an outer edge. They were still alive, choking on air.

"Fish?"

"His catch, he said." Em turned back to the mouth of the cave, where she was peering through a narrow crack. "We're part of it."

"Part of what?"

"His catch. We're to wait here and die like the fish, then he's going to eat us."

Daniel groaned. His stomach burned with fear and hunger. "How can you be so calm?"

"Because we'll take longer than fish to die. As soon as he returns, I'll offer him some gold to set us free. I wanted to wait until you were conscious, so I didn't have to carry you out like a sack of potatoes."

"Potatoes . . ." Daniel said.

"Mashed with butter and chives."

Daniel eyed the flapping net. "Deep-fried chips with battered fish."

Em sat back on her haunches, feeling in her pocket where she had stored the gold for safekeeping. "We'll be down to one piece of gold after this," she said.

"Maybe we'll find the Snow Witch soon. The fisherman might be friendly." Daniel pulled out the crumpled packet of cigarettes he had bought when they left Vologda.

"You aren't going to smoke at a time like this," Em said, irritated.

He opened the packet. Within were eight mashed cigarettes, which had been soaked then dried again. "No. But if he's what I think he is, then these might come in useful."

"Oh?"

"You didn't happen to see his feet?"

"They were bare. I only had a glimpse of them."

"I bet he has extremely long toes," Daniel said, calling up from memory Nanny Rima's stories about water spirits. "I think he's a vodyanoy. A fisherman demon. He won't just leave us here to die, Em, he'll drown us when he's ready. He has a house on the bottom of the riverbed. He'll want to take us there."

"And the cigarettes?"

"A vodyanoy is vicious and unforgiving, but he'll love tobacco." Daniel began ripping the filters off the cigarettes and casting them onto the cave floor.

Em turned back to the crack of daylight. "Ah, he's there."

Daniel crawled over to join her, peering out. Sitting among the reeds, dangling his net in the water, was the black-haired creature they had met in the woods.

"Should we call him over?" Em said.

"You do it."

Em gave him a wry smile, then turned to the opening. "Hey! Vodyanoy! Come here, I want to make a deal with you."

The creature turned. Despite his hulking figure, he had a human face smothered under his enormous black beard. He stood and approached, and Daniel could see his features were mottled with algae. The skin around his temples and jaw was dry and almost scaly. His glassy, protuberant eyes fixed on them through the gap above the boulder.

"What do you want?" he asked.

"We have gold," Em said.

"Well, give it to me."

"Not for nothing. You have to let us go and promise not to drown us."

He scowled. "Is it much gold?"

"A gold earring. Finely made and beautiful. On your ear it would gleam like the sun," Daniel offered.

The vodyanoy scratched his greasy hair. He shrugged. "I suppose it's a fair deal." He leaned forward and grunted the boulder aside, then barred the way with his hand outstretched. "The gold first."

Em dropped the earring onto his palm.

"Ah," he said, holding it up to look through it. "Very pretty." He pushed it through his earlobe and a squirt of black blood popped out. "Go on, then. Go away."

They climbed out of the cave and into the mottled sunshine on the riverbank. "Do you know where the Snow Witch lives?" Em asked, dusting herself off.

"I'm not answering any questions. Not without more gold."

"What about tobacco?" Daniel said, offering a cigarette.

The vodyanoy took the cigarette curiously, sniffed it deeply. The hairs in his nostrils twitched, and an almost-seraphic smile came to his face. He nodded. "I'm Bolotnik," he said. "Your names?"

"Em and Daniel," Daniel said, chancing a glance at the creature's toes. They were as long as his fingers. "We're from Mir. We're lost and we're looking for the Snow Witch."

Bolotnik screwed his face up. "Snow Witch . . . Snow Witch . . . - Can't say I know of her."

"Are you certain?" Em said. "East and east and north a-ways?"

"Ohhh," said the creature, nodding with dawning understanding. "Oh, the Snow Witch. Yes, yes. You're too far north now. You need to go south a-ways."

"She's south of here?"

"No, she's north of here, but you have to go south to go around the Dead Forest. Not a man or beast can survive in there. It's full of revenants. All those in the history of Mir who have died an unfortunate death gather there."

Em and Daniel exchanged glances. The Dead Forest. "That's a lot of revenants," Em said.

"I was just going to fry up some fish," Bolotnik said. He peered at Daniel hopefully. "If you've got another of those sticks of tobacco, you can join me."

Daniel's mouth grew moist. "Oh, yes," he said.

"Wait, wait," Em said. "Don't you live on the riverbed? We can't follow you down there."

"No, I'm banished from home for two days. I'm in trouble with my wife. Too much vodka with the swamp spirits." He waved a dismissive hand. "You don't want to hear of it. I'm cooking up here on the surface tonight."

"Well then," Em smiled. "We'd be delighted."

Bolotnik was ambivalent about their company. He made them sit at least six feet away from him, citing the fact that they smelled like Mir and he couldn't eat with that smell around. Em was grateful for the distance, because he glanced at her across the fire from time to time with a barely disguised expression of desire. She wasn't sure if he wanted to eat her or rape her, but Em was keen to avoid either possibility.

The fish was wonderful. She and Daniel both ate beyond politeness, leaving the vodyanoy with raised eyebrows, gathering the net with his latest catch protectively against his side.

"We need more information," Em said, licking her fingers and repressing a burp. "Would you help us?"

He shrugged. "It's not in my nature to help Mir folk, but nor is it in my nature to go back on a deal. As long as I keep the gold, as long as there's tobacco for me, I'll help."

Daniel counted out his last few cigarettes and handed them to Bolotnik, who hid a pleased smile.

"The Snow Witch," he said. "Tell us everything you know."

"She lives in the north, on the crystal lake in a grand palace." He peeled some tobacco and popped it into his mouth. "She rages all day and all night against her family, who she believes forsook her in an hour of need. She's hideous to behold. Most people have to turn away."

"How do we get there?" Em said.

"Go south, go around the Dead Forest. You'll know it when you see it. Then east until you reach the first frost plains. Somewhere around there . . . north and north . . ." He trailed off. "It's a long way."

Em's heart sank. "It is?"

"You probably won't make it."

"So, south," Em said, ignoring his last comment. "Follow the river downstream."

"Yes, on the western side, not the eastern because that's directly through the Dead Forest."

"I understand."

"You'll run into russalki. And lots of swamp spirits . . ." He snapped his fingers. "You'll be safer on the water than on the land. I can lend you a boat."

"You'd do that?"

"Let me see . . . you've already given me gold and tobacco." The vodyanoy seemed coy, glancing away bashfully. "What else could such a pretty girl give me in exchange for a boat?"

Daniel was looking at her expectantly, and Em had the distinct feeling she had missed some nuance of the conversation.

"We don't have anything else—," she began.

"I'd never tell my wife. She's already cross enough."

Daniel leaned on her, whispering in her ear, "He wants a kiss."

"A kiss?" Em said, too loudly and too aghast.

"I won't bite you if that's what you're worried about," Bolotnik protested, wiping the back of his hand over his dirty beard. "And you'll get a boat for your trouble. And a stock of fresh fish. And a magic fire that burns even when it's wet."

Em had to admit that this was a lot of assistance. "Just one kiss—," she started.

"That's all I'd ask," he said, surly again. "I have a wife, you know."

Em realized half-heartedly that it was hardly the only occasion she'd offered kisses without love. "Well, then. I suppose you should kiss me."

The vodyanoy bared his teeth in a smile, then beckoned her grandly. "Come here, then. I'm not going to come after you. I'm not desperate."

Em cleared her throat as she stood, smoothing down her clothes and tucking her hair behind her ears. She crossed the distance between them and knelt in front of him, where his face was turned up to hers in the firelight, grinning.

"Mmmm," he said, "pretty Mir girl." Then he took a deep breath and held it, and Em realized this was to cover the Mir smell he had complained of.

"Now," he said urgently, his breath stopped up in his throat. She closed her eyes and leaned in, felt the brush of scaly lips, the tentative lick of his slimy tongue. She wondered if he was tasting her and regretting the decision to let them go. Then he pushed her away and released his breath. Em climbed to her feet and returned to her place next to Daniel, while Bolotnik squeezed his hands into tight, coy fists. The inky substance he had sprayed in their eyes was leaking from his palms. Em shuddered and gave thanks it was over.

Daniel was staring at her. "What did you do to her?" he said to Bolotnik.

Em grew alarmed. "Why? What's happened?"

"It's your mouth, Em," Daniel said, leaning over and reaching a tentative thumb to her lips. He rubbed his thumb hard over her bottom lip, as a mother might rub a smudge off a grubby child.

Em pulled back, irritated. "What about my mouth?"

"Your lips are black," Bolotnik said.

"Black?"

Em wiped her mouth vigorously, but Daniel shook his head. "Still there."

"It will fade in a day or two," Bolotnik said proudly. "It's just a little of me rubbed off on you. Everyone you see will know you've been kissing me. Pretty little Mir girl."

"Your side of the bargain now," Em said, annoyed but smoothing her voice. "A boat, and some fish. And we'd like our furs back too. We'll leave this evening."

"Leave in the morning," Bolotnik said. "I'll have to fish all night." He nodded at Daniel. "You can help me while the Mir girl sleeps."

"My name's Em," she muttered.

"Go and get your furs," he said. "I hung them back a few hundred feet in the sun. They should be dry by now. Just don't let my wife see you. If you see a headless old witch with fat knees, run."

"How would she see me with no head?"

"Don't underestimate Skazki folk." He chuckled and pulled a net from under his cloak. "Come on, boy. Let's go fishing."

With the fire at his back, the wide night sky dusted starry above him and the oily dark of the river laid at his feet, Daniel felt an odd, dislocated sense of calm. He should not be calm; his whole world was in chaos. He was spending the evening in the company of a huge, hostile water demon, and tomorrow he had to set out on a river journey through treacherous lands in search of a malevolent witch whom he may never find. And yet, fishing in Skazki was like fishing in Mir. A meditative task.

"You're not catching much," Bolotnik huffed.

"I'm not very good at this."

"Never been fishing before?"

"Not with a net. Only with a rod." Usually he only caught one or two and threw them back anyway, unable to bear their pathetic flapping deaths. He didn't admit that to Bolotnik, who would have pointed out, rightly, that they had to be dead before they could be eaten.

Bolotnik cast his net again, his fingers working the long strings that dragged it through the water. Then he was still, waiting. Calmness came to the water again. The vodyanoy stretched out his legs, wriggling his long bare toes. "Tell me about Mir girls," he said, indicating the sleeping Em behind them. "Are they all as pretty as that one?"

Daniel considered his fishing companion by the firelight. "Some are. Some aren't."

"Any prettier?"

Daniel checked that Em was fast asleep. "There's one I know," he said. "More beautiful than sunrise."

"Tell me."

"Rosa," Daniel said.

"Rosa," Bolotnik repeated, turning the word over in his mouth in a way that made it sound filthy. "What does she look like?"

"She has long black hair, and blue eyes as dark as the ocean, warm arms, curves and hollows . . ." He trailed off, embarrassed.

Bolotnik was grinning at him. In the flickering light, the grin looked malevolent. Yet the conversation was as ordinary as any fishing-trip conversation. "Have you poked her, then?"

Daniel suppressed a laugh. "None of your business."

Bolotnik shrugged, returning his attention to his net. "Of course you've poked her," he muttered. "It's only me has to poke a headless sow who never stops nagging."

Daniel let the quiet resume for a while. The pile of fish beside them grew higher.

"How do we return your boat to you when we're finished with it?" Daniel asked.

"It will return itself. Just leave it in the water with the oars drawn inside." He grinned again. "Make sure it doesn't return with you in it. By then, our bargain will no longer be current, and I'll take you to my wife so she can eat you."

"You mean 'meet you'?"

"You heard me right."

Dawn glimmered in the east. "Time to load up the boat," he said to Bolotnik.

"One last warning," he said. "Beware the russalki. They haunt the river for miles. Don't let them find out your name, because they'll use it and they're irresistible. More beautiful than any Mir girl." Bolotnik indicated Em with a nod. "She'll be safe. It's young men they want."

"Okay," Daniel said, "I'll be careful."

With the daylight they loaded up the long, shallow rowboat. Bolotnik arranged a circle of flat stones carefully on the bottom of the wooden boat, and rubbed his hands over it to start a fire.

"It won't burn the wood, and it won't go out," he said. "It's the same fire I use down under the water, river-flame."

Em climbed into the boat, shrinking into her fur against the morning cold. Daniel threw in a dozen fish gathered on a hook, and Bolotnik pushed them off. Daniel picked up the oars and they began to move. The bump of oars and water echoed between the banks. Searing beams of dawn shot through the trees around the next bend, refracting purple and orange on the river.

"Thank you for your help," he called to Bolotnik.

The gruff vodyanoy was already turning away, a hairy black figure growing distant on the bank, as Em and Daniel set off downriver to the next uncertain bend of their journey.

Eighteen

The little boat was cramped and uncomfortable, but they were sun-warm and well fed as they passed their first morning on the river. By the afternoon, though, a new discomfort had settled in for Em. She held off saying anything as long as she could, but finally told her traveling companion.

"Daniel," she said, "I need to pee."

Daniel pulled the oars in and they clattered against the wood panels of the boat, splashing Em's ankles. "Go over the side. I can look the other way."

"No. We'll have to pull into the bank."

"But—"

"I'm not worried about appearing inelegant, Daniel. I can't stand up and aim like you. I'm worried about falling in, or capsizing the boat."

Daniel turned to look over his shoulder in the direction they were traveling. "I can see a shallow incline a couple of hundred feet ahead. Can you hold on?"

"Yes. I'm not six."

Daniel dipped the oars again and rowed vigorously. Em stretched her legs out on either side of the stockpile of fish that lay beside the magic fire. A low yellow flame licked over the stones, never quite high enough to warm the chill from her bones. The boat itself was moldy and narrow, and she was having trouble getting comfortable among the hard surfaces and confined spaces. Daniel, with his long legs, was probably finding it infinitely worse. They cruised with the current over dark silvery water, accompanied by dank smells and fish smells, and the odd sharp smell of smoke from the magic fire: a cross between peat and sulfur. The banks of the river rose high and fell low, fir and larch grew densely, the occasional stand of willows dragging their long, sad arms into the water. Hordes of mosquitoes clouded around them, landing black and stinging on her wrists and knuckles.

Daniel lifted one oar and maneuvered the boat to shore. It

thumped softly against the bank, and Daniel hooked his arm around an overhanging branch to pull it in tight.

"Can you get out here?" he asked.

"Should be fine." She stood, felt the boat tilt, steadied herself, then pulled herself out using the branch. Her feet landed safely on the ground.

"I won't be long," she said.

Daniel was tying a rope to the branch. "Take your time."

Em picked her way across marshy ground, trampling tiny colored flowers on weedy stems and flicking bugs off her neck. The trees ahead looked to provide some privacy, and she chose a suitable one to relieve herself behind. She glanced about as she did, and caught sight of an old fishing net caught over a low branch about twenty feet away. She re-dressed and moved toward it. One thing Bolotnik hadn't given them was a means of catching their own fish. This one looked half-rotted and tangled, but it might come in handy. As she approached, she noticed that an old wooden bucket was turned up on the ground next to it. It was broken, moldy and had no handle, but would make a fantastic on-board toilet so they didn't have to keep getting in and out of the boat. She had already reached for it before her brain engaged and it occurred to her that it was highly suspicious that these objects were here. The thought was too late. The fine thread attached to the base of the bucket glinted; the net descended and thumped down onto her body.

"Damn," she muttered, angry at herself, trying to shrug the net off. She was tangled in it somehow. There was no way of knowing if the trap had been laid years in the past or just that morning. "Daniel," she called out, "I need you."

"I'm coming," he replied, and she heard footsteps but couldn't be sure they were his. She pulled the net off one arm, found it snarled over her shoulder, and tried again. As she touched it, she felt a slither of movement between her fingers. This was no ordinary net. What she had mistaken for an old, moldy, impossibly tangled fishing net now proved itself to be a sophisticated trap. Knots touched other knots and formed new junctions with a sticky sucking noise. The harder she tried to loosen herself, the tighter she became ensnared. The warmth of her skin made the rope liquefy and re- solve, her struggles made it slither and twist.

"Daniel, quick!" she called, hoping that imbuing her voice with an edge of panic would make him come faster.

He appeared around the trunk of a fir tree. His face grew alarmed as he saw her struggling with the trap, and his alarm fright- ened her. He raced toward her, reaching out his fingers.

"No, don't touch it," she said forcefully. "You'd just get caught in it too. It seems to like the warmth of human skin. Find a stick, see if you can lift it off with that. Preferably before whoever made it comes back for it."

Daniel searched on the ground and seized on a thick stick, which he poked toward the net. "This is very old," he said, relaxing a little. "The bucket too. It's probably been here for years."

"Do you think so?"

"Yes, certainly. The bucket probably once held fish. I remember making a trap like this for a bird when I was fifteen." He gently poked the stick under the net over her shoulders and lifted. "Raise your arms," he said. "We'll have to try to get it off carefully."

She raised her arms slowly, as Daniel inched the net up higher and higher. He released her left arm, then her right. The net now hung over her head and face.

"It's tangled in my hair," she said.

"We'll get it off your face first," he replied, the stick coming dan- gerously close to poking her eyes out. "Can you close your eyes?"

She did as he asked, not quite trusting him with the stick. A bird cried out an alarm deep in the forest and Em felt keenly that they should be moving away from here. The net began to peel off her face, the stick grazed her brow.

"Sorry," Daniel said.

"It's okay. I think we should hurry."

"Lean over."

She leaned to the side, opening her eyes. The net hung heavy in her hair, and Daniel pushed it off. It landed with a soft whump in the undergrowth. A puff of decayed leaf matter rose. Em crouched to take the bucket, breaking the thread that attached it to the net. "Nice work, Daniel," she said. "I thought I might be wearing that all the way home."

"It would have matched the black lipstick nicely," he said.

Em wiped the back of her hand against her mouth. She had forgotten the stain Bolotnik's lips had left on hers. "Is it fading?" she asked.

Daniel peered closer. "Doesn't seem to be. Maybe a little."

She held the bucket up, triumphant. "Toilet," she said. "An unpleasant, moldy, fish-scented one."

"I've used worse in London."

Em relished the relative safety of the boat as they headed back toward the riverbank. At least out on the river they could see where they were going and what was coming for them. She was brushing a mosquito from her neck when Daniel seized her upper arm and pulled her behind a tree.

"What?"

"Shh," he said sharply, indicating with a nod toward their boat.

About two feet in front of it was a strange crouching figure. It took Em a few moments to make sense of it. Thickset, large-bosomed, fat doughy arms, no head. She moved closer to the boat, crouching lower.

"It's Bolotnik's wife," she said. "It has to be."

"What's she doing?"

"If I didn't know better I'd say she's sniffing the boat."

"Without a nose?"

Em tried to get a better view of her. Where her head should have been, the neck was grown over with the same doughy pale skin. A few straggling hairs grew there, around a saggy flap of skin that may have masked an opening. "What are we going to do?"

"Wait and see. She might leave it and wander off."

"She must know it's her husband's boat. What if she takes it with her?"

Bolotnik's wife turned sharply then, as though she'd heard them.

"Okay, if she can hear and smell, she can also see," Em whispered, pressing her mouth close to Daniel's ear. "We can't let her find us, especially as she'll be able to tell with one look at me that I've been kissing her husband."

Daniel exhaled softly, knocking his head gently on the trunk. "I am so sick of this," he said. "I feel I'm going to lose my mind if I have to keep living with this fear."

She touched his wrist. "We've survived this far," she said, trying to sound reassuring.

"Through luck and gold. Both will run out eventually."

Em inclined her head in the direction of the river. "What's she doing?"

Daniel carefully bent around the tree. An instant later he was on his feet, pulling Em up too. "She saw me, she's coming," he said and started to run.

Em took to her heels after Daniel, then caught up to him and pulled him behind a tree.

"Stop!" she hissed.

"What?"

Em dropped her voice as low as she could. "We can't keep running. We need the boat."

Daniel shook his head, his shoulders lifting: *what can we do?*

"The net."

Daniel turned his face to her and nodded. Up this close, Em could see he was pale and shaking. Would he never grow used to the constant cycle of panic and action? A hundred years ago, men his age were dodging bullets on battlefields. Had they been unable to manage their fear too? Was Daniel's generation too softened by progress for reckless heroics?

"It's okay," she whispered. With a gentle incline of her head, she signaled that they should inch their way back to the glade where they had left the net.

Quietly, miming instructions to the other, Em and Daniel each found a sturdy stick to pick up the net. Em's was a young branch, broken by the wind perhaps, about three feet long and three inches across. Daniel's was slightly larger. They each caught an end of the net and held it up, walking apart to spread it wide. Then, with a nod from Daniel to tell her he was ready, Em called out, "We're over here!"

Footsteps thundered toward them. Em peered out from behind a tree. The headless woman uttered a bellow, which sent the flap on her headless neck fluttering open so the sound could spit through the blowhole. "Mir woman," she said. "I've smelled you and heard you, and now I see you!"

"Come and get me then," Em called.

"Have you been kissing my husband?"

"Yes." Em braced herself as the distance between them closed. She could see fine yellow spines lining the woman's arms, like the needles on a poisonous fish. Her body was large and powerfully built, and her lack of a head was very little handicap. "Yes, I kissed him, and I'd do it again."

Bolotnik's wife doubled her speed, leaking enraged gasps. Daniel, standing parallel to Em, was poised to move on her signal. The woman drew closer, Em took a deep breath, signaled to Daniel he should move.

He stepped out, stretching the net across the woman's path. She skidded, but the muddy ground prevented her from slowing in time. She landed with a whump in the net, cursing and gasping.

Daniel and Em leapt out, wrapping the net tightly around her.

"Let me go, foul Mir folk! I'll kill you, my husband will eat you."

"Quick, Em, let's get out of here."

Taking a deep breath, Bolotnik's wife puffed up, and the yellow spines on her arms became erect and sharp. One sliced through Em's sleeve and into her wrist, leaving a hot trail of pain. They also sliced at the net, sawing into the rope. She relaxed and breathed in again, puffing up and cutting at the net.

"She's going to get free!" Em called.

"We should run."

"She's quick, she'll follow us." Em had already loosened her stick from the net, and took a swing at Bolotnik's wife. Without a head to aim for, her blow landed in the woman's back. She gasped, fell to her knees, her cutting spines withdrawing.

"Em, we should run."

"She'll just follow us," Em said. "I'm sick of running away." Another blow. The enraged woman was taking another breath to puff out her spines, but Em knocked the wind out of her. A groan came out of the blowhole, followed by a seeping yellow substance. Em's stick splintered in half and she tossed it into the undergrowth. She reached for a large rock to wield instead.

Daniel hefted his stick and took aim as well. Em had the white-hot sensation that matters had swung entirely out of control, as they hammered the woman's body but she refused to fall, refused to stop puffing her spines. The net was shredding apart, as Em and Daniel rained blow after sickening blow on Bolotnik's wife, and blood and yellow discharge stained the ropes and the ground beneath them. An oily, fishy smell pervaded the air.

Finally, finally, the headless body slipped to the ground. Em thumped her again and again, until Daniel caught her wrist in his hand and shouted, "Em, stop!"

Em looked up at him, dazed. "Why are you shouting at me?"

"I said it four times, you didn't hear me. She's dead."

"Dead?" Em stared at the crumpled, beaten body, genuinely surprised. She tried to catch her breath. "Dead?"

"What did you think would happen?" he said, throwing his stick away in disgust.

Em leaned against a tree trunk, dropping her rock. "Oh."

"Back to the boat," he said. "Before Bolotnik comes and finds us."

They left the ruined body of Bolotnik's wife and the shreds of the sticky net in the stinking undergrowth and ran back down to the boat. Em seized her bucket, the consolation prize in this horrific adventure, and threw it into the boat ahead of her. Daniel untied the rope and pushed off with the oars. They were still catching their breath five minutes later, still unable to speak.

Finally, Daniel said, "I feel sick."

Em closed her eyes tight then opened them again. "I can still smell that oily yellow goo. Was that her blood?"

"She had blood too. It was something else. It was—oh God, Em. Look at your arm."

Em looked down. Her wrist, where the spine had cut into her, was oozing the same yellowish fluid. She leaned over the side of the boat and let it drag through the water. "She got me," she said.

"What if it's poison?"

Em pulled her arm out of the water and pushed her sleeve up to examine the wound more closely. The cut was shallow, but wide, and the yellow substance was mingled with her own blood in the wound. She tore a strip off the bottom of her pants and dabbed at it gingerly. The yellow seeped onto the cloth. She squeezed the wound gently, wincing from the pain. Squiggles of yellow fled from her touch, sinking into her blood until they became invisible. "There's not much," she said. "I don't feel ill. It's probably not poison." She glanced up and saw very clearly on Daniel's face how much he would hate to lose her now. Not because of any special fondness, simply for fear of being alone.

Daniel pulled the oars in and leaned forward on his knees, his hands over his face. Em tried to ignore this display of emotion, dabbing at the wound and examining how her body felt. Was that strange sick feeling a result of poison in a wound? Or was it a result of having beaten a woman to death? Daniel breathed in his sobs, and eventually raised his head, looking off into the middle distance as though distracted. This attempt to appear as though he hadn't been crying touched her far more than his tears, and she said, "Daniel, please take some small comfort. We are still alive. We still have the bear. This may yet work out."

"Em, I don't think it will. I think we're probably going to die."

She watched him, wordlessly.

"Em? Did you hear what I said?"

"I've known that since we arrived," she said.

He shook his head, that now-familiar expression of puzzlement on his face. "But you said—"

"I said all kinds of things, Daniel, because your fear was a liability. It still is. But you're right. We're probably going to die."

"How can you stand it?" he said, his voice constricted with swallowed hysteria. "How can you be calm and keep going? Are you even human?"

Em recoiled from his accusatory question, anger flaring inside her. She had been asked that before—by her ex-husband, countless co-workers, her own mother—and had always hated it. "I am what I am," she said forcefully. "You know nothing about me."

Daniel clapped his mouth shut, chastened. "I'm sorry."

"Just keep rowing."

He picked up the oars and did as she said.

"I don't want to die any more than you do, Daniel," she continued. "I'm particularly unnerved by the possibility that my death may be extremely unpleasant. It's not my way to dwell on these things. Fear and love, sadness, joy . . . I do have feelings, but they are transient and don't take root. I've always been this way."

Daniel frowned. "I don't understand."

"You wouldn't. I've never met anybody else who can, because I've never met anybody else like me."

He watched her, and she watched him. The boat slid through the water and the sun moved behind clouds. The oars beat and pulled at the water, clunking softly.

"Well, then," he said at last, in a quiet, resigned tone, "explain it to me."

"It's not that easy." Em tucked her hair behind her ears, searching for the right words. "It's like explaining color to a blind man."

"Try."

She thought about it a few moments, then ventured forth. "Do you know what permafrost is?" she asked.

"I think so," he replied, obviously perplexed. "The layer of frozen soil in cold places. Like Russia."

"Yes. It thaws very infrequently, very briefly. Nothing much grows in it. A few hardy shrubs, lots of surface vegetation like lichen and so on."

"Why are we talking about permafrost?"

"Because that's what I'm like."

"You're frozen?"

"You must admit, you find me cold," she laughed, "but it's far more complex than that."

His eyes were puzzled, but his expression was determined. "Go on. Explain it."

"Daniel, I don't *feel* things the way other people do. At least I'm fairly sure I don't, because you all sound like you're talking in another language when you speak of love, or passion, or . . . anything." She glanced away, watching the ripples that arrowed out behind the oars. "I've never felt fear as anything beyond a moderately sophisticated survival instinct. I've never felt anything catastrophic enough to call love, not even for my own child. My relationships with others have been shrubs and moss, never monstrous fruit-bearing trees." She pulled her knees up to her chest, certain she hadn't made herself understood. "My heart is like permafrost," she said. "Cold and barren, not the rich black soil of the south."

Daniel fell silent for a long time, and she glanced up to see if he was staring at her with the same disgust and fear that others had displayed. He wasn't. He was looking at her, and he said, "That's very sad."

She held up a hand to stop his pity. "Spare me."

"It explains a lot about you. How you are with people, that odd detachment." He smiled apologetically. "I don't mean to be rude."

"You're not. You're just telling it as you see it."

"How come you've never mentioned it before?"

Em sighed. "It's not that it's a secret," she said, "but it's not an ideal conversation opener either, and I don't really get close enough to people to feel I should reveal so much of myself."

A rush of summer air hissed over the treetops, dimpling the water and bringing her skin out in gooseflesh. Her arm ached and she was sorry she'd told Daniel. They needed to rely on each other, and if he was suspicious of her now . . .

"But you married," he said, as though the thought had popped hot and urgent into his head. "You had a child."

"It was an experiment. A disastrous one. I'd heard so many women talk in rapturous tones about children, I thought that if anything could awaken feeling in me, that would be it. I chose a suitable husband, I bore his child. I still felt . . . not nothing. I just felt very little."

"Have you spoken to a doctor? A psychiatrist?"

Em bristled. "No. I'm not dangerous or murderous or psychotic. I know right from wrong. I feel pity quite strongly, especially for those who suffer from emotional trauma." *Slaves to feeling, like you*, she wanted to say but didn't. "I'm certainly sickened by what we did this morning . . ." She trailed off. "It was the only practical thing to do."

Daniel kept drawing on the oars. They made a rhythmic thump and swish, and Em felt strangely light. "Do you hate me now, Daniel?" she asked.

"No," he said.

She noticed the corners of his mouth twitching upward. "What is it?" she said.

He chuckled. "I shouldn't laugh. I don't mean to be—"

"What?" She smiled tentatively. Nobody had ever found her situation funny before.

"We're like two rejects from Oz, Em. You don't have a heart, and I have no courage."

She allowed herself a stifled laugh. "I'm glad you're not afraid of me," she said.

He shrugged. "No matter what you are," he replied, "I'm glad we're in this together."

Em leaned her chin on her knees, relieved. "So am I."

The river was wide and gleamed like a dark mirror. Daniel couldn't grow used to life on the boat. He couldn't get comfortable, he was sick of the taste of fish, he hated going to the toilet in a bucket, and the wind sheering over the water negated the warmth of the ring of magic fire between him and Em. But at least they were moving; hopefully closer to the Snow Witch and home.

Late on the second afternoon they glimpsed the hem of the Dead Forest. Bolotnik had been right: they could recognize it on sight. The tall trees were crowded on top of each other, and sinuous shadows slid in and out of the narrow spaces, winding around the tree trunks. Their whispers layered and layered, so that the further along the river Daniel and Em traveled, the more the forest moaned in one mournful voice.

"I don't understand," Em said to Daniel, instinctively dropping her voice to a whisper. "I thought these dead people . . . what did you call them?"

"Revenants."

"I thought revenants haunted the places where they died."

"They do. And they're here as well. Nanny Rima always told me that the dead travel in a blink."

"We should be quiet," Em said. "We don't want to attract attention."

Daniel agreed and fell silent, and the shadows grew long and night came, morning followed, and so on as he and Em silently glided past the lightless forest.

Another two days passed, and the silence of the river seeped into his blood and organs and calmed him. He rowed, feeling the rhythm sink into his muscles. Sometimes he quietly passed the oars to Em for an hour or two and lay back in the boat to watch the clouded sky move above him, as it had moved above the gaze of every traveler before him. The days grew rhythmic too, the clunk and pull of the oars in the morning, the drifting stillness in the afternoon when they both rested their tired bodies. Often, he gazed at the dark forest and thought about death, and began to accept it. Sometimes it felt like he and Em would be caught on the river forever, never seeing the end of the Dead Forest. They ran out of food again, but didn't speak of it.

Finally the trees thinned, the shadows grew paler and the whispers grew softer. The east bank was giving way to flat fields dotted with stands of larch leading their eyes to a distant haze of hills, and Em and Daniel began to speak again.

"We'll have to travel a little further on land into the east," Em said, "past the southern front of the Dead Forest."

"Bolotnik spoke of frost plains."

"We'll know when we get there." Em tugged her sleeve down over her left wrist, where Bolotnik's wife had scratched her. She hadn't complained of it, so Daniel assumed it was healing normally. Thank God. He didn't want to contemplate continuing this journey alone. "When do you want to pull the boat in?"

"Let's finish the day on the river, make sure we're entirely clear of the forest," Daniel said, stretching his arms above his head. He felt a series of pops up his spine as his muscles decompressed. "Though I'm sick of rowing."

"You'll be sick of walking again before long," Em said.

The boat continued downstream, and the river narrowed and the banks grew steep. Em talked about going back to the flat lands, but Daniel didn't want to take any chances. "Perhaps one more night on the boat?" he said.

"I suppose I can survive. I'm hungry though."

"Me too." On cue, his stomach growled.

"Perhaps we can—" Em stopped suddenly, her body erect. "Listen," she said.

Daniel stilled himself and listened. Voices.

"More revenants?" Em asked.

"It's coming from the west bank," said Daniel. "Not the forest."

"What are they saying?"

Female voices calling out, a word here, a word there. Then, a high girlish giggle: Daniel gasped involuntarily. A sensation as warm and sweet and clinging as honey surged in his blood. Inexpressible promises lurked in that laughter.

"Russalki," he breathed. "Oh, Em, we're in trouble. Whatever you do, don't say my name."

Em nodded, serious. "Right, so we're safe as long as I don't say your name?"

"I hope so. Can you hear what they're saying?"

Em shook her head. The boat slid forward, and the voices became more distinct.

Boris!

Vladimir!

Zoryn! Oh, Zoryn! Laughter, like shallow water over gleaming stones.

Eduard! Anastas! Evgeny!

"Names?" said Em. "Are they calling out names?"

"Men's names," Daniel added, "in hope that a man of that name will pass and become ensnared. Once they have your name, they're irresistible."

Igor! Demyan!

The voices promised . . . something he had wanted all his life, some unutterable magic thing that his skin dreamed of, some flowering painful heat that had always resided inside him but had never yet been brought to consciousness.

"You're okay now, right?" Em said, leaning forward with an expression of concern. "You look—"

Daniel shook off the distraction. "I should be fine. We'll just keep rowing, get away from this bend in the river. They haunt small sections, form communities. An hour or so downstream, we'll be safe. *I'll* be safe."

Florenti! Oh, Florenti, do *come to me!*

Kiryl! Oleg!

The soft voices continued, caught on a breeze and amplified between the high riverbanks. Daniel bit his lip hard. He tasted blood.

"Let's keep your mind occupied," Em said. "Tell me everything you can about russalki."

The way ahead grew narrower, vines and overhanging branches crowding onto the water. Daniel cast his mind back to Nanny Rima's stories.

"They're young, beautiful women. Usually suicides or murder victims. Behind the laughter lies a great sadness . . . a great *angry* sadness which is dangerous. They want to be loved, but they're unpredictable. Some of the tales tell of russalki who marry men and live half the year on the land. Then they pine for the water and begin to resent their lovers and their children and drown them for spite."

The voices were fading behind them now, the river widening. Daniel filled his lungs with a deep, shaking breath, calm slowly restoring itself to his body. "Sounds like we're past the worst of it."

Em nodded, hunching forward to warm her hands on the low fire. She looked small and pale, and Daniel thought about what she had told him, before the long silence. That she had never felt love. He had spent a long time feeling intimidated by her, but now he just felt sorry for her. For himself, too, because no matter how fond of her he grew, they had already become as close as they were ever going to be.

"Fish," she said softly.

"What?"

She sat upright, hands on the edge of the boat, peering over. "Fish. There."

Daniel looked where she was pointing. A school of fat silver fish were keeping pace with the boat, close to the surface.

"Get the bucket," Em said.

"The toilet bucket?"

"They're close enough to catch. We can cook the germs off." Em leaned forward and grabbed the oars. "Quick, they're splitting off in the other direction."

Daniel seized the bucket and stood unsteadily, leaning his spare hand on the edge of the boat. "Steer me a little closer, Em."

Em did as he asked and he leaned out, casting the bucket into the water. The fish wisely swished away from him. He was put in mind of one of those arcade machines, where grasping the prize with the mechanical claw seemed so easy until actually put to the test. He pulled the bucket in, thought about giving up. Hunger nibbled his stomach and a second later he was trying again, leaning out as far as he safely could—

Sylvestr!

The clear piercing voice broke the air. A shock of surprise and desire jolted Daniel, who began to pitch over.

"Daniel!" Em called, lurching forward to grab his leg. The boat dipped dangerously close to the water.

Daniel!

Daniel!

Daniel! Daniel! Daniel!

In a moment, the woods along the bank were ringing with a dozen voices, all calling his name.

Daniel landed with a thump back in the boat, which righted immediately. His skin prickled with fear and desire.

"I'm sorry! God! What have I done?" cried Em as the voices rang across the water.

Daniel, come to me!

Daniel? Tinkling laughter, the most desirable thing he'd ever heard. Searing desire bloomed again, more intense this time. His body was a slave to it; his skin prickled from his scalp to his toes, heat rushed to his groin, making his balls ache and his cock grow hard.

"Em . . . ," he started, fear chasing the desire.

"Don't listen to them," she said. "Put your fingers in your ears."

Em's voice was growing indistinct. A sharp hot nausea overwhelmed him, dragging at his stomach, plucking his skin. The only thing he could think of that would relieve the discomfort was to plunge into the water. He imagined that the moment his body hit the water, he would experience an instant orgasm, more powerful than an Atlantic current.

"Sit down!" Em ordered, pushing his shoulders. He hadn't even realized he was standing. She forced him onto the floor of the boat, tearing off her fur cloak and wrapping it around his head. "Don't listen to them, listen to silence."

The russalki voices were muted now. She had wrapped his ears in fur, was pulling his cloak off him to make a second layer, which she draped over his head. Darkness and muffled quiet descended. He breathed, screwing his nose at the rank smell of the fur. Far off, far off . . .

Daniel!

Dozens of them, quiet as butterfly wings on a still day, but there all the same. He pulled his hands up against his face, bit into his palms. The boat was moving swiftly. Em was rowing hard. He stayed under the dark quiet and tried to focus on other sounds. His own breathing, his rapid heart. All over his body, the waves of hot and cold ran. Whenever that faint whisper of his name hushed past his ears, a longing more inexorable than death pulled at him, chilling his skin, filling his mind with visions of lips and breasts and warm wet places to plunge into.

Em kicked him, said something he couldn't quite hear. She thrust his hands over his ears, and all he heard was ringing silence.

She kicked him again a few moments later. Then she was pulling the furs off him.

"They've stopped," she said.

Daniel took a gulp of fresh air. All he could hear now in the woods were distant birds. Relief spread through him.

"Are you okay?" she asked.

"I think so. A bit shook up."

"I'm sorry." She indicated the water. "We lost our toilet."

The mundanity of her complaint cut through his befuddled state. "Do you need it right now?"

Em shook her head. "I can last. I think we should stay aboard for another day at least, make sure we're well and truly out of russalki territory."

Daniel took the oars. "Let's move fast. The more distance I put between them and me, the better." The boat slid quickly through the water, and Daniel felt a sense of loss that grew sadder with each oar stroke. He pulled further and further away from unutterable pleasures, beyond the dreams of any man, and never to be offered again.

Three hours past the russalki, Em knew it was her turn to row. How, then, was she to tell Daniel she couldn't? That the wound inflicted by Bolotnik's wife was agonizingly hot and, she was fairly certain, festering with slow-moving poison? Escaping the cries of the russalki had hurt her, pulled the wound open afresh as she'd rowed as hard as she could. She had to rest it.

"Can we drift for a while?" she said to him. "I'm tired."

"I'll keep rowing then."

"No, take a break. We haven't heard any voices for hours. I'm sure we're in safe waters again."

Daniel dropped the oars and they drifted slowly. Em pressed her palm discreetly over the wound; the pressure relieved some of the boiling ache. Half an hour passed, and Daniel was about to pick up the oars again when the boat became suddenly still.

Em sat up and peered into the water. "That's odd. The current is still moving."

Daniel lifted the oars and pulled hard. They barely moved a foot.

"What's happening?" Em said.

An eerie rhythm echoed between the banks, wood knocking on water, water sucking against the current. In front of her, their magic ring of fire flickered and went out. Then the boat began moving upstream, back the way they came.

"Bolotnik," said Daniel. "He's found out what we did to his wife."

"Holy shit!" Em cried as the boat began speeding upstream. "He's recalled the boat. What do we do?"

"Jump. Before we're back among the russalki." He was already climbing to his feet. The boat was skimming fast now, almost without touching the water.

Em climbed to her feet and dived in a second behind Daniel. The water was cold and sour, and her furs dragged her down. She swam behind Daniel to the bank, where they climbed up a rocky outcrop and onto dry land. While Daniel lay panting, she watched the boat disappear around the bend.

"He's days away," Daniel was saying. "I don't think he can catch us now."

Em wrapped her arms around her knees and shivered. "At least we've had a wash."

"Our clothes too."

"We have to get out of them. We have to start a roaring fire and dry off properly."

Hunger and desperation made them casual, and they risked collecting wild mushrooms to cook as the light bled from the sky. Em had stripped down to her blouse and pants, Daniel to boxers and a T-shirt. The bear made an odd lumpy bulge under his shirt. Their fire, built with an abundance of enthusiasm, was nearly four feet high. Em sat as close to it as she could. The rest of their clothes hung behind her on a branch. The sky was clear, which meant moonlight and cold breezes.

"Well, we're not dead," Daniel said, licking mushroom juice from his fingers.

"Not yet, anyway," she replied, touching her wrist. "Would the food have tasted foul if it was poisonous?"

"I don't know," he shrugged, "but at least we won't die of hunger."

"Daniel, would you mind if I took the first sleep tonight?" Em said. "I'm tired and headachy and feeling unwell."

He looked at her sharply. "Not from the mushrooms?"

"No, I've been like it all day."

"How is that wound?"

"Oh, healing up okay. Don't worry."

Daniel frowned, then nodded slowly. "Of course, have a good sleep. You'll feel better."

"Wake me, won't you?" she said. "After six hours, just like usual?"

"Just get some rest. We're warm and we've eaten and I'm feeling calm."

Em settled on the soft grass, nursing her sore wrist in front of her. She closed her eyes and told sleep to come. The pain wanted to keep it at bay, but Em could always close down those signals to the brain which kept it alert. She just had to let her body take the sleep it needed. One breath, two breaths . . . *quiet and still.* Slowly, she fell asleep.

When she woke, though, it was in a rush.

Daniel wasn't there. She sat up. Some noise had woken her, but what? She peered off into the dark and saw Daniel about two hundred feet away. Perhaps he was taking a late-night pee.

Then she heard it. A woman's laugh, high and girlish.

"Wait!" she called after him, scrambling to her feet.

Daniel! Daniel!

"No, don't follow her!"

Daniel stopped, turned, his face in shadow. Em dashed toward him.

Before she could reach him, a sinuous figure with long pale hair had seized him, and dived into the water.

Nineteen

Rosa, no longer able to rely on herself to wake, now relied on the sun. Each night she left her curtain parted so the warm shaft of six o'clock light would traverse her pillow and tickle her eyes open. Since the morning tiredness had become relentless, she had slept through the start of Makhar's lessons too many times. She determined to fight it, though, and was this morning already dressed and furnished with a cup of coffee. Her mother's notebooks spread out before her, Rosa lay on her bed to spend some time with the books before work.

It was simple. If she had no magic, then she had to rely on her brains. These notebooks contained magical secrets: why write them in code otherwise? If Rosa could crack the code, she would have something to use to improve her situation. If she could find her mother's charm bracelet, even better.

The letters swam in front of her, their meaning impenetrable. She had a sheet of paper next to her where she scribbled her notes. She tried rearranging letters, tried a numerical sequence, looked for regular clusters of letters that might signify names or other important words.

Got nowhere.

One thing she kept coming back to, though, was the final page of the first notebook. On it, her mother had written two paragraphs with a space between them. Four lines in each, punctuated at the end like poetry. Rosa was certain that this was a poem, and that if she could just figure out which one, she could crack the code. But which poem? Her mother was very fond of poetry, and had named a number of favorites over the years: Mayakovski, Lermontov, Akhmatova. There was nothing to say, either, that this wasn't a poem of her own composition, written in code out of artistic timidity.

Rosa heard a bang, a thud and a yelp outside. Her window was ajar to release the morning bee invasion. She stood and looked out. Over at the hive, Ilya hopped about, rubbing his foot, panicky bees swarming around him. A frame lay cracked on the grass.

She climbed down off the bed and left the guesthouse, crossing the dewy lawn in bare feet and with the sun in her hair. Ilya looked up, and made a gesture that she should stay away.

"Bees are in a bad mood," he called.

"Come here, then. Let me look at your foot."

Ilya approached, peeling off his veil and gloves. He limped slightly, but Rosa didn't care about his foot particularly. It was the rest of his body she found intriguing.

"Here," she said, crouching in front of him. "Let me see." She had her hand around his ankle and was already loosening his shoelace.

He winced. "I dropped the corner on my toe."

"I hope it's not broken," Rosa said, removing his shoe and peeling off his sock. She pushed the leg of his jeans up over his calf, letting the fingers of her right hand close firmly around the hard muscle. "Does this hurt?" she said, manipulating his toes.

"A little."

"I don't think anything's broken. Just bruised." She gazed up at him under her lashes. Her face was level with his crotch and this made him blush. "You should get some ice on it. To stop the swelling."

"Rosa? Ilya?"

Rosa looked over her shoulder. Anatoly stood near the garden, watching them. Rosa felt her body tense and grow warm.

Ilya pulled away, and she got to her feet. "Come on, Ilya," she said. "I'll help you back to the house."

"I can walk."

"No, just lean on me," she said, slipping her arm firmly around his waist. She felt his muscles tighten, then relax as he leaned into her. He was very warm and very hard and all her senses flared with electricity. Her fingers pressed into his ribs. "Hold me very tightly," she said, dropping her voice to a whisper.

Ilya said nothing, but Anatoly was with them in an instant, leading Ilya off and clucking about Rosa not being strong enough to help him. She laughed and let Ilya go, turned her eyes to the kitchen window where Ludmilla was staring at her icily.

Makhar came banging out of the house, shouting with excitement about Ilya's injury. He turned to Rosa and called, "Where are your shoes, Roshka?"

Rosa looked down. Her feet were damp and cold with dew. The linked pattern of decorative cuts now stretched halfway around her ankle. The early ones had faded to pink, the more recent were crimson. She counted them with her eyes. Eighteen. Time was crushing her.

"Roshka?" said Makhar, who had come to her side and was now tugging her hand.

"I'll just put some on and come up for lessons. Poetry today, Makhar."

He made a face and dashed back inside.

When she joined him, the morning's excitement had died away to nothing. Ilya, his toe bandaged, had been dispatched to the laundry to mend a leaking tap. Anatoly was on the phone to a buyer, and Ludmilla was scrubbing the bath. Makhar waited at the table.

"Why poetry?" were his first words.

"Because we can't do maths forever," she said. "Do you have any poetry books in the house?"

Makhar pointed to the well-worn hutch where dozens of grubby-spined books were shoved carelessly. "Up there," he said.

Rosa approached the hutch, sliding past Anatoly where he leaned on the kitchen bench, talking in serious tones. The day book was open in front of him, and he tapped a pen on it restlessly. He gave her a look that she was at a loss to understand. Was it anger? Or jealousy? Or desire? Perhaps it was all three. In any case, she chose to ignore it. She found a dog-eared treasury of Russian poetry in the hutch and brought it back to the table.

Rosa was distracted that morning, flicking through the poetry book in spare moments. "I'm looking for a special poem, Makhar. Is this the only poetry book you have?" she asked the boy, who answered with a decisive nod and returned to composing his own poem, an ode to space pirates from New York.

There had been a poem her mother had recited to her as a child, something about a butterfly and a cliff and loneliness, but Rosa couldn't call to memory much more than a shred of a line, and certainly not its title or author. Again and again she tortured her memory, then cursed herself for being unable to recall it. She hated it when her brain failed her. It made her feel strangled and helpless.

It was late in the week, mid-morning, when Elizavetta came out of hiding. Makhar had run off to find Ludmilla, to give her a phone message from the bakery in town. Rosa sat at the table to wait for him in still sunlight with the smells of honey and lingering sleep all around her. She heard the door open in the hallway, and turned, expecting Anatoly or Ilya. Anyone but Elizavetta.

Her pale face peered around the threshold. She ascertained that Rosa was alone, and shuffled down the hallway. Her wrist bones jutted from her skin, her eyes were hollow and shadowed.

Rosa leapt from her seat. "Let me help you," she said. "Luda is outside."

Elizavetta brushed her off. "It's not my mother I wish to speak to. It's you."

Rosa stood back, surprised, as Elizavetta fell into a chair at the kitchen table.

"Me?" she said.

Elizavetta raised her pale eyebrows. "Is it such a surprise? You've lived here for weeks and we've barely spoken. I thought it time that I ask you some questions."

Rosa sat down. "Questions?"

"I hear a lot. Lying there all day, and the walls are like paper in this house. I hear a lot of things, and some of them I don't like." The pupils in her blue eyes were shrunk to pinpoints. Rosa compared this shriveled girl to the healthy, smiling woman in the photographs with Nikita. No wonder Anatoly was desperate. She looked as though only a fine curtain hung between her and death, as though she might slip through it at any breath.

"You'd better explain," Rosa said. "I don't know what you mean."

"Really? Then I'll tell you. The last two nights I have heard my mother and father talk about you, and about how you have set your sights on my husband."

Rosa was momentarily confused, was about to say, "Nikita?" when she realized that Elizavetta meant Ilya.

"Is it true?" Elizavetta said.

"What do you care if it's true?" Rosa replied with a shrug. "You don't want him."

"He's *my* husband," she replied petulantly.

Rosa stood and walked to the window. She could see Ludmilla and Makhar. He danced about while she pegged clothes on an old rope strung between two lemon trees. Rosa turned and dropped her voice low. "Elizavetta, you are too busy with your first husband to pay any attention to your second."

Elizavetta's face snapped into a scowl. If the girl had possessed any shred of energy, she may have risen and slapped Rosa's face. Instead, she made a spitting noise, then said, "What do you know about me? Nothing. What do you know about Nikita? Nothing."

"I know more than Anatoly," Rosa said. "I know that the reason Nikita won't cross over is because you won't release him."

"That's nonsense."

"Anatoly is a powerful volkhv. He is so full of magic that his blood tastes of it. Yet he can't banish one simple revenant, the spirit of a sullen boy. He thinks there's something wrong with his zagovor, but I know the real problem. You're going to Nikita willingly, but nobody around here—not Ilya, especially not your father—can see that."

Elizavetta dropped her head and muttered, "What goes on in this house is none of your business."

"What I do with Ilya is none of your business."

"Yes it is. He's my husband." Her head was up again, her pale eyes blazing.

"What do you want him for? You don't love him, you never speak to him, you don't share his bed."

Elizavetta sniffed dismissively. "What's the point of sharing a bed? He can't fulfil his duties in that department. As to why I want him? I want him because he's mine."

"So he's there if you change your mind about Nikita?"

Elizavetta's eyebrows shot up, and Rosa realized she had hit on a vein of truth.

"Is that it? Are you tired of your illness? Are you tired of the caress of moonlight?" Rosa sat on the table in front of her. "Do you worry that you won't love Nikita forever?"

"Don't use his name. Your mouth isn't fit for it." Elizavetta pulled herself to her feet, brushing off Rosa's offer of assistance once again. "I can manage. I don't need your help."

"At least tell your father the truth. Tell him he wastes his time. Tell him you won't let Nikita go."

"You stay out of this," Elizavetta said, as she shuffled weakly up the hall. "It's not your business."

Rosa lowered herself off the table and took a deep breath. It *was* her business. If Anatoly knew the truth, that Nikita wouldn't go no matter how many spells were fired at him, then Rosa might be able to get her magic back.

Makhar clattered back into the house, wearing clothes pegs on his ears. "Look, Roshka," he said, "aren't I beautiful?"

Rosa didn't intend to avoid Anatoly forever. She only intended to register her displeasure with him, maybe even make him nervous that she might leave. By the end of the week, he was knocking at the door of her guesthouse after dinner. She quickly hid her mother's books under her pillow, and opened the door.

"Good evening, Anatoly," she said with a smile. "Come in. I thought I might see you one night this week."

He closed the door behind him, wearing a surly expression. "It seems to me that this week you haven't wanted much to do with me."

"That's right."

"Up until now, you've been very eager to work at my elbow, to learn my zagovory and see me do my magic. What has changed?"

"I've realized that you are stealing my magic."

Anatoly looked stunned.

"Yes, Anatoly. When I am working at your elbow you are sucking magic from me as sure as a fox sucks the contents of an egg."

"I am not, Rosa," he said, finding his voice. "I swear I am not."

Rosa realized that his surprise was not a result of being discovered, but of being accused.

He turned his palms up. "How could you think such a thing, Rosa? When you are at my elbow, I am helping you build your repertoire of spells and incantations. I am helping you to grow. I am certainly not stealing magic." He took three fingers and made a cross over his chest. "I swear it."

Puzzlement momentarily stole her words. Could she be wrong? Only a volkhv knew how dangerous it was to swear to a lie.

"Rosa, what made you think that?"

"I . . . my magic is diminishing."

"I explained that. It's only a temporary setback. It will surge back, stronger than ever." He made an emphatic fist. "I promise you. You must not give up, Rosa. It could be only days away."

Confused and tired, Rosa palmed her eyes. "I'm sorry, Anatoly . . . I thought . . . But what about Ilya?"

Anatoly's eyes grew dark. He moved further into the guesthouse, and Rosa fought the urge to shrink toward the armchair.

"What about him?" Anatoly said. "Why concern yourself with him at all?"

"He's the seventh son of the seventh son. Yet he has no magic."

"And I'm accused of theft again?"

"Not by Ilya. He has said nothing," Rosa said. "I just thought . . ."

"As to his being a seventh son of a seventh son, not every man of that birth possesses latent magic. The lore tells that, if he should possess it, it will be stronger than seven men's combined." He wagged a finger. "You have been jumping to conclusions, Rosa."

Rosa crossed her arms protectively over her chest, realized that the stance made her look timid, and uncrossed them again. "I'm only looking out for myself, Anatoly," she said.

Anatoly's somber expression broke into a smile. "Ah. I see." He advanced, holding out his left palm. "Do you see this cut on my palm?"

She peered closely, but could see nothing but calloused skin. "No."

"That's right, Rosa, but the other night, I sliced it open and you touched it."

"Was it your left palm?" She reached for his right to check, but it was whole as well.

"Still looking for Anatoly to play tricks on you?" he said, his fingers tightening on her hand and holding her. "Rosa, your touch healed me."

Rosa pulled her eyebrows close together, trying not to sound skeptical. "It did?"

"You see for yourself, I have no scars. This means your magic is returning to you." He held her in his gaze, and Rosa felt a frisson of expectation and desire shiver up through the floorboards and pass through both of them. His thumb stroked her palm. "We must resume our instruction very soon."

Rosa withdrew her hand. He let go without resistance. "All right, then. Tomorrow."

"I look forward to it." He was glancing around her room, almost as though he could sense that there was competing magic in there somewhere.

Rosa pointedly ignored his curiosity, turned to the electric kettle. "Would you like me to make you a cup of coffee?"

He waved her suggestion away. "I never drink the stuff. I should get back to the house." He moved, then stopped and cleared his throat. "Ah, Rosa. One other thing."

"Yes?"

"Stay away from Ilya."

Rosa almost laughed, then realized he was serious. "Oh? Why?"

"He's trouble. Trust me." This was thrown over his shoulder as he walked to the door.

Rosa hid a smile. Anatoly's jealousy thrilled her. His warning added fresh layers of excitement to the idea of Ilya, his smooth young body and his strange mismatched eyes. "You don't have to worry about me," she said. "I'm well used to dealing with trouble."

She put out her hand to open the door, and he grabbed her wrist forcefully. "I'm serious, Rosa. This isn't a joke."

"I know," she said, smiling at him, "I'm not laughing." She

silently dared him not to let her go, to crush the bones of her wrist until they ached.

But he didn't. He released her and opened the door a little. His tone was low and thick, his breath tickling her ear. "Rosa, you—"

"Papa?" A little voice in the gloom outside.

Rosa peered out to see Makhar at the bottom of the stairs. "Hello, Makhar," she said, and realized her voice sounded constricted and guilty. How must the scene have looked to the little boy? Anatoly's lips close to her ear, Rosa's body inclined toward the older man's, her eyes turned up and smiling. Dangerous flirtations were amusing around adults, but too sad for children. "How long have you been there?"

He held out a book. "I found this. Under my bed. It's poetry, so you could find the one you were looking for." He wouldn't meet her eye, and Anatoly caught his spare hand.

Rosa took the book. "Thank you, Makhar."

"Come on, boy," said Anatoly gruffly. "Back to the house." About a hundred feet away, Makhar broke from Anatoly's grasp and ran back toward Rosa.

"Makhar!" called Anatoly.

"What is it?" Rosa said, crouching to be at the little boy's level.

"You aren't as pretty as my mama," he said in a harsh whisper, then ran off to rejoin his father.

Rosa watched him, feeling vaguely depressed. Anatoly's secret visit had upset the boy, and it had upset her too. Now she had to reassess the situation. Was accusing Anatoly of stealing her magic a way to deal with the disappointment of losing it just when she felt she was making progress? She closed the door and turned the heavy poetry book over in her hands. *Five Hundred Great Russian Poems.* It had to be in here.

"Here we go again," she said. She made coffee and pulled out her pages of notes and her mother's books.

It had been a warm day, giving way to a balmy night. Rosa heard the first rumble in the distance shortly after ten, and by eleven a storm was full upon her little guesthouse. The rain drove hard against the panes, and the roof rattled in the wind. The hollow of cold air the storm dragged in its wake had her climbing into bed to work, pulling the blankets up into her lap as she forced her mind onto the code once more.

An hour had passed before Rosa discovered an index of first lines in the back of the poetry book. She skimmed them all, recalling the old poem about the butterfly and the cliff from her memory. What had been the first line? Something about a golden butterfly? Her eyes darted, looking for the word *butterfly*, and didn't find it. But the word *cliff* did jump out from time to time. She decided to go backward through the index, looking for cliffs, and had returned to the second page of the index before she found the line: "A little golden cloud slept on the breast of a giant cliff."

"That's it," she breathed. It was a cloud, not a butterfly. The poem was called "The Cliff" and was written by Mikhail Lermontov. She thumbed through the book to find the right page, then read the poem under her breath. She tapped the page. "That's it." A rush of familiarity as she read it all the way through. Her mother must have recited it for her hundreds of times, while smoothing the blankets over her shoulder in bed at night, or sitting on the tiny patio of their townhouse in the brief summer sunshine.

Rosa contained her excitement. It was certainly the poem she had been trying to remember, but it might not be the one written in her mother's book. She flipped the book open. The poem matched the structure of the coded piece: two stanzas, four lines each. Rosa quickly scribbled the code on a separate piece of paper, and interspersed the poem line by line. Now things didn't seem so easy. Letters she expected to see repeated weren't. She threw the books aside and tapped her feet against each other. Frustration on top of frustration, and the unrelenting tiredness was now descending too. Outside, the downpour continued, though the wind had died off. She thought about Daniel, and wondered if he was wet, or cold, or even dead. Determined, she flipped her mother's book over again. It was upside-down, and this fresh perspective caught Rosa's eye.

The patterns were there. They were just backward.

Rosa pulled out a fresh sheet of paper, copying out the code again. This time she wrote the poem in, line by line, but with the first word at the end of the line and worked right to left.

Now she transcribed it; found herself working faster and faster as the code appeared. Leave out the vowels, this letter substituted for that, this number of words and then a change of substituted letter . . . By midnight she had it.

Her tiredness melted away like the clouds overhead. A fever of excitement gripped her. She copied out the key for the code then turned to the first page of her mother's book, translating the first line.

To make bread rise quickly. She flipped the page.

To show the face of a beloved in a dream.

To determine whether a journey will be safe.

On and on she went through the book, translating the first line of each page, filling in the missing vowels: *to keep a fire burning in the hearth; to make a man impotent; to help babies sleep at night; to spy on your neighbor unseen.* There were close to a hundred spells, all there for Rosa to learn now that she had the code.

Rosa realized that her mother's repeated recital of "The Cliff" over the years was born of more than just love of the words. She was programming it into Rosa's brain, so that, if the notebooks should one day fall into her daughter's hands, she would be able to decipher them.

Beyond that, Rosa understood at last how much her mother had been steeped in magic. She had once thought that Ellena was a dabbler, a collector of lucky charms and tea-leaf tales. Now another truth was apparent: the strength her mother possessed, the command of magic, all hidden away for the sake of Rosa's father and a life in the free West. Toward the end, when Ellena could no longer be relied on for coherent words or sentences, she had garbled bits and pieces of spells and magical advice, but Rosa had barely paid heed. She had imagined them all the product of an ailing mind, of the disease that was closing down her mother's brain: light by reluctant light, door by reluctant door. Yet Ellena had magic to rival Anatoly's. No wonder Anatoly didn't want Rosa's bracelet anywhere near him.

And, in an unexpected moment between thoughts, Rosa made

a connection. Tarabarshchina. The magician's cipher of which Anatoly had spoken. This was it. Those scribbled, impenetrable marks Rosa had seen in the margins of the day book—Anatoly's magical notes. Now she would be able to read them.

Rosa put the books aside and turned off the light. She stood on the bed, gazing into the drenched garden. All the lights were off at the house. The Chenchikovs were sleeping. She felt like a kid before Christmas. Tomorrow, as soon as she could get her hands on the day book, Anatoly's secrets would come to her.

Twenty

Makhar was not the friendly little boy he had been just twenty-four hours past. With a surly expression that made him resemble his father so much it almost made Rosa laugh, he waited for her at the kitchen table, kicking the underside restively.

"What do you want to start with this morning, Makhar?" she asked, hoping to win back his favor.

He shrugged, silent.

"Maths? You like maths."

"It's all right."

"We could make up a shopping list to add up."

He shrugged again, and Rosa took the chair next to him and turned him to face her.

"Makhar, are you upset with me?"

He nodded, the angry set of his mouth quivering toward sadness.

"Please don't be upset with me. I've done nothing bad."

"The second lady said that, and Papa nearly left."

The second lady? So Anatoly hadn't been lying about his previous affairs. "Your papa isn't going to leave you, and certainly not for me. He loves your mama."

"Then why does he make her so sad?"

"I'm sure he doesn't mean to. Sometimes adults are . . ." She searched for the right words. "Sometimes we can be insensitive, or jealous, or emotional. I promise you, I'm not trying to steal your papa. He's teaching me some things, that's all."

"Like you teach me?"

"Just like that."

"Is he teaching you maths?"

Rosa smiled. "No. Other things." She tapped his exercise book. "Enough of this. It's time you did some work."

"Can we play the shopping list game?"

"Of course." Rosa eyed the day book where it lay in the hutch. "I've got an idea. Let's go back through the day book and look for all Luda's shopping lists, and work out how much money Luda has spent in the last six months. Maybe we can do a percentage? How much for bread, how much for eggs, and so on."

"That sounds like fun," he said, racing to the hutch and returning with the day book clasped against his chest. He thumbed through the pages and Rosa leaned into him to look over his head. His tanned fingers scanned down the list, scribbling down prices for bread and milk and vegetables. Meanwhile, Rosa put her mind to Anatoly's coded messages. On this page, there were three in a list, in small writing above the date. The cipher was no longer fresh in her mind; sleep had intervened. She concentrated on the first line: two words. Counted the letters in her head.

Move bees.

Makhar flipped the page. "Next one, Rosa," he said.

"You just keep going," she replied. "You're doing great."

Move bees turned up again. Underneath it, *protect fire.* They were the only two on that page. Makhar was flipping back through the book again. Two again. *Move bees* and *Hide Rosa.* She checked the date. It was the day that she and Anatoly had buried Luda's button in the ant hill. It clicked into place. Just as the day book documented all their daily tasks, it also documented what daily magic Anatoly had performed. No spells, no secrets. A record for practical purposes and nothing more.

Disappointment set in. No grand mystery here.

As Makhar worked backward through the book, two annotations kept cropping up again and again. *Move bees* was obvious. Anatoly used his magic like other beekeepers used smoke, to control bees. The other was not so obvious in its meaning: *Shift.* And yet it appeared on almost every second page.

Shift. Shift what? And shift it where?

Makhar had worked all the way to January, and Rosa set him up with a page for calculations and a pie graph to start work on. She sat on the other side of the table with the day book, and searched Anatoly's notes more thoroughly.

All the magic they had done together was there. She turned back to the date she had first arrived, and found a note that said: *Hide bracelet 549.* Well, she knew he'd hidden it, but where? What did the number signify?

"What are you reading?" Makhar said curiously.

Her head snapped up, and she flipped the pages over guiltily. "It says here you're going to the dentist tomorrow," she said, pointing at the note for the following day.

Makhar made a face. "Does it?"

She turned the book around to show him.

"Yuck," he said. "I hate the dentist. All those drills."

"At least you won't have classes. Will Luda take you?"

"We all go, even Elizavetta. The dentist only comes to town twice a year." His face brightened. "Will you come too, Rosa? Papa says that Russian dentists are the best in the world."

At least she was back in his favor. "I had a check-up just last month in St. Petersburg," she said. "I guess I'll be home alone."

He showed her his pie graph, already measured and divided. "Can I color it in?" he asked.

"Let's leave it until the day after tomorrow," she said. "There was a big storm last night. I bet there are puddles."

"And mud," he said, in a very serious voice.

"We'll call it a science lesson," she said, shooting out of her chair. "Fetch your coat."

Rosa heard them leaving the next morning: doors banging, the car engine warming up, Ludmilla's voice snippy with anxiety, and Elizavetta's exasperated weak tone. It was a hot morning, and Rosa had woken with a thin layer of sleep still clinging to her. As soon as all was silent outside, she went up to the house for a long shower.

It was a luxury to stand under the shower until the hot water ran cold. Normally she had to hurry in and out. In the kitchen she lazed at the table in a wedge of sunshine, eating toast with honey and drinking two cups of coffee while she checked every page of Anatoly's day book for clues to her bracelet's whereabouts. There were none.

The morning was warming toward eleven o'clock when she heard a thump. She sat up, flicking her damp hair off her shoulders, and listened. Nothing further.

It had sounded as though it was coming from the shed on the far side of the house. A glimmer of danger: what if a thief, knowing that the Chenchikovs were all away at the dentist, had chosen this morning to break in? Nobody would expect to find Rosa here. Or would they? What about that oily bartender who knew she was staying with Anatoly? Miles from anywhere, completely alone, her vulnerability prickled over her skin.

Rosa closed the day book and went to investigate.

She strode down the hallway and through the laundry to the back door of the house. She stopped to listen at the threshold. There was definitely someone in the shed, trying to be quiet, but betraying himself with the occasional soft clatter and thud. As she moved closer, she could hear the sound of running water. She crossed the grass and threw open the door.

Ilya turned sharply. "Oh, Rosa," he said. "I wasn't expecting you."

"What are you doing here?" She glanced around the shed, which was filled with plastic tubs and bits and pieces of equipment. Cobwebs were caught in corners and the benches were made of rough-hewn, unfinished wood. Ilya himself was stripped to his jeans and a singlet as he worked at the deep stone sinks. A homemade tattoo of a heart, in faded blue ink, decorated his right arm. "Aren't you supposed to be at the dentist?"

"Yes," he said, twisting the tap off, "but Elizavetta wouldn't have me in the car with her. She's upset with me for some reason."

Rosa felt a twinge of guilt, soon cast aside. She moved inside the shed. The concrete floor was sticky with honey, which clung to the soles of her bare feet. "So you've been hiding here all morning?"

Ilya brushed his hair out of his eyes with the back of his hand. "Not hiding. Working. Anatoly wants all these drums cleaned up before he gets back."

"Not hiding?"

He smiled, glanced away. "Well, Anatoly did tell me not to leave the shed. And to work quietly." He picked up another plastic drum, and Rosa admired the way the muscles on the back of his arm moved. His skin was silky and olive, lightly tanned. "Anyway I'd better get back to it."

Rosa hitched herself up onto the bench nearby. "You mind if I stay?"

Ilya shrugged. "No," he said guardedly.

"I won't tell Anatoly."

"I'm not worried about that," he muttered, but Rosa knew he was lying.

"I want to ask you something," she said. "Anatoly has hidden my bracelet, and I really want to get it back. I know that the number 549 is significant, but I don't know what it means."

Ilya didn't stop working, picked up another drum and lowered it into the sink. "He numbers his trees," Ilya said.

"His trees?"

"Every tree on this property, including the woodlands right out to the road."

"Is there a map?"

"Only in his mind."

"How do you know this?"

"He told me. He makes no secret of it."

"So he's hidden my bracelet in a tree?"

"I've said this before: you'll never find it. If Anatoly wants it to stay hidden, it will."

"Would you help me?"

He looked up, amused. "I don't know what help I would be. I just told you—"

"I don't believe that. I believe I can find it. I'll work out a way."

Ilya didn't answer. He stacked six drums inside each other and put them aside, reached for another.

"How do you feel about Anatoly forbidding us to spend time together?" she asked.

"He hasn't forbidden it."

"Yes, he has. Not directly. He warned me that you were trouble. I should stay away from you."

Ilya looked puzzled. "He did?"

"What has he said about me?"

He hesitated a few moments before answering. "That you might be a liar. That you like to manipulate people."

"I wouldn't lie to you," she replied. "I've no reason to."

"And the other accusation?"

"Anatoly is describing himself. Unfounded accusations are always drawn from personal experience." Rosa lowered herself from the bench. "We don't have to listen to Anatoly." She grasped his hand.

"Rosa, let me go, my hands are all sticky."

She pulled him toward her and he caught his breath. She took a hand in each of hers, placed one over her heart, the other she held to her mouth. Her tongue darted out. "Your fingers taste like honey," she said. "I'd like to taste the rest of you."

He pulled his hand away. "Rosa . . ."

"He won't know, Ilya. Anatoly won't know, nobody will know."

"Can't he . . . read minds?"

Rosa shook her head. "He may sense some things, but he has no way to confirm them." She picked up his hand again, this time sliding it under her blouse. His fingers closed over her breast and she felt the warm, liquid rush of longing.

"Oh, God," he said, his strange eyes fluttering closed as he fought with terror and desire. Then he opened them again. "Rosa, I can't."

"Yes, you can."

"No, you don't understand. I *can't*. I haven't been able to since I married Elizavetta, I—"

"Shh," she said, putting a finger to his lips. "I do understand. Elizavetta told me, but it's not true."

"It *is* true. I should know, I've—"

"It's not real, Ilya. It's an enchantment."

"How do you know?"

"I know." Her hand skimmed down his firm stomach and pressed into the front of his jeans. "You see, you're strong and hard."

"It always starts this way, but as soon as . . ."

Rosa smiled at him. "Then let it be an experiment. I don't care if you can't fuck me, Ilya, but I bet you can."

Ilya held her in his gaze for a moment. Then he pulled her violently toward him. She tipped back her head and he lay furious hot kisses all over her throat. Grasping her hair, he pressed his mouth against hers. She felt the years of frustration in him then, and closed her own fingers around the back of his neck to hang on tight. As his body stiffened and his caresses grew fierce, her body yielded and softened to accommodate him. She slid her hands under his singlet and let them butterfly over his ribs and chest, then fumbled at his zip to release him from his jeans. With a swift, practiced movement, she had removed her knickers and kicked them off, and guided his hands under her skirt and over her hips.

"Rosa," he moaned softly over her ears, "Rosa, Rosa."

Her hands were back in his hair. "I know, I know. Isn't it wonderful? Don't you feel alive?" His skin was on fire, his face was flushed, and she kissed him and breathed in the intensity of his passion to burn bright in her lungs. She performed a neat half-pirouette in his arms and leaned against the bench to guide him inside her. He sank into her, cupping her breasts in his rough hands, his hot breath tickling her ear. Sensations in her body deepened and gathered, gathered lower, bunched up to almost unbearable intensity. She cried out as the sweet release shuddered through her. Seconds later, Ilya did the same.

A few moments passed as they leaned on the bench, collecting their breath. Then Rosa laughed, spun round and caught him in her arms to say to him, "I told you so."

Elizavetta's room was dark and hot. Ilya pushed the window open and parted the curtain, while Rosa slid under the bed to search.

"I don't understand. What are you looking for?"

Rosa sneezed. Dust lay thick here, and there was very little room between the floor and the bed. The mattress was visible between the wooden slats of the frame. "Come here and I'll show you."

He joined her. They lay on their backs; arm to arm. Rosa's hair trailed in the dust and she squeezed his hand. "We're looking for a needle."

"A needle?"

"Yes, like a sewing needle. I read about it in my mother's notebooks. A sewing needle, threaded with a strand from a dead man's shirt and knotted. Stick it into a mattress and it would make any man who lies in that bed impotent."

"But why would Anatoly want me to be impotent?"

"Anatoly wouldn't. Elizavetta would."

"Elizavetta can do magic?"

"She's a volkhv's daughter, she probably has some ability. Just as you'd expect a musician's daughter to be able to hold a tune." A glint caught her eye. She reached up and plucked a needle from the mattress. "There."

Ilya took it from her and examined it. "This is the reason?"

"You were under an enchantment, Ilya. It was never your problem." She inched out from under the bed and stood, brushing dust from her long hair.

Ilya joined her and they flopped down on Elizavetta's bed. Ilya ran the thread through his fingers over and over.

"Why would she do this?" he said at last.

"You really don't know?"

He turned on his side, confusion and sadness spread across his features. "No, I don't."

"She still loves Nikita, Ilya. She never stopped loving him."

"I don't expect her to stop loving him. He was her first husband, it's only natural. But as long as she loves me too . . ." Then he sighed, rolled onto his back and laid his arm across his eyes.

Rosa watched him as a minute ticked past, wondering all the while about how Anatoly had managed to find a new husband for Elizavetta so conveniently, and how he had convinced the two of them to marry.

"Ilya," she said gently, lifting his arm and snuggling into his side, "don't be sad."

"This isn't where I expected to find myself. In a half-marriage on a bee farm with a crazy volkhv for a father-in-law. I wanted to do other things. Travel, maybe, see a big city."

"You may yet. You're only twenty."

"It feels as though I'm trapped."

"Life has unpredictable currents. And strong ones." She took his hand in hers and stroked his fingers. "Sometimes it's worth swimming."

"I loved her, Rosa. I may still love her . . . or perhaps one day love her again."

"Did she ever say she loved you?"

"Oh, yes. It was instant. We were married within two months."

"Anatoly was happy about that?"

Ilya kissed Rosa's hand and laid it upon his chest. "Anatoly was very happy. He thought it would help her get over Nikita."

Rosa considered this. It was true: if Elizavetta fell in love again, then Nikita would finally lose his hold over her. But there were few loves more tenacious than first loves.

"You never slept with her? Not even once?"

"On the wedding night, something changed in Elizavetta. She was very moody, crying for no reason. She insisted we just hold each other, nothing more. The following night, too. By the end of the week, when she finally said yes, I was incapable. She was unforgiving, she made jokes . . . It wasn't a pleasant time."

"She was already turning cold toward you?"

"A little. Yes."

"Did you find it odd?"

He took a deep breath before replying, and Rosa felt his chest lift beneath her cheek. "She's ill," he said softly.

Rosa sat up and looked down at him. Her long hair trailed over his face. "Do you feel guilty now?" she asked, smiling.

Ilya shook his head. "No regrets." His fingers crept up under her blouse, lingering over her soft stomach and moving up to brush her nipple.

Rosa closed her eyes. The first breaking of the taboo was always more satisfying than its inevitable echo, but it usually took seven repeats before the thrill was gone completely.

Ilya rucked up her skirt and closed his hands around her buttocks. "Where's your underwear?" he asked.

"I left some clothes over at the shed," she said.

"Don't let Anatoly find them."

She amused herself imagining what Anatoly would think if he did. Or how he would react if he walked in right now: his big body all trembling with outrage, his hard hands pressed into her soft shoulders to pull her and Ilya apart. She bent her face to Ilya's and kissed him deeply, allowing her tongue to slide against his. "Shall we make sure the enchantment has truly been removed from this bed?" she asked.

"I'd like that," he said.

Rosa found her discarded clothes in the shed and finished dressing herself. Ilya had stayed at the house to take a shower. Rosa already recognized in him the first signs of a man who feels guilt over illicit sex: moodiness, reticence, obsession with scrubbing her scent off his skin. She didn't mind, she had been through it all before. The worst ones were the men who declared they loved her desperately and had imminent plans to leave their wives. Nobody was forever, not for Rosa.

As she left the shed, she cast her gaze down toward the stream, where the high brick wall gave way to water. Surely Anatoly was more likely to hide her bracelet in the secret grove he used for magic. She could count the trees, perhaps. Or just look for knotholes that might be good for hiding.

Rosa headed for the stream, then inched around the brick wall on the stepping stones. Anatoly's secret grove waited, beyond the bank and the big spruce tree. She gazed around. There were dozens of trees, disappearing off into the distance where they joined with the woodlands at the entrance to the farm. If she started counting, where would she start? She flapped her arms helplessly. Somewhere in these woods was tree number 549, and somewhere in tree number 549 was her mother's bracelet, and somewhere in her mother's bracelet was . . . Rosa didn't know, though she hoped that the bracelet would help her grow her magic again, and quickly. Too much time had passed already. She didn't believe Daniel and Em could last indefinitely without her.

A warm breeze sighed in the branches. Rosa looked up. The sun's rays dazzled around the treetops, so that when she closed her eyes she could still see their silhouettes outlined in electric green. A plane's engine droned in the distance, and she wondered where it was going. Where was she going? Once she had found Daniel and brought him safely home? They couldn't be together, nothing had changed there. She couldn't stay much longer with Uncle Vasily: they already grew too close. Where could she go next? The questions made her heart feel icy, as thoughts of the future always did. And yet, the future was racing toward her with every heartbeat. With her eyes closed, she could see so clearly into the empty ribs of existence.

Rosa snapped her eyes open and headed back toward the wall. She stopped a moment to look at the spruce, the twelve knives embedded within its trunk. Then she looked down at the muddy ground, and realized she was looking at many sets of footprints. Her own were light. Anatoly's were heavy, as though he had hit the ground here with great force: running, or jumping? And they were on all sides, facing all directions, multiple sets of them.

A glimmer of recognition in the back of her mind: something she had read in her mother's notebooks.

Rosa seized a stick and obscured her own footprints, then hurried back to the guesthouse. Careful to keep her muddy feet off the bedspread, she began scanning pages.

Rosa remembered the first time she met Anatoly, how his rapid ease of movement had been at odds with his great hulking body as he'd run from her. Certainly such flexibility and strength was derived from magic, not nature. She returned her attention to the book in front of her. Her own handwriting was scrawled between lines and in margins, notes translating her mother's neat rows of cipher. Within seconds she had found it.

Twelve knives embedded in a tree, twelve somersaults over the knives, twelve incantations about the rapid transformations witnessed in nature.

A zagovor for shape-shifting.

Rosa understood now the repeated *shift* in Anatoly's day book. It referred to a physically demanding branch of sorcery that only the strongest volkhv could accomplish: to change himself into another creature.

And then, for Rosa, it all fell into place.

Twenty-one

The molten dream had started on land, and Daniel half expected that collision with the water would jolt him out of it, restore him to the sharply focused reality that he knew, deep down, he should try to hang on to.

But the russalka knew his name. More than that, she knew the truth about his name: that underneath the brittle, mundane outer layer it was a powerful incantation.

He heard a splash far away. He heard a giggle, muffled by the weight of the river. Cold sizzled on his skin and his lungs strained. Then she was there, turning him and tumbling him, catching him in warm arms and pressing her lips to his. He opened his mouth and air poured in, dizzying him. Her lips vanished, her arms too. He fell a long time, bubbles fizzed around him, dark violent currents swam between his legs and over his torso.

Then, suddenly, air. Cold air, and he was being dragged, dripping, onto the bank.

A pale figure, clouded in night shadow, knelt over him, listening to his heart. Her head was turned away.

"I am Lobasta," she whispered against his heart, and her voice was like a mist that vibrated down through his heart valves, flooding his veins and setting every nerve alight. His body ached. She lifted his shirt, and her feather-light fingertips traced patterns on his stomach. "Oh, Daniel," she said, turning her head to him. He caught a glimpse of perfect pale features and huge green eyes, then her hair fell to cover her face and she had pressed her lips to his throat. All practicality had long ago fled, and now her kisses turned his remaining thoughts to streams of honey and he barely noticed as she pulled off his shirt, untied the bear and threw it with a *whump* onto the bank.

The trees bent in a rush of wind, and moonlight fell on them. She seemed almost to be made of moonlight, her luminous paleness flickered with the movement of the branches. A shadow moved nearby, and another woman knelt beside him.

"He's mine," Lobasta said.

"I don't want to keep him," the other woman said mournfully. "I just want to play."

"Me too," said another.

They fluttered around him, touching him and pulling at his clothes.

"You can play," Lobasta said grudgingly, "but I'm keeping him."

Their voices were spells, their touches sweet electricity. He realized that he was naked, but couldn't remember the awkward routine of having his clothes removed. The night air was cold on his skin, but they chased his shivers with their hot mouths and soft caresses. A beautiful face descended, and his mouth was filled with her mouth, her tongue. Her long hair drifted over his face and he couldn't see anything beyond a cloud of dark mist and moonlight refracted. A firm, wet pressure had captured his cock, and two soft breasts were pressed into his ribs. They were all moaning his name over and over, and he came before he could open his mouth to cry out.

But they didn't let him go. They reconfigured, kneeling over him to rouse him again with their mouths, parting their pale legs over his face, rolling him to probe every secret inch of his body, and the hot ache rose through him again. And again. Dawn broke, the sun revealed the pale green radiance of their skin and hair, the membranous thinness of their eyelids, the polished softness of their bellies and breasts, and all sense was lost to him in a fusion of aching, ever-renewing desire and searing, thundering fulfillment.

Em waited for dawn. It was the only practical thing to do.

So far as she could determine, Daniel wasn't in mortal danger from the russalki until they had tired of him. There was no point in running about in the dark in the woods looking for him, or diving into the lightless river. So she sat by the fire, clutching her knees to her chest, nursing her aching wrist and waiting for daylight.

She mused while she watched the flames. Daniel was probably not suffering. By now, he would be deep in that trance to which he had almost succumbed the previous day on the boat. The russalki were probably treating him lovingly. It wasn't as though he was captured by a hungry leshii or a mantis-like wizard who wanted to make candles from his skin. Under other circumstances, she may have even left Daniel to his fate. They were probably going to die anyway, and dying of pleasure was infinitely preferable to dying of hunger, or cold, or from an aching wound that wouldn't heal. But the bear had disappeared with Daniel, and it was her last hope for a passage home.

With the dawn, Em followed Daniel's tracks in the muddy bank down to where she had last seen him. Another set of footprints—small bare feet—joined his, then both disappeared into the river. Em peered across to the other bank. She could make out a brown lump that might have been Daniel's fur cloak.

She was a good swimmer, but didn't relish jumping into the water and being cold and wet for hours after. More importantly, she had no idea what she'd do if she found the russalki. She needed help, and knew that her last piece of gold ensured she would find it.

Or rather, that help would find her.

The first glimmers of sunlight were streaking up through the woods when she found a glade not far from the river's edge. The trees around her were huge and ancient, and her smallness seemed intensified by comparison. She clutched her gold ring in her right hand, held it in front of her. This had been her wedding ring. After the divorce, she had switched it from her left hand to her right although not from any emotional attachment: it had cost too much money to relegate it to the back of her drawer. She cleared her throat, working out what to say.

"Ah . . ." she started, then realized she would have to speak much louder. "I have gold!" she called, and heard her voice echo around the quiet wood, attracting the attention of a nearby blackbird who hopped down to a low branch to stare at her. "I have gold and I need help. The first person . . ." That wasn't the right word, but she wasn't sure how else to phrase it. "The first . . . demon or spirit to reach me can have the gold in exchange for protection and assistance." She fell silent, waiting, realizing she had no way to prepare herself for what might happen next.

High in the treetops, a wind swirled. At first it was little more than a tickle, the points of a half-dozen fir trees beginning to circle clockwise. Then, next to them, another group moved counterclockwise. This time it was a distinct, muscular movement, as though ligaments and joints grew inside the trees and were flexing in preparation for some athletic feat. A blast of cold air shot up beside Em, streaking into the sky and raging in the branches. Within it, veins of pale iridescent purple and green tangled and fought. She shivered and caught her breath. Another on the other side. She stood her ground, eyes ahead, skin prickling with full realization of her helplessness. A flurry of birds took to the sky, wings frantic. A freezing gust gathered into a column behind her, sending the woods into a frenzy: the howling of gushing air through branches, the creak and pop of twigs, the cold flurry of fallen pine needles in slow whirlwinds. The woods had come alive as unseen spirits fought among themselves to be the first to reach her.

In an instant, it stopped. Stillness, heavier than before. The air around her tightened, froze. The temperature dropped and the sky snapped and popped.

"Where is the gold?"

Em turned. Behind her stood a man, and the shock of his sudden, unperceived presence was equaled only by the shock of his appearance.

He was a head taller than her, with dark curling hair and a strong, almost hooked nose. Despite this, or perhaps because of it, he was intensely attractive, with cool blue eyes and a wide mouth. He was almost naked. A skirt of feathers and furs was wrapped low on his hips, exposing a body as hard and smooth and perfectly proportioned as a sculpture. A double arch of feathers curved above his shoulders.

He stood very still and regarded her, as she regarded him.

"The gold," he said.

She held out the ring on her opened palm. "Take it," she said.

"Place it on the ground. It is best if I do not touch you."

Em did as he asked, and he bent to pick the ring up, revealing a pair of enormous wings—white and spotted black like the wings of a snow owl—which sprouted between his muscular shoulder blades.

He stood and caught her staring at him. "My appearance makes you curious?"

"You must be cold," she said with a smile, glancing at his bare feet.

"There is nobody colder than me." He appraised the ring. "Mir gold, it's very beautiful."

"It's yours if you help me."

"Of course I'll help you." He smiled, but the deep arch of his dark brows rendered the smile menacing. He slipped the ring onto his pinky finger. "My name is Morozko."

"And what are you?"

Morozko shook his head. "I don't understand what you mean."

"I'm a Mir woman, Bolotnik was a vodyanoy, Vikhor was a leshii. What are you?"

"I'm Morozko. There's only one of me." He flexed and the wings opened. They were easily ten feet across, dazzling as snow, and an icy chill radiated from them, frosting her skin beneath her clothes. He folded them again. "I am the father of frost."

Em took a deep breath. "Morozko, I thank you for your help. I'm on a journey, but my traveling companion has been stolen by russalki. I think I know where he is. I just have to know how to get him back safely."

Morozko listened, blinking slowly. Em found herself wishing he would stand a little further off. "Mir woman," he said carefully, "this is not your greatest problem."

"I'm sorry?"

"Continuing your journey, rescuing your companion. They are small problems. You have a far greater one of which you are unaware."

A twinge of dread touched her heart. "What do you mean?"

He nodded toward her wrist. "That poison is killing you."

Em turned her wrist over and inched back her sleeve gingerly. The wound was still raw. It ached and seeped, but Em had been heartened by the fact that it had grown no worse. She had even started to think it would slowly heal by itself. "Really?"

"Who struck you this blow? A swamp spirit?" His lip curled. "They are the foulest of creatures, their poison is as slow and deadly as stagnant slime. You will die from this wound. It will be agonizing and unpleasant. Your companion, if rescued, will have to go on alone."

Em stared at her cut wrist, a rush of surreal dread momentarily taking her breath.

"Unless . . . ," he began.

"Unless what?" she said, returning her attention to him.

"I could freeze it. Frozen poison doesn't travel."

She held out her wrist. "Go on."

"Are you certain?"

"Certain that I don't want to die from swamp poison? Yes."

"I must warn you, though, that once I've touched you, I will always be able to find you." His smile softened the portent of the words. "It's nothing you need to fear, because I have no cruel intent toward you. I am not a flesh-eater like the others. Those who bear my mark . . . I always own a little piece of them."

Em offered her wrist again. "At least I'll be alive for you to find."

"What is your name?" he asked.

Em hesitated. "Em," she said.

"I am cold, Em. If you allow me to touch you, you will be cold too. From here on, cold will live inside you."

Em hesitated, understanding that this decision was not to be made lightly. The alternative was to die slowly of blood poisoning. She nodded. "I want you to freeze it," she said. "I'm not ready to die yet."

"Hold very still," he said.

Em clenched her fist and held her arm perfectly steady. Morozko took a step closer, and she felt the cold exuding from his hard body and shivering across her skin. He reached out, extending his index finger. He touched the very tip of it to the edge of the wound, and Em jumped. Freezing electricity.

"Still," he said again, soothingly.

She took a breath and focused her mind. It would hurt, but then it would be over. The needlepoint of icy pain returned as he ran the tip of his finger across the cut. Her body shuddered, her organs shivered inside her, her jaw trembled. The searing cold drew up her wrist, then stopped when he took his hand away. She looked closely at the wound. It was white and sealed over. Frozen.

"Can it thaw?" she said. "In front of a fire?"

"No. Never. It's for always."

Em realized that, despite the withdrawal of his icy touch, she was still very cold. "What about the rest of me? If I sit in the sun, will I feel more comfortable?"

"No, but now cold can never hurt you. You can't die of it, or freeze off your toes. You needn't fear the cold." He tilted his head almost imperceptibly. "Nor will you ever feel warm again."

Despite what he had said, she pulled her cloak around her tighter, as though it could help. "Maybe I will if I get back to Mir. Maybe enchantments can't cross the veil."

"I cannot answer with any certainty. Nobody I've touched has ever returned to Mir." He nodded once, his black curls falling forward. "It's time for me to go."

"Wait! What about Daniel? The russalki?"

"You already have your gold's worth of help. I don't like to interfere with the russalki."

"How can I help him?"

"Can you swim?"

She nodded.

"You needn't be afraid of the icy depths of the river now. Just go and take him. They're weak and stupid." He extended his wings behind him. They beat slowly, sending a blast of cold air over her. "Good-bye. Until I see you again." The wings flapped and he extended his arms along them. He coiled into a half-crouching position, then with a grunt launched himself upward. It was an incredibly athletic movement, muscles and sinews flexing and contracting under his pale skin: a man's movement, not a bird's. Then the wings caught the air, they beat and he rose and flew up into the treetops, briefly blocking the sun, disappearing beyond her sight.

Em had the odd, unfamiliar sensation that she had lost something.

She pulled up her sleeve, looked at the wound again, touched it with her finger. Frozen solid. A cold ache drew down inside her, and she longed to sit in the sun and find a little warmth and comfort.

But that was gone forever.

Em returned to the campsite and kicked over the fire. She stripped off her cloak and left it behind. It made no difference to her body temperature, so she may as well be without it weighing her down. It was odd, the coldness inside her. As though she had swallowed a handful of snow, its chill prickles spreading out into her blood. Rather than her body regaining its heat with time, the twitch of cold lingered. She unconsciously pressed her shoulder blades toward each other, and a shiver fluttered through her again. Along with warmth, she had lost stillness.

She dived into the water and surfaced, breaststroking her way across to the other side. The current pulled her slowly off course, and she reached the opposite bank about twenty feet downstream of Daniel's fur cloak. She returned by foot, picked up the cloak and folded it over her arm. He would need it, when she found him.

Daniel had indicated that the russalki didn't like to be too far from the water, so it was reasonable to assume that sticking to the bank of the river was her best option for finding him. But should she move upstream, back to where they had passed through the colony of russalki the previous day? Or downstream, in the direction they had brought him to remove his cloak? They were already three hours ahead of her, so she had to make the right decision.

Em searched the muddy ground. Footprints led back into the water. They had swum with him, but in which direction?

She looked left, right, at the ground again. Had no idea which way to go.

Downstream.

The word popped into her head with a cold hiss. It reminded her of the noise of car tires driving through a freezing puddle. The frozen line on her wrist tingled, and she felt again the echo of Morozko's touch.

"Downstream?" she whispered to the dawn. There was no reply.

She turned and headed downstream.

An hour's journey away, she found the rest of Daniel's clothes, cast haphazardly along the bank. She bent to pick them up. The sling lay amongst it all, empty. So the russalki had the bear. She tried to make sense of the prints in the mud, but they were chaotic and illegible.

Em straightened, hooking Daniel's clothes over her frozen forearm. She gazed off down the river. Quiet trees hung over it, the odd silver-violet of the sky lending their green leaves a bruised luster. A misty haze hung over the river, obscuring the bends in the distance. How far had the russalki taken Daniel, and were they still on the move? If they were swimming with the current, they could be miles ahead of her. She could be following them for days before she caught up with them. The further south she went, the further she moved off the path to the Snow Witch.

"Damn Daniel," she muttered, then remembered it was her fault that the russalki had his name to bind him. She shivered, wishing the sunlight slanting through the trees could penetrate her skin. Her best hope was that the russalki would take Daniel to a fixed location, home in a pond or a cave. If they stopped, even for half a day, that would give Em a chance to catch up.

Her stomach growled, her heart was cold and her body ached. But Em kept moving. Downstream, as Morozko had instructed.

As the dream continued, Daniel began to forget about Before. Life above the water had been cruel, intractable. Now Lobasta had helped him cross into a violet- and green-dappled world buzzing with pleasures. Beyond the surface, the sun had risen, and the light pierced the water and refracted into daydreaming shards that quivered around him. The russalki swam with him downstream, passing his pliant body from one set of arms to another. Their hair trailed in his mouth, their soft breasts crushed against his back, and their lips pressed into his lips every few seconds, pushing sweet breath into his lungs and sending tiny bubbles fizzing around his face. With their breath came more than air to keep his lungs moving, but a forgetting mist, erasing his thoughts of how he came to be here, or whether he should try to escape, even of who he was. If they didn't repeat his name over and over, he would have forgotten it by now.

Eventually—hours or moments later—they dragged him onto the bank again. They rolled his body between theirs, laughing and singing his name, playing with him the way kittens play with a ball of wool. Sensual pleasures embraced him, and more time passed without him knowing. The sky grew dim, the last of the daylight was vanishing. Lobasta took his hand and walked him to the water's edge.

"What is it?" she asked him.

He regarded her dumbly, no understanding of what she meant.

"Down there." She pointed to the water. He saw only dim currents.

"Ah," she said, then passed her fingers over his eyes. "You need a second sight."

It was like a dark cloud breaking open onto blue sky. Now he could see into the water, as though it was lit by phosphorescence. A carved figure rested on a rock beneath the surface, between billowing weed and darting fish. It was a golden bear.

"I don't know," he said, but couldn't feel the words pass his lips.

Lobasta understood him all the same.

"Think harder," she said.

"A bear," he replied, then time grew elastic again and it was deep in the night. The girls all around him were sleeping, their soft white limbs flung out casually. He lay tight between them, naked, but not cold. Their combined body heat kept him warm. The river flowed past, midges settled their delicate feet over his torso. He felt no stinging pain, as though his skin was now alive only to pleasure.

The vision of the bear niggled at the back of his mind. Something important . . . he couldn't quite catch it. A sinuous arm wound about his throat, dragging him up into a warm lap. It was Lobasta.

"You're awake," she said, delighted.

He tried to speak, but no words emerged, and soon his mouth was filled again with warm wet kisses.

It was close to dawn when the thought came to him again. The bear, which Lobasta had stored down in the rock pool, who was she?

She.

Somebody had given him to her. A beautiful face crossed his mind, but melded in his imagination with Lobasta's face.

"Who are you thinking of?" Lobasta said, her eyebrows twitching with anger.

He shook his head, realized his skin was prickling with cold.

"The bear," Lobasta said. "Where did you find her?"

A word insinuated itself into his mind. Rose?

"What's he doing?"

"Why does he twitch so?"

"He's cold. Is our spell broken?"

At once the word was on his tongue, and for the first time since this sensuous dream began, he heard his own voice. "Rosa!" It was a hoarse, desperate cry, and it frightened him. The dream shattered, he was freezing and wet.

"Throw him in the water!"

"He has betrayed us!"

Lobasta was sobbing. Daniel tried to climb to his feet, but his body was too weak.

Insistent hands closed on him, dragged him roughly. He hit the water with a splash, and began to sink. A spark of instinct made him move his legs and arms, propel himself to the surface.

Then Lobasta was there again, her lips closing onto his. He expected the sweet breath that he had grown used to since they took him, opened his mouth willingly.

But instead of pleasant air, a pall of black fog poured into him. A harpy's shriek sounded in his ears, and he fell: under water, under consciousness.

As the sun climbed high in the violet sky and sent trembling shafts of light across the river, Em kept moving. She followed the bank past rock pools and shallow cliffs, and then down into flat muddy fields and through trees and rotting undergrowth. She was hungry, but didn't stop to forage for food. Anyway, the cold inside her made the hunger mild by comparison. Here and there she would see signs that the russalki had passed this way. A long silken hair caught on a branch and glinting in the sun, or skidding footprints in and out of the water. Once she thought she heard laughter, far ahead of her.

With determination, Em closed the distance. As the day bloomed and then faded, she moved and didn't rest. Even though she had walked for hours and sometimes she had run, her body temperature had not risen even a fraction. Frost lived under her skin, the marrow in her bones was iced over.

The irony was not lost on her: people had always said she was cold.

The wound, however, had started to heal. It itched, didn't appear so red and raw, and the pain had withdrawn. The yellow substance had frozen to white and, while taking a brief rest, Em had picked up a pointed twig and scraped some of the poison out. When the skin healed up, she didn't want the poison trapped inside. Hope still lived in her: one day, she might be back home. Perhaps then she could thaw.

The shadows grew long and the sun sank in a splash of golds and greens. Voices were carried up the river to her, and she knew she was close. Perhaps they would stop and camp for the night. She moved slower now, trying to be quiet. Dusk had settled, night was a shade away. Laughter ahead, female voices, not Daniel's.

Em clung to the shadows of the trees. The bank of the river sloped away onto a little flat outcrop, perhaps a hundred feet distant. Grass grew down to the edge of the rocks, and below them was a still pool, six feet across. This is where the russalki had stopped.

At first Em couldn't see Daniel. Daylight had fled, and branches and bushes blocked her sightline. She counted three or four girls, though. They moved about, fussing and giggling. She inched a little closer, crouched beside a fallen tree, and peered over. No, there were only three: one pale blonde, one with streaming ginger hair, and a third who appeared almost green. Lying between them, looking as though he was already dead, was Daniel.

No, not dead. His head lolled to the side and his eyes were glassy, but he was alive, his gaze tracking one of the girls.

All of them were completely naked, but didn't appear to be suffering from the evening cold.

The redhead moved, sat on the outcrop and dangled her feet in the water. She called something back to the others, and there were more giggles. Daniel had closed his eyes.

Em placed Daniel's clothes on the ground, sat on them and watched for a while. How could she get near enough to take Daniel away from them when they were all crowded so close? Morozko had said they weren't strong, but they outnumbered her and, besides, Daniel would resist going.

"Think, Em, think," she muttered. A net? Rope? She had neither of those things. She had only her hands and her brain.

Of course. Just wait until they slept.

She relaxed against the log, turning her back and gazing at the first pale stars glimmering above. The russalki had probably stopped to rest for the night. Once they were sleeping, Em would steal down there and drag Daniel away. But if they woke . . .

Daniel, if he wasn't under their spell, could help himself. He was only vulnerable to his name, so Em would have to ensure he couldn't hear them say it. She picked up the edge of his woollen scarf, and unpicked a thread. Earplugs, then. Maybe even some mud to clap over his ears. The activity would keep her busy.

She glanced over her shoulder, and saw that the blond russalka had taken Daniel to the water's edge. He was glassy-eyed and cadaverous, barely able to move his own limbs, as though the person he had been was buried under flesh and bone. She wanted to turn her gaze away, not see him so naked and depleted. But the russalka was pointing at the water and asking something. Em couldn't make out the words, but thought she might have said, "What is it?"

There was a long pause; Daniel looked confused. He mumbled something.

The russalka whispered in his ear. He drew his brows down, concentrating, then said, "A bear."

Em drew a little gasp. The bear was in the rock pool. Her plans would have to involve recovering it as well as Daniel.

The russalka was asking Daniel more questions, but he had closed his eyes, and the other girls gathered around him and laid him down on the bank. They hovered over him, pressing their bodies and mouths against him, and Em turned away. To see him naked was one thing, to watch him take part in group sex was quite another.

She yawned. Soon the russalki would tire and then sleep, but she couldn't. If she and Daniel were oblivious at the same time, they could wake up somewhere far worse, perhaps leaving the bear in the possession of the russalki. She watched the movement of the branches in the evening breeze. There was no point in her building a fire: she had nothing to cook and no use for heat. So instead she hugged her knees and ran over her plans in her head.

There was a long period of quiet, and Em watched the encampment with eager interest. Daniel slept; two of the russalki slept. But the third, the blond one whom Em had come to regard as the leader, sat up and gazed at Daniel. It was difficult to see her features clearly in the dark and at such a distance, but Em was fairly certain the girl was in love with Daniel. Her gaze never left him, her breasts rose and fell in melodramatic sighs, her hands went over and over to his ribs and chest, forlorn thumbs extending childlike into the hollows of his throat and armpits. Daniel would stir, she would kiss him and he would sleep again.

The night was very long. Em had suffered through hunger and she had suffered through cold, and learned that the body could endure them well enough with an act of will. But tiredness . . . Sleep was insistently pressing on her brain. *Put your head down, close your eyes, give up consciousness.*

She paced. She leaned upright against a tree. She did star-jumps. She recited poems under her breath. She thought up complicated sentences and translated them into as many languages as she could. Still the blond russalka stayed awake. Em was starting to think she might have to go down there and drag Daniel off, taking her chances with his new lover.

But then Daniel woke and with his awakening all the other russalki woke too. They purred and fondled and probed him, and she kicked a rock and muttered, "Shit, shit," and looked away.

The night had grown still, and their voices rose up to her on the ridge. The girls made tiny gasps of giggled pleasure, but Daniel sounded like an animal: incoherent grunts and moans, as though he no longer possessed any consciousness of his dignity or humanity. It made her think that perhaps Daniel was already lost, that he wouldn't be returning from this adventure. In that case, it made sense for her to get the bear first and worry about Daniel later.

The orgy went on and on, and Em sat with her head in her hands trying not to listen. She sneaked one curious peek, but was rewarded only with the sight of flailing limbs and cascading hair. It had been a long time since she had thought about sex. Not because she didn't enjoy it: she was as much attracted to bodily pleasure as anyone. Rather, sexual relationships rose out of other relationships, the kind of relationships that she couldn't form. The problem of what to do with erotic urges had plagued her for many years. Was she to make love to a piece of machinery, or pay a handsome stranger? Neither option had felt like her style, so she had simply willed herself to be dead to those urges. Any glimmer of physical desire was greeted with a quick and certain mental blockage, the way thieves are met with steel security screens in banks.

Behind her, the quiet settled again. She turned. Daniel lay spent on the grass, two russalki curled around him stroking his hair. The blond one sat and watched them, idly dangling her foot in the pool.

Em decided that the instant the other two were asleep, she would take her chances with their leader and steal the bear. As for Daniel . . . she could decide what to do about him later.

She stood, collecting her tools and readying herself. She left Daniel's clothes safely on dry land, and backed down the ridge and out to the edge of the river.

By the time she got there, some commotion had started. Voices were raised, Daniel's among them. She thought she heard him call Rosa's name, and then there were the sounds of struggle and a splash. Em hesitated only half an instant, not sure whether to go back up to the ridge to see what was happening, or to dive in as planned.

Dive. The cold hiss again, and she realized Morozko was still close in her thoughts.

She plunged into the water.

It was dark and freezing, but she didn't fear the cold. She swam fast, stopped to see ahead of her, and swam again. Daniel was not on the bank. The blond russalka was pulling herself out of the river. Adrenalin lit a fire in Em's muscles, and she propelled herself through the water. Ahead, a thrashing limb, sinking.

Two seconds later she had him. There was shouting up on land. She hooked her arm around Daniel's throat and swam away with him.

"Daniel!"

"Daniel!"

Daniel, unconscious but operating on dull instinct, struggled weakly against her. He slipped under water. She picked him up under the arms again, swam against the current. She glanced over her shoulder at the russalki, thought she saw three hags instead of three beautiful temptresses. Took a deep breath and plunged herself and Daniel under the water, away from their cries.

Seconds later they surfaced.

Daniel had inhaled water, his lips were white. She dragged him up onto the bank and laid him on his stomach, sitting on his back. She quickly filled his ears with mud as the russalki's cries continued. She pressed down, crushing her knees into his ribs. Water spurted out of his nose and mouth.

She flipped him over. Airways clear. Not breathing. Pressing her mouth over his, she pushed air into his lungs.

Nothing.

More air.

Nothing.

More air.

He coughed. More water trickled from his mouth. His lungs began to work on their own. Em pressed her head to his chest. His heartbeat was surprisingly slow and rhythmic.

But he was not conscious.

She slapped his face gently, pinched him. But when she peeled back his eyelids, only the whites of his eyes were showing.

Daniel was alive, but dead to the world.

Em picked him up and dragged him further into the woods. The cold air had brought his skin into goosebumps. She returned to the ridge for his clothes. From here, she could see the three russalki, sitting on their rock and sobbing into their hands. The blond one, in particular, was wailing and calling Daniel's name. Em went back to Daniel and dressed him, bringing her breathing under control.

The russalki weren't hunters. As long as Daniel couldn't hear their cries, he was safe. She settled him under his almost-dry fur and built a fire. Daniel's lighter was low on lighter fluid; she had to flick it two or three times to get a tiny flame that wouldn't catch on the pile of leaves she had made. It was the last on a long list of difficulties, but Em found herself bubbling over with anger.

"Damn it!" she shouted and flung the lighter away from her. Ten seconds later she was crawling around in the undergrowth, trying to find it. With shaking hands, she touched the flame to the leaves again; this time it caught.

When the fire was crackling low, the sun had broken over the horizon. Em's eyes were sore and gritty, and she left Daniel and made her way back down to the ridge. The russalki leaned on each other now, mournfully gazing out over the river. They would see her if she came to take the bear. Unless she stayed underwater. Could she hold her breath that long?

Em drove her fingernails into her palms. Weariness, heavy as six feet of soil, made her sag. It was all too hard. She was exhausted. But she had to have the bear. Birds sang their morning songs, fresh daylight glinted on dew. Em walked through the moist shadows to the edge of the river and took a deep, deep breath.

Then dived in.

Before a quarter of her journey had passed she was already dying to breathe. The water was dirty and sunless, the pool seemed a million miles away. She focused and stayed steady on her path. In the gloom, she could see fish darting, weed twisting slowly. A shaft of light broke the surface just ahead, letting her know she was moving toward the treeless bend where the russalki sat. Her lungs felt blocked and her throat felt hard. She could see the algae-covered rocks where they sloped underwater, and swam for them. She longed to surface, to take a huge gulp of air.

Then she saw it, sitting in a green-tinted beam of refracted sunlight. The bear. The light played over her golden surface and her open eyes met Em's as she smiled smugly and waited to be collected.

Em's fingers closed on the bear. A small triumph. She needed to breathe. She couldn't continue another moment without air, or she would black out and her body would draw in two lungs full of water. She turned, tried to swim as far as she could before she surfaced. Her body, operating on instinct, arrowed up to the air.

She breathed.

"There's the woman!"

"She has our treasure!"

The russalki had spotted her and were climbing to their feet. Again, they had transformed: the sweet, full breasts had turned into wizened sacs, the creamy complexions sagged with wrinkles. Em dashed for the bank, heard them splash into the water behind her. She beat them to shore, ran up into the woods to find Daniel, still unconscious, by the fire.

Fire. Water.

Em knew nothing about Russian folklore, but knew these elements were each other's enemies. She cracked open Daniel's lighter, poured the remaining lighter fluid onto the end of a big stick and touched it to the flames. She turned, the burning torch firmly in her right hand, the bear curled against her ribs with her left. The russalki skidded to a halt when they saw her. They were girls again, beautiful and wet-eyed, with sad trembling mouths.

"Oh, let us keep him."

"We didn't mean to hurt him."

"Get back," Em said. "Leave him alone. Leave me alone." She warily crouched next to Daniel. "I'm taking him with me."

The girls backed away, tears quivering on their lashes. The lighter fluid was burning off quickly, she only had a few moments to scare them away. In front of them, a fall of leaves. Hopefully they were dry enough to catch. She flung the torch into the pile of leaves, and the girls cringed back as flame leapt up in front of them.

"Go!" she said. "Go, or I'll set you all alight."

Shrieking, clutching each other, their skirt drooping to wrinkles, they fled. None of them looked back.

The fire was moving, catching on more deadfall. So much the better. It would put a screen between Daniel and any of the russalki if they dared to return. The flames moved slowly, but she knew she had to get out quickly. She crouched next to Daniel, got his arm around her shoulder and stumbled forward, away from the fire, away from the river. She hoped to get him as far from the russalki as she could before she decided what to do next. But he was heavy, a dead weight, and she was weary.

She stopped every ten minutes and rested, then dragged him a little further. She tried lying him down in the crackling under-growth and pulling him by his feet, and progressed quite a distance like that until she accidentally smacked his head against a protrud-ing rock.

She dropped him, sat down to rest her exhausted body, and thought.

The woods were quiet, the trees wide spaced, allowing in the sunlight. Ahead of her was a ridge. Impossible to drag Daniel up there. She couldn't head back to the river; she wasn't heading north again toward the Dead Forest, and she didn't want to go any further south, away from the Snow Witch.

She glanced at Daniel. His face was peaceful, his eyelids faintly purple, his pulse a soft flutter against his throat. He knew no pain, no hunger, no cold.

"I can't leave you here," she said, but already she was glancing around for a sheltered place. The bear seemed to be watching her, pleased with the new plan. About fifty feet away, a fallen log, col-lapsed on one side but with one intact curve: enough to keep off the rain if it fell, enough to hide Daniel from the greedy eyes of the for-est demons.

Kneeling, she dragged him over and tucked him into the hollow.

She collected twigs and leaves, took her time working to hide him properly, make him warm, hang his fur over the gap and remove him completely from sight. Then she bent to the ground and found handfuls of mud to smear over the bear. If nobody suspected she was made of gold, they would allow Em to keep her. It gave Em an odd shine of satisfaction to pack mud into the bear's eyes and smiling mouth.

Finally, Em knelt next to the log and leaned forward, feeling she should say something but not sure what.

"I'll make a deal with you, Daniel," she whispered, pressing her cheek against the flaking wood. "I'll walk until nightfall to see if I can find help, and then I'll come back for you. If there is nobody to find, then I'll just keep going and I'll search for the Snow Witch alone." She patted the log. "I'm sorry."

Then she rose and walked toward the east.

Twenty-two

Lack of sleep made the day nightmarishly long. Em forced her legs to keep moving, even though her brain was incapable of anything but dazed delayed reactions. She stumbled over rocks and walked into trees. As much as she tried to control them, her thoughts kept returning to the fallen log with Daniel packed safely inside. What if he woke from his enchantment? Would he come after her? Or wait for days for her return, more faithful than she by nature? Along the way, she had been arranging stones into piles—beacons to Daniel of where she had traveled—every three hundred feet or so.

The woods thinned, then plains unfolded, with only loose stands of trees dotted across them. Long yellow grass waved in the breeze, blazed under the sun. Grass seeds clung to her clothes and itched and insects darted around her. The ground was less stony, so she twisted the long grass stalks into knots, marking her path. From every ridge she scanned for civilization; in every hollow she convinced herself she'd never see another living creature again.

She was worn out by late afternoon, but didn't dare sit still for fear of falling asleep. Stopping to catch her breath, hands on her knees and weary head hanging forward, she thought about returning to Daniel, maybe even getting back on the river and following it toward the grassy fields they had seen, where they had been so positive they would be nearer the Snow Witch.

Keep moving east.

Again, the icy voice prickling in her mind.

So she kept moving, east if the sun setting directly behind her was any indication. Nightfall was less than an hour away, and Daniel was still helpless back there in his hollow.

Then, at last, she crested a rise and her nose twitched. Smoke. She could smell smoke.

She had found somebody. But who?

Renewed hope invigorated her muscles. She began to run.

After half an hour she returned to a walk. Then half an hour after that, a reluctant dragging of the feet. A little cottage had come into view under the thin glow of the moon: an unpainted wooden building, stained with centuries, the door black with mildew. Behind it, woodland. She had no idea what kind of creature lived here, and she had no gold to bargain with.

Well, perhaps that wasn't entirely true.

Em circled the cottage. She passed a half-fallen stable with a skinny horse inside, and a shed full of old rubbish and a dilapidated cart. She moved a few feet into the woods, stopping to hide the muddy bear carefully under a bush. Then she dusted the dried mud off her hands and took a deep breath, striding toward the front door of the cottage.

She rapped four times, hard.

"Who is it?" A weedy voice from within.

"A stranger. I need your help."

"Go away."

"I won't hurt you, I—" Em leaned on the door and, realizing it wasn't closed, pushed it open. She took a step inside the single, dim room. Smoke filled the air, stinging her eyes as it rushed past her to escape out the door. The walls were streaked with soot. There was no light except for the open fire, and she could make out the silhouettes of three figures.

"I'm lost," she said. "My friend is under an enchantment."

The largest figure, a man of about fifty, stood up and turned to her. In the dark, she thought her vision deceived her.

But no, she really was seeing a face that was perfectly normal but for one defect: no eyes. Instead, little scarred hollows.

"You should leave," he said with a scowl.

The woman—Em presumed this man's wife—was bent to the fire, stirring a pot of meat stew. The greasy, gamey smell made Em's mouth water. "Strangers aren't welcome here." Then she turned to Em with the same empty hollows in her face. The third person, a son of about teenage years, didn't bother to turn. He rocked back and forth in his chair by the fire, saying nothing. Em took a hesitant step forward to check if he was scarred the same way as his parents. He was, but only on one side. His right eye was still intact.

"Don't come any closer," the man said.

"Please," she said, spreading out her hands, then realized they couldn't see the gesture. "I'm sorry to walk in on you like this, but I am desperate." She scanned the dark room again. Apart from two straw mattresses and the chair their son sat in, it appeared they owned no furniture. A few pots and pans and tools were stacked in corners. The people themselves had no features that made them different from herself: no bark-like skin or fish eyes or green hair. "Are you human?" she asked.

"What sort of question—," started the wife.

"I'm from Mir," Em said. "Are you from Mir, too?"

The woman inched close to the man and felt for his hand. Em took their silence as confirmation.

"Please help me. I'm like you," she said. "My name is Em."

"I'm Mirra," the woman said cautiously. "This is my husband Artur and our son Slava. We can't help you."

"Please. My friend Daniel . . . he's unconscious, enchanted by russalki. I've hidden him as best I can, but I'm afraid a leshii will find him and I just want to bring him somewhere warm where he can recover—"

"Stop, stop," said Artur. "Why should we help you? You would bring us into danger, and you offer us nothing in return."

"What can I offer you?"

"Gold."

"I thought only the enchanted creatures wanted gold."

"So they do, and we have to deal with them," Mirra said.

Em thought about the bear, tucked away in the woods. Was it possible to cut off the bear's nose, or her foot, or some small portion of her? What if the Snow Witch only valued her intact? No, if anybody was going to be mauled for gold, it was going to be Em.

She had one gold filling and crown, her second-to-last molar on the left of her jaw.

"Do you have any gold?" Artur was asking.

She looked at him clutching his wife's hand, the firelight creating unnatural shadows in the hollows where his eyes should have been. Daniel, unconscious and alone, needed her help.

"Yes, I have," she said. "But it might be hard to get to."

Without even a swig of brandy to dull the edges of her pain receptors, Em was duly handed a pair of rusted pliers and told to remove the tooth.

Using her index finger, she carefully felt along her jawline, counting the teeth with her fingertip to make sure she had the right one. Then she inserted the pliers and fastened them around the tooth. Sour metal and dirt. She closed her eyes. She was cold, exhausted, hungry. She wanted to weep. She braced herself.

She couldn't do it.

"I'm sorry," she said, removing the pliers so they could hear her, "but you'll have to do it for me."

"I can't see to do it," Artur said, suspicious that she would renege on their deal.

"If I line the pliers up on the right tooth, all you have to do is pull."

"Slava," Artur barked to the young man. "Give up your chair for the lady."

"Better if you do it with her lying down," Mirra suggested, "then I can hold her head."

This was a nightmare. Em's thighs trembled as she lowered herself to the hard, soot-streaked floorboards. Once again she found the tooth and attached the pliers, then she guided Artur's fingers to the handles.

Mirra's hard hands closed over Em's forehead, pinning her head to the ground. She wanted to entreat Artur to do it quickly, but couldn't speak with the pliers in her mouth. The sight of him, pink hollows under his brows, grim-faced in the firelight, made her close her eyes and wish for the pain to be over quickly.

He pulled. Em fought back a shout of pain. He pulled harder, and she felt the tooth loosen. Her jaw was reluctant to let it go. Hot spirals of pain rushed up her cheek and into her skull. Even her eye sockets ached. One more wrench and the tooth came free, sucking from its socket with a shuddering creak. Em tasted blood, her tongue instinctively moving to the hole to apply pressure.

"There!" Artur said. "Now, Mirra, show this to Slava. I need his good eye to confirm this is really gold."

Em sat up, both hands pressed hard against her jaw. The pain was white hot, and her head throbbed sharply. Mirra clutched the tooth in her right hand, opening her palm to Slava. Em had thought him brainless, but his eye fixed keenly on the tooth.

"Shiny, shiny," he said. "Shiny gold."

Mirra snatched it from his grasping fingers and he moaned and cried and rocked back and forth again. Mirra turned an apologetic smile to Em. "He'll be quiet soon," she said. "We try to ignore him when he's noisy."

Em was in too much pain to care about the noise. Her eyes watered and she couldn't stand up. Slowly, slowly, it began to dull, leaving her with a hot ache stretched across her jaw.

"Where is this friend of yours hidden?" Artur was saying, and Em realized he had taken his bearskin coat off a hook and was shrugging into it.

"I can show you," she said, then realized that she couldn't travel. She was bone-weary, in pain, stricken with hunger and the unrelenting cold of her blood. "Or you can follow my path back there," she said. "I twisted grass, I left stacks of stones. I . . ." She hung her head. "I can't go another step."

Artur tapped Slava on the shoulder. "Get up, boy. Go out and bring the horse and cart round. Young woman, if you give us the directions and tell us exactly where this friend of yours is, we'll go fetch him. You stay here with Mirra. She'll make you food and give you a warm place to rest."

"Thank you," Em managed.

Within minutes, Artur and Slava had left, Em's directions carefully memorized. Mirra served up a steaming dish of rabbit stew and Em, despite her sore mouth, ate it gratefully. She sat on the floor next to the fire, her skin hopeful though her heart knew the heat wouldn't reach into her, while Mirra sat in the chair and mended socks. Her fingers found holes, threaded needles, made neat stitches all without the assistance of her eyes.

"How long have you all been blind?" Em asked.

"That would be a long and unpleasant story," Mirra said, lips drawn so tight that her hairy chin puckered. "You should rest."

"I can't. I mean, I can't sleep. If I did . . ." Em was almost too tired to form sentences. "I can listen. You could tell me your story. I must stay awake."

Mirra sighed and put her mending aside. She rubbed her knuckles and shook her head sadly. "Do you think it's better to be alive and miserable than to be dead?" she asked.

Em thought about Morozko's touch, and how it had saved her life but filled her veins with frost. "I think so," Em said. "Where are you from?"

"From Mir, as you guessed. We have been living here for sixty years now. We were originally from Chechnya, but in 1944 Stalin had our whole village sent to Siberia. Other communities went too. There were thousands of us in exile."

"How did you get here?"

"Many of us exiled Mir folk came across. We're common in this part of Skazki. One hundred miles out of Irkutsk, there is a crossing."

"A crossing?"

"Through the veil. There are twenty-seven crossings dotted over Russia. The thrice-nine lands of Skazki."

"So you're saying there are twenty-seven ways out of here?"

"Yes. If you can find them, if you have sufficient magic to cross the veil."

Em was excited now. Maybe they didn't need the Snow Witch. "What do they look like? Is there one nearby?"

"About eighty miles north of here, right on the eastern edge of the Dead Forest. It's where we first entered Skazki."

Despite all her physical discomforts, Em was beginning to hope again. Eighty miles: she could be there in under a week.

"They're difficult to see," Mirra continued. "Impossible for me, of course. Best to see them at night, when the colors are brightest. Or if you have magic in your eyes: the second sight."

As soon as Daniel was back, she could make her way up there. Perhaps she could persuade Artur to part with his horse and cart. She had no more gold, but maybe she wouldn't need the bear.

"Many people, many good people came through that entrance when we did," Mirra said, her voice dropping sadly.

Em tapped her forehead. What was she thinking? Of course she needed the bear. Magic for the crossing. Then how else could she get the horse and cart? Steal it? If only Daniel was here, awake and alert and able to help. He'd know something for sure. He understood all about this enchanted logic.

Em glanced up. An expectant silence hung in the air. Mirra must have asked a question. "I'm sorry, what did you say?" Em said.

"You were silent a long time. I thought you might have fallen asleep."

"No, no. I shouldn't sleep. Mirra, if there are so many crossings back to Mir, why hasn't anyone told us before? Everyone we spoke to said there was no way back."

"Leshii? Vodyanoy? Witches? They don't want you to go back. They want to hunt you."

Em leaned forward eagerly. "Tell me your story. You came here sixty years ago?" She pushed aside her tiredness and focused intently on Mirra's tale, in case it contained more vital information.

"Give or take a few years. We came because we were starving to death in Mir, and because Slava was sick and dying. We were told that your own death couldn't find you here, and we gave everything we had—except our horse—to a local volkhv to help us cross. We had a daughter then, a tiny girl of three.

"The volkhv was sending people over in the hundreds, getting very rich no doubt. We arrived and spread out, grateful for the milder weather, the possibility of living long, long lives. Friends of ours went west immediately, in search of water. They survived two hours in the Dead Forest. We heard their cries as they were slaughtered. We learned very quickly to stay away from the woods, then to stay away from the water. We learned very quickly there was, in fact, nowhere safe for us. We built our house here and huddled inside it and hoped for the best.

"Slava had been dying of a stomach ailment, but almost as soon as we arrived he grew stronger. Or at least, he grew no worse. For that, we had to be happy. We had our lives, we had a roof over our heads and woods to hunt in. We had our freedom. Or so we thought, because we hadn't reckoned on Egibinicha.

"That's how she introduced herself, but I know now that she has many names, all of them evil. A witch, foul to look upon, a heart woven of snakes and a soul formed of flies. She killed and ate my daughter." Mirra hung her head and the firelight glowed against her gray-streaked hair. "Without eyes, I can shed no tears for her."

Em let the silence sit for a while, gently massaging her jaw. The pain was constant but dull. The quiet crackle of the fire was soothing. Outside, rain fell, its rhythmic pattering restful. She feared sleep, so she prompted Mirra to keep talking. "How did you lose your eyes?"

"Egibinicha took them. First mine, one at a time. Payment, she said, for allowing us to live. These woods belong to her, and all that dare to live in them must make the payments she asks for. In return, we can hunt the woods, and she protects us from the leshii."

"She takes payment in eyes?"

Mirra shook her head. "Not just eyes. All manner of things. She took our eyes when we displeased her. We try very hard not to displease her. She left Slava with one eye so he could continue to hunt, but the pain and the distress of losing his other sent him mad."

Em stood up and paced.

"Are you worried for your friend?" Mirra asked.

She stole a long glance at Mirra's face, the way the firelight made deformed shadows in the hollows under her eyebrows. "I'm worried I'll fall asleep," Em said. "My friend and I are under an enchantment. If we sleep at the same time, we could wake up anywhere."

"Who put you under this enchantment?"

"I'm not sure. Have you ever heard of the Snow Witch?"

Mirra frowned. "No. But witches are to be feared greatly."

Em shook her arms and stretched them over her head. All her nerves and muscles were singing to her to lie down. *Sleep, sleep.* Mirra fell silent and Em paced, making plans and calculations. Eighty miles north, on the edge of the Dead Forest, there was a crossing between Skazki and Mir. It made much more sense to forget about the Snow Witch, and head for the exit. She'd still have to bring the bear, of course. It was the enchanted ticket to enable them to cross. She allowed the fog of despair to lift. Daniel might be better in a few days, and they would be well fed before they set out. They could make it. She glanced at Mirra. The woman was nodding into her chest, and Em didn't want to disturb her, but being inside the sleeping house with its soothing sounds was a danger to her. She left the gloomy room behind her, and went out into the cold rain to wait.

They would be hours yet, but she feared nothing from the cold, and the discomfort would ensure she didn't drift off unexpectedly. She sat with her back leaning against the front door, gazing out across the misted fields. The door creaked open behind her and Mirra stuck her head out.

"Em?" she called.

"I'm right here," said Em, tugging the hem of the woman's skirt.

"You don't want me to make a bed for you?"

"No. I have to stay awake."

"You'll freeze out here in the rain."

"No, I won't." Em stood and ushered Mirra back inside. "Go to bed. I'll be fine. I'll wait here for them to return."

The insistent rhythm of the rain, hour after hour, took its toll on her wakefulness. Despite intense discomfort, her body kept crying for inertia. Em wouldn't give in. She paced and, when pacing became soporific, she recited television scripts. She might have been amused by the situation, under other circumstances: pacing in the rain in Russian fairyland, talking to nobody about the sex lives of North Sea puffins. But exhaustion had dulled her sense of humor, along with all her other wits. Two nights without sleep, and who knew how many more she had to endure. As long as Daniel was unconscious, she had to stay awake.

Daylight was just a shade away when the cart finally became visible. Em walked out to greet them.

Artur and Slava had oilskin cloaks on, but Daniel was curled, still unconscious, under his sodden fur in the cart. Artur sat in the back with him.

"Has he woken at all?" she asked Artur.

"I cannot see to know," he replied, as Em jogged along beside him. "I didn't feel him stir. Ask Slava."

"Slava?" she said, turning her attention to the younger man, who was on horseback. "Has he stirred? Has he opened his eyes?"

"Once, a little," Slava said. "Once, a little. Once, a little." He repeated the phrase over and over, stuck in a senseless loop.

Once. A little.

Em knew, then—she *knew*—that this would work out. Daniel was coming up. As soon as he did, she could seize a few hours' sleep and they could be on their way. To the exit, just eighty miles north of here.

Slava pulled the horse and cart around the back of the cottage, and he and Artur carried Daniel inside. The rain had eased, and the sky was brightening.

Mirra woke when they arrived, and she helped Em with Daniel while Artur and Slava curled up on a mattress and slept. Em was grateful for the activity. Hope had given her a second wind. They stripped Daniel of his wet clothes, and Em hung them with his fur outside, under the narrow eaves. The drizzle still misted over the clothes, but Em hoped that the rising sun would soon burn through the clouds and dry them.

Mirra brought blankets, and they wrapped Daniel and dragged him close to the fire. Mirra poured off a little broth from the previous night's stew, and Em sat Daniel in her arms and tried to get a few drops down his throat. He stirred, grunted, drank a mouthful, then lapsed back into unconsciousness.

Very promising.

"Have you heard of an enchantment like this before, Mirra?" Em asked, as she settled Daniel once again, smoothing his hair from his sleeping brow.

"I'm not certain." Mirra sat back and turned her blind face to Em. "Russalki did it to him, you say?"

"Russalki."

"Then you have little to fear. They meant to drown him, I suppose. They only wanted him to sleep long enough that he couldn't escape the water. He will come out of it eventually."

"How soon?"

Mirra shrugged. "There is no way of knowing."

Em rubbed her eyes. "I just want to sleep."

Mirra reached out, feeling for Em's hand. Em thought that it might be a gesture of affection, but Mirra squeezed her fingers so hard it hurt. "You have been treated lightly by Skazki," she said, her voice growing bitter. "Do not complain to me of sleep." Then she released Em's hand and stood up. "I go to fetch water."

"I'll come with you. I need to keep busy."

"As you wish."

Em filled the day laboring with Mirra—fetching water, uprooting vegetables from a scrawny patch behind the shed, bringing in wood for the fire, feeding and watering the horse—and every time she entered the house, she hoped she would see Daniel sitting up, eating soup and ready for action. When she asked Slava if Daniel had stirred again, he went back into his "once, a little" loop. Artur said he'd heard Daniel mutter something incoherent, but nothing else.

For Em, all her physical discomforts had blurred into each other. She was tired because she was cold, she was cold because her jaw ached, her jaw ached because she was tired. Weariness was lead in her veins, and had robbed her of all precision of speech and movement. She longed for oblivion, but clung stubbornly to wakefulness.

Daniel stirred around nightfall. He muttered something in English, and it had been so long since Em had heard the language that she couldn't make sense of it. Then his eyelids fluttered once, and he fell back under.

It must be soon. It must be soon.

Phrases got stuck on repeat in her head, until she was nearly as asinine as Slava. She was a zombie, barely able to go through the motions, dropping her food and bumping her elbows on walls.

Day flickered out, night relaxed into place. The fields outside were dark under clear skies, and all her hosts were sleeping quietly inside. Em walked around and around outside the house, fighting sleep. As soon as Daniel was awake, she could rest. Then they'd have to be on their way. *Eighty miles north. Eighty miles north.*

Em stopped where Daniel's clothes were hung to dry. The fur cloak was still sodden, so she decided to take it inside and hold it by the fire a while. The activity would keep her awake, and Daniel would need dry, warm things when they got going again.

She crept in, careful not to wake the family. She crouched by Daniel, whose eyes were flicking back and forth under his lids. Dreaming. How she longed to dream. She stood, spreading the cloak between her arms in front of the fire. After five minutes her shoulders ached. That was good, that was a ward against sleep. She yawned, shifted her weight, lost her balance.

Dropped the cloak on the fire.

"Shit!" she cried out, reaching for it, snatching the edge and pulling it free. It was too wet to catch alight, but a far worse outcome had resulted.

The fire had gone out.

Her shout woke the family. An instant later, Mirra's querulous voice in the dark: "I can't hear the fire."

"The fire's out, the fire's out, the fire's out," Slava began, droning into a panicked chant. "It's out, it's out, it's out."

Artur crawled across the floor to the hearth, his hand reaching toward the mouth of the fireplace. "What have you done!" he cried. "Our fire! We cannot live without fire!"

"Calm down, calm down. I'll light another one," she said.

"We can't just light a new fire, the old one has been with us all these years," Mirra said. "It's never once gone out. It protects us from those who would hunt us. You have destroyed our safety with your carelessness."

"I'm sorry, I didn't mean to."

"She'll have to go to Bone-Legs," Artur said, his voice dropping to a portentous rumble. "For Bone-Legs' fire is where the last spark in this hearth came from."

"Bone-Legs, Bone-Legs," Slava chanted.

Em, mentally fatigued as she was, had trouble following all this. "Who is Bone-Legs?" she asked.

"Our neighbor," Mirra said quickly. "Artur is right, you'll have to go to Bone-Legs for fire."

"Does she live close? Couldn't I just start a fire for you? I can rub two sticks together."

"No," Artur snapped, "this is not just any fire."

"It's very close," Mirra said, smoothing over his words with a practical tone. "Just a little way into the woods. Follow the path. The first house you come to."

Em dropped the damp fur. "All right, if you're sure—"

"Bone-Legs, Bone-Legs," Slava repeated, and Em was made suspicious by his smile. It was childishly mean, the expression of a little boy taking pleasure in another's punishment.

"Do I just knock on her door?"

"Say Artur and Mirra sent you. Say we need fire. She'll work out the rest." They were already pushing her out the door, their eyeless faces anxious and grim. "Go, go. Do not leave us too long without fire."

Em found herself outside in the soft dark, the door slammed shut behind her. She turned and headed toward the woods, setting her feet on the path to Bone-Legs' house.

Under shadowed gradations of sleep and dreams, Daniel was becoming aware of himself again. He had been tucked away in a hollow, then cast into the back of a cart. Finally, he had heard Em's voice and tried to fight his way back up to her. He was cold and his body ached, but there was a fire nearby and soothing sounds around him. The shadows were lifting, but he was bound in a cocoon of immobility. Wakefulness flickered on and off, words heard here and there dappled into comprehension.

Then, the fire went out. He felt a cold hole where it had been. And shouting voices.

Em's voice, then a door closing.

The voices of the others—who were they? where had she left him?—and the shadows were weighing on him again, pressing him back under.

"You ought not have sent her to Egibinicha."

"What else could we do? Old Bone-Legs will have Slava's eye if we ask her ourselves."

"We could have built our own fire."

"Only Egibinicha's fire will keep away the spirits."

He was losing his grip on consciousness again, but panic spiked his heart. Egibinicha. Old Bone-Legs. Em didn't know, she had never heard the stories, but Daniel had, and he knew those names. They were names used so her real name, which was taboo, need never be spoken.

The most powerful and malevolent witch in all of Russian folklore: Baba Yaga.

Twenty-three

There was a time to move and a time to stand still, and Rosa knew that she had stayed too long with the Chenchikovs. A month had passed, and she couldn't spare another. Her suspicions of Anatoly grew rapidly. He was powerful and dangerous; and powerful, dangerous men could twist logic to make themselves appear innocent.

When you are at my elbow, I am certainly not stealing magic.

But Rosa was not always at his elbow.

She was armed now: with her suspicions, with the tarabarshchina, with a clue to the location of her mother's bracelet. Somehow, this week, she had to make a move.

Constant tiredness was taking its toll, her mind was distracted and Makhar had noticed.

"Roshka? Is there something wrong?" he asked, after she had made her third mistake in his long division corrections.

Is something wrong? What was she to tell the boy? That his father was a thief? "I can't concentrate today," she said. She needed a cigarette, her fingers danced on the tabletop. "How about another science trip? Into the woods?"

"Will there still be mud? We could collect worms," he replied.

"Let's go and see," she said. "Just let me go back to my guesthouse for cigarettes."

"Cigarettes are bad for you," he said with a frown.

"Are you going to wait here or come with me?"

"I'll come with you."

He ambled alongside her as she crossed the garden to the guesthouse and back. They stopped to tell Ludmilla they were going for a walk in the woods.

"I'd prefer it if you didn't smoke around my son," Ludmilla called after her, seeing that Rosa clutched a packet of cigarettes.

"Sure," Rosa said, waving. "Come on, Makhar."

She lit a cigarette as Makhar locked the gate behind them. The first drag was heaven, and she took a moment to savor it.

Makhar was pouting.

"What?" she said.

"I don't want you to die of cancer."

"I won't."

"You might."

She shook her head. "I promise you, I absolutely won't. I know for sure." They wound into the woods.

"What's it like?" Makhar asked. "Smoking?"

Rosa shrugged.

"Can I try?" he asked.

"Sure." She handed him the cigarette. He took a shallow puff and coughed loudly.

"It's horrible," he said, but made no move to relinquish the cigarette.

Rosa lit another. "Oh, yeah. It's horrible. No mistake."

Makhar puffed again, jamming the cigarette between pouted lips like a miniature rock star. He struck a pose, no doubt learned from American music clips. "Do I look cool, Rosa?"

She felt a twinge of guilt. "Don't smoke it if it's horrible."

"Hey look, what a great stick."

The cigarette was cast aside as he pounced eagerly on a long, crooked stick in the undergrowth.

Rosa squashed the butt with her shoe and admired his new prize. "That is a great stick," she conceded.

He began to hobble, leaning on the stick for support. "I'm an old lady," he said.

"Are you the kind of old lady that collects worms for science class?"

"Yes, I collect them and then I eat them." He lifted the stick and beat it rhythmically on the trees as they passed, muttering a little tune. Rosa walked along beside him, too preoccupied to notice at first the words of the song. He did it every time they were in the woods for science. It had never seemed significant, but slowly it dawned on her what he was singing.

"One hundred and two and turn to the left; six on the left then move to the right." He swapped his stick from one hand to the other.

"One hundred and eight, one hundred and nine, all of the trees in the woodland are mine."

"Makhar," she said, grasping his free hand and pulling him roughly to a stop.

"Yes, Roshka?"

She crouched in front of him. "What are you singing?"

"A song my papa taught me." He looked taken aback, and Rosa realized her sudden crazed enthusiasm must have frightened him.

Anticipation bubbled, but she smoothed her voice. "Do all these trees have a number?"

He nodded, wide-eyed.

"And you know all the numbers?"

He nodded again.

"Can you tell me the numbers?"

He shook his head this time, then twisted his lips thoughtfully. "I don't know."

"It's just, I've thought of a great maths game we could play."

"I love maths games."

"I know. So, I could give you sums to do in your head, and you'd have to find the tree which has the same number as the answer."

He beamed. "That sounds like fun."

"I'm sure your papa wouldn't mind if we played it. It's not like I'll remember how the trees are numbered. It sounds very complex . . ." She pulled a dopey expression.

Makhar laughed. "Don't, Roshka. You're not so pretty when you make that face."

"All right then, what's twenty-three squared?"

He nodded once then set off with a determined gait deeper into the woods. Rosa followed. The sky was gray and she feared rain would set in before much longer. That would drive them inside. She had to get him to the right tree quickly, but without arousing suspicion.

"When did you learn all the numbers?" she asked him as she finished her cigarette and mashed it against a tree.

"When I was very little." A self-important nod followed. "Papa says one day I might have to take over the woods and the farm." He stopped and whacked his stick against a tree. "There," he said.

"Add thirty-one," she said.

He moved further. She waited where she stood. "Here," he said.

"Take away the square root of one hundred and twenty-one."

Makhar tapped his stick, singing his song low. "Here," he said, pointing to a broad birch. Its arms stretched toward the dull sky. A knothole, about four inches across, hid under one of the branches. This was it, tree number 549.

Rain began to spit down. "Last sum, then," she said. "Add four fifteens."

He strode off, tapping his stick. Rosa reached up and into the knothole. Inside was gritty and damp, and a beetle skittered across her palm as she felt around. Nothing. But before the disappointment set in, she remembered that Anatoly would have hidden the bracelet with magic. Magic that could trick her fingers. She slid her hand in again, feeling grit, twigs . . . no, not twigs. Something cold and hard: her mother's bracelet, still entwined with the one Daniel had given her. She didn't pull it out into daylight. Anatoly would sense it if she brought it back to the farm. For now, it would have to stay where it was.

How would she find this tree again? There were hundreds like it in the woods.

Rosa turned and scanned around her. Rocks that looked like other rocks; fallen logs that looked like other fallen logs. A bird skimmed by close to her head, landed on a nearby branch to chirp at her. She reached into her pocket for her cigarettes. No more until next Monday when Ilya went to town again, but they would be sacrificed to a good cause. Following Makhar, she tore them into pieces and left them in a trail behind her, resting them on rocks and logs and branches. White flecks barely noticeable except to someone seeking them, all the way back to the farm.

Soon it would be time to try the veil again. There remained only a few further things for her to wrap up.

That evening, the wind picked up and howled over the eaves of her guesthouse, making mad dancers of the trees in the woods. Rosa settled herself in bed with her mother's notebooks to transcribe, and a bottomless cup of coffee to keep her awake. Shortly after midnight she heard a thud over at the house, and stood up on her bed to peer out the window. Ilya had stolen from the house, but the wind had caught the door and slammed it shut. He paused, tensed against Anatoly's temper, to see if anyone came for him.

Two seconds passed. Three. Nobody stirred. His hair lifted as the wind rushed over him. Then he made his way around the house and off, Rosa presumed, toward the woods.

Poor Ilya. Every windy night was a torture to him, believing that his wife's dead husband was hovering nearby. Rosa tried to concentrate on her work, but found she couldn't. Ilya was out there alone.

Damn it, she had started to care.

Rosa pulled on a coat and closed the guesthouse door quietly behind her. The wind tangled her hair, and sped the clouds across the moonless sky. She followed the fence around and let herself out the gate. From here, she could already see Ilya. He was barefoot and in pajamas—a gray T-shirt and long cotton pants—and he stood as if in a trance gazing into the trees.

She hurried across and touched his arm. He jumped, and whirled around.

"I'm sorry to frighten you," she said.

"What are you doing here?"

"It's too cold to be out here dressed like this, Ilya."

"Leave me be. I think he's here tonight."

"Nikita? And what will you do if you find him?"

Ilya's face hardened. "I'm not afraid of him."

Rosa was reminded of how young Ilya was, and she took his elbow. "I'm sure you could best him in a fight if he was alive, but he's not. The dead are full of tricks and mischief." She tugged him toward her. "Come in out of the wind. Look, you're covered in goosebumps."

He made a feeble attempt to shrug her off, but she held him firm.

"Be reasonable, Ilya. There's nothing you can do. You know that."

He turned with a huffed sigh, and allowed himself to be led back through the gate. "He'll have her tonight. He'll steal my wife from her bed and tomorrow she'll be weaker and sicker."

"You may be wrong. This may just be an ordinary windy night." But Rosa could sense it, too, something black and needy in the shadows. It was best if they were both safely inside. "Come back to my guesthouse," Rosa said, squeezing his hand. "I'll make you very warm."

The faint buzz and knock of a bee trapped in the window greeted them on their arrival. Rosa led Ilya to the bed and shrugged out of her coat. The pool of lamplight was yellow and dim.

"How do they get in?" he asked, looking up at the bee.

"They hang around your window, too?" Rosa asked, realizing he suspected nothing.

"Yes, they do."

"I expect they find an opening and just force their way in," she said, keeping her voice very even. She sat astride Ilya's thighs and began to unbutton her blouse. "I'll let him out later."

"*Her*," Ilya said. "All the worker bees are female."

"Whatever." Rosa's kisses silenced him, and she made good on her promise to warm his blood. Afterward, she released the trapped bee and switched off the lamp. Ilya's warm, smooth body waited for her under the covers, and she snuggled into his side while he stroked her hair. The wind shuddered over the roof.

At length, he said, "I shouldn't fall asleep here, Rosa."

"I know." She adjusted her position so she could see his face in the dark. "Let's sit up and talk then."

"What about?"

"About us, about anything." She touched his brow. "Tell me about your family. Six brothers! Did you fight a lot?"

"No. I was the youngest, I was . . . different to them. They left me alone."

"How were you different?"

"I was sick a lot as a child. I spent a lot of time with my mother."

"What kind of sick?"

"Fevers. Fits. Heart problems."

"You wouldn't know it now. You're healthy as a horse."

"I know. I grew out of it."

"When you were a teenager?" she asked. "Did it get worse around your thirteenth birthday, then gradually better after that?"

She could see him smile in the dark. "How did you know that?"

"I've heard of that kind of thing before." Magic, in vast quantities, was unwieldy in a child's body. Puberty could bring the onset of new powers, and an adult body to store it all. She didn't say any of this to Ilya, who moved his fingers absently in gentle circles on her shoulder.

"Why don't you tell me of your family," he said. "Do you have brothers or sisters?"

"No. Just me."

"And your mother and father? Do they live in Russia or in Canada?"

"They live nowhere. My mother died a couple of years ago. My father when I was eight."

"You're an orphan," he said softly, almost wonderingly. "I think it might explain you, the way you are."

"I doubt it."

"How did they die?"

"My mother from illness, my father by accident." She sat up, pulling the covers against her chest. "It was winter and he took me ice-skating on the frozen lake at the bottom of our street. Mama was home cooking dinner. We were expecting guests. She wanted me out of the house because she was busy and I was bored, so she insisted I be taken outside to burn off some energy. It was late afternoon and my father sat on a bench nearby and I took to the ice, only it was too thin and I skated right through it, into the freezing water." She flicked her hair over her shoulder and wished she hadn't torn up all her cigarettes, wished she had kept just one for emergencies. "Papa came in after me. I survived, he didn't." Rosa heard her own brittle tone, but was powerless to temper it. The only alternative was to cry, and she wouldn't do that.

"I'm very sorry," Ilya said.

"It's all in the past." The past had been endured, and the wounds were painless if they weren't prodded. It was the future that weighed on her, crushed her.

"Rosa?" Ilya said. "You look as if you might cry."

"I won't," she said, shaking her head. "Ilya, don't you think it a terrible thing that we'll die one day?"

"It's a terrible thing, but I don't think about it," he said. "I try to think of brighter things. You live now. You're beautiful and clever and young, and your body is still warm and full of hot blood." He pulled her down beside him and ran his index finger in soft circles over her stomach.

"You know this can't go on," she murmured.

"I know," he said.

But Rosa suspected they were talking about two different things.

The next morning, the house was in uproar when Rosa arrived for breakfast. Makhar was crying and hanging around Elizavetta's door, while Ludmilla shushed him and told him to get out of the way. Anatoly was barking down the phone to somebody. Ilya hovered uncertainly, not meeting Rosa's eye.

When Elizavetta was finally drawn from her room, Rosa understood. The young woman was very, very ill. Her eyes were glassy, but her gaze was beatific. She seemed wholly unaware of the chaos around her, shuffling on her bony legs down the hallway while resting on Ludmilla's arm. Rosa wisely stepped out of the way, taking Makhar by the arm and rubbing his shoulder softly.

Ludmilla lowered Elizavetta to a chair and went to Anatoly's side, gesturing anxiously.

"Water," croaked Elizavetta, and Makhar ran to the sink for a cup.

Elizavetta tried to stand by herself, but immediately lost her balance. Rosa was closest, so caught her elbow.

"You should sit," Rosa said.

"As if you care!" Elizavetta gave her a nasty smile, then lowered her voice so only Rosa could hear. "Soon I will be dead and happy. Then you can have my husband, if you still want him. And anything else of mine that's left behind."

"Don't talk to her!" Ludmilla cried, gathering Elizavetta in her arms. "She must conserve her energy."

Makhar returned with a cup of water, but Elizavetta brushed it aside. Rosa took him under her wing, pressing him close against her.

A sheen of sweat beaded Anatoly's brow. "The doctor will see her as soon as we get there," he said to Ludmilla as he slammed down the phone.

"He can't help," Elizavetta said.

"I won't hear it," Ludmilla said, visibly upset but retaining her irritable tone. "Ilya, help us get her in the car."

"She's right," Anatoly said, running his shaking hands through his hair mournfully.

"All of you, stop it. Let's just get her in the car and off to the doctor," Ludmilla snapped.

The agitation drew out of the room as they left, Ludmilla calling over her shoulder that Rosa was to mind Makhar until they returned. Rosa stroked Makhar's hair as she watched them go. Anatoly seemed much smaller than usual. She thought about the wicked things he had done, and found she couldn't blame him. Who wouldn't sacrifice a stranger's happiness for the happiness of a loved one?

She sat Makhar at the table and pulled out his English book, but he couldn't concentrate.

"Elizavetta looked very pale, didn't she?" he said, kicking the underside of the table.

Not just pale: transparent. Rosa smiled. "She'll be fine. You're not to worry." She stroked his fair hair away from his forehead. "The doctor will know what to do."

"No doctor can make her better, Roshka. Papa said so."

"You probably misheard." She tapped the page in front of her. "Come on, you have to fill in these blanks with the right word in English."

"I can't concentrate, Rosa. Like you, yesterday."

"Do you want to walk in the woods again?"

He shook his snowy head. "I want to go and sit by the gate and watch for the car."

"They'll be hours."

"I'll take my marbles."

"Do you want me to come?"

Again, he shook his head.

"Okay," she said, squeezing his hand, "but when Elizavetta comes home, we'll finish these exercises."

He shot out of his chair and went clattering out of the house. Rosa stood by the kitchen window and watched him run up the front path and out to the gate. *When Elizavetta comes home.* Rosa knew that if Elizavetta came home, it would be because she was sent home to die. There was nothing left in the girl.

She turned, leaning against the sink, and eyed the hutch. Perhaps the time uninterrupted could be put to good use.

Rosa flipped open Anatoly's day book, and read as she paced. She could read the tarabarshchina almost as easily as uncoded language by now, and she flicked through quickly, checking every entry. Most of it was benign information about bees and business deals. When she had reached the beginning of the book, she began to wonder what Anatoly had been up to the previous year, when Nikita had been killed and Ilya had come along.

She sat on the floor in front of the hutch and pulled the bottom doors open. Inside was a confusion of old papers and account books, food-splattered recipe books, Makhar's drawings and boxes of photographs. Right at the bottom, she found last year's day book.

The house was very quiet and still. A clock ticked in Anatoly's room down at the end of the hall, and dust motes were suspended in the weak sunlight struggling through the grimy kitchen window. Rosa made herself comfortable on the sticky floorboards, leafing carefully through the book, looking for evidence to incriminate Anatoly. She knew she would find it.

And she did.

Here, just a year ago. Wedged between two mundane spells for water purification and moving bees. *Ilya love Elizavetta. Elizavetta love Ilya.*

Anatoly had put them both under a love spell. He must have known the best way to break Nikita's hold on Elizavetta would be if she gave her heart to another. Because it wasn't real love—rather, the manufactured love of enchantment—Elizavetta had been unable to let Nikita go and her wedding night had been impossible. She had tired of Ilya. Only he was still under the spell.

Sighing, Rosa slid the book back into place. She couldn't leave Ilya suffering under the enchantment, and they were easy enough to break. Usually, finding out one had been tricked into love was enough to undo it; she didn't know if she wanted to be responsible for the family turmoil that would follow.

She slammed the cupboard door, stood and went in search of Makhar. It would all depend on what happened tonight, when she tried to cross the veil again. If she made it, she could sort the Chenchikovs out on her return. If not, then more drastic measures would be called for. And whether or not Ilya ran away from the farm would be the least of anyone's concerns.

Summer was turning toward her zenith, and the nights were growing very short. Not long after the sun had faded from the sky Rosa found herself, flashlight in hand, heading for the woods.

The beam picked up the pale remains of her cigarettes, and she tracked them through the still woods to the birch tree that housed her mother's bracelet. In the dark, its silvery bark appeared ghostly and shadows gathered in the crevice around the knothole. Gingerly, Rosa reached inside for the bracelet, then fastened it around her wrist.

She had no idea how much or how little of her own magic remained in her body, but was certain her mother's bracelet would help. The sky was still warm, the trees breathed softly around her. Waist-high saplings brushed against her, the uneven ground slowing her pace as she neared the edge of the wood. Then the field opened up, dark and tranquil under the indigo sky. The buzz and snap of the veil was just beyond her senses; she concentrated and brought it into sight.

Rosa crossed the field, stood with her arms above her head and willed her mother's magic into her body. "Sister moon," she said, "I beseech you. Tsar air, I beg your aid. On a small green island in the cold sea, the youngest of three sons was born. His name was Daniel, and he fell in love with a rose whose bloom would all too soon fade from this world. She led him far away, and far away. Too far away . . ." Rosa's eyes were drawn out across the field into the inky mist of night beyond. "He has crossed the veil from this world to the next. As he has crossed, so may I cross this veil. My word is firm, so it shall be."

She stepped forward. The veil shuddered and stretched and started to disintegrate.

Then it breathed and re-formed, as elastic and impenetrable as ever.

"Damn!" Rosa muttered, flapping her arms helplessly at her sides. Although she had tried to temper her expectations, she simply couldn't believe she was still standing on this side of the veil.

Rosa knew now that her mother's bracelet wasn't enough. She knew too that her own magic was being sucked out of her by Anatoly. There was simply not enough power in her body to cross the veil. It was like trying to start a car with a nine-volt battery.

She took a moment to compose herself. An owl swooped past and into the field, rose again with a squirming mouse in its beak and took to the sky on starlight gray wings. A soft breeze rippled over the grass, and the veil shifted and settled.

"I'm coming, Daniel," she said quietly. "I *am* coming." She turned back toward the Chenchikovs' farm. She knew what she had to do.

Anatoly had always said he would like to get inside her.

Twenty-four

Serious business and sexual feeling repelled each other for Rosa, and so it was that as she watched Ilya, who was unaware of her presence in the shed, he was no longer desirable. The sunlight through the paint-spattered window made a hopeful patch on the unfinished wooden floor. Ilya's hands were engaged in nailing together a sagging honey frame. He looked very young and very vulnerable.

"Ilya?"

He looked up, and a smile came to his mismatched eyes. "Rosa." Then he frowned. "Anatoly didn't see you come out here?"

She shook her head and advanced toward him. "I was careful. I've left Makhar with enough sums to keep him busy for a time. I needed to speak with you."

He wiped his hands on his jeans and folded his arms. "It sounds serious."

"It is serious."

"Go on."

She leaned on the bench, a respectful distance away from him. "Ilya, you have been enchanted."

His eyebrows twitched, and Rosa could see the spell was already leaving him. His body relaxed, almost imperceptibly, around his shoulders and jaw.

"What do you mean? The impotence spell?"

"Far more powerful. I can read Anatoly's cipher. I found a note from this time last year. He put you under a zagovor, so that you would love Elizavetta."

His puzzled expression grew disbelieving. "No!"

"Can you feel it, Ilya? Can you feel it withdrawing from your body? An enchantment like this cannot stand up to truth. You know it's true."

"I . . ." He closed his eyes and pinched the bridge of his nose. "I feel so strange."

"You feel yourself again. Am I right?"

"I feel as though I'm bleeding somewhere. I'm losing something . . ." His face lost its color and Rosa hurried over.

"Are you dizzy?" She helped him to sit on the floorboards, crouching next to him. "Take a few moments to catch your breath. It will pass. Your body is so used to the magic pressing on it, you might feel faint or light-headed."

Under her hand, she could feel his back rising and falling as he breathed deeply. At last, he looked up.

"What's happening to me, Rosa?"

"Ilya, Anatoly has not treated either of us kindly. You least of all. You've been under an enchantment these twelve months, and now you know it."

"How can this be?"

"Tell me, how do you feel about Elizavetta now? Has the enchantment left you?"

"I feel . . ." He paused, his lips parted, for a long time. Words wouldn't come.

"Do you still love her?"

He shook his head. "I did just this morning. When I looked in on her and she was asleep in her bed. She is so ill now, and I felt such a pang of fear. But now . . . it's as though I imagined it."

"Anatoly orchestrated it all. And there's more."

He looked into her eyes, his own gaze frightened. "What else has he done to me?"

"You are the seventh son of a seventh son. You were overflowing with magic. He has stolen it all."

Ilya shook his head. "I had no magic."

"You had so much magic it gave you fevers and fits as a child. You had so much magic one of your eyes changed color. You could have been a powerful magician."

"I never wanted to be a magician."

"He has taken it without asking. Mine too. He has stranded me here with nothing. He does it to save his daughter, but she won't be saved. She still loves Nikita, and his spirit draws her. With her permission. She's beyond saving."

"She's near death."

"She longs for death, which makes Anatoly more desperate." She touched his knee, but it was a motherly pat, not a lover's caress. "I think you should leave the farm."

"Where would I go?"

"You would go to my Uncle Vasily in St. Petersburg. He'll take care of you. He'll give you a job and help you find somewhere to live. He'll do all of this if you bring him news of me . . . I have no good news to give him, but he'll thank you all the same."

Ilya touched her fingers, but he too had felt the electricity between them grow cold. "I have no transport."

"Take Anatoly's car."

"Anatoly will need it."

"Luda can't drive. Once Anatoly is gone, they will have no use for it."

"Where is Anatoly going?"

She tilted her head and smiled tightly. "Better if you don't know." Rosa stood and helped him to his feet. "Tonight, Ilya. It must all happen tonight."

Ilya sighed, and his eyes fluttered closed for a moment. "I'm afraid of him."

"Don't be afraid. Meet me here at eleven. I'll take care of everything." She squeezed his hand. "You will be free."

He gathered his determination, nodding once. "Thank you, Rosa."

"And I thank you, Ilya." She stretched up to kiss his cheek. He turned his lips toward her and met her mouth. It wasn't a passionate kiss, just one human pressing another's flesh, as anonymous as elbows bumping on a crowded tram.

But Makhar saw it.

"Rosa! Ilya!"

"How long have you been there?" Ilya said, as the little boy was running away, crying.

"I'll go," Rosa said, dashing off after him.

Makhar was already disappearing behind the back of the house.

"Makhar! Wait!" she called, doubling her speed.

Too late. Makhar was wailing into Ludmilla's apron as she stood by the clothesline. Her hands were in his hair, but her gaze was firmly on Rosa.

"Is what the child says true?" she asked, icily.

"I don't know what he said," Rosa replied.

Anatoly appeared then, looking like a portly spaceman in his bee suit. "What's wrong?" he demanded.

"Makhar saw Rosa and Ilya kissing in the shed," Ludmilla said stonily. "I told you no good would come of having the girl here."

Rosa advanced toward Makhar, tried to pry him gently away from Ludmilla. "Makhar, sweet boy. You don't understand."

"Get away!" he shouted. His face was pink and tear-streaked. "Ilya is married to my sister. You will steal him and then Elizavetta will have no one."

"I won't—"

"Leave my son alone," said Ludmilla. "You have done enough damage to my daughter."

Ilya had reluctantly joined them. "Luda, it wasn't as it seemed . . ." he started, then trailed off because guilt had made him speechless.

Anatoly stepped in, barking orders. "Ilya, back to the shed. Makhar, Luda, go inside and finish lessons. Rosa, you go to the guesthouse. I will talk to you all in turn." He caressed Makhar's hair. "Calm yourself, little one. It isn't as bad as all that."

"But Ilya will go away—"

"Ilya is going nowhere." He fixed Rosa with a stern glance and she could have laughed. Anatoly thought he controlled the situation, still thought she relied upon him. Instead of laughing, she feigned a contrite expression and returned wordlessly to the guesthouse.

She paced—through excitement, not fear—for the half hour it took Anatoly to arrive. She had deliberately left her mother's bracelet in the guesthouse, though carefully tucked away in her suitcase, to goad Anatoly's suspicions.

When he did arrive, he thundered up the stairs and pushed the door open without knocking. He slammed it behind him and glowered at her. She stood her ground, eyeing him coolly, expressionless.

"What were you thinking?" he demanded.

"I wasn't thinking. Not of you, anyway," she said, all innocence.

"How long have you been fucking him?"

"I haven't. We shared one kiss, this morning. Makhar saw it and that was unfortunate."

"You're lying."

She shrugged. "You are very certain."

He broke his gaze and paced. The floorboards squeaked under his heavy footsteps. As he approached the bed, with the suitcases lying beneath it, he paused a moment. His eyelids twitched and Rosa knew he had sensed extra magic in the room, though he didn't mention it.

"Luda is demanding I send you away," he said. "Today."

"I believe Luda is probably relieved I was kissing Ilya and not you."

"She's furious."

"I believe you are furious for the same reason that Luda is relieved."

Anatoly stopped and gave her a black scowl. "You are wrong if you think that I can be so easily led by the pizzle. You have underestimated me."

"Perhaps I have. In the past." She smiled. "Come, Anatoly. No harm is done. It was just a little kiss. Ilya is an attractive boy. You can't blame me. Nor can you blame him. His wife is unlikely to offer her affections and—"

"His wife," Anatoly roared, "is my daughter. My mortally sick daughter. Do you understand? She will never break free of the revenant if she has nobody else to love."

Rosa bit her tongue. "I'm sorry, Anatoly. Please don't send me away." As if he would. He could smell magic and he wanted it. He wouldn't let her out of his sight until he'd drained every last drop from her.

"Well," he rumbled, all fatherly and stern, "we shall have to see about that."

"Please, let me stay. Soon, perhaps, I'll be able to cross the veil and then you won't have to worry about me anymore."

He shrugged and sat on her bed, spreading his hands across his wide knees. "Perhaps I can smooth things over with Luda."

"Anatoly, sometimes I don't think I can cross the veil." She dropped her head so her hair hid her face. "I don't think anyone can."

"You need just a little more magic. And it will grow—"

"I don't think even you can."

"Of course I can."

She dropped to her knees beside him, resting her fingers on the backs of his hands. "Then take me across it. Please, I'm begging you. It's already been so long."

"Soon, Rosa, you will have the power to do it yourself."

"Soon? When? I've already been here a month."

"You can't rush these things—"

"Ah, pish!" she said, standing and walking away from him. "I think Luda is right. I think I should leave."

"No. Stay," he said, his voice momentarily betraying his panic. It was quickly smoothed over. "You can't give up. You're so close, Rosa. Your lover needs you."

"If you're certain. I'd like to stay. I think there's so much more you can give me."

He stood. "I'll speak with Luda."

"Thank you, Anatoly."

He left, this time closing the door softly behind him.

"Thank you for nothing," she muttered in English, and started preparations for her adventure.

Dear Uncle Vasily,

I am deeply sorry to offer you only a flimsy sheet of paper, when I know you long for a far more substantial and human connection. This young man, Ilya Andreev Stepanov, has been a good friend to me. He is a hard worker and a decent person. Please find him a job at one of your developments, and see if someone has a room for him to stay in until he is on his feet. And please, don't blame him for the contents of this letter. He is only a messenger. It's me dealing the blow.

I do not think I will ever see you again. I never meant to become so close to your heart: I avoid such closeness for reasons which will soon become clear. But one's own blood attracts and binds, and now I regret loving you so much. Loving anybody.

Is all this strange to you, Uncle Vasily, or have you guessed? Of course you have, you are a clever man. You have long been fond of drawing comparisons between my mother and me; you know we are similar. I can't bear that I must share her fate, and I am determined that nobody else should have to.

I know what you will say. I know you will flap your arms about and roar and tug your lip, but my will is immoveable.

There remain only practical matters. I am taking much from the Chenchikov family. Could you ensure that a decent amount of money is sent to Ludmilla Chenchikova? A large sum to start, then perhaps some continuing small pension? She has very little and her daughter is dying.

Lastly, do not come looking for me. You won't find me, and you will serve my memory better to stay in your comfortable home and enjoy your life. Perhaps even find love. Dare I suggest that you may find it somewhere other than where you have, until now, been seeking it?

Do you remember me telling you that bear was a blessing? It seems that I didn't know the difference between a blessing and a curse. I think I do now.

I am not often frightened, Uncle Vasily. Indeed, I believe you think me almost fearless, but there is one thing of which I am frightened beyond anything, and that is losing myself. I hope to find a place, beyond the veil, where I can remain Rosa; even if it means I am lost to life. Lost to you.

Please understand.

Yours with love and more love,

Roshka.

It was a quarter past eleven, and Rosa had started to think Ilya might not come. He slipped through the door to the shed at last, flushed and jittery.

"Anatoly went to bed very late," he said. "I wanted to wait until they were asleep."

"Anatoly rises again at midnight," Rosa said sharply. "You must be out of here before then."

Ilya gave her a puzzled look and she waved his curiosity away. "It would do me no good to explain to you now. Here." She handed him an envelope, with Vasily's address on the front. "This is where you are going. Give this letter to my uncle, and he'll take care of you."

"Are you certain?"

"I am. We have to be very quiet now, quieter than these cobwebs. We can't start the car, in case they hear the engine. We'll have to release the brake and push it out onto the track."

He nodded, slinging his duffel bag over his shoulder. "Let's do it, then."

They stole around the shed to the car. With Rosa steering and Ilya pushing, they moved it silently past the house and out the gate, then around onto the overgrown track that eventually led down to the road. When they were a safe distance from the house, Rosa started the car.

"Thank you, Rosa," Ilya said breathlessly, as they changed places and he slid into the driver's seat.

"Thank you, Ilya," she said, brushing her lips lightly across his cheek. "I wish you good luck on your journey."

"And I wish you good luck on yours." He pressed his hand over his heart. "I am excited but also afraid. Anatoly might follow me."

"He won't," she said. "I guarantee it." She tapped the roof of the car. "Go. Remember me."

"I will."

The car revved and then pulled off, tires crackling over rocks and fallen leaves. Rosa watched until the taillights disappeared around the bend, then took a deep breath. Her stomach was itchy with excitement. She had to be back in bed by midnight.

She had packed, but not because she was taking anything with her. Rather, there was a finality in packing her things and stacking the cases neatly at the foot of the bed. She had chosen clothes for her journey—a blue velvet jacket and black lace skirt—which would be all but hidden by the heavy overcoat slung over the chair waiting for her. Daniel liked her in blue.

Rosa held her breath between her teeth for a moment. *Daniel.* Was he still alive?

Of course he was. The urgency wouldn't still be in her if he had died.

She got into bed and pulled up the covers, careful to hide the wrist that was adorned with her mother's bracelet. She closed her eyes to wait.

It must have been midnight. The faint hum and tap of a bee inside her window. She stilled her heart and breathing. Let it bump around for a few minutes before sitting up and switching on the light.

"Oh, poor little thing," she said. "Are you trapped? Let me help you out."

She stood on the bed, as she always did to open the window for a bee, but she didn't open the window.

Swiftly, without a moment's hesitation, she snatched the bee into her hand. It bumped about inside her fist, buzzing angrily. She wasn't afraid of it stinging her. This bee, she knew, had a strong instinct for self-preservation.

"I'm sorry, but there is only one way to do this," she said, and she opened her mouth and threw the bee in. It battered itself behind her clenched teeth. She picked up a cup and filled it with cooled water from the kettle, then, careful not to open her teeth too wide, filled her mouth with water.

And down went the bee. She felt it knocking and vibrating all the way down her throat, down her gullet, then finally into her stomach. "Got you," she said.

Something caught her eye and she looked down. Across the floor spread two shadows: hers, feminine and slight, and another hulking, male shadow.

"Come on, Anatoly," she said, seizing her overcoat and heading for the woods, the field, the veil which would now bend to her will. "We're going on an adventure."

Twenty-five

Em paused at the edge of the woods, waiting for her eyes to adjust properly to the dark. The path was narrow: a dirt track, really, less than a foot across. Around it were tightly packed spruce trees, tall and skeletal with drooping limbs and mottled bark that made Em think of disease and decay. The smell was pungent: the clean spike of the spruce fighting with an unpleasant smell of rot and damp. She moved between the trees, her weary legs protesting every step. *Sleep, sleep,* her body cried.

"Forget sleep," she said. "Concentrate." Artur and Mirra said that Bone-Legs lived only a short distance into the woods, but she couldn't see any glow of light that would indicate a house nearby. She stumbled over a rock, righted herself, and kept moving.

A dip in the road, then a gentle rise, and she saw Bone-Legs' house. The trees squeezed right up against it, shadowing the eaves. Em stopped for a moment and looked. It was a strange, round building sitting up on odd skinny stumps. She moved closer, peering into the dark. They looked like giant birds' legs, the clawed feet driven into the ground, with grass sprouting like feathers around the knuckles. A dirty bone-colored set of stairs led up to the front door, but Em didn't approach. Something held her back.

The smell of the place made her feel sick. Acrid and oily. Burning. Like roasting flesh. The light from inside was strange: flickering and flaring, as though there was an enormous bonfire burning within. The sound, too, was extraordinary. A pressure had gathered around her ears, a high-pitched whine, beyond the range of ordinary human hearing, intensifying nearby.

Yet it was more than what she could smell and see and hear that held her in the shadows. A profound unease, located just below her navel. An instinct that told her not to go a step closer.

"This is ridiculous," she said. Exhaustion was taking its toll, that was all. How could she think straight when she was so tired she couldn't even walk straight? Artur and Mirra had been clear: they had to have fire from Bone-Legs. No other fire would do. As Daniel needed somewhere to stay until he was recovered, and as Em needed specific directions to the crossing by the Dead Forest, it would pay to keep them happy. She glanced up at the cottage again. It was just an old lady's house.

She started up the front path.

Don't go in there.

"Oh, shut up," she muttered. She didn't know where these voices in her head came from, but they multiplied the more tired she became. What she had to do now was get the fire, go back to Daniel, wait for him to wake, then go home.

Then sleep and sleep and sleep . . .

Em lifted her hand and rapped hard on the door. A second later it opened.

"Hello—," she started, then realized that nobody stood on the other side. She hesitated, looked behind her. Noticed that the stairs she had just climbed were not bone-colored but actually bones. Dirty, moldy old bones that looked like they had been pilfered from centuries-old graves.

"Come in," a weak voice called from within.

Just an old lady.

"Hello?" Em said, moving into a narrow, dark hallway. "Artur and Mirra sent me. I'm looking for Bone-Legs."

"Oh, nobody calls me that anymore."

Em snapped her head around. It sounded like the voice had come from a different direction. In front of her, the hallway split into three, down twisted corridors of shadow. How was this possible? The cottage seemed so small from the outside. Light beckoned at the end of the corridor on her right, so she headed that way.

"Artur and Mirra sent me," she called again. "Your neighbors. I'm here to get some fire for them."

"They call me Baba Yaga."

This time the voice came from directly behind her, but she turned and found she was still alone in the corridor. The name, however, touched her. She had heard it before . . . somewhere . . .

Not just an old lady.

She was nearly at the end of the corridor, and took the last bend

into the light-filled space. The fire was enormous, built like a bonfire in the center of a round room. Its flames shot up to the ceiling,
which was scorched black but didn't catch. Smoke choked her. The
floorboards, rough and unpolished, were stained brown and black
with blood. The stench was unbearable. Body parts were strewn
from one end of the room to the other. A bloodied arm, gnawed at
the shoulder, lay at her feet. Flies buzzed about, their black wings
vibrating with excitement at the feast laid on for them. Em took a
step back, turned to run.

And found her way blocked by a monster.

She screamed. She had never screamed before in her life, and
hadn't realized what a physically demanding act it was. Her lungs,
her throat, her stomach all ached with it. Shocked to the heart.

The creature before her was a foot taller than her with a head
resembling a lump of granite carved like a witch's face, thick black
hair-like fur sprouting across the square brow, no discernible neck,
a hunched back with long skinny arms hanging from it, and spidery,
bony legs with huge hairy feet splayed outward. Her eyes were white
and dead and her teeth, which she had bared, appeared to be formed
of sharp metal spikes.

Em jumped backward, feeling for the wall. The creature was
frozen, watching her. Em found her way around the fire and to the
back wall, all the time hoping that Baba Yaga wasn't real, that she
was just an apparition thrown up from her overtired mind. She
chanced a look over her shoulder, saw a doorway, edged toward it,
her heart pounding out of her chest.

Unhurriedly, Baba Yaga followed. Her movements were horrible
to watch: almost birdlike, with her head flicking, agitated, from side
to side. The pressure on Em's ears intensified again. A not-really-
there ringing, which made her feel as though her eardrums would
burst. She turned and ran for the door.

Em had only a moment to register that the door handle was
made out of finger bones, that a cage suspended from the roof of the
corridor contained a semi-decayed human head. She ran down the
corridor, expecting to find a back door. Instead she found more corridors.

This can't be. The corridors snaked off from each other, and there was no way of telling how far they stretched away. Em heard the scratch and shuffle of footsteps behind her, muffled by the bubble of pressure over her ears. She chose a corridor and ran, pulled up sharp when she realized the corridor was narrowing in front of her, pulsing like a biological thing—a length of intestine or a fat earthworm—and slipping from side to side so that the exit was obscured then revealed.

The thing was after her. She had to go.

She ran, fighting the sticky walls of the corridor. Wherever she touched the wall, it sucked at her skin coldly. She struggled against it, finally emerging into a dark room with close walls. In front of her, four doors waited, each with a handle made of bones.

Em went to the first and threw it open. Thickly packed mud, with a narrow opening drilled through it. A tunnel. Em crouched and peered in. The tunnel narrowed dramatically. She had a feeling that if she crawled in there, it would press the air from her lungs and make her easy prey. She moved to the next door, which opened onto a raging bonfire. Flame licked out and scorched her hand. She slammed the door closed and hurried to the next. This time, three steps down to a dark, stinking stream of water. Em took two steps then backed out again. It was impossible to tell how deep the water was, or would become.

She heard the monster behind her and took her chances on the fourth door, shutting herself into a freezing corridor where the air crackled with frost. A faint phosphorous light lit the dark space. Stalactites of ice hung from the ceiling. The cold didn't bother her and she kept running.

And running.

And two minutes later she was still running and getting nowhere. The corridor stretched off into infinity, a nightmare made manifest. No light but the light of ice, no end but being captured by the horrid creature behind her. Angry spitting noises followed her, as the corridor bent and she kept running. She slid, knocked the wall, realized it was made of ice.

"Ice," she whispered to herself, and her breath was a fog in front of her. Panting, she began to smile. "It's ice." This was a trap. Baba Yaga had intended to chase her in here to perish: anybody else would have succumbed to the cold by now. Em took a deep breath. This was surely a temperature that could stop lungs moving, yet she was immune. She flattened her body against the ice wall and waited in the dim blue-gray light for her pursuer.

A moment later, the witch came hurtling around the bend. Not expecting Em to be there waiting, she ran a few steps past her before screeching and turning, her feet slipping on the cold ground. By this time, Em was already away, back in the direction she had come. She flew up the corridor, slamming the door on Baba Yaga's approach. She turned the handle of bones, then snapped it off for good measure. Baba Yaga thundered on the door. Em didn't pause. She fought her way through the pulsing corridor and through the bonfire room, then clattered down the bone stairs.

Crunching, grinding, angry sounds followed her. The beast was in there, and still on her tail. Em plunged off the path and into the woods to catch her breath. From behind a tree, she saw Baba Yaga throw the door to her cottage open. She stood on the top step, head moving birdlike on her hunched shoulders as she scanned the area. Then the creature opened her mouth and let out a screech like nothing Em had ever heard.

It was as though that pressure she had felt on her ears was gathered up, sucking the air from the world around it, then violently unleashed. The screech went on and on, vibrating in invisible concentric circles through the woods. Branches shook and cracked, birds fell dead from their perches. Em's head felt like it would split in two, her brain seemed to shudder and her teeth all jumped in her head. When the sound finally stopped, Baba Yaga stood for a moment at the top of her stairs, white eyes wide and unblinking. Then she took one step out, and Em realized she was hovering in the air.

"Oh, God, she can fly," Em groaned, picking herself up to flee again. She took one glance back, and saw Baba Yaga—her back pillar-straight—propelling her way through the air with some invisible oar clutched between her spindly fingers. Em picked up her pace. Branches whipped her face, rocks kicked at the soles of her feet. She suspected getting back to the cottage would offer her no protection, but she had to run anyway and find Daniel. She understood, with a deep primitive instinct, that she couldn't let this creature catch her.

A horrific screeching noise roused Daniel momentarily. The inertia that had gripped him fled and he sat up and opened his eyes.

Two people he didn't know were hovering near the door of the tiny, dark cottage he was in.

All at once, his body collapsed under him again, and he landed with a thump on the floor. He couldn't move, and sleep was encroaching on his senses. Something was wrong. Where was Em?

"She'll come for us, she's angry," the woman was saying.

"How did the Mir woman get away?"

"It signifies nothing. It's us Bone-Legs will punish."

"What if we offer to help?"

"Get Slava to go out after the woman. Then the witch will know we're on her side. That the woman was an offering."

"Yes, yes. Throw her friend out, too. Bone-Legs can have them both."

"Slava!"

Darkness came, then fluttered off again. He felt rough hands under his armpits, his feet being dragged across the floor.

"Hey, be careful," he tried to say, but no words came out, just an incoherent groan.

He fell under again, and was at peace once more. Then something broke through the dark haze, a pleading voice.

"You must try to wake up, Daniel."

"Em," he said. Or tried to say. He moved his limbs; they all went in the wrong directions. Her arm was around his back, pulling him to his feet. He dropped his weight on her and tried to move his legs again. Found his feet could shuffle if he didn't concentrate on them too hard.

"Good, good. Quickly now. If you can."

He ran into something. She cried out. He still couldn't open his eyes or talk, and he feared the inertia returning.

"Hold this," she said, thrusting something into the crook of his arm. He pressed it against his ribs, wondering what it was, where he was, who he was . . .

"You're doing great. A little further . . ."

Then her voice faded out and he was lying down again, slipping under. Far away, he felt her hands pummeling him, then that sensation was dissolving too. The soft peace of sleep returned.

As long as Daniel had been semi-awake, Em had allowed herself to believe they would get out of this alive. But now that he had lapsed into unconsciousness again, she felt hope run through her fingers.

He lay in the grass next to her, the bear still pressed against his side. The ringing pressure in her ears told her Baba Yaga was drawing closer, and away in the moonlit field she could see Slava. He only had one eye, so she had managed to sneak by in his blind spot so far, but he would soon spy her standing here next to Daniel.

So don't stand.

"Yes, of course," she muttered, crouching so that the long grass hid her. She pulled Daniel a little way, to a hedge surrounded by rocks. She tucked Daniel under it, threw herself on top of him and pulled the damp fur over the both of them. Her elbows drilled into damp ground, her head rested on Daniel's shoulder.

"Think, Em, think," she said, pressing a hand over her eyes. It wouldn't be long before they found her. The witch and the boy had no light, but she was stuck in one place unless she abandoned Daniel. She was easy prey. And what would they do to her when they got her? She shuddered, and envied Daniel his unconsciousness. She was too weary to run, too weary to fight, and too weary to think about how close she had felt—just hours ago—to escaping home to Mir.

Then the solution occurred to her: if she and Daniel slept at the same time, the bear would move them.

They might end up in snowfields, or in a village of hostile revenants, or on a leshii's breakfast table. They might also end up safely in empty fields. The fact was, if Em didn't do it, she and Daniel would be returning to Baba Yaga's charnel house to have their throats bitten open and their bones sucked for marrow.

Em gathered the bear against her and closed her eyes. It didn't cross her mind for an instant that she might have difficulty sleeping. She was mortally weary, and her body needed to rest: all she had to do was let it. Daniel's body was warm beneath her, though she was unable to leach the warmth into herself. She matched the rhythm of her breath to his, and felt her heart slow. One breath, two breaths . . .

Be quiet and still.

Just as she began to slip away, another consideration occurred to her, the one she had been too tired to think through. If she and Daniel left this place, they left behind their chance to escape through the crossing at the Dead Forest.

It was too late. Sleep, victory finally within its grasp, rushed on top of her.

"Thank God," she said. Though maybe not aloud.

Her body sank toward unknown places.

Twenty-six

I wonder where the Golden Bear will take them next, don't you? A cave under the earth where only blind worms and flesh-eating bats live? A frozen wasteland where the horizon is endless and the white ice is uninterrupted by comfort? The bottom of a deep lake, where the weight of water crushes lungs like a bear crushes butterflies? Or, have you considered this: perhaps the Golden Bear's deeds are not capricious at all, perhaps she *wants* to return to the Snow Witch.

The Snow Witch. You must wonder about her, I know. I tell Totchka many stories, but none of the Snow Witch. If ever there was a thing to echo in a child's nightmares, it is the Snow Witch. Such horrors! No need to put those horrors in my little girl's imagination, for she has already suffered and seen enough. Nor have I told her stories of the Golden Bear, for many of her stories are steeped in blood and cruelty. Like this one.

Imagine a May morning in Moscow, 1682. The night before brought a violent storm: a bad omen. People are still clearing branches and debris from their paths. The logs that line the thoroughfares are part sunk into mud, the whole is a stinking mess. It is Monday, and Monday is an unlucky day for Russians. Some folk already wear their nerves ragged anticipating more bad luck on such a day. Imagine the sound of carts and wagons, musicians and jugglers, shouting street vendors and braying animals at market. Then, cutting across the noisy streets, bells begin to ring all of a sudden. The tocsin: its awful clang and din, pealing out its dread foreboding to all.

Gathering sounds of marching now, footsteps and hoofbeats reverberating through the streets. Folk peer out of windows and doorways, to see the awesome Streltsy regiments moving past, determination set on their brows. Their brightly colored uniforms catch the sun, their yellow boots are splattered with mud. Their pikes and banners are raised, and their cannon follow them. These are the Tsar's own guard, grown fat and corrupt from years of indulgence. Now is a time of confusion, for there are two Tsars:

half-brothers too young to rule who have become the pawns of their warring families. The elder Tsar, Vanya, is partially blind and simple-brained. The younger Tsar, Petr, is only ten years old, but one day he will be known as Petr the Great. And it is Petr's family who, on this day, will see their own blood spilled on the ground in violent revolt.

The Streltsy pour into the Kremlin and up the hill to Cathedral Square where they mass before the Facets Palace. The Red Staircase itself appears to tremble with fear. Murder's dark promise lurks in this mob; one whiff of blood could ignite them.

"Death to the Naryshkins, for they have killed the Tsar!"

"Vanya is poisoned. We will avenge his death!"

"Show yourselves, or every boyar in the Kremlin will be put to the blade!"

Inside, a young mother trembles. Her darling son, Petr, looks at her with frightened eyes.

"What do they mean, Mama? Vanya is alive and well. I saw him just this morning at Matins."

His mother, her knuckles white as they wrap around her son's shoulder, feels her stomach turn to water. "Somebody has started a rumor. One that will kill us all."

People are shouting at Petr's mother: her brothers and uncles, frightened nursemaids and servants. They all say the same thing: take the boy to the staircase, find Vanya and present him too. The Streltsy must see that they are in error.

The Golden Bear watches the people running back and forth up the rich corridors, their bright fine clothes at odds with their pale haunted expressions. Torture and death await them, the Streltsy have revolted! Little Petr begins to cry, somebody hurries Vanya into the room and thrusts him toward Petr's mother.

"Go. Now," says her brother. "Take both boys. Tell them all is well."

She cannot make her legs move. Somebody pushes her. It is too much for Vanya, who clings to her hand and wets his breeches. Somehow, she finds herself standing at the top of the staircase. Her body trembles as though it intends to fall to pieces. She cannot make her voice work. The Streltsy shout and jostle and she wants to flee. She must protect Petr, who hides his face in her side.

"Listen to me!" she shouts, and all heads turn to her, their black intentions thick and oily in their eyes.

She holds Vanya's hand aloft, and the boy emits one loud, pitiable sob. His eyelids flutter anxiously over his half-sighted eyes.

"Here is Vanya. You see? He is safe and well. And here is his half-brother, Petr, my son and your Tsar."

A ripple of astonishment. Two of the commanders advance up the staircase for a closer inspection, declare it is indeed Vanya.

Something still isn't quite right. As though, like dogs promised flesh, the denial through reason cannot quench the foretaste. All may be well, perhaps, if only . . .

One of the boyars, affronted at their threats, strides out onto the balcony and begins to berate the Streltsy. Only disaster can proceed from here.

The soldiers pour up the staircase. The woman and her two young charges are pushed aside, and cling to each other on the edge of the balcony. The boyar is seized and flung over the edge onto the waiting pikes of those below. The mob dismembers him, mashes his body to pulp. Then, hungry for more, they begin to howl the names of others. Soldiers raid the palace, dragging the accused traitors, screaming and struggling, to be thrown upon the pikes. Vanya is blessed in his blindness, he can see only the few inches in front of him. Petr's mother closes her eyes to pray and pray and pray. Little Petr, however, watches it all, and sees his dearest uncle, an old man with only good in his heart, torn to pieces, his body savaged and violated.

Inside the palace, frightened people hide under beds, in closets and under staircases. Pikes are driven through mattresses, the court dwarfs are enlisted to help find traitors, everything is in an uproar of fear and blood. Some are tortured for hours before finally giving up their spirit, on racks and fires in shadowy dungeons. Cruelty reigns over all.

Who is responsible for this carnage? The Golden Bear knows, for she has seen it all come into being. She knows precisely who set into motion this revolt. First, the order was given by this plump-faced woman you see sitting before you now, hands folded on her lap as she waits quietly by the deep window in the Terem palace. Her name is Sofya and, after today's events, she now controls Russia as its Regent. She is plain, tending to fat, with a nose too long for her delicate face and deep-set eyes under heavy brows. Her gaze is dark, her hair mousy and thin. She seems harmless, does she not? Perhaps you might think her a pathetic creature, because Sofya dies for the love of a man whom she cannot have. A man whose influence upon her is so strong that, to please him, she will consent to have members of her own family slaughtered.

So perhaps we should say it is this man, Prince Golitsyn, upon whom the blame for such savagery should be laid. He is ambitious, he is vain and believes that only he knows what is best for Russia. Here he sits in his stone palace in Moscow, surrounded by the ornaments of the West of which he is so fond: silver plate and Venetian mirrors, clocks, watches and gadgets. He is soft-eyed and fair-haired, dashing and intelligent. Yet . . . I see no cruelty in his mien. Is he, then, to be thought responsible for the day's horrors? No, for he too was acting on the advice of another. A shadowy figure who has been circulating at court in recent times, a familiar face to the Golden Bear. Indeed, by now, to us. It is the Secret Ambassador.

How did this all begin? Let us turn back a little while in time, and see.

The Secret Ambassador grows desperate as the years pass. The connection between Mir and Skazki, which he hoped to improve through the introduction of Skazki blood into the Russian royal line, grows ever more tenuous. He has discovered that Mokosha's blood is not necessarily passed on to every Romanov infant. Quite the opposite. The blood chooses just one child, and not always the most suitable to rule.

It is easy to spot the child who has the Skazki blood. Of course, the Secret Ambassador can sense it with his subtle magic, but a far more obvious indicator exists: each of them develops a strong, almost obsessive, attachment to the Golden Bear. As though their veins yearn for any connection with the magical realm of her birth. Thus Mikhail is introduced to his secret history and accepts his responsibility to reproduce the Skazki blood. And while his son and successor, the Tsar Alexis, proves to be a difficult and overly religious man, he spawns thirteen children from his first wife. The Secret Ambassador counts them, watching in anticipation. Only one child has Skazki in her: the third daughter, Sofya. Sentenced by tradition to remain unmarried and childless. When Alexis's second wife bears a single child, little Petr, he is all-Mir. The rule of Russia is certain to fall to him, and he with no connection to Skazki! Too precarious!

The Secret Ambassador takes himself to see Sofya in the gloomy confines of her chambers. Here is the Golden Bear, smiling and watching, knowing everything. The Secret Ambassador dismisses Sofya's two female dwarfs with a snarl and a baring of teeth. How he hates this fashion for dwarfs in service, as though the powerful magic of a domovoi can be replaced so easily with a tiny human.

Sofya is her father's daughter and she wants nothing to do with magic and secrets.

"I will not listen to you, stranger," she says. "God is my master, His displeasure is not to be provoked. It would bring me no health in my flesh, nor rest in my bones."

The Secret Ambassador has been observing the Tsarevna for some time. She is intelligent and decisive, she is ambitious and yearns for life beyond these walls. And she is in love with Prince Golitsyn. Nothing can come of this love. Golitsyn has a wife, and even if that wife could be put aside in a nunnery, Sofya cannot marry. As the Tsar's sister, there is no man in Russia of high enough birth to be suitable as her match, and the public would never allow marriage to a foreigner. So she is confined to the Terem with her sisters and aunts, to live out her days in perpetual virginity, invisible to the world. She wants something different. Oh, how she *wants* it. She longs for a public life, for power, for passions that tear her clothes and bruise her skin. And Golitsyn wants to rule Russia. And between her desire and his, the Secret Ambassador finds a way to put Sofya in control.

Prince Golitsyn arrives at the dark chamber late in the afternoon. The windows are too thick to allow in the light, so every alcove is illuminated with candles. The waxy smoke hangs under the low ceiling, smudging the white arches and the painted carvings. A scratched mirror glints dully; a carved chest stands in dusty silence; the chairs and sofa wear their faded gold thread apologetically. Where good lighting would show up the dirt and clutter in here, the dimness lends a ruined glamour. Sofya is surprised to see Prince Golitsyn. Her heavy brow quivers, hopeful. She sets aside her embroidery and says, "Why have you come here?"

He falls to his knees before her, as the Secret Ambassador has instructed. He clasps her doughy hands in his. "Sofya, we must act."

"Act?"

"We must undo the Naryshkins. You should be Regent, not Petr's mother. She is a fool. You are wise and clever."

"I won't think of shedding blood," Sofya says, setting her jaw. "Don't ask me to think it, little father. Only they are blessed who have not walked in the company of the ungodly." How she adores the touch of his soft hands on hers. Until now, the most comfort she has stolen from his body is the meaningless brush of his passing in a small space.

"Many things are unthinkable until they are enacted," he says, and he turns her left hand over and brushes his thumb across her palm.

She is suddenly alive with knowing, and it feels as though every part of her body is opening up to him. He rises, places a hand on each of her shoulders, and leans in to kiss her.

Golitsyn experiences none of the delight and anticipation that Sofya feels. While he doesn't find her repulsive, this moment is filled with awkwardness. Her body is too big for his tastes and her features too coarse. Her skin is salty and her breath smells of potato soup. Her white flesh pours out of his hands as he tries to mold pleasure onto it. Under the dusty canopy of her dark bed, he performs the task as the Secret Ambassador has dictated it. If he should get a child upon the woman, all the better for the Secret Ambassador. Golitsyn only wants power for himself, and once Sofya is satisfied, his mind turns back to that objective.

"My light," he says, covering her gently with an ermine blanket, "we cannot allow Petr's family to gain the upper hand."

"Must we talk of politics?" she complains, pushing off the blanket so that her large breasts are liberated to the deepening evening. Dust hangs in the dark; the thick oily smell of tallow candles is faint.

"You are the most suited to be Regent. You know that. We have spoken of it before. You must act decisively. The Streltsy are on your side. Vanya is older than Petr, but Vanya is unable to rule on his own." He kisses her bosom and murmurs against her heart. "Sofya, you are destined to rule."

Sofya has been softened by lovemaking. Through tender persuasion, violent fates are sealed. The revolt goes ahead and Sofya learns that once blood is spilled, it can never be recalled into the veins of the dead.

The Secret Ambassador has relied too heavily on Golitsyn as his intermediary. The prince is a dreamer and a weakling. So shocked by the savagery of the revolt is he that he retires to his country estate to take comfort in his wife and children and gather his thoughts.

How is the Secret Ambassador to influence Sofya, the ruler of Russia, when she is so suspicious of Skazki ways and magic?

The migration of the soul from one body to another is the Secret Ambassador's special magic. He can use it to shift his shape, possess the body of another, or elude his own death.

He decides he must take the body of a Mir man, somebody the Tsarevna already trusts. From behind the eyes of the Golden Bear he watches court for a few weeks, finally selecting Fedya Shaklovity, a junior clerk whom Sofya favors. This young man, who has done nothing to harm the Secret Ambassador, must give up his life. Only one soul can inhabit a single body at a time, and Shaklovity's displaced spirit, with no place left for it to go, is soon to shiver through the veil and away.

The Secret Ambassador is long since past any qualms about the fate of individuals. The fate of Skazki must be ensured: Stasya's blood must stay in Mir, the ties cannot be allowed to slip completely, and one day . . . one day . . . perhaps the magic world will be asked to return in full-round, rather than in shadows and whispers.

In the German suburbs, there is a house owned by a wealthy merchant who has returned to Saxony to look after his ill parents. The Secret Ambassador finds the cellar of this house, knowing it will be visited only by dust and mildew as the years pass. It is here that he ensconces himself, preparing for the magic he must perform. He sits cross-legged on the dirt floor among sacks of moldering potatoes and begins the humming that puts him in his trance. The floor is cold and a rat skitters across his legs. The humming pulls him and stretches him, as though he is a puppet connected to the sky by a piece of elastic beneath his ribs. A sense of dislocation reverberates through his body, as though he is at once himself and not himself, at once abstract and material. The world around him grows shadowed, then quickly dazzlingly alight as he pulls away from his body with a wrench of ligaments and veins, and vibrates for a moment on the veil.

He is free, but only briefly. The Secret Ambassador needs a means of transport for his soul, and the only transport for a soul is a body. He dives down toward the rat, possessing its cramped body and directing its skittering feet toward the Kremlin. If anyone should come across this miserable cellar, they will find only a cold, slumped man, humming a mindless tune to the passing years.

Shaklovity is on the way to the Terem's audience chamber, where flattering portraits of all the current Tsarevnas adorn the walls. He is unsuspecting, light of foot. What man of sense and bearing would notice a rat scurrying toward him, much less feel afraid of it? The Secret Ambassador lines up Shaklovity, propels himself forward: out of the rat, into the man.

A struggle ensues as the man is knocked to the ground by invisible forces. Shaklovity grabs at his chest, gibbering. Inside this body it is crowded; the Secret Ambassador sinks, fusing into muscle and bone. The struggle continues in Shaklovity's mind now, which is not willing to give up its spirit easily. The Mir man pushes against the Secret Ambassador, but the Secret Ambassador's spirit is fiery and eternal and blinding. Fedor Shaklovity is squeezed out of his body, and sent away to be carried on the whim of light.

The world is different through another's senses. While everything looks as it always has, the Secret Ambassador notes that the air feels lighter, the sound of boots on flagstones is sharper, that Sofya smells sweeter. When she arrives at the audience chamber, her soft gaze is careworn and vulnerable.

"My friend," she says, holding out her hands for him to clasp, "someone said you were unwell. That you collapsed just outside."

"A little fall, nothing to worry about," he replies with a smile.

"You look ill. Your eyes are very pale."

The Secret Ambassador smiles inwardly. A soul will always keep its own gaze, even in another's body: it is true that eyes are windows. Most folk see only what they've always seen, or make excuses for dissimilarity. Sofya does not see who is really lurking behind Shaklovity's gaze. The Golden Bear does, and she feels frightened. She is unsettled to discover that the connection between soul and vessel is not absolute; there is something wholly unnatural about a spirit misplaced.

The Secret Ambassador is now a worm in the ear of the Regent. He fills Sofya with ambition, with schemes, with ideas beyond her station. He orchestrates secret assignations for her with Prince Golitsyn, hoping fervently that she will bear his child and keep Petr off the throne. Sofya does not grow a child, but she does thrive and grow fat. She surrounds herself with luxuries and drapes her generous body in bright, beautiful clothes and jewels: Armenian silk and embroidered velvets, sparkling wristbands catching her sleeves, glossy pearls adorning her hair. The Secret Ambassador manages his anxiety; she is still young, there is time for children. Her half-simple brother, Vanya, wants little to do with power and willingly allows Sofya to take the nation into her hands.

Despite the Secret Ambassador's counsel, Sofya is too soft. God has made her submissive: she raises her hands in His name and sidelines worldly thought. She feels no sense of urgency about Petr, although he is destined to take his rightful place as the ruler of Russia one day. She ignores warnings and sends him a play army, allows him to roam about, dismisses him as nothing but a silly boy. Golitsyn is her other weakness. She indulges him, and he is an indecisive wastrel. He leads bad military campaigns and she rewards him with honors; he refuses to put aside his wife in a nunnery, and she smiles pleasantly and says she understands. Sofya is content. These years shine for her, and she never pauses long to think of the changes that will ring in darker times.

It is Petr, of course, who changes. All boys become men.

It is a warm July morning, the day that marks the Feast of Our Lady of Kazan. Sofya takes her usual place in the Cathedral of the Assumption, at Vanya's side, close to the Metropolitan with his dark embroidered robes and white headdress. Petr and his entourage arrive. It has been some months since Sofya last saw Petr. He has been away at his palace at Kolomonskoe. He looks different, and Sofya can't, at first, decide what it is. It isn't his height—the boy has been well over six feet tall since his fifteenth birthday—nor is it his soft beard, which he trims neatly in the European fashion.

It is in his bearing. For the first time, Sofya sees evidence that the boy knows his power. A cold knot of realization tightens within her. Shaklovity has told her a dozen times, and she has not listened. She will lose power, she will lose Golitsyn and she will lose her freedom. This is inevitable.

Sofya watches Petr with sidelong glances from her seat at the front of the cathedral. The robes of red and gold, the jeweled icons; the delicious bells and chants twining together and echoing above her. She sees Petr glancing her way from near the door, muttering with his cronies. Sofya finds she cannot keep her mind on the service. *Forgive me, God. Be my defender; break the teeth of my enemies.* Her brother looms large in her thoughts, an emptied fate beckons. After the service she rises to join the royal procession. To her dismay, Petr breaks from his place in the procession and walks over to her.

"Sister," he says coldly, "a word with you."

She turns, and feels all eyes drawn to them. What a sight they must make: she, short and round; he, six and a half feet tall. She barely comes up to his chest, and has to turn her face upward to meet his fish-eyed gaze. He watches her silently for a moment, his face ticking and twitching as it had done ever since the day he witnessed the revolt of the Streltsy.

"Can it not wait until after the procession?" she says, feeling sweat form on her palms.

"No, for the procession itself is the problem." He indicates. Vanya, head bent as he awaits the cue to start walking. "It is right for the two Tsars to walk in this procession, but not for you."

"What do you mean? I have entered this holy place with faith, reverence and fear in the Lord. I use my tongue to magnify His name. I belong here as much as you."

"No. You are only a caretaker, and you are a woman and as such should be confined behind closed doors."

"I am more than a caretaker," she protests, realizing it is foolish to do so in this place, but unable to stop herself. What else is she to do? Obey his orders? "I have governed this country well and devotedly these seven years—"

"As Regent. Not as Tsar. That honor belongs only to Vanya and me."

"Are you suggesting—"

"All I am suggesting, *sister*, is that you remember your place."

Sofya glances around quickly, trying to gauge the mood of the gathering. She grows flushed and flustered. Defiantly, she seizes the icon from the hands of the Metropolitan, holding it proudly. "I will not step out of the procession," she says.

Petr's face screws up in a scowl. "Then I will." He turns and strides away. A murmur of disapproval chases itself around the cathedral. The Tsar not in the procession? It isn't right. It is bad luck. What is the Tsarevna thinking?

She is thinking about her future, of course, and how it is about to catch up with her.

Petr's challenge to Sofya is the talk of Moscow. Of course, the Secret Ambassador learns of it and feels the full weight of his frustration with Sofya. He arranges to meet her and Golitsyn in her private apartments. When he arrives, Golitsyn awaits him alone. A musky smell hangs in the air.

"Where is the Tsarevna?" asks the Secret Ambassador.

"She dresses herself," Golitsyn says, not meeting his eye.

The Secret Ambassador rightly places the odor as the scent of lovemaking. Golitsyn is graying, his skin fits him not so firmly as it once did, and a dullness grows in his eyes. Years of obligatory love have worn him down. He smoothes his clothes and sags into a chair.

"It is not over yet," the Secret Ambassador whispers.

"What do you mean, Shaklovity?" Golitsyn asks, running a hand through his thin hair.

Sofya flounces in. Her bright blue sarafan is embroidered with gold thread, and a gown of purple velvet is stretched over it. Her pale hair is unbound, but she wears a gold scarf tied in it. Every plump finger is adorned with rings of silver and amber. She glances slyly at Golitsyn, then offers the Secret Ambassador a serious expression.

"Shaklovity, your letter had a tone of urgency—"

"Matters have become urgent. It is time," he tells them, "to end this decisively. Sofya, you are the rightful heir to the throne. You are Alexis's daughter, you have ruled fairly and well. You must depose your half-brother, marry Prince Golitsyn and bear many children."

Prince Golitsyn's expression of distaste is too evident. Sofya glances away from it, blinking rapidly. The awkwardness seems to echo against the stone walls and return to them magnified.

"I don't see how it can be done," she says.

The Secret Ambassador gathers shadows around him, adding weight to his words. "The same as it was done before, but more thoroughly. Not a single Naryshkin should be left alive, and certainly not Petr."

"You wish to assassinate him?" Golitsyn says, and the tremor in his voice tells the Secret Ambassador he fights a battle that he cannot win.

"His mother's a whore. For all we know he's not even really Alexis's son."

Sofya is desperate, yet she cannot countenance more blood on her hands. She still suffers nightmares from the first revolt. *Help me, save me, have mercy on me, and keep me, Lord, by your grace.* On the one hand, the Secret Ambassador's suggestion strikes precisely at the heart of her ambitions; on the other, she cannot bear to think of more bloodshed. The warring pressures of ambition and godliness squeeze her hard, and she flies into a rage. Her face is mottled pink, and her bosom twitches. "And what of my full brother, Vanya?" she asks. "Am I to kill him, too! Would you make me commit fratricide?" She turns away and walks five paces to a carved ebony dresser, where she leans over and breathes heavily. The Secret Ambassador sees her shoulders shake.

"No, no. Vanya doesn't want to be Tsar, you know that. He wants only a quiet home and a comfortable life."

"You go too far, Shaklovity," she says, evidently trying to keep her voice under control. "We are not killers." She turns and points a trembling finger at him. "Not another word of it. I have too much murder in my memory already."

Poor Sofya. She cannot be cruel, and for that she loses everything. Perhaps it is true that a woman cannot rule.

The end comes for her softly and weakly, not with a sudden thunderous rush. At the Secret Ambassador's will, rumors and intrigues fly, a storm of innuendo builds. Rather than bringing a revolt, it brings only confusion. Golitsyn leaves Sofya, the Patriarch defects to Petr's side, a number of commanders of the Streltsy throw in their lot with the Naryshkins and, before long, the foreign guard too. Sofya bends her neck to Petr's judgment and is sent to the Novodevichy Convent where her hair is shorn and her unwieldy body is enfolded in plain black robes.

Shaklovity is delivered into the enemy's hands.

The Secret Ambassador finds himself trapped in a body intended for the torture chamber. Ordinarily this wouldn't trouble him, for he need only hum for a short time and he can jump from Shaklovity's body, but his captors, incensed by the first of the toneless humming, force a bit between his teeth. It tastes like old blood and mold and it keeps his lips from vibrating against one another. The chamber is dark and damp, and the screams of other poor souls fill the air. The

Secret Ambassador is perplexed. He tries to hum in his throat, but the vibration is not fine enough for magic.

His torturers first lay him on the ground and sit on his head and knees, beating him up and down with the baton until all his ribs are broken. He hopes that they will remove the bit to take a confession from him, but these torturers are not interested in what he has to say. This torture is not for interrogation, it is simply a prelude to his execution. Hot coals are forced into his ears, his shoulders are dislocated, the *knout* tears the skin from his back, and the Secret Ambassador is trapped through this agony in a claustrophobic and broken body.

Once removed to the block, the bit is torn from his mouth and he begins to hum. He summons all his self-control not to shout in pain when his hands and feet are chopped off. He feels the dislocation of body and soul begin. He can see a duck waddling in dirty puddles beside the stone wall of the Kremlin. A crowd has gathered to watch his death; they shout and throw mud. Still he hums. The axe is raised, its shadow falls, its bite on his skin—

Then he is away, out and over the crowd, directing himself awkwardly into the duck and waddling down to the German suburbs. There, he finds his own cold body and walks in it once more.

What alarm he feels as he walks over fields and through forests, along rivers and over hills. Everywhere he goes he sees signs that Skazki's power is weakening: the family that doesn't leave blini and vodka for the domovoi, the girls who haven't learned midwinter divination from their mothers, the youths who do not plow the crossroads to protect their livestock. Certainly, there are many who do, but Mir is giving up on magic as surely as the years are passing. Petr legislates against charms, enchantments and other superstitions. Sofya, last of the Skazki blood, is confined to a convent. Is he doomed only to wait for news of her death so he can return to his homeland and let the connection falter and dissolve? A last attempt, then, at winning her to his side.

Sofya's rooms at the convent are comfortable enough, with cushions and warm furs, many candles in gilt holders and tapestries to stop the cold from leaching out of the stone walls, but the rooms are empty of voices, of laughter and whispered promises. Sofya lives by herself here. She sees the nuns once a day for supper, but they do not converse about love or about freedom. Outside her chamber window, hung in the most advantageous position for viewing, are ninety-five rotting corpses—the bodies of the men who dared to plot against Petr in Sofya's name. The crows come and peck at them, bits drop off onto the stone walk below, and the ripe smell seeps through cracks under the windows to linger around her while she sleeps.

When the Secret Ambassador steals into her chambers, sunlight sends its first streaks over the horizon. The nearest body, hanging on its beam, is silhouetted by dawn. It slowly turns on its rope: north to south, south to north, creaking. The Secret Ambassador sits on the edge of a chair, elbows on his knees, while he waits for Sofya to return from Matins.

Sofya, divested of her regal splendor, appears smaller than remembered when she arrives.

"I hadn't expected to see your kind here," she says, closing the door firmly behind her. "Especially not in a place of holiness." Secretly, she is glad to see somebody. Alone, she grows bitter. She has lost her freedom and somewhere along the way she has lost her spirit.

"Listen to me, Tsarevna," the Secret Ambassador says, "not all is lost for you."

"Don't fill my head with your heathen nonsense."

"Sofya, you carry in your veins the blood of Skazki, the other world you fear so much. You are its daughter."

"I won't listen."

"The Golden Bear, the favored ornament of your childhood, was made in Skazki. You treasured it because you recognized it as being of your own kind."

A sense of familiarity resonates in Sofya. That bear: how she had loved it. "I should like to see that bear again," she says.

"And so you shall, when you are crowned Empress of all the Russias."

"These dreams are long since gone cold, Secret Ambassador."
She paces to the window, tries to look past the dark bodies that line
her view. "What need have I for power? It won't fill the emptiness."

"If power doesn't interest you, then what of love? I could bring a
man to you, to implant his seed. Children, Sofya, little babies to
hold and keep as your own."

She bends her head to the window, her forehead touching the
cool panes. "A man? What man?"

"Somebody tall and strong, with hot skin—"

"Golitsyn?"

The Secret Ambassador hesitates.

"He is gone," she says. "I know. Banished to the Siberian snowfields. I will not see him again." She turns, tilts her head to one side.
Her brows are very dark and heavy. "No other man will ever touch
me. My skin would die from sadness."

The Secret Ambassador entertains a brief fantasy of forcing
himself upon her, raping her, but he cannot father a child. The old
gods that made him ensured he couldn't reproduce and bring another like him into the world, as much as he likes to indulge himself
in Mir flesh. He wants to weep into his palms. All is lost! Skazki
blood will die with her. The worlds will forever remain apart. Skazki will fade away to watercolor pictures.

Sofya, seeing his distress, softens for a moment.

"Secret Ambassador," she says, "I fought to change my fate. In
vain. I find now that the sour taste of acceptance diminishes over
time. Perhaps now is the moment to taste it for yourself."

Ah, how the Secret Ambassador wants to crush this woman! He
does not. He has a cruel streak, but his intellect can override it. He
leaves Sofya, and he returns to his own world to brood and to wait.

The years pass, as years do.

What do you think he did with those years? I know, because I am
well acquainted with the Secret Ambassador.

He sat in his warm cottage in Skazki, alone. He tried to prepare
himself for the inevitable final sunset. But one morning, his senses
prickled with knowing.

He drew a hand over his mirror, and saw Petr's daughter, Anne. She lived in a grand new city called St. Petersburg, and under her arm she carried a Golden Bear.

What a fool the Secret Ambassador had been! For what feature, if strong enough to be noted, does not occasionally skip a generation, only to return decades later.

And so he watched as Mokosha's blood returned. Anne to little Petr, little Petr to Pavel. The Secret Ambassador visited when he could, to watch, to make contact with Mokosha's descendants and let them know of the heavy responsibility that hung around their shoulders. All of them dismissed him kindly but firmly.

Then, wonder of wonders, three brothers in the one brood began to fight over the Golden Bear as if it were Mir's greatest treasure. Konstantin, Nikolai, Aleksandr.

In Aleksandr, the Secret Ambassador found one of Skazki's greatest allies, and her greatest traitor.

But that is a story for another time.

I have spent too much of the night in telling tales. Morning rushes upon me, Totchka begins to stir in the gray of dawn. The fire has settled low, and my hands are cold. Anticipation heats my veins, though, for soon Rosa will be here. I can sense her nearby. At any moment she will spot my little cottage from the ridge and come down to visit me. I look forward to her arrival very much. Rosa and I, I'm certain, will be able to help each other.

You see, nobody knows the truth about Rosa Kovalenka. Except for me.

PART THREE

Sensation take me, drown my soul,
Give me oblivion.
In the dreaming universe
Pour me, crush me,
Grant me my extinction.

—FYODOR TYUTCHEV

Twenty-seven

Daniel woke to silence.

Dazed, he opened his eyes. They were dazzled by sunlight, streaming through long grass. He turned his face away.

Not quite silence.

The throb of his head.

The gentle breeze whispering across the grass.

Em's breathing.

She lay half on top of him, her cheek resting on his chest, fast asleep. He reached out tentatively, drew back his fingers when he realized she was strangely cold.

She must be dead.

No, she couldn't be dead. She was breathing.

He touched her cheek again. No warmth at all in her skin. Her eyelids flickered and he withdrew his hand.

"Daniel?" she said groggily. The bear was nestled in the crook of her arm.

"I'm right here," he said.

She took a moment, then slowly sat up, putting the bear aside. "Are you okay?" she asked.

"I'm fine," he said, though his head ached and his eyes felt acutely sensitive to the glare of the morning sun. "You?"

"I'm sorry, I had to sleep. It was the only way to escape that monster."

Daniel glanced around. All he could see was grass, so he stood up. The grass was green and pale yellow, waist-high, waving softly. He turned in a circle. As far as he could see, the landscape didn't change.

He turned to Em, who was standing next to him. "Any idea where the hell we are?"

Em gazed at the landscape. The breeze lifted a strand of her hair and brushed it against her cheek. She pushed it behind her ear. "This is the middle of nowhere," she said. "I mean, really."

Daniel checked the ground at his feet. A damp fur, the golden bear. Nothing else.

"And we have nothing?"

"Nothing. No lighter, no food, no firewood, no water."

"Only a golden bear and one fur."

"Perhaps we won't need it." She shielded her eyes against the sun. "It's sunny here."

"I'm certain it will be cold at night." Daniel measured the endless sky, blue tinged with pulsing violet. His eyeballs shivered, and other colors sprang to life. Veins of gold and throbbing green. Just as quickly the sensation fled.

"Then we'll have to find shelter before nightfall," Em said. But she didn't move and neither did Daniel. Both stood, still as statues, gazing out toward the endless horizon of grassland.

Finally, Daniel said, "Which way?"

Em shrugged and Daniel noticed that she looked haggard and pale. "I have no idea. East and east and north-a-ways?"

He shook his head. "We're somewhere else now. Another of the thrice-nine lands. Who knows which direction is right from here?"

"Okay. But it's sunny, so we're in the south. We could head north at least?"

"I don't know. Perhaps we're not in the south. Skazki is made up of stories and fairytale places. We could be anywhere."

Em puffed out her cheeks and sighed. "It's a start," she said. "We can't stand here forever."

They headed north. Em related to Daniel what had happened while he was unconscious. He listened with an increasing sense of terrified wonder, and embarrassed guilt.

"You had to go through all that," he said, "while I just lay there like a dead weight."

"It wasn't your fault."

"You were so close to a crossing . . . You could have gone without me."

"I wouldn't have made it alone. We might find another crossing."

"What would we be looking for exactly?"

"I don't really know. Mirra said they're easier to see at night, or with second sight."

Daniel frowned; some dim memory was trying to struggle to consciousness. It wouldn't come.

"We have to count our blessings," Em was saying. "We've managed to survive this far, without any deadly consequences."

"You almost didn't," he said. "How is your wrist now?"

She stopped and turned to him, holding out her wrist for him to inspect. He slid his palm underneath it to support it. Again he was struck by the chill of her skin.

"It's healed up beautifully," he said.

"You can feel it, though, can't you?" she said. "The cold. I've been like that ever since he touched me. My blood is cold. My muscles are cold. I can't feel the sun on my cheeks, though I can see it's blazing down." Her voice was tight, sad.

He was unsettled by her sadness. He'd taken her emotional stability for granted. "Maybe when we get back . . ."

"Yeah. Sure. When we get back."

They moved on in silence. The long grass sighed like waves around them as the sun climbed high and hot in the violet sky.

At first Rosa thought nothing had happened. Yes, she had felt the veil part, she had seen the flash of colored light skitter across her field of vision.

This place, on the other side of the veil, looked precisely like the place she had left behind. She stood uncertainly, and the bee bumped inside her.

"Sit still," she said, and the bee obeyed.

She glanced left and right. Her senses prickled. Faint music, a sliver of dark light over the ground. Yes, this was somewhere different. She could smell it, hear it. Gray shadows moved as the air shivered; pale stars and a quarter moon were the only light. Forty feet away, she paused near a lone birch sapling. A strand of colored wool, tied around a branch, was flapping in the breeze.

Rosa unpicked the knot and ran it over her fingers. In the dark, the purple and red were dulled, but she still recognized it. The scarf that Daniel had been wearing when he left.

"He's been here," she said. "He's left a trail."

The bee didn't respond.

Rosa wound the wool over her knuckles and peered into the darkness for the next marker. She moved slowly, her gaze examining every shrub and tree. The second one took her twenty minutes to find, the third one even longer. She followed them as the dark dissolved and morning was left in its wake, finally arriving at a stream just as the sun broke over the horizon.

She crouched on the bank, scooping cool water into her mouth. She tied her hair in a knot at her neck and gazed across the stream. No more colored markers fluttering in the dawn light. Where had he gone from here?

A rustle behind her caught her attention. She stood and turned, looking back the way she had come. The woods were sparse, sundappled. A shadow moved in the distance, clung to a tree and waited. Up high, the wind circled in the treetops.

Her skin prickled. The moment of anticipation was intense, violently sweet. She was about to see something amazing, and she wanted to be completely alert for it.

Then it burst from cover. A grizzled man, nearly seven feet tall, skin like bark and hair like dried grass, roaring and barreling toward her. A leshii.

Her heart started. The wind howled, sweeping everything into its brutal arms. Branches snapped and birds flapped from the trees in fear. Rosa leapt back, turned and dashed into the stream. At its deepest point it only came up to her waist. She frantically unwound a strand of colored wool, knotting it and repeating the zagovor.

"As I travel on the road . . . in the fields . . . shit!" She stumbled over a loose rock, steadied herself and clambered out on the opposite bank. The leshii was gaining on her. She quickly ran through the rest of the spell, tied the last knot, then turned to face her pursuer.

"Come on then, barkface," she called, brandishing the protection knot. The wind whipped her hair loose and tugged at her clothes.

He didn't slow, and she had a few brief moments to observe him. What a wonder! She had read of such creatures, but never hoped to see one in the flesh. Her head spun with excitement. The creature approached, was almost upon her.

She threw down the knot. "None shall come near me, my word is firm! So shall it be."

Crash!

The creature tripped on some invisible barrier, thundered to the ground with a yell. The wind abruptly stopped, and she ran as hard as she could, over a ridge and down into open fields.

When ten minutes had passed with no return of the leshii, she slowed and caught her breath.

"Thanks, Anatoly," she said.

The bee buzzed angrily inside her.

"Yeah, yeah. I know you're pissed."

She stretched her arms over her head and turned to survey the countryside. More trees, more grass, more bushes. Hills and hollows, long grass moving shadowy and bright at the behest of the wind. No houses. Dark clouds were moving in, adding a glum chill to the morning and swallowing Anatoly's shadow.

Where was Daniel? More importantly, had he been set upon by a leshii in these woods too? If so, how had he survived?

Maybe he hadn't survived.

"I refuse to believe he's dead," she muttered, pulling another strand of wool off her wrist and knotting it ready for an emergency. She spoke her spell as she walked, following her instincts to the northeast.

As she walked, she made protection knots, tying them around her wrists to use later. A drizzle started to fall, and she pulled up her hood. Before long it had turned to rain, and she hunched down inside her coat and grumbled about it. Despite the discomfort, she had a distinct feeling she was heading in the right direction, and she was happy to trust in it.

An hour passed in the rain before she discovered what was leading her. Over a ridge and down in the valley she saw it: a brightly painted cottage.

At first, she couldn't pick why it looked different to the surrounding area. Then she realized that a bubble of brightness clung to the building. Sunlight shone on its walls, even though rain and dark clouds engulfed the rest of the countryside. She opened her second sight and saw that the bubble extended out at least twenty feet from the walls and swirled with dazzling colors. This was powerful magic.

She hurried toward the cottage, admiring the neat blue paint, the decorated wooden shutters. A bird sat on the eaves, cleaning its feathers. Tidy garden beds lined the path. She didn't know who lived here, but she knew without a doubt she was being invited in.

As if to confirm this, the door opened as she approached. She slipped into the bubble of brightness, out of the rain. Sunlight warmed her face as she pushed off her hood. A figure moved to the door, his face flaring into shadow as the sun hit her eyes. But his voice was friendly, even relieved.

"Welcome, Rosa," he said. "I've been waiting for you."

As the day wore on and the afternoon grew bright, Em and Daniel continued their journey across the undulating, treeless plains. Cloud shadows were the only changing feature of the landscape. Em's feet were moving, but distance telescoped to nothing: she may as well have been walking on the spot. Each low rise was greeted by another identical vista, shimmering green-gold grass stretching away for miles. The sunlight was brilliant, and Daniel was perspiring. Em longed for some of that warmth, but it was three A.M.–cold in her blood, and her elbows were drawn close to her body to brace against it.

"You know what I hate the most?" Daniel said.

"What?"

"I can't stop wondering if we'd headed south whether we'd have found something by now."

"But if we turn around and go back, food or shelter, or maybe, even a crossing, may be just over the next rise."

"Exactly. That's exactly what I think."

"We are nowhere. And we have no idea how close we are to anywhere." She turned her palms up. "We just have to be decisive and keep moving, and don't think about what might have been. We can't slip into despair. Come on, let's play a game to take your mind off it. List all the foreign swear words you know."

"Nothing's as good as English to swear in," he said, swatting a fly from his cheek. "I've yet to find a word as good as 'fuck' to express so many emotions: fear, amazement, anger . . ."

"I've always been fond of the way Germans use 'ass' for everything: ass-busy, ass-cold."

Daniel shrugged. "I don't have the heart for word games, Em."

"Talk to me about something else then."

"I don't have the heart for conversation." He scratched the back of his head. "Sorry. I'm hungry, I'm thirsty."

Em scanned around. "Looks like grass for dinner. And muddy puddles for aperitifs."

They stopped while the sun sank, to rest and nibble the juicy ends of grass stalks. It was nothing like food; perhaps not even digestible, but it seemed to lift their spirits. Em's jaw ached so she chewed cautiously. She could feel with her tongue a tender swelling where her tooth used to be. The temperature plunged and Daniel suggested they keep moving.

"Walking will warm me up, and we're more likely to see a crossing at night," he said.

"You're right. We'll rest in daylight, move in the dark."

As they continued through the grass, Em felt the first glimmerings of a desolation so hot and real that it made her want to cry. The fields stretching on forever, the dull shadows of night, the faint glow of a quarter moon. The ache of hunger, the shudder of cold, the maddening irritation of the grass seeds that worked their way under her clothes and itched against her skin. They may as well have been wandering in outer space, tracing impossible distances from anyone or anything. Her body felt frail and skinny, her ribs ached. Night settled in, the grass whispered around them, and the stars offered their pitiful warmth grudgingly.

Then, as they were cresting a low rise, Daniel said, "I see something."

Em's head snapped up. She could see it too. A white figure, standing in the field in the distance.

"What is it?"

"A person?"

"It's standing very still."

"It looks like a statue."

"A statue isn't much use to us."

"But it might mean there's civilization of some sort around here."

They hurried down the slope and across the field. The white figure was still. Odd that it was just standing there in the wide, distant nowhere. Incongruous, like the out-of-place detail in an otherwise pleasant dream that adds a sinister undertone to the whole. Only starlight and summer breezes touched the figure.

"Somebody must have carved it," she said to Daniel. "Somebody's been here."

"But when? It might be centuries old."

As they drew nearer, Em could see more detail. "She," she said. "It's a statue of a woman."

Down the slope they went, foot after foot, as they had done for miles already. They approached the statue, and Daniel drew a sharp gasp.

"What?" Em said, slowing her pace and hanging back.

"Oh, no. Em, this is too weird."

"What's wrong?" She peered through the dark at the statue. It was an old woman with closed eyes, wearing a peasant dress and a headscarf pulled low over her brow.

"That's Nanny Rima."

She turned. "What?"

"That . . . it's Nanny Rima. My Russian nanny."

Em grabbed his elbow and they inched forward, pausing a tentative two feet from the statue.

"This must be some kind of hallucination," he said, almost under his breath.

Em glanced from the statue to Daniel, and back again. "Why would there be a statue of your Russian nanny standing in the middle of the steppe?"

Silence reigned for a few moments between them, as the wind shivered over the grass.

"What do we do?" Em asked at last.

Daniel shook his head. "I don't know."

Em considered the statue. "She has a kind face," she said, and reached out to brush the statue's cheek with the back of her hand.

Ah!

A gasp, the sudden exhalation of a long-held breath. Color flooded into the statue's face and her eyes fluttered open.

Em jumped back. Daniel yelped in fear.

"Ha! Fooled you!" the old woman cackled, raising her hands in delight.

Daniel was backing away.

"No, no. Don't run. I'm not going to hurt you."

Em caught Daniel's wrist and held him next to her. "Who are you?"

"I don't know," the woman said. "I don't have a name, but I can whistle a merry tune. Listen." With a quick breath, she launched into a Russian folk tune that Em half-recognized. It was an eerie note in the gray darkness, and she could feel Daniel pulling on her hand.

"We should go," he said. "We don't know what she'll do to us."

"I won't do anything to you!" the old woman protested. "Ha! Why are you so afraid of me?"

Em offered the woman a smile. "You resemble somebody Daniel once knew."

"Yes, yes, of course I do. I stole her face out of his memory as you were coming down the slope. Neither of you could bear to look at me otherwise. *Polevoi* aren't known for their beauty."

Em looked at Daniel, who nodded. "Polevoi. Field spirit," he said. "Mostly harmless."

"Of course I'm harmless. I told you that. What was the woman's name?" the polevoi asked.

"Nanny Rima," Daniel replied.

"Then that name will suit me just fine, thank you." She reached out to grasp Daniel's hand. Her gnarled knuckles squeezed his fingers tight. "Dear boy."

Daniel started to smile, then checked himself. "Where are we?" he asked.

"In the middle of a grass plain."

"We need food and clean water," Em said. "We have nothing to offer you in return for your help."

Rima waved her hand. "Ah, I want nothing from you. I'd like to help. Follow me." She turned and headed northwest.

Em and Daniel exchanged glances.

"Your call," Em said.

"I think we should follow her," Daniel said.

"Okay."

They fell into step just behind her, as she started whistling the melancholy tune again. Em allowed herself to hope, just a little, that they might soon have a warm meal in front of them.

The tune quivered away to nothing. Rima sighed and said, "That one always makes me sad."

"It's beautiful," Em said. "Do you live nearby?"

"I live right here," Rima said. "Wherever I am is where I live."

"So you're not taking us to a house?"

"No."

"Then where?"

"I know where to find food and wood for a fire, and I know a crystal stream of pure, clear water by a shady grove." Her voice grew almost rapturous. "You just follow me."

"How well do you know this area, then?" Daniel asked.

"It's inscribed in my heart. I'm part of it." She slowed so that Em and Daniel were forced to walk beside her. She smiled a grandmotherly smile. "You want more than food and water, don't you?"

"We want to get home," Em said. "Home to Mir. We have two options: either we find the Snow Witch—"

"The Snow Witch!"

"You know of her?"

"Yes, yes. She's the most important person in Skazki. They say that her death would bring about the ruin of us all." Rima clicked her tongue. "Oh, the Snow Witch! I know of her!"

"We need to find her," Daniel said.

"Impossible. You're in the wrong land."

"The wrong land?"

"You'd need to find a crossing."

"That's our other option. Find a crossing and use it to get back to Mir."

Rima shook her head. "Well, you can't simply tell a crossing where you'd like it to go. It will take you where it wants to take you."

"What do you mean?"

"They cross each other all over the place, between all the lands, between Skazki and Mir. Too complicated to explain, I'm afraid."

"Try me," Em said, keeping the exasperation out of her voice.

"It's all right, though, because you're in luck. I know where there's a crossing nearby, direct to Mir, no complications."

Relief flooded through her. She heard Daniel sigh.

"Really?" Em said.

"Yes, yes. I'm not lying. Not lying even a little."

"Can you take us there?"

"I'm taking you there now. A few hours. Maybe a little more. Just follow me." She lifted her face to the sky and sniffed the air. "You know, there's rain coming. Clouds closing in." She turned and gave them a shadowy smile. "Stay by me, won't you?"

Twenty-eight

Rosa raised her hand to shield her eyes from the sun and considered the man in front of her. He was very tall, dressed in black trousers and a peasant smock knotted at the hips. He had long gray hair tied loosely at his neck, a full gray beard and a large, hooked nose. It was impossible to tell his age. He resembled a man of seventy, except for his eyes, which betrayed centuries of knowledge: they were a peculiar gray-blue color, very pale and with small pupils. Wolf's eyes, she thought, right before recognition swiped her.

"Oh," she said.

He gave her a wolfish smile. "You know me, don't you?"

"I've seen photographs."

"Pah, cameras! I wish they'd never been invented. I once had anonymity. Though I suppose you think I've aged?"

"Not as much as you should have," she laughed.

"There are many impossible things here, Rosa." He held out his hand and she took it boldly. "Call me Papa Grigory," he said, gently tugging her hand. "Come."

"Thank you, Papa Grigory."

He led her over the threshold and into a neat one-room cottage. The area was large, with a gleaming colored stove, a rough-hewn table, faded rugs and a huge wooden bed. The room smelled of lavender and dust. Sitting at the table, drawing with the deformed stump of a crayon, was a little girl of about six years old.

"Hello," Rosa said as the little girl looked up.

The child peered at her from under suspicious brows. Her eyes were dark, her hair chestnut brown. She had thin wrists, dark shadows under her eyes, pale skin, and an oddly swollen throat. She looked ill, and the wheezy coughing fit that followed confirmed it.

Papa Grigory was unperturbed by the cough. "Rosa, this is my little girl. Her name is Totchka. Totchka, say hello."

Totchka caught her breath and, unsmiling, said, "Hello, Rosa."

"Good girl. That's my good girl," said Grigory, smoothing the child's hair. "Now, I have to talk to Rosa. Why don't you go outside and play with your seashells?"

Totchka grudgingly pushed her chair back and climbed to her feet. "Don't leave the light," Grigory said. "Stay in the garden. It's wet out there."

"Yes, Papa," she said, lifting a bucket of seashells that sat by the door and wandering out into the garden.

"I collected them on the shores of the Mediterranean," Grigory said, turning to Rosa. "I never knew they'd be so useful. She spends hours with them pretending to be at the seaside, spotting imaginary boats. I wish I could take her to the sea, give her real details to fill her imagination."

"Can't you?"

He shook his head sadly and indicated she should sit. "Totchka can't leave Skazki. She would die."

"Skazki?"

"That is where you are."

Rosa took a seat. "And I came from . . . ?"

"Mir."

"Of course," she said, smiling. "How do you know who I am?"

"The bear. I've been alert to all three of you since she chose you."

Rosa's heart leapt. "Daniel? He's still alive?"

"Oh yes. Lost, exhausted, but still alive. His friend Em, too. She's a wily one."

Sweet relief in her veins. Daniel was alive.

Grigory wandered over to the kitchen bench. "Have you eaten anything since your adventure started?"

"Only a volkhv," she said.

He laughed as he sliced bread and cheese. "Not very tasty, I imagine."

"Bitter," Rosa said as he placed a plate of food on the table and sat across from her. "Thank you."

"I expect you have questions."

Rosa took a slice of bread. "About a million. I don't even know where to start. I need to find Daniel."

"I want you to find Daniel, too, and I will help you. It will be simple, and you must bring him and the Golden Bear back here. He has set himself on a perilous path. He believes he must take the Golden Bear to the Snow Witch."

"Who's the Snow Witch?"

"Only the most hideous and dangerous creature in all of Skazki." His voice dropped to a low rumble and his pupils contracted to pinpoints. His hands moved nervously on the tabletop. "If the Snow Witch should catch Daniel, she will fill his mind with icy nightmares until his brain turns on itself in distress. She will drink his blood because she likes the taste of his fear. She will split open his white chest and feast on his ardent heart. Fear her, Rosa. She is a monster."

A wave of fear for Daniel swept over her. "Daniel doesn't know this?"

"He's defenseless against her." Papa Grigory smiled, his mood changing suddenly, sending deep lines arrowing from his eyes. "You aren't to worry, I'm certain he will be safe. You'll find him before she does." He rose again, full of some nervous energy that couldn't endure inertia. He opened the stove and poked the embers, scratched at a carbon smudge on the painted tiles.

Rosa finished eating and brushed crumbs from her fingers. She turned to the window, and watched Totchka through the thick panes. The little girl was hunched over her bucket at the very edge of the sunlight's circle, laying out shells in neat rows.

"Is she from Mir?" Rosa asked.

Grigory walked to the window and looked out. "Yes. I saved her from a cruel illness. Ninety years ago."

Rosa told herself not to be surprised. This was a land of impossibilities. "She's still a child?"

Grigory turned and leaned his back against the window. "Yes, she's still a child. She will always remain a child, because she was fated to die as a child. In Skazki, her own death can't find her."

"And what is her own death?"

"Diphtheria. Like her mother and brothers. A poor family living in a basement near Moika Canal in St. Petersburg. If I hadn't happened by, that death would have found her. Now you see why she can't go back to Mir."

Rosa considered this, and a glimmer of an idea began to sing to her. "Is it . . . can my death find me here?"

Grigory shook his head. "No, Rosa. The only death that can find you here is a death not-your-own."

The room seemed to pulse with light. A burden, too long laid across her heart, grew light. *It can't find me here.* The future was suddenly filled with possibilities.

"Rosa?"

She looked up at Grigory, who had moved to stand beside her. "Sit down," she said, smiling. "You're making me nervous."

He eased into his chair, but his fingertips still moved, brushing delicate arabesques on the table. "Rosa, if the Snow Witch gets the Golden Bear, terrible things will happen."

"What terrible things?"

"All the horrors of Skazki will be released into Mir. Leshii will stalk the highways, fire demons will descend on the cities, witches and wizards will travel wherever they please and indulge their hideous appetites. From Russia they will find their way to every curve of the globe. Nobody will be safe in Mir. There are only twenty-seven volkhvy to watch the crossings. Twenty-seven men against an army of monsters! It cannot be allowed to happen."

The bee buzzed and bumped in her stomach. She laid her hand across her belly and said, "Shh, Anatoly. I can't concentrate."

"He is frantic because he knows it is true." Grigory leaned forward and placed a gentle hand over Rosa's fingers. She felt herself trapped in his powerful, unwavering gaze. "All of Mir's hopes rest with you, Rosa Kovalenka. You must intercept Daniel and Em and take the bear back to Mir. Hide her where nobody will ever find her."

"Of course," she said. "Of course I'll do it. I'll leave now, if you tell me which way to go."

"Tomorrow," he said, "at first light. There are preparations to be made, and you should rest and eat well. Skazki is a harsh land. No-body should wander into it without due caution."

"Fine. Whatever you say," she said. "I'll leave tomorrow."

Night turned into morning, and morning grew into daylight, and Em and Daniel were still following Nanny Rima through the noth-ingness. The sky was leaden. Although Daniel was glad it wasn't raining, the clouds obscured any light from the sun. Direction was meaningless; north could be anywhere. The road to forever was a sea of long grass, sealed to a sweep of dark-gray sky. It seemed they were inside rather than outside, in a vast enclosed space from which there was no escape.

"How far now, Rima?" he asked. He was trying to be on his guard around the polevoi, but this was proving difficult. Nanny Rima was one of his fondest memories, and the creature leading them looked identical. Except for the odd, birdlike eyes.

"Not far."

Em sighed and stopped. "I need to rest."

Daniel turned to her. "You can't go any further?"

"She's been saying 'not far' for hours."

"I'm not lying to you!" Rima said. "It's *not far*. It's not my prob-lem if Mir bodies feel the distance more than Skazki bodies."

Em looked pointedly at Daniel. "A short rest. Please."

Rima nodded, suddenly sympathetic. "Of course, little one. Of course you can rest, poor girl."

Em lowered herself carefully, and Daniel sat with her. As soon as stillness hit him, he wondered how he was ever going to stand up again. His thighs trembled and his heart gasped in relief. Rima paced around them in a circle, whistling melancholy tunes and chattering.

"I've just remembered that on the way to the Mir crossing, there's a field of wild mushrooms! Won't they be delicious? Wonder-ful rabbit hunting there, too. You know, I can charm a rabbit into my hands." She crouched and feigned an elaborate beckoning ges-ture. "We'll split him open, stuff him with mushrooms and roast him until his flesh is so tender it falls off the bone."

Daniel realized he was salivating.

"And a crystal stream, water so sweet you'd swear it had honey in it. Honey! Of course, there are wild bees on the way. In a wood just a little way from here. We'll stop and eat honey." She clapped her hands together. "What a feast we'll have!"

"It sounds wonderful, Rima," Daniel said. "How far do you think? In miles?"

She turned her bird eyes on him, blinked once. "What are miles?"

He and Em exchanged glances.

"How many hours then?" Em asked.

"As many as it takes. Not long. By nightfall, certainly."

"Let's get going," Em said, struggling to her feet.

"But, Em, you're tired," said Daniel.

"I'm tired of being in Skazki. The sooner we leave, the sooner we get home."

The day gave way to evening, the stars hid behind the thick layer of clouds. Em was slow, walking with difficulty. Daniel held her elbow and tried to help her along, and was startled by the narrow distance across the back of her arm. Every time he whispered to her that she should rest, she drew her mouth into a line and shook her head and said, "It'll be worth it. We'll eat, we'll find a crossing."

Rima clucked about slow walkers making the journey too long, but nothing could hasten Em's steps.

But then, somewhere in the darkest wedge of night, Em stopped.

"Em?" Daniel asked.

She was standing stock still, staring at the ground. Her shoulders were shaking.

"Em," he said again, panicking. "Are you all right?"

Rima had stopped too, and was standing back with a half-smile on her face.

Em looked up, her eyes glittering in the dark. "I've seen this rock before."

"What?"

"This rock," she said, jabbing her finger toward the ground. "I've seen it before. She's leading us in circles!"

"Oh no! No!" Rima cried. "It's not true. All rocks look alike, it's dark. I'm not leading you in circles. I'm leading you toward home and comfort."

Daniel's attention flicked from one woman to the other. "Are you sure, Em?"

"Of course I'm sure. I never forget anything. I have seen this rock before. We passed here in the early afternoon. She's led us in a big circle."

"I have not! You're the one who's making this journey hard. You're too slow. You always have to stop to drink from puddles, and now you're going crazy with tiredness and hunger. It's a different rock."

"And look!" said Em, warming to her subject now. "The grass here is bent. Somebody has walked here recently. Us!"

"The wind bends the grass. Walk five feet in any direction and you'll see bent grass, and other rocks." Rima turned to Daniel. "Tell her she's seeing things. I'm trying to help you."

Daniel wavered. Ordinarily he'd trust Em, but she looked sick and shaky. The polevoi had promised them the two things they wanted most in the world: sustenance and a way home. It would be foolish to get her off-side if Em's exhaustion was making her hysterical.

"I think we need to rest," he said cautiously.

"No," moaned Rima. "No rest. Keep going and we'll be there. Soon."

He shook his head. "Em's going to have to sleep."

Rima snapped her fingers. "I'll show you. I'll go on ahead and find some mushrooms and bring them back for you to taste. Then you'll see I'm not lying."

Daniel helped Em to the ground. "There's no need for that. Em will rest, and then we'll move on."

"I insist," Rima said. "Wait right here. I'll be back in no time."

Daniel felt a twinge of concern as Rima's white figure disappeared into the dark, her melancholy song dwindling to nothing on the summer breeze.

Em was resting her head on her knees. "I'm sorry, Daniel. Maybe I was wrong."

"Get some sleep, Em," he said, smoothing her hair. "By the time you wake, she might be back with mushrooms."

"I don't trust her."

"Poisonous mushrooms, then," he joked.

She lifted her head and smiled wryly. "I'd still eat them."

He nodded wearily. "So would I."

Em lay on her side in the long grass, and Daniel sat close beside her, huddling under the fur. No warmth to take comfort in from Em's body. He watched her as she fell asleep, then cast his gaze over the wide dull nothing that surrounded them. A breeze tickled the grass, sending ripples of gray movement across the plains. He rested his chin on his knees and waited for Rima.

Em rose slowly to consciousness. Her hands were folded beneath her head and shoulder, and she felt something hard under her fingers. A rock? She moved her fingers to brush it away, but it was stuck to her.

She sat up, rubbed her shoulder. The hard lump was her bone, jutting through skin. Daniel was sitting, his back to her, watching the clouds dissolve on the dawn sky.

"Daniel?" she said.

He turned. "She didn't come back."

Em could have wept. No wild mushrooms, no juicy roasted rabbit, no honey, no clean water.

"We shouldn't have trusted her," she said.

"If we wait here . . . maybe . . ."

Em shook her head and brushed stray hair from her eyes.

"We headed northwest, Daniel. The sun's rising there . . ." She jabbed her finger toward the intensifying glow in the east. "That means we're now facing southeast. She led us in circles. She got us lost on purpose. We're probably right back where we started."

Daniel sagged into his knees. "Why *did* we trust her, Em?"

"Because we're desperate," Em said, brushing grass seeds off her clothes.

Daniel turned his gaze back to the sky, and Em noticed he was squinting and drawing his brows down, then shaking his head as if to clear his vision.

"What are you doing?" she asked.

"Ever since I woke up from the russalki's enchantment, my eyes have been doing strange things."

"What kind of strange?"

"It's as though . . ." He squinted again. "It's as though I can see an extra layer of air. With colors. Now that the clouds have gone, I can see the sky has streaks of gold through it. Can you see that?"

Em looked at the sky. It was more violet-hued than the sky at home, but there were no streaks of unusual color. "No."

"I wonder what it is," he muttered, turning his hands over in front of his eyes and peering at them. "It's strange."

"Something the russalki did to you? To see underwater?"

Daniel's head jerked up. "Oh. I remember. Lobasta wanted me to see the bear, in the rock pool. She said . . ." He drew his brows down in concentration. "So much of it is a blur."

Em glanced away discreetly. She had seen and heard too much of what the russalki did to Daniel, and didn't want to see his embarrassment if he remembered too.

He fell silent. She turned back.

"Daniel?"

"She said she was giving me a second sight."

Em drew a breath, then smiled. "And with second sight, you can find a crossing."

"I can find a crossing."

Em felt laughter bubbling up. "We can find a crossing. You have second sight. We can probably find other things, too. Turn it on . . . go on. Can you spot any food out there? Which direction should we go?"

Daniel spun in a slow circle, squinting like a schoolboy at a multiplication problem. "Food . . . water . . . come on." He returned to his original position and shook his head sadly. "I don't sense anything. Maybe it's not working right."

"You probably need to practice. Just try to find the direction we should travel. Just turn off the thinking part of your brain and see what happens."

"That way," he said, without hesitation, indicating east.

She nodded. "Good work."

"Em, are you okay to walk?"

She wasn't okay. She could feel her body starting to close down, her poor heart protesting, her muscles and bones trembling. But there was nothing else she could do.

"Let's move for a few hours and see what happens," she said. "We might be closer to home than we think."

While the rain intensified outside, the comfort bubble around Papa Grigory's cottage stayed warm and dry. Night did come, but it was soft and forgiving, not the miserable cold of a windy, rain-soaked Russian night. Rosa sat at the wooden table while Grigory told Totchka a long story about Princess Vasilisa the beautiful.

Rosa was warm, comfortable, hopeful, and a little impatient.

Finally, the little girl dragged under by sleep, Grigory joined her at the table.

"She is a beautiful child, isn't she?" he said, sighing, his gaze still attached to Totchka.

Rosa didn't reply. In truth, she thought Totchka grim-faced and unfriendly, but parents were always blind to their children's faults. She indicated the collection of dolls lined up at the end of Totchka's bed. Their linen heads were faceless. "Why don't her dolls have faces?" she asked.

"She's superstitious. Her mother once told her that bad magic could get into dolls with faces and make them come alive." He shook his head, smiling. "She doesn't outgrow her childhood fears, even though I've promised that nothing of the sort could ever happen to her here. I protect her from everything bad."

"Like rain?"

"Sometimes I let a little rain in. I'm thinking of opening the sky tonight. The garden needs watering."

"How do you do it?"

Grigory turned his attention to her, twitching his eyebrows comically and feigning an ominous voice. "Magic. Haven't you heard the tales about me?"

Rosa laughed. "That's powerful magic. You have the bubble around the cottage the whole time?"

"Yes."

"Isn't that exhausting?"

"How else do you think an ageless creature like myself has aged so dramatically?" he said. "For centuries, I resembled a man of forty. In the short time I have been blessed with Totchka's love, I have grown wrinkled and spotted."

"Will you die?"

He shook his head. "I can't die."

Totchka stirred and his eyes were drawn back to her. "My immortality once made me fearless. I never realized until I met Totchka that one could fear something much more than one's own death," he said. "I love her so dearly. It grows every day." He smiled at Rosa. "Impossibly."

"You must adore her to expend so much energy on magic sunshine."

"The circle of light protects us from more than inclement weather, Rosa. Skazki is dangerous. It teems with hungry spirits, and Totchka is defenseless. She wouldn't survive a week without it, without me."

Rosa's eyes went to the window, but all she could see were reflections: the warm glow of candlelight, her own pale face. "How long would I survive, Grigory?"

"That would depend. Are you going to set Anatoly free?"

"Eventually." A bump and buzz in her stomach. "Though he doesn't deserve it. I have no magic of my own now. It's all gone."

"Then you would be almost defenseless in Skazki too."

"Almost defenseless. But my own death couldn't find me."

"Well now, Rosa. What about these questions?" Papa Grigory said, but his expression betrayed no puzzlement. "What do you want to tell me?"

"Nothing. Just yet." She tapped her fingers on the tabletop. "I'm keen to go. Must I wait until morning? What if Daniel needs me before then?"

"We need to make preparations."

"We spent all day baking bread and packing."

"You need to rest. You can have my side of the bed. I'll sleep on the floor."

Rosa glanced at the warm bed, the sleeping hump of the little girl's shoulder. It did look inviting, and she was tired.

"Go, Rosa. Sleep. I have a few things to take care of."

Rosa woke in the dark, her head too full of thoughts to regain sleep. Totchka slumbered on, untroubled. Rosa sat up and allowed her eyes to adjust to the dark. She could make out the shape of the table and the chairs. The stove popped and cracked softly. Papa Grigory was nowhere in sight. She quietly folded back the covers and rose, stopping to smooth the blanket over Totchka's shoulder. The little girl muttered in her sleep, then settled. Rosa watched her a moment, wondering why a man like Grigory had adopted such an odd creature as his daughter. He clearly adored her.

Curious, she laid her hand gently across the crown of Totchka's head and focused her second sight, sent it like a searching beam into the girl's farthest memories. Totchka made an expression of irritation that passed as quickly as it arrived. Her furrowed brow was momentarily so much like Grigory's that Rosa nearly laughed: it was as though living in close proximity for so long had given them the family similarities that blood couldn't provide. Rosa closed her eyes, drew distinct impressions of a messy birth. A name came to her: Mila. A father? No, only a shadow there. Then another impression: cold, in the open air. A wailing baby on a church step. Being passed into callous hands. A brief, cruel childhood marred by illness. Then the tall man with the beard. Grigory.

Rosa opened her eyes. The impressions told her little, except that Totchka had led a miserable existence until Grigory had taken her in. But still, what explained the connection between them? Grigory must have seen many people suffer, why had Totchka's suffering in particular touched him so deeply? Was love that much of a mystery?

Rosa tiptoed across the cottage to the front door, then stole out into the garden. Rain fell lightly, warm drops on her cheeks and nose. She couldn't see Grigory anywhere, but movement outside the bubble caught her eye. Was that him in the trees? Hesitantly, she took a step outside the protective circle. Cold, wet wind on her right leg; sweet, balmy rain on her left. She almost drew back inside the bubble. It was late and she was tired, but she was curious. The freezing downpour soaked her in two seconds. Arms crossed over her chest against the cold, she called, "Papa Grigory?"

"Over here," he said.

She followed his voice into a broad stand of trees, and found him bent over a large dark shape. "What are you doing?" she asked.

Grigory straightened. His hair was soaked. She could see, now, that he stood next to a huge pile of deadfall. Branches and twigs and leaves piled to shoulder height in the middle of a ring of trees.

"You can help," he said. "We have to clear this away."

"Why?"

"There's something underneath it that you'll need for your journey." He bent over the pile again, throwing off debris.

"Can't we do it in the morning? Or when the rain lets up?"

"It's good to suffer from time to time, Rosa," he said, heaving a branch onto the ground. "It reminds you you're alive."

Rosa helped him in dragging branches from the pile, parting overgrown vines and clearing heaps of leaf matter. Her hands were muddy, her clothes were soaked, but her heart was pounding from the vigorous activity.

"So what are we looking for under here?" Rosa asked.

"A sleigh," said Grigory, not pausing from his work.

"A sleigh?"

"You can't go on foot. You'll never catch up with them. Only I have the power to collapse the crossings. And I'm not leaving Totchka."

"And what's going to pull it?"

"It pulls itself through the sky." He braced himself and began to roll a huge log out of the way. "Come, Rosa, help me with this one."

She moved to the other side and put her shoulder to the log. Rain ran down her cheeks and her neck, her hair clung to her face.

She pushed as hard as she could, straining the muscles in her arms and back, and the log began to give.

"There!" said Papa Grigory, and the log rolled, pulling a veil of vines and dead leaves behind it. Beneath, exposed now to the rain, was the front end of a black sleigh. Its curved bow was painted with two enormous bird eyes, and came to a black point that resembled a beak.

"This is Voron," he said, stroking the curves lovingly. "Raven son-of-Raven. He's been in my family for years."

Rosa nodded, peeling back some more vines. "It's beautiful. Doesn't it get damaged out here?"

"No, it remains always new." He scratched a smudge off the bar. "This sleigh will take you wherever you want to go."

Rosa cleared debris from around the skis, unable to hide her pleasure. A magic sleigh to travel a land of wonders.

"Voron pleases you, Rosa?"

"Oh, yes. I can't wait to go."

Grigory suddenly stopped what he was doing, his head snapping up. "Can you hear that?" he asked.

"What? No." Rosa tuned into the darkness, could only hear rain.

"Totchka. She's crying." He dropped his handful of twigs and started toward the cottage.

Rosa hurried behind him. "What do you think is wrong?"

"Her cough sometimes wakes her up. What I wouldn't give to make her better."

Rosa followed him in the dark, thinking about Anatoly and his daughter. Elizavetta may even be dead by the time Anatoly returned. She felt a twinge of guilt.

"I'm sure she's all right," Rosa said.

"If she wakes and I'm not there, it panics her," Grigory answered, as they stepped back into the bubble and out of the heavy rain.

Totchka was at the door in her nightdress, looking thin and frightened. "Papa! Where were you?"

"Hush, child. All is well. Return to your bed," he said, ushering Totchka back into the warm cottage.

"I can't sleep now. I'll have nightmares."

Rosa closed the door behind them.

"Then let me change into some dry clothes and I'll tell you a story."

Totchka, sniffling, agreed to this. Grigory gave Rosa one of his shirts to change into, and she hung her own clothes by the fire and climbed into bed next to the little girl.

Papa Grigory pulled up a chair and he stroked his beard and made hums and hahs of consideration.

"Which story, now?" he asked.

"The French king!" Totchka said. "Mother Moist Earth and the French king. You know it's my favorite."

"Very well," said Grigory. "Lie still and listen quietly."

Twenty-nine

"In a certain land, at a certain time, there lived a great and noble Tsar named Aleksandr, who ruled over his people wisely and lovingly," Papa Grigory began.

"Aleksandr," Totchka breathed with a rapturous smile, pulling the blankets up to her chin. "He was very handsome," she said to Rosa.

"Aleksandr was so special," continued Grigory, "because he was the half-blood prince of a magic kingdom. In days long ago, a beautiful magical princess had come and blessed his family. His ancestors had rejected their magical blood, but Aleksandr did not. He was thrilled by it, and he kept close by his side a Golden Bear which had been made in the magic kingdom."

"Tell me more about the bear," Totchka said, her eyes widening as though she really wanted to know and really wanted Grigory to keep it from her, too. Rosa thought she'd very much like to hear more about the bear, but Grigory was dismissive.

"They are stories for another time, Totchka," he said. "Not for such a little girl as you."

Totchka whined and pouted, and Rosa had the distinct sense that this particular game had been played out between them many times.

"Now, Aleksandr honored his magic blood by installing at his court a wise and powerful man from the magic kingdom. What was his name, Totchka?"

"The Secret Ambassador," Totchka replied solemnly.

"Indeed it was," Grigory said, reaching out to smooth her hair.

"Tell me about where Aleksandr and the Secret Ambassador lived, Papa," Totchka said.

"Aleksandr lived in a grand and beautiful city on the gulf, called St. Petersburg. Its avenues were broad and clean, and the stone buildings were painted in gorgeous hues. Nowhere in the world were there larger parks, more beautiful ironwork, brighter canals or more glittering domes and towering spires. What a city! Aleksandr's palace was the crowning glory, adorned inside with so much gold, so many fine objects and precious things that it cannot be told in a tale, or written with a pen.

"The Secret Ambassador had his own special lodgings at this palace, and consulted with Aleksandr nearly every day. Not for more than a thousand years had an ambassador from the magic kingdom had such intimate and powerful influence in the affairs of the kingdom of men.

"But bright lights produce dark shadows, and there were many close to Aleksandr who thought the Secret Ambassador a mystical fool. Especially one wicked, wicked woman, the Tsar's own sister."

"Ekaterina!" Totchka said with a scowl.

"Yes, Ekaterina. She was the most beautiful princess in Russia. When she opened her window to look at the bright day, even the wind sighed in longing. When she grew sad, even the rainclouds cried. Everyone was in love with her, even Aleksandr himself, her own brother.

"He mooned over her, wrote long love letters, trembled at her disapproval and jumped like a pup at her good grace. 'Ekaterina Pavlovna,' he would say, 'what would you have me do to make you love me?'

" 'Dear brother,' she replied. 'I already love you, as is fit for a sister. But, should you wish to please me further, you can tame a little bluebird to sit at my window, so I may be greeted by him every morning.'

"Aleksandr duly arranged her wish: he found a bird-tamer and a bird, and the tamer spent weeks and months at the task. Then, when it was complete, Ekaterina only huffed and said she was no longer fond of bluebirds.

" 'Well, then, Ekaterina Pavlovna,' Aleksandr said, 'what would you have me do to make you love me?'

" 'Dear brother, I already love you, as is fit for a sister. But, should you wish to please me further, you can build me a garden seat of larkspur and jessamine, so I may sit on it on sunny afternoons.'

"And so, Aleksandr hired a carpenter, bought the flowers and the lacquer, and the craftsman spent weeks and months at the task.

Then, when it was complete, Ekaterina only huffed and said she was no longer fond of larkspur and jessamine.

"'Well, then, Ekaterina Pavlovna,' Aleksandr said, 'what would you have me do to make you love me?'

"'Dear brother, I already love you, as is fit for a sister. But, should you wish to please me further, you can assemble me an orchestra of beautiful virgins playing silver instruments so I may listen to the purest music there is.'

"What do you think Aleksandr did, Totchka?"

"He found the orchestra, and had the instruments made, and taught them the songs himself, because he was very musical," Totchka said, her little girl's voice mimicking Grigory's storytelling meticulousness. "Then Ekaterina didn't want the music anymore."

"Just so," Grigory said, "because she was impossible to please, though Aleksandr never saw this.

"Ekaterina wanted too much from Tsar Aleksandr, but the Secret Ambassador wanted only one thing from him. He wanted the magic kingdom to be invited back into the lives of the kingdom of men. If Tsar Aleksandr would only make a declaration of brotherly love for his half-blood magical family, then the Secret Ambassador need fear no longer that his magic kingdom would wither and die. Aleksandr said he would think about it but, in truth, he was so concerned about his sister's love that he put off giving an answer for weeks and months and years. He enjoyed the fruits of his youth, and was very happy.

"But not all was well in Aleksandr's world, because in the west, there was a great emperor. The mighty commander of the greatest army ever known, and his name was . . ."

Grigory looked to Totchka again, who gave a theatrical shudder and spat the name, "Napoleon."

"Yes, the French king. Napoleon, a man in love with death. Kingdom after kingdom fell to his Grand Army. Napoleon was of lowly birth and the fire in his belly was white-hot. Mighty ambition drove him, he would stop at nothing. This is why he was one of Mir's most famous captains. This is why Aleksandr was so afraid of him."

Totchka settled under her blankets, her fingers twining in her own hair as Grigory shifted in his chair and continued his tale.

"Do you know where Tilsit is, Totchka?" asked Papa Grigory.

The little girl nodded. "It's in Eastern Prussia. I've never been there."

"I have," said Rosa. "It's part of Russia now. It's called Sovetsk. I think it's quite famous for cheese." She smiled at Totchka. "The river's very pretty."

Totchka wore admiration in her eyes for Rosa. "You have seen the Memel River? Where Napoleon met Aleksandr?"

"Yes," Rosa said, "although it's called something else now. The Niemen, I think."

"Just so," said Grigory. "And it was precisely there that the two great princes met to discuss peace. It has long been said that Napoleon and Aleksandr met alone, but it isn't true. For the Secret Ambassador was there."

"He was hiding," said Totchka, watching Rosa now, "in the Golden Bear."

Rosa returned her attention to Papa Grigory. "Ah, the mysterious Golden Bear."

He gave her a weak smile. "Just so, yes. The Secret Ambassador peeled out of himself and sat in that Golden Bear, watching the whole exchange."

Papa Grigory stopped for a moment to take a breath, or maybe to add a dramatic pause. Rosa considered him, and wondered about this Secret Ambassador character.

"It was a warm summer's afternoon. The light was hot upon the land. A specially made raft had been built and anchored precisely in the middle of the river. On board was a gaily colored pavilion with bright streamers fluttering from its peaks in the wind, and the royal emblems of each country emblazoned in glittering thread. Tsar Aleksandr went across to the raft on a little boat with only the bear for company. Napoleon met him, and they went inside.

"'I want no gifts from you,' Napoleon said, indicating the bear.

"'She is no gift, she is my lucky charm,' Aleksandr replied, and

Napoleon raised his eyebrows but thought little more of it, because there isn't a race on the earth as superstitious as the Rus.

"In the pavilion, a great feast had been laid out. Far too much for two men. Partridge and spatchcock, peach pies and cream pastries, fine wines and sweet cheeses. They picked at pieces, but both were too full of passions to need food. Napoleon had gorged on steely ambition, Aleksandr on bitter fear.

"'You are pale, my friend,' Napoleon said.

"'It is only the light.'

"'There is no need for fear. You see, I smile at you.' The French king bared his teeth. 'We both hate the English, Aleksandr. Common enemies make firm friends.'

"To Aleksandr's relief, Napoleon outlined an informal treaty, where he and Aleksandr would be common enemies against the English. They embraced like brothers, and all might have been well . . . ," said Grigory. "Yes, all might have been well but for one small problem."

Totchka sat up, eyes aglow. "Yes, yes. Napoleon wanted to marry Ekaterina, didn't he? Aleksandr said no."

"That is right, little one, but you make me wonder why you need me to tell the tale if you know it so well. Napoleon did indeed ask for the hand of Aleksandr's favorite sister. What a match it would have been! How safe it would have made the folk of Russia! But Aleksandr had too many hot thoughts about his sister and could not bear the idea of the French king having her.

"He roared and paced. His advisers danced about like little birds, desperate to change his mind.

"'Your majesty, your majesty, Napoleon promises to leave us be if we will only relinquish your sister.'

"'No, no, a thousand times no,' Aleksandr said. 'I will not let him marry her if he promises me two thousand fine horses. I will not let him marry her if he promises me all of Prussia. I will not let him marry her if he promises me the moon and all the stars.'

"His refusals echoed about the streets of St. Petersburg, through the thick forests to Siberia, down the rivers to Moscow, and across the steppes of Central Asia. Goodwill had dissolved between Napoleon and Aleksandr. Soon, the French king's hungry gaze would turn to Russia.

"And so it did. In the summer, Napoleon crossed the river with six hundred thousand men and over a thousand cannon. His army was black as a black raven, and no matter where one stood, one could not see end nor edge of it. The most brutal, hardened soldiers from France, Germany, Holland, Scotland, Ireland, Italy, Poland, Hungary and Portugal. Aleksandr could field only a poor army, less than a third the size of the Grand Army, and their fate already looked to be sealed. The Grand Army began to move, their bronze eagles held high, driving everything before them. All was surely lost.

"Aleksandr turned to his advisers in their fine kaftans, sitting in their high-backed chairs, or pacing the floor of the great hall. They panicked, they pouted, they shouted, they shivered, they quivered, they quailed. But the Secret Ambassador was as strong as steel. He pounded his staff on the tiles and cried, 'Enough!'

"All eyes were on him, as he rose to his full height and turned his blazing eyes on the Tsar.

"'Aleksandr, Napoleon has more than half a million men. True, this appears to be to his advantage. You have three great allies. First, the goodwill of your people, who love their Mother Russia passionately and will die to defend her. Second, the vast spaces of the land to retreat into, drawing the French king further and further toward his ruin. Third, all your magical half-brothers and sisters from the land of Skazki. We will mount our steeds of wind and fire, we will ride to the open fields, we will fight for Mother Moist Earth, and die for her. We will come to your aid if I only give the word.'"

Grigory paused, laying his long hands on his knees. "The word was given," he whispered, "and so the greatest military defeat in Mir's history was brought into being.

"Aleksandr's army engaged then retreated, engaged then retreated, pulling the Grand Army into the trap. Napoleon did not see this; he thought he was winning. He thought Moscow would be his, easily and freely. But when he paused on Sparrow Hill, looking down on the mighty ramparts and gilded domes of the ancient city, he felt his first twinge of doubt. Had it not been too easy? Was Moscow not too quiet?"

Grigory stopped and smiled. Totchka nodded. "Napoleon waited, didn't he, Papa? He waited for days for word from Aleksandr. Up on Sparrow Hill."

"Just so. Aleksandr sent no word. No deputation of surrender, no promise to fight on. Aleksandr sent him nothing but silence. Puzzled, Napoleon sent his advance guards down to the city. They returned with news impossible to believe.

"Moscow was empty. No vendors tended their street stalls. No publicans poured vodka in their taverns. No prostitutes lifted their skirts in alleyways. Empty. Echoing and empty.

"Napoleon rode down to the Kremlin. Nobody greeted him. An ominous silence waited, and the marching feet and hooves echoed gravely around. They set up camp, and then the Secret Ambassador began to work his powerful magic.

"First, he called upon the fire demons of Skazki, opened a crossing and encouraged them to pour forth. In every corner of the city, fires broke out. The demons of wind and air came next, fanning the flames, sending embers flying out of the city and across the fields, scorching the earth across which Napoleon would have to return.

"Moscow was burning! Buildings, food, amenities, all consumed by magical flames. Napoleon had never met such adversity. The few people who were left in the city would rather burn their grain than sell it to the French king, and so it was that his army felt the pinch of hunger and the cold caress of disease.

"Napoleon waited too long. Too long. Aleksandr's silence was absolute. No word was sent from St. Petersburg. Too late Napoleon ordered a retreat from Moscow. By then, Aleksandr's army had re-grouped. By then, the Secret Ambassador had enlisted Mother Moist Earth herself to finish the Grand Army off.

"Perhaps they were unconcerned when they first set off from Moscow. Certainly, they had hardly any food and only summer uni-forms on. But the weather was mild and they had home on their minds. It seemed a straight road to travel. But on that road were the black swamp and the crooked birch to trap the Grand Army. All the grasses and meadows tangled together; all the colored flowers dropped their petals; and all the dark woods bent their heads down to the earth. Magic was alive on that road, the magic of our Mother.

"She is a cruel spirit, Mother Moist Earth, and she feels anger deep in her bowels. She sent the rain first: cold, miserable downpours which churned the ground to sucking mud. Fire demons had been ahead of her, scorching the earth black and it congealed to tar with the rains. Knee-deep in the cold filth were Napoleon's men. Their starving horses could not move. Misery marched among them. And then, Mother sent the cold: temperatures plunged deep and deep below frozen, a cold that sent fingers blue and white, that froze the blood in men's hearts and the air in their lungs."

"Tell the best part, Papa," Totchka exclaimed. "With the artillery."

"Ah, yes. The gunners couldn't operate their cannon because their hands and feet had frozen off," Grigory said, and Totchka laughed and clapped her hands together gleefully.

"Across the miles, Aleksandr's voice carried on an ill wind to Napoleon. 'Go,' he said to the French king. 'You've made enough young wives widows, you've made enough infants orphans, you've quenched your thirst on the blood, and ground your teeth on the bones of the Rus. No more. Go.'

"While the Grand Army was limping away, small bands of Russian troops picked at them, emboldened by the knowledge that the very earth they loved so much was their ally. By the time Napoleon crossed the river out of Russia, the Grand Army was reduced to a handful of sad, ruined cripples. Less than one in twenty men had survived. The others had been swallowed in the snow and mud, their bones a sacrifice to appease the great spirit of the Mother."

Totchka settled under again, suppressing a yawn. "Then what happened, Papa?"

"Then Aleksandr was so grateful that he clasped the Secret Ambassador to his bosom. 'My dear friend,' he said, 'in repayment, I will give you what you have always wanted from me. Tomorrow at midnight, I will hold a secret ceremony and I will swear you three promises.'

"The Secret Ambassador was almost too excited to button his

shirt the next evening. Here was the promise upon which he had
been waiting, for surely Aleksandr meant to grant him his dearest
wish—the reunification of the kingdoms of magic and men.

"The great hall was ablaze with candles. The dim light flickered
over the friezes of saints. Here, the goddess Mokosha's face under
the Virgin Mary's veil; there, a wooden crucifix carved with the
eyes of a leshii. Aleksandr wore dark colors, as did his closest advisers. The Secret Ambassador advanced up the hall between sparse
rows of men, glancing at the faces. These men were all allies; none
of the nay-sayers had been invited. In the flickering amber light,
Aleksandr asked the Secret Ambassador to kneel. He held aloft the
Golden Bear and said, 'Tonight, in this court of shadows, I swear
three times.

" 'First, I swear that the Russian people honor and love you for
your part in saving Russia from the French king.

" 'Second, I swear that under my rule no penalty shall ever be
paid for the worship of magical creatures from your dear kingdom.

" 'Third . . .' Aleksandr paused, smiling. 'Dear friend, what a
pleasure it is to grant you your dearest wish. I swear that as long as a
drop of my half-magic blood lives on, the kingdom of men and the
kingdom of magic will—'

" 'Stop this!' A door slammed open. The Secret Ambassador's
head whipped up, and his heart, prepared for joy, was now stained
with uncertainty. Ekaterina, in her long nightshirt, hair flowing
behind her, strode into the room.

" 'Go on, Aleksandr,' said the Secret Ambassador, close to tears.
'Please. Don't listen to her.'

"Ekaterina pushed her way through the crowd and ascended the
shallow staircase, where she wrenched the Golden Bear from Aleksandr's hands. 'What nonsense is this? Are you mad? You cannot
swear upon such a heathen object.' Here, she threw the bear across
the floor. 'And you certainly cannot swear to allow heathen monsters free reign in our kingdom. Yes, yes, your secret has been let
slip, brother, and in good time too. What were you thinking? I am
most displeased.'

"The Secret Ambassador was still hopeful. Foolish old man. He should have known that all was lost, and indeed it was when Aleksandr mumbled an end to his sentence: 'As long as a drop of my half-magic blood lives on, the kingdom of men and the kingdom of magic will remain as they always have.' And then he went too far. 'When the last drop is extinguished, then I can help you no more, Secret Ambassador.'

"A bolt of shock speared into the Secret Ambassador's heart. How he wept and wailed!

"Aleksandr took the Secret Ambassador aside much later. He promised he would think more about it. Weeks turned into months and years. The folk of Skazki enjoyed freer crossing and much happy hunting in Mir. Still the Secret Ambassador waited on the final promise. At last, angry, the Secret Ambassador organized a secret meeting. Aleksandr didn't arrive, indeed nobody ever saw or heard from the Tsar again.

"At this place the story of the Tsar Aleksandr and the French king has come to an end. Now, Totchka, it is time to sleep."

"No, no, tell me first . . . what will happen on the day when the last drop of half-magic blood dies?"

"It is too awful to speak of," Grigory said, his face darkening. "Monsters will roam free, cold will settle over everything. You aren't to think of it, Totchka, for it will not happen."

Totchka smiled uncertainly. "Really, Papa?"

"I have always made you that promise, little one. And I shall keep it." He glanced at Rosa. "Now, sleep."

Totchka yawned. "Another story?"

"No, precious child. Sleep now."

Totchka's eyes closed, and Rosa settled next to her. She was tired, but excited. Sleep came in fits and starts, her dreams quivering in and out of wakefulness, leaving her confused and restless. At one point, deep in the night, a strange noise woke her. At first, she thought it was just Grigory sighing. Then, she could hear crying. A woman or a child, but far off and quiet.

Rosa turned on her side and slowly cracked an eyelid open.

Grigory sat at the table and in his hands was a shining mirror. He hunched over it, sighing. The sobs appeared to be coming from the mirror's surface. Then Grigory shifted, putting his back between her and his activity. She closed her eyes and tried to sleep again, wondering about Grigory's secrets. Somewhere in the hour before dawn, sleep finally caught her in its firm grasp, and she knew nothing again until the morning.

Thirty

"She's still sleeping."

"Then wake her up."

Rosa's eyes flickered open. Totchka leaned close, her sticky index finger about to jab Rosa in the eye.

"I'm awake," Rosa said, gently brushing aside the little girl's hand. "What time is it?"

Totchka frowned in puzzlement, and Rosa presumed that time didn't mean the same here in the protective bubble of Papa Grigory's cottage.

"Is the sun up?" she asked instead, sitting up. She noticed that Totchka wore a too-large headdress: a decorated kokoshnik that didn't match her plain brown dress.

"Oh, yes," Totchka said. "It's been up for hours. Papa said I wasn't to wake you until it was nearly time to go. He says your journey will be tiring and dangerous. So I let you sleep late."

Rosa's eyes sought out Grigory. He was busy in a far corner, organizing colored fabrics on hooks.

"Thanks," Rosa said. "I like your hat."

"It's *your* hat," Totchka said, pulling off the headdress and handing it over.

Rosa took it curiously, ran her fingertip over the fine intricate beading. "I don't think I'll be needing a kokoshnik."

"Rosa," Grigory growled. "You'll do as you're told."

Rosa shrugged, threw back the covers and put the hat on, modeling it for Totchka with only Grigory's shirt for an accompaniment, which left her knees exposed to the cool of morning. Totchka laughed and Grigory turned to smile at them.

"Take a closer look at it, Rosa," he said. "It's special."

Rosa realized that the fabrics Grigory was fussing with were actually clothes. She pulled the kokoshnik off her head and examined the patterns. Triple-pearl clusters hung at every inch. The peak was decorated with the shapes of a circle and an apple embroidered in gold thread.

"Where did you get this?" she asked.

"I've always had it," he said cryptically. "These clothes too. A hero's costume . . . or should I say, a heroine?" He moved to stand next to her, indicating the embroidered apple. "You see? The apple rolling over the saucer is the symbol of travel in distant lands. Nine drops of pearls, three pearls in each group, represent the twenty-seven lands of Skazki." He took Rosa by the hand and led her to the clothes. "And here is the rest of your costume."

"I don't want to wear fancy clothes," she said. "I just want to wear my blue jacket." She indicated where it was hanging over the chair near the stove. "Daniel likes me in blue."

"Heroes wear red, not blue," Grigory said firmly. "You must be dressed properly for your journey." He pushed the door open and Rosa saw Voron, the sleigh, waiting in the front garden. "We shall equip you fit for a hero's journey through the lands of Skazki."

By mid-morning, the sleigh was packed and Totchka and Grigory were fussing around her as she waited, in her underwear, to be dressed for the journey.

"First," said Grigory, "the fiery sarafan." He held out the dress for her to step into. It was made of deep red silk, embroidered with gold brocade. "Here," he said, indicating the pattern across the bottom of the skirt, "is the six-winged fire dragon. May his flames keep you warm wherever you go. The sun, the moon and the stars decorate the sleeves, so that they may always illuminate your way."

Rosa allowed Totchka to tie the dress across her bust. Little bells hung at the ends of the ties.

"Listen," the little girl said, rattling the bells. No sound. "They are magic bells, for they will always be silent until danger lurks near."

Papa Grigory held out a wide belt, which he wrapped around Rosa's hips. "This dreaming girdle will help you while you sleep. It will send you dreamed warnings of danger, or good counsel when you are lost or confused." He touched her mother's bracelet, still wound together with the one Daniel had given her. "You already have some of your mother's magic, and a link to find your lover." He touched her other wrist. "Here, you have three protection knots remaining. I shall give you another charm to hang about your throat." He reached into his pocket and withdrew a leather strap. Hanging from it was a spearhead.

"A thunder arrow," Rosa said, reaching for it. "Is it flint?"

"It's made from a fallen star," Totchka said, eager to correct her. "Isn't it, Papa Grigory?"

"A fallen star, just so," he said, knotting it around Rosa's neck. "*Sata*, Rosa. You know what that is?"

"A meteorite," she said. "Yes, I know."

"I found it myself out in the northeastern forests. All the trees for a hundred miles had been flattened like grass. You wear a star about your neck, Rosa. Few could bear its weight, but you are special."

Rosa touched the spearhead reverently.

"Last," Grigory said, "these shoes." He held up a pair of leather shoes, which Rosa could tell at a glance were far too small.

"They won't fit," she said.

Grigory frowned. "This costume has been waiting here for centuries. For you. Everything else fits."

Rosa sat and pushed her toes into the shoe to demonstrate. "See? Far too small. What are they, anyway? Lucky shoes?"

Grigory's dark expression told her she had been too flippant. "They are death shoes, Rosa. Should you fail, should you die, these shoes will take your spirit back to the one place you can know great happiness. You will avoid the fate of other revenants."

The thought moved her temporarily to silence. What would be the one place she could know great happiness? In Vasily's kitchen eating fried eggs with her uncle? Sitting with Daniel late on a summer night on his tiny back patio? Or could she go further back in time? Back to the first precious years on Prince Edward Island, years of gentle mists and rustling green, her parents happy and in love, all the ugly twists of fate as yet unanticipated?

"She can tie them on her belt, Papa," Totchka said, "then put them on if she dies."

"If she is dead, she can't put her shoes on," Papa said.

The puzzled frown again touched Totchka's face, and Rosa realized she understood death no more than she understood time.

"She's right in a way," Rosa said. "I'll get some kind of warning from the bells. I can squeeze into them if I have to. Tie them on my belt."

And so she was finally ready to leave, her battered lace-up black boots in odd contrast to the traditional costume. She took heavy furs for Daniel and Em, as Grigory said they had lost most of their supplies. The sleigh was packed, the sun gleamed dully on its black curves. Her heart was in her throat with anticipation. Grigory helped her into the padded black velvet seat.

"Voron will take you wherever you want to go. You must find Daniel yourself, the same way you've found him before." He touched the bracelet. "Return to me soon, Rosa, with that damned Golden Bear. I think I know how to reward you." His eyes met hers, their strange paleness shrewd.

Yes, he knew.

"I'll do my best," she said.

Grigory smacked the side of the sleigh once. "Up, Voron," he said. "Rosa's in charge now."

The first tilt into the air nearly unseated her; she held on and the sleigh lifted upward. Her stomach dropped, her spine turned to water. Voron arrowed through the protective bubble around Grigory's house, speeding her into cool violet air. Laughter bubbled on her lips as the wind rushed onto her cheeks and sent her hair streaming. At first she clutched the bar in front of her, then released it, felt the giddy half-falling sensation of being skyborne. She risked a glance behind her, was thrilled by the steepness of the angle. Below, she could see Totchka and Grigory waving, doll-faced miniatures with white hands. She watched them until they disappeared behind her and the sleigh leveled off.

Rosa held out her wrist, her fingers searching for the swallow charm on her mother's bracelet. She opened her second sight, was dazzled by the veins of silver and gold that ran through the sky.

"Which way?" she asked.

The swallow turned, then stopped to point: "Northeast, Voron," she said.

The sleigh bobbed, tilted, turned, then sped off into the clouds.

Em was dying, and Daniel couldn't deny it any longer.

She pushed on bravely through the endless grass, but all the color had fled from her cheeks and her breathing was coming in shuddering rasps. He insisted that they rest around twilight, afraid that her heart would simply stop if she went any further.

"You have to rest," he said. "Sleep a little while. I can scout ahead and see if there's any food."

"Sure," she said, gratefully. "I'll rest a little while." She lowered herself to the ground and lay on her back, her hand over her heart, and closed her eyes.

A tide of dread and sorrow washed through him. She would die; he would be alone. Then he would die too. This was the end, certainly. They hadn't eaten in days, and had only drunk from muddy puddles. Em had started complaining of stomach cramps, and would almost certainly have vomited if there was anything inside her to get out.

Daniel moved on, knotting grass stalks as he went so he could find his way back. In every direction, there was nothing but more grass stretching away on indifferent fields that led to nowhere. The sun set as he crested a low rise. He hoped to see something, anything: a stand of trees, the gleam of a river, a distant village. Anything but more grass.

This time, surely.

His heart sank as he topped the rise. More grass, as far as he could see. Another hill to taunt him in the distance. He opened his freshly acquired second sight, scanning for crossings. Nothing. Just sky.

For days it had been the same: the constant hope that the landscape would change, the constant cruel disappointment. He couldn't escape, even in his dreams, which were filled with vast grassy steppes, under dull twilit skies, rolling on endlessly and endlessly to the end of time.

He turned and headed back to Em.

She opened her eyes as he sat beside her. "Didn't find anything?"

"No."

"I didn't think you would, but I was still hoping."

"I wonder when we'll stop hoping."

"Maybe we never will. Maybe hope is biological. A survival instinct." She didn't sit up. The grass formed a sheer curtain around her so he couldn't clearly see the haggard death's mask her face wore.

"I'm sure we'll find something tomorrow," he mumbled.

"I'm not so sure, Daniel." She sighed. "Let's play a game, keep our minds off it."

"I can't play games, Em —"

"For me. Please, Daniel. I can't bear to just lie here watching the stars appear and wondering if I'm going to die before the sun comes up."

"Em, don't say that."

"Why not say it? I can feel it. I can feel my body shutting down. I know it's coming."

"Are you afraid?"

"Of course I am. My body's sending me a million signals, telling me to keep going, to survive. I can't bear to listen to it anymore. Go on, list me five shades of blue."

Daniel smiled weakly and answered her questions as night deepened overhead and the stars shone. Five perennial flowers, five tropical fruits, five Spencer Tracy films, five capital cities in the southern hemisphere, five great female rulers. Finally, she said, "Now list me five things you'll miss if you never get back home."

There were five million. "I'm not sure."

"Go on. You first, then me."

Daniel considered, wriggling into a sitting position so that he could see Em better under the darkening sky. "All right. First, I'll miss food. Curries and beer in particular. Second, I'll miss music. I'll miss my Beatles collection. Third, I'll miss London. I'll miss the orange lights through the mist on winter mornings. Fourth, I'll miss my own bed, with the hollow in the middle where I fit perfectly and the smell of the washing powder they use at the local laundromat. And fifth . . ." He trailed off, the game suddenly becoming far too serious.

"Go on," she said.

"I'll miss Rosa," he said, "although I didn't have her anyway."

"But you always had the possibility."

"Yes," he said. "That's it." He sighed and leaned forward to grasp his knees. "Now you."

Em was quiet for a while, thinking about it. "I'll miss shopping. I'll miss my house, and my garden . . ." Another silence, then she said, "I guess I don't have as much to miss as you."

The wind shifted across the grass, a sinuous movement. On their first day out here, Daniel had admired the breeze's progress as beautiful: now it put his nerves on edge, and he longed for the calm of stillness instead of the itch of movement. He longed for vertical structures to hide beneath instead of this endless horizontal exposure.

"How about regrets," Em said. "What will you regret?"

"Em, we're talking like dead people."

"We are dead people," she said lightly. "You know that."

"I'll regret that I didn't fly."

"I'll regret that I didn't love."

"I'll regret that I did." He laughed and it turned into a sob. He swallowed hard, determined to stay brave. The breeze moved across the grass again, sighing its barely audible sigh.

"Sometimes," Em said slowly, "I hear a man's voice in my head."

"What does he say?"

"I'm exhausted and sick when I hear this voice. I've heard it before, and it wasn't a hallucination. At least, I don't think it was."

"What are you talking about?" Daniel was concerned. Usually Em was perfectly coherent, no matter what the circumstances.

"He's speaking to me now," she continued.

"What does he say?" Daniel asked again, a little slower.

"He says, 'Morning won't come without me.'"

"What does that mean?"

"I don't know." She closed her eyes. "I don't mean to get your hopes up."

"You haven't."

Em was silent a long time. Daniel waited for her to speak again, then panicked and thought she might be dead. A quick check of the pulse at her wrist told him she wasn't, but it also woke her up.

"Sorry," he said, when her eyes flickered open and she caught him in her gaze.

She grasped his fingers in her own. "Hold on to me, Daniel."

"I will." He didn't let go as she fell asleep once more.

Voron flew at the same speed Rosa flew in her dreams, coasting and dipping over currents, chasing its own shadow over gentle rolling hills and stands of trees. The sleigh was made of iron and wood, but sometimes under her fingers she thought she could feel the twist of lithe sinews, or the swell and shrink of breath. The sky sped past as they crossed a forest, and smoke rose into the air. Rosa looked down, but could see nothing through the trees. Was it burning wood or burning flesh she could smell? It was hard to remember she was in hostile territory when she felt such exhilaration.

"Isn't this fun, Anatoly?" she shouted.

Anatoly was still. Perhaps he'd given up fighting her. Her senses prickled, and she snapped her head up. Ahead, the sky was splintered. A crossing.

"Are we going through there?" she asked. Voron didn't waver in his path. The veil draped the sky, miles in each direction. "I guess we are."

She braced herself as the sleigh shot through the veil, sending fragments of colored light exploding into the air, shuddering through her and pushing her breath back down her throat. Then, she was simply *elsewhere*. The sky was twilit colors of blue and gray, and a great glittering river snaked below her.

Water. The thought made her throat feel dry. Time to try a landing on Voron.

"Voron," she said. "Down."

The sleigh bobbed lightly on the air, coasting rather than propelling forward. Then the descent began, slowly drifting fractionally side to side like a feather. They settled in the long grass on the riverbank and Rosa climbed down. The route to the water's edge was rocky, and the sarafan became the most impractical thing she had ever worn. She tucked the sides up into her underwear so the skirt hung around her knees rather than her ankles. The stars and moons on the skirt glowed faintly, adding a pale blue light to the dusk as she made her way down to the water.

Rosa crouched there, scooping handfuls of water into her mouth. Behind her, up on the bank, she heard a rustle but when she stood to look around, there was nothing but Voron, his metal beak gleaming faintly in the twilight. She smiled. "If I didn't know better, Voron, I'd say you were alive." Voron remained silent.

She turned back to the water, casting her gaze over the opposite bank. The smell came again and this time she knew: smoke weighed down with the fatty odor of burning flesh. Down here on the ground, the danger seemed much closer. She switched into her second sight, sending it through the trees to discover where the smell emanated from. Too distant.

Then movement in the water caught her eye. She stepped back, her gaze searching into the river. A pale, dead-eyed thing was staring back at her. She let out a little shriek and scrambled back onto the bank. The swamp spirit launched itself up out of the water, rotted white hands reaching for her hair. Rosa kicked out, got away, and ran for Voron.

"Up, Voron, up!" she cried, and the sleigh lurched and lifted, as though it knew the danger. The swamp spirit, weedy hair clinging thinly to its wrinkled scalp, caught the back of one of the skis and took to the sky with them.

"Get off!" Rosa screamed, as she felt the sleigh's weight shift and start to shudder. The creature was going to pull them out of the sky, and they were already up a hundred feet. Rosa's eyes scanned the sleigh for a heavy object to beat the thing off, then she tore the thunder arrow from around her neck.

"I said, get off!" she shouted, as she thumped the swamp spirit's fingers with the lump of rock. As she did so, a thunderous roar cracked around her, splitting the air and echoing metallically in her ears. The creature lost its grip and fell. Voron, divested of the burden, shot upward. Rosa watched as the swamp spirit spun through the sky, a white

blur, then landed in a crumpled heap on the grass below. She retied
the thunder arrow around her neck, feeling her heart slow.

Rosa settled back in her seat, knees curled up to her chest.
Grigory said that, so far, Daniel and Em had survived in Skazki:
how? She had been attacked by a leshii and a swamp spirit and had
had to use magic to protect herself. They had no magic. Perhaps Em
was as strong as she was smart.

Perhaps Rosa had underestimated Daniel.

As she pondered this, a dislocated but familiar sound reached
her ears. Bells. Complex patterns and combinations of high and low
chimes, coming to her on the breeze. Below, the landscape was
changing. Flat lands gave way to low mountains; snow, half-melted
and dirty, gathered on rises. The bells grew louder, echoing through
the peaks and valleys. Up ahead, on a flat hilltop, she could make out
the outline of a towered building, golden cupolas gleaming in the
dark. The trajectory that she and Voron were on meant that it would
pass directly underneath them. The clouds grew close, a flurry of
snowflakes caught in her hair. She was glad for the sarafan's enchanted warmth, because she could feel the temperature dropping
steadily. Mists blurred their path, then cleared again, as the bells
reached a deafening volume. The building was directly in front of
her: a palace, painted bright colors and topped with golden domes
and clattering bell towers. Pagan symbols and frescoes were outlined in gold on every surface: bears and bulls, winged dragons and
darting fish. Then it was rushing beneath them and behind. She
turned to look at it, curiosity an itch deep inside her.

"Voron," she said, "go back."

Voron veered to the right, turning back in a circle.

"Go round," she said, before they had reached the towers again.

Voron began to circle the palace, and Rosa watched it from the
side of the sleigh as they passed once, twice, three times.

"What is it?" she whispered. It looked like a Russian Orthodox
cathedral, with its onion domes and gold decorative towers. But
there were no crosses; no saints on the white and blue paintwork.
The square that surrounded it was paved in gray stone, smattered
with grubby melting snow.

She tapped Voron's iron shoulder. "Down, Voron."

The sleigh slowed, sharpened its angle, and dipped toward the square. Rosa played absently with the protection knots at her wrist.

Voron skidded into a bank of snow in the empty square. The bells sounded frantic, stuck on a loop. The cold air made the sound harsh. The ground was slippery with ice, and a chill wind flapped at her clothes. Snowflakes spun around her as she crossed the square. She felt small and young. The twilight here was purple, but had not yet deepened toward night. Pale stars tried their hardest to shine between the clouds. Huge carved wooden doors towered above her and she stopped to catch her breath, gazing at the elaborate shapes of celestial bodies, animal spirits, vines and antlers that an artist had chiseled from the wood. Her heart was fast, the familiar sizzle of adrenalin in her chest. She pushed one of the doors open, letting a crack of snowy twilight into a dark entry hall. Empty. Rosa slipped inside, leaving the door open behind her. High windows admitted a little light. A wide staircase swept away from her up to an empty landing. No furniture, no rich ornaments, just a grand hollowness.

"Hello?" she called.

The door creaked behind her. She glanced over her shoulder. A disembodied voice boomed through the room.

"Did Koschey send you?"

Rosa slowly searched the room with her gaze. "Show yourself."

"You have Koschey's sleigh," said another voice.

"I only know him as Papa Grigory," Rosa said evenly, although her mind was ticking over quickly. *Koschey, the deathless.* It explained a great many things about Grigory. "He didn't send me here. I came of my own free will."

Disembodied laughter in the chill emptiness. "Does Koschey know you have such a strong free will?"

"Who are you?"

"Come up the stairs," the first voice said. "We're in the throne room at the end of the hall."

Rosa backed toward the door. "No thanks. I'd best be on my way."

A sudden blast of wind slammed the door shut, muting the roar of the bells. Rosa tried the handle, but it wouldn't budge.

"We simply won't take no for an answer," said the second, quieter voice.

"Come, little Mir girl. We'll tell you about Koschey."

"Just follow the stairs."

She shouldn't be here. She shouldn't have stopped. She was supposed to find Daniel. And yet, she wanted more than anything to meet the occupants of the castle.

"I'll only stay a minute," she said, unwinding a protection knot across her knuckles. She took a deep breath and started up the staircase.

Em was cold, but she had always been cold. Now she felt life retreating from her, shriveling into a weak pulse somewhere deep inside her. She had thought that death would be an expanding sensation, not this uncomfortable contracting. She slept fitfully, always surprised when she woke again to see the stars, to see Daniel's hunched back as he sat next to her, gazing out across the fields.

No, the cold was different.

She sat up. Daniel turned to her.

Prickling across her skin, icy and sharp.

"He's coming," she breathed.

"Who?"

The wind wailed, slowly, a moaned promise, closer and closer. The sky churned to the freezing movement of his wings. Daniel's hair whipped about as he looked around, alarmed.

"Morozko."

"Who? What do you mean?" His words were caught at his lips and tossed aside by the wind.

She struggled to her feet and turned, her hair blowing into her eyes. In the distance, a white figure against the gray dawn. She was reminded of old paintings, angels emerging from apocalyptic skies. Overwhelmed, she lost her balance and fell. Daniel caught her and lowered her to the ground.

"Em, be careful."

"It's going to be okay. He's coming."

Footsteps. Cold. She saw Daniel shudder. She closed her eyes.

"Who are you?" Daniel said.

"Don't touch me," said Morozko. "It's dangerous."

Then his icy arms were around her. She opened her eyes. He had her cradled in his strong embrace, pressed against his chest. "I'm here, you're safe," he said. "There's food and clean water not ten miles from here."

"I can't walk," she said.

"Then I'll carry you."

Thirty-one

The sun rose and dazzled Em's eyes as Morozko led them back toward the southeast and over a hill to the edge of a wood. A glistening stream rushed over rocks, field mushrooms grew in abundance. Daniel built a fire while Morozko hunted in the trees. Em waited, still too weak to move, breathing relief and hope anew. They still might make it home.

"This is a lot harder without a lighter," Daniel said, furiously rubbing sticks together over a pile of dead leaves.

"Leave it for Morozko. He can probably start a fire."

"No, I think I'm finally getting . . . there." Sparks smoldered in the leaves. He poked them gingerly with a stick. "Yes, that looks good." He looked up at Em. "So, how much do you know about him?"

"I know that he's saved me twice now."

"Morozko is the father of the frost. Though none of the stories Rima told me had him looking like that." He hitched a thumb toward the wood, where Morozko's lithe and muscular body slipped in and out of sight between trees. "He took pity on a mortal woman who was dying of exposure."

"Perhaps it's his speciality." She laughed weakly. "I don't care. I've drunk fresh water, we're going to eat properly, we have shade to rest under. I don't care what happens next."

"You don't?"

"It can't be worse than dying on the steppe." Her eyes went to the woods again. Morozko was very still now, and the curve of his lower back beneath his wings seemed hard and inviting to the touch. A sudden movement, a pounce. Then he was returning to the fire with a pheasant, its head dangling on a broken neck.

"Food," he said, handing the bird to Daniel. "I'll take care of Em."

Daniel took the bird, but Em could see his eyes were suspicious. Why not? They had been chased, injured and led astray by every creature they had met. Morozko sat with Em, pulling her into his cold embrace. She knew he was different, though. She knew he was going to be her savior.

"Rest a little longer, Em," he said, laying her head on his chest and stroking her hair. An echo of memory, from her childhood. Her mother held her like this, but she would always struggle away. She felt no desire to struggle away from Morozko. A little girl, wrapped in his embrace. "There will be food soon, and I will stay here with you a day or two until you regain some strength."

"Thank you," she said, and her ribs fluttered. An unfamiliar feeling. A vulnerability of the fingertips, a weakness in the chest. Perhaps she would feel better after she'd eaten.

In the end, Em could only eat very little. Her stomach cramped and threatened to send the mushrooms straight back up. But the clean water and small amount of food had made her feel alive again, instead of half-dead. She sat by the side of the stream with Morozko, watching the sunlight on the water and feeling an inexplicable sense of excited joy.

Daniel came to crouch next to her. "I need to sleep," he said.

"Of course," she replied. How had she not thought of it? Daniel hadn't slept the previous day. "I'll stay awake."

Morozko waved a dismissive hand at Daniel. "Take yourself off under the trees. Sleep as long as you like, and I'll ensure the safety of your companion."

Again, Daniel's suspicion was only thinly veiled. He nodded, and moved to the cover of the trees. Em watched as he curled into a ball and closed his eyes.

A few minutes later, Morozko said, "He's asleep."

"How do you know?"

"I can tell. Are you in love with him?"

Em almost laughed. "I'm in love with nobody."

"Is that so?"

"I've never loved," she said. "I've never felt anything." Em watched the sky. The morning brightened, white clouds material-ized and transformed. She sighed, comfortable and glad to be alive.

"I can never repay you," she said. "You've saved my life."

"The price will be paid in time."

"What price? I'll pay anything." She thought about the bear, slung under Daniel's clothes. They needed it to get home, but if Morozko asked for it . . . It was strange, the thought of giving up everything for him was pleasant: a kind of martyrdom where the burden of making decisions, of going forward, was lifted from her finally.

"Something's happening to you," Morozko said, his eyes narrowing as he examined her face. His skin was as smooth as marble. "I think you are starting to feel."

His comment confused her, but she was recovering from near-death and couldn't be blamed if she wasn't herself. So she sat silently, enjoying the morning and trusting she'd be well again soon.

Rosa stood uncertainly at the top of the stairs, peering into the gloom. At the end of the long hallway, a door opened and amber light spilled out onto the stone tiles. Dust danced slowly, turning bright and dark in the glow. The voices no longer echoed about: they obviously came from the opened room.

"Come on, then," the first voice said, "don't be afraid."

Rosa advanced up the hall, straightening her spine and preparing herself to run at any moment. She paused at the door, peering around the corner into the throne room. It was lit with dozens of candles, the light glinting dully off dirty gold objects junked into corners and across dusty surfaces: cups and crosses, knots and icons. Two men sat within, side by side on a long carved bench. A wooden throne gathered dust on a riser, under a window that commanded a view of twilit skies. The men were dressed in traditional Russian costume. The first, a dark-haired man with a pointed beard and dramatically Slavic eyes, wore stain-spattered robes of gold and orange. His corpulent companion, with red-gold hair and a curling beard, was dressed in blue.

The dark-haired man stood. "What is your name, friend of Koschey?"

"I don't know that I'm a friend of Koschey," she replied. Superstitious about revealing her name, she said, "You can call me Mir girl."

"Why do you have his raven sleigh?" asked the second man.

"He loaned it to me. I have to . . . tell me who you are first. I won't say another word until you do."

They exchanged glances. The dark man nodded. "I was once known as Perun. My companion's name is Veles."

Rosa gasped an incredulous laugh. "You're . . . ?" Perun, the king of the pagan gods, deity of war and thunder. This slight, untidy man? And Veles, god of cattle and trade, music and wealth. "You don't look like gods."

"And you don't look like Koschey; although you arrived in his sleigh, you're wearing clothes made by his hand, and you've got the same ugly gleam in your eyes as him," Veles said, his round face flushing red.

Slow down, Rosa. "But, Perun and Veles are . . . Why are you sitting in a dirty room in an empty palace alone?"

"We're not alone, we have each other," Veles said. He turned to his companion. "She doesn't believe us, brother."

"Then we shall make her believe," Perun said, pride gathering in his voice. "Silly Mir girl." He rose, and Rosa could see the effort it took to straighten joints and mobilize muscles. Once he was up, though, his bearing was tall, his movements graceful. He strode to the window and unlatched the shutter. Cold air rushed in. With a guttural gasp and a powerful throw of his arm, blinding lightning split the sky. Simultaneously, thunder boomed down on the palace, rattling the shutters, shaking the walls, dislodging crosses and icons hung on the wall and setting the dirty treasures dancing and jittering against each other. Rosa couldn't keep the smile from her lips. Wax, loosened by the shuddering, poured down from the wheel of candles above Rosa, narrowly missing her shoulder. It pooled quietly, as the thunder died off and all was still.

Perun closed the shutter. "It's too cold to have the window open," he said, returning to his seat and lowering himself gently. He nursed the arm he'd used for magic against his chest, as though the effort had strained the muscles.

"You're right, brother," said Veles, reaching out to rub his arm. "Let us stay warm."

"If you're Perun and Veles, what are you doing here?" She gestured around.

"We're waiting," said Veles.

"Waiting for what?" she asked.

"We'll ask the questions," Perun said. "Sit down."

Rosa lowered herself to the floor. It was smeared with centuries of soot and dust. The pool of wax smelled thick and fatty. She tucked her dress under her knees, but knew it would be filthy by the time she left.

"Explain to me," Perun said, "how you come to have Koschey's sleigh if, as you maintain, he didn't send you here to spy on us."

"Grigory loaned me the sleigh to find somebody. I saw your palace and was curious, so I came down to look."

"Who were you meant to find?"

"My lover."

"He's lost in Skazki? Why does Koschey care?"

Rosa hesitated. Grigory hadn't forbidden her from talking about her reasons for being here, and Perun and Veles had as much to gain from her finding Daniel as she did. They might offer assistance. "My lover has the Golden Bear, and I have to stop him from taking it to the Snow Witch."

Perun and Veles emitted twin gasps.

"Do you hear what she says, brother?"

"I do. The Snow Witch may finally have her wish."

"The Mir girl may stop her. Koschey has told lies."

"Koschey is always interfering!"

"We should have never let him have so much power. We should never have let him spend so much time in Mir."

"He became part-human! Some even say he fathered a child."

"He doesn't know it. The mother hid the baby with enchantments."

"Somebody more responsible should have been sent." Veles looked as though he might rise from his seat, then he sagged down again. "But I hadn't the energy for Mir myself."

"Stop, stop!" Rosa said, holding up her hand. "You're talking too fast. Explain what you mean. What lies have I been told?"

"You tell us," Veles said, jabbing a chubby finger at her. "Why must the Snow Witch not have her bear? What tale has Koschey told you?"

"That all the horrors of Skazki will be unleashed on Mir," Rosa said.

Perun and Veles regarded each other with expressions of resigned displeasure. They shook their heads, made tutting noises, like an old married couple who had long since grown blind to each other's infirmities and grime.

"What then?" Rosa asked.

Perun turned his dark, expressive eyes to her. "The fate he has you imagine can never be. Once we did roam in the wide world, but we have long since been confined to this land of blood and colors."

"Koschey has lied to you. He deals in lies."

"The truth is, Mir girl, that when the Snow Witch has the bear, the two worlds will separate finally and permanently. Do you understand what this means?"

Rosa shook her head. "No."

Perun struck the items off on his fingers. "No more Skazki creatures can hunt in Mir. They will starve and die out. No more Mir creatures can live in Skazki. Koschey's ugly little daughter will be sent home. That is why he lied to you."

It took a few moments for this to sink in. Grigory had lied to her? She didn't want to believe it. What if Perun was lying to her?

"If what you say is true," she asked slowly, "what will happen to you? You don't hunt for food in Mir."

Veles shook his head sadly. "It has already been happening to us for over a thousand years. We're fading to nothing."

Perun opened his hands, gesturing weakly. "Look around you. This was once a grand palace, wrought of stone and wood. Then the new religion came, and we were renamed as saints and prophets. What did they call us, Veles?"

Veles squinted toward the ceiling, bringing back the recollection. "I was Saint Vlasii," he said. "Christians carried icons of me into cattle fields on holy days. You were the Holy Prophet, the thunder-maker, ascending to heaven on a fiery chariot."

Perun rolled his eyes. "If I could have lived in heaven instead of here, believe me, I would have."

"The new religion raised white towers and cupolas of gold around us," Veles said. "Slowly and slowly, we are being forgotten."

"To be forgotten is worse than to forget," Perun said, his head drooping. "Our glory dissipates daily. I can no longer keep the sun in the sky. This is our twilight."

"We grow dim. When the ties between the worlds are permanently severed, it will all be over."

"You'll die?" Rosa asked.

"Death can be glorious," Perun said, his chest puffing out. "Amid the clang of arms in battle, or in the white heat of martyrdom, or at the end of a noble quest which has changed worlds. No, we won't die. We'll just slip away into oblivion, forget ourselves."

Rosa felt her body grow cold, her worst fear named aloud. "How can you stand it?" she asked. "Don't you fear it?"

A long silence ensued, and Perun's eyes went to the window and gazed at distant stars. Finally, with a sigh, he said, "I'm tired."

"You needn't worry," she said. "I can stop the Snow Witch getting her bear."

"It is time for us to go," Perun said. "Let us go."

"I don't understand," Rosa said. "You want to fade away?"

"We want to surrender to fate," Veles said. "Time is too long. You wouldn't understand."

Silence fell. The years weighed heavily in the room, and Rosa felt it. Dust moved, candles dripped; darkness layered on darkness. Her thoughts were half-formed and rapid.

"I see you thinking," Perun said. "Who do you believe? Koschey or us?"

"At least go to see the Snow Witch," Veles advised. "Once you see her, all will be clear."

Perun narrowed his eyes at her. "Koschey has given you his sleigh, has he also given you weapons?"

She pulled the thunder arrow out and showed him. "Only this."

Perun leaned forward, closing his hand over it. She felt a numbing tingle around her neck, like a mild electric shock. Then it was gone.

"I have sown the power of the elements in your arrow," he said, his hand falling away. "It can undo Grigory's enchantment."

"We are more powerful than him," Veles said. "Though he would never admit it."

"Go now," Perun said.

Rosa climbed to her feet. "Yes, I've already stayed too long."

"Make the right decision, Mir girl," Perun said. "Consider what we've told you."

Confused and inexplicably tired, Rosa left the throne room, clattered down the stairs and back out into the snowy twilight. Voron waited, the velvet seat soft and warm.

"Up," she said, and the sleigh took to the sky, putting thousands of feet of freezing air between her and the two old men. She thought for a long time, found herself growing more and more weary.

"If I lie down a little while, Voron, will you keep me on track to find Daniel?" she asked.

There was no answer, but she lay down anyway. Almost as soon as her head hit the padded seat, she drifted off.

Dark. Sweat. Hot steel. Blood. Jewels. Torn flesh. Colored ribbons. Frost. Ice. Pain. Wrenching pain. Where are they? Why does nobody come for me?

Rosa's eyelids fluttered open briefly, and then she was sliding back into sleep. The sleigh's cadence soothed her. Just before she went under, she thought she could hear the sound of giant wings flapping on the still twilight air.

Morozko's attentions toward Em were suspicious to Daniel, but Em had fallen under some kind of spell. Yes, Morozko had brought them to food and safety. Yes, he tended to Em with infinite care and caution. But every other creature they had met was hostile unless paid. So far they had paid Morozko nothing, and Daniel was afraid that when the price was named, it would be too high.

Adding fuel to his suspicions was the fact that all afternoon, since Daniel had woken, Morozko had kept him busy away from the camp. First collecting firewood, then hunting for eggs, and finally searching up and down the edges of the stream for *poputnik* leaves, which he insisted would ease Em's stomach cramps and allow her to eat properly.

Through all this, Em looked dazed and weak. She had lost her usual sharp-eyed practicality, smiling and gazing at Morozko as though she were a thirteen-year-old girl, and he the gorgeous friend of an older brother.

In the late afternoon, when Morozko left to hunt, Daniel sat with Em to persuade her to his way of thinking.

"Are you feeling better?" he asked.

"The poputnik has helped," she said. "I'm holding down food. I feel a lot stronger." She smiled, tucking her hair behind her ears. "We are so lucky that Morozko found us."

"Are we?"

Her expression was puzzled. "What do you mean?"

Daniel dropped his voice to a whisper, leaning forward. "I'm worried, Em. How do we know he doesn't intend to harm us?"

"Of course he doesn't," she replied sharply.

"How do you know that?"

"I just know. I . . ." She searched about for words. "I feel it."

"You *feel* it?"

"Yes. Very strongly. I feel good things when I look at him."

"I don't. If I look at him with the second sight, I see shadows on his brow. I feel suspicions, resentments."

"And why should your feelings matter more than mine?"

"Because you've never *felt* anything before. You've always been practical and thoughtful." He touched her shoulder, withdrew his touch when he realized how cold she had become. Only inanimate objects should be that cold: chilled peaches or refrigerated cadavers. "Em, think about it. It doesn't make sense."

"What makes sense in Skazki? It's been chaos since we arrived."

Daniel shook his head, growing exasperated. "You're behaving so strangely, Em. It's like you're falling in love with him."

She snorted. "Very funny. I didn't complain when you wanted to follow the polevoi, even though I could see that you were fooled by her. Just because she looked like Nanny Rima."

"This is different. He's dangerous."

"No, he's not." She held her palm out in a stop gesture. "I don't want to talk about this nonsense anymore. I'm weak, I've been sick. We'll discuss it later."

In her rebuff, she was a little more like the old Em, and it was enough reassurance to make him back off, resolve to try later.

Hopefully, before it was too late.

Morning light came. Em sat by the fire, gazing at the glowing embers. Once, not too long ago, it had bothered her that the fire could provide her no comfort. Now, she relished it. As though the cold was infinitely preferable to warmth. It made her smile.

Daniel was in the woods, collecting mushrooms for breakfast. Morozko stood by the stream, dark curls falling forward over his bent head. Early light stained his skin. His folded white wings curved gracefully on his hard back: a painting come to life. She smiled again. She was smiling a lot lately; probably grateful that she was still alive. Grateful that home was a possibility again.

Though home without Morozko seemed something of an empty idea. Em rose, and walked toward him.

"Hello," she said, trailing a finger over his upper arm. "Do you need company?"

He turned and smiled, and she was breathtaken by his terrible beauty. Breathtaken. What was happening to her? She wanted him, of course. He was supremely sexually attractive. She didn't want him the way that she'd wanted the others, where their faces and names were irrelevant. No, she imagined that if she could make love to Morozko it might awaken something in her. Something she didn't have a grammar to express. In fact, if she concentrated on the feeling very hard, she realized that sex needn't even be part of it.

"What do you want, Em?" he asked, cutting into her thoughts before they could venture too far into uncharted territory.

"I just wanted to . . ." She trailed off, uncertain. Something about his voice frightened her.

"No, I mean, *what do you want?*"

She shook her head. "I want to give you something," she said, her words pouring out in a rush. "You've done so much for me. And Daniel."

"What do you want to give me?"

"Gold."

"You gave me gold once before." He opened his mouth and lifted his tongue. In the space beneath, her gold wedding ring rested.

"I have more. Well . . ." She glanced over her shoulder. "Daniel has it. It's a bear."

Morozko's shoulders flexed forward, and Em could feel the movement under her fingers. He didn't feel as cold as he once felt.

"A bear?" he said, an expression of anticipation crossing his face. "A bear made of gold? Where did you get it?"

"Would you like to see it?"

Morozko smiled, taking her hand. "I'll see it soon enough. Tell me, why do you want to give me this bear?"

"I . . . because you . . ."

"I'll ask you again: *what do you want?* Don't answer me with trivia. In your gut, in your sinews, what do you want?"

Em opened her mouth. The word "you" begged to emerge. Her brain engaged, the word stayed in.

His voice dropped so low she almost didn't hear him. "You are starting to feel."

Em laughed. "I'm not. I'm the same as I ever was."

"You are falling in love with me."

"I'm . . ." Words fought with her tongue.

"Like attracts like," he said. "I doubt anyone else could have awoken feeling in you."

"This is silly." She felt embarrassed. Young and foolish.

"Are you not curious, Em? About love?"

Em concentrated. She didn't like herself all speechless and vulnerable. "Of course, from time to time."

His fingers locked with hers. He squeezed her hand hard. "I can make you feel, now you've opened your heart to me a little."

"This makes no sense."

"You said you were curious."

A falling sensation fluttered over her. "Yes," she said. "Yes, I'm curious, but . . ."

He dropped her hand and turned his shoulder away. "I don't want to force you."

"No! Really, I'm curious. I just . . ." She rubbed the center of her forehead. "I'm confused."

Once again, he picked up both her hands. His fingers locked between hers, like a trap closing. "I am interested to see how deep these new feelings flow, but you must understand it could be dangerous."

She tried to laugh dismissively, but could feel the fear flicker across her own expression. "You're talking in riddles."

"Prepare, Em. You can drop my hands any time." He loosened his grip to demonstrate. "In fact, you should make sure you drop them before too long. My soul is colder than my skin. You don't want the cold to go all the way to your heart."

She was about to open her mouth to say "What do you mean?" when a barrage of sensations rocketed into her. She gasped and closed her eyes, let the images unfold.

It was the sweetest joy. Love? How would she know, she'd never felt it before. But this was all over her body: prickling her skin, thudding in her muscles and bones. She'd imagined love to be more isolated, more of a sharp flutter in the chest and nothing more.

"What is it?" she said, but the words came out fuddled and muddy.

"It will stop when you're ready to stop, but it won't return."

So was it love? The thundering rollercoaster continued, dipping and soaring in her body. A simple test would solve the confusion. Children were said to rouse the deepest love, so she reeled back in her mind for memories, for Rubin's birth. At first the flashes were of the pain, the overly bright hospital room, but then a white-hot moment: the tiny body of an infant cradled in her hands.

Far away, she heard herself gasp for air. She may have even sobbed. Sensation rose like a tide, pulses of light and dark bruised her. The image led to another, and another, unbidden. The dam had cracked, and now she waited for the floodwaters to crush her. Her mother, her father . . . *my father, I loved him* . . . even Daniel, his pale anxious face arousing such sweet weakness inside her. *I love him. I love them all.* Most of all, it was her son who came to her. Only snatches—after all, she had spent so little time with him—but the most wondrous painful joy came with them. She loved him more than truth, more than light, more than breath. The curve of his plump cheek made her ache, the light of his crooked smile sent bolts of electricity to her heart, the smell of his freshly washed hair made her want to abandon everything and lie down, his warm body curled in her arms, forever and forever and forever . . .

"Em! What's happening?" This was Daniel's voice, but it was far away, and the alarm in his words couldn't touch her. She was pounding with joy, glued to the feeling, never wanted to come back.

"She can let go whenever she wants. Don't come any closer."

"Let her go!"

"As you wish."

The tide began to withdraw, Morozko's fingers were leaving hers.

"No!" she screamed, tightening her grip, vicious as a beast. She pulled hard on Morozko's hands, and the feelings came back.

"You have chosen then," he said.

"Em, let go!"

How could she let go? How could she go back to not feeling this way ever again? Years on top of empty years lay behind her. Was that her future too? She couldn't bear it. She crushed Morozko's fingers in hers, and this time behind the glittering feelings of love, she felt the first tendril of ice touch her heart.

"It's going to kill you," Morozko said, somewhere between sad and resigned.

Oh, the sweet ache of it. Oh, the unspeakable joy. Her heart hurt anyway. What was one more spear of frosty pain?

"Ah, well," Morozko said, "there are worse ways to die."

"I won't let go," she gasped. Her voice echoed in her own dark mind, but she couldn't hear it aloud. Shadows gathered on the periphery. She feasted on the feelings, ignoring the growing stab of pain. Somewhere, far away, two men were shouting at each other. It hardly mattered. She loved more than truth, more than light, more than breath.

And so she let go of all three.

First truth.

Then light.

Then breath.

Daniel pulled up sharply as Em dropped to the ground, pale and blue around the lips.

Morozko turned to him. Dark light stained his eyes. "She's dead," he said.

Em? Dead? Impossible.

"The bear," Morozko said, extending his hand. "Give it to me."

Daniel folded his arms across his middle, feeling the lump of the bear against his ribs. He remembered what Em had said: *She's our ticket home . . . Guard her with your life.*

"No," said Daniel. Involuntarily, his second sight switched on, and Morozko's features were washed in icy blues and dull gray shadows. He turned to run.

"You can't run from me!" Morozko called, amused disbelief in his voice.

Daniel did run. Panicked, he headed into the open grassland rather than the shadowed forest. The frost demon was behind him, gaining on him every second, his freezing aura extending ever closer.

Thirty-two

Day and night were all the same for Rosa. She had lost track, because the sun's course through the sky no longer marked time. On each occasion that she slipped through the veil, it was a different time of day over a different landscape. The snowy twilight of Perun and Veles' world gave way to the arctic gleam of ice and black water, then to the rich green of the black-soil woods, then to wide miles of spruce forest, where all she saw for an entire day were the tips of trees. It created in her a kind of jetlag, where she was unable to hold her eyes open in full sun, or she sat up all night on the velvet seat on Voron's back, gazing in awestruck wonder at the million stars and the endless magical landscape to which they lent their pale light.

On the fourth day, Voron broke through a crossing into a violet dawn that glowed over a vast steppe. She gazed around in all directions. As far as she could see, nothing. She leaned back in her seat and unwrapped another pancake, humming a tune to herself. The wind streamed through her hair and was starting to make her ears ache. She pulled her headdress down over them, and longed for a pair of earmuffs instead of the richly decorated kokoshnik.

The sun glimmered over the horizon, and its orange light caught on moving water. A river? She sat up and peered into the hazy distance. A narrow stream, trees bending around it and leading back into a sparse forest.

He's here.

The feeling was so strong it nearly took her breath away. This was it. Months at the Chenchikovs' farm, days of travel, and finally, Daniel was nearby. It seemed almost impossible, a wish so dear it couldn't possibly be granted. She stood carefully, leaning over the front bar of the sleigh. Movement in the grass. Two figures. Daniel was one. The other was a winged man. Not Em.

Then the little bells that laced the front of her dress started chiming urgently.

Her heart missed a beat. Daniel was fleeing. He was in danger.

"Down, Voron!" she shouted, thumping the bar and nearly losing her balance. "Down, between them."

Voron hesitated. The angle was too steep.

"Down!" she commanded.

Voron plunged from the sky. She held on to the bar as the sleigh tipped almost vertically toward the ground, speeding so fast that the sound of rushing air nearly deafened her. The pit of her stomach dissolved. The headdress was torn from her hair and tumbled away into the sky. A hundred feet from the ground, Voron swooped into landing position, skidding roughly to a stop in front of the winged demon.

"Stop!" she shouted, jumping from the sleigh and unwinding a protection knot from her arm.

The demon kept running, barreling toward her with a snarl and a baring of his teeth. She threw the knot on the ground. The creature stumbled, fell.

"Daniel!" she shouted.

Daniel stopped. Turned. His mouth dropped in astonishment. Rosa glanced back to the demon. It had stood and now rose into the air, beating its wings and taking off after Daniel once again.

"Leave him alone!" she shouted. Her hand went to the thunder arrow. A fallen star should fell a demon, especially a star imbued with the earthly power of lightning. She ripped it from her neck, took aim and shot it into the sky. It struck the demon on the shoulder. A crack of thunder boomed out of the sky, splitting her hearing and sending harsh echoes for miles. He tumbled, his wings rolling into each other, feathers flying. With a sickening *whump* he hit the ground.

Rosa ran toward Daniel, who stood, stunned, frozen in the distance. As she drew closer, she could see what a toll Skazki had taken on him. He was haggard, thin, he'd grown a sparse beard and his skin was tanned. But he was still Daniel, with dark dreamy eyes and an uncertain brow. She loved him, even though she knew she would have to let him go.

"Rosa!" he gasped, as they crashed into each other, sobbing and shuddering into each other's hair and shoulders.

Rosa stood back after a moment to examine him. "I've come to rescue you," she said.

"Morozko . . . ," he began, then took a frightened step back.

Rosa turned. Morozko had risen to his feet, and limped toward them, rubbing his shoulder. His eyes rounded with wonder as he took in her costume, the girdle and the sarafan, the shoes at her belt and the design of stars and dragons.

"Who are you?" he said, his voice laced with awe. "Why do you ride in Koschey's sleigh? You smell like a Mir woman, but you're dressed like a *bogatyra*. You wield the thunder arrow like a god and the stars glow on your clothes."

"You stay back," she said, imbuing her voice with a vicious confidence she certainly didn't feel. "I have many more weapons that Koschey has given me."

"I'm an old friend of Koschey's," Morozko said. "He would not want you to use them against me."

"Then stay back. Stay away from him."

Morozko indicated Daniel with his good arm. "He has the Golden Bear. I thought to take it, to return it to Koschey."

"That's why I'm here," she said. "Grigory sent me. We're returning to him immediately with the bear. On the sleigh."

"Forgive me. If I'd known I would never have tried to stop you." He offered her the thunder arrow, which she tied once more around her neck. He considered Daniel over Rosa's head. "I'm sorry about your traveling companion."

Rosa turned to Daniel. "Em? Where is she?"

Daniel's face spoke for him, his disbelief and shock plain around his eyes and mouth.

Rosa felt a rush of cold prickles. "No. Not here, Daniel. Not here. She'll wander revenant forever. Where is she? Take me to her, straightaway."

"Back toward the stream," Daniel said.

"I'll lead you," Morozko said, turning with his wings folded behind him.

Like a funeral procession they returned to the site of Em's death. Morozko, marble-cold with snowy wings. Rosa, black-haired and dressed in crimson. Daniel, dirty and clothed in brown. The gray sky lowered over the yellow-green grass, and the hidden sun glared across it all.

At the side of the stream, in muddy grass, Em lay crumpled in a heap. Rosa felt for a pulse, but there was nothing. Morozko knelt beside her, and Rosa could feel the intense cold that radiated from him.

"I didn't intend to kill her," he said to Rosa. "She was a creature unlike any I'd known. I was curious. I explored her. It ended badly."

She turned her gaze to his, and saw distress in his eyes.

"She survived so long here, on her wits."

"She didn't have her wits at the last." He dropped his head.

Rosa returned her attention to Em's body. She closed her eyes, opening her second sight and ranging it around. Nearby, but fading fast, there was a tiny glow of warmth.

"She's around still," Rosa said, clearing her vision. "She hasn't joined the revenants yet."

"You can bring her back to life?" Daniel said, incredulous.

"No. No, Daniel," she replied, regretting arousing any false hope. The anticipation in his face made her sad and she had to look away. "Death is forever. But . . ." She untied the shoes at her waist, realizing now who they were for. "Here," she said, handing one to Daniel, "help me get these on her."

"What are they?"

"Quickly now. They'll take her soul to the one place she can find great joy."

Daniel hurried, Rosa too. Then she laid her hands over Em's heart and closed her eyes again.

Calmly, quietly, she began, "I beseech the moon and all the stars . . ." She knew the zagovor, having heard Anatoly chant it to Nikita's revenant spirit. She had none of his impassioned fury. She didn't need it. The shoes would take Em where she needed to go. This was just to make it simpler.

"My word is firm," she finished. "So it shall be."

The warm light that had been fading suddenly bloomed into

brightness on her second vision, nearly knocking Rosa over. Daniel gasped. He could see it too, and Rosa wondered how long he'd had the second sight. The light dazzled for a moment, then, with a sound that might have been a sigh of relief or an unstructured humming melody, it extinguished to black.

Rosa opened her eyes.

"What do we do with her body?" Daniel said. "We can't leave it here for witches or wolves."

"She's not in it anymore, Daniel," Rosa said.

"But still . . ."

"I'll take her," Morozko said. "I'll take her back to the ice caves with me. Nothing will touch her there."

Rosa and Daniel watched as Morozko folded Em's body gently in his arms, easing her head gingerly onto his bruised shoulder. Then, with an athletic leap, he took to the sky and spiraled up toward the clouds. They watched until he disappeared from view.

Rosa turned to Daniel. He was fighting tears.

She took his hand. "Come on," she said. "Let's get away from here."

Voron waited. Rosa climbed in, but Daniel hesitated.

"Daniel," she asked. "Not still afraid of flying?"

He shook his head, smiling ruefully. "Yes, I am." He took a step onto the sleigh. "But I'm coming with you."

Rosa's here. Rosa's here.

It was what Daniel had dreamed about every day since his arrival in Skazki, and now that she was finally here he could scarcely believe it. No matter that the sky beneath the sleigh was miles deep, that he clung to the side of the sleigh until his knuckles threatened to break through his skin. Rosa was beside him, and he felt a first glimmer of the possibility that he might be happy again sometime.

Em's death was a sad weight on his heart. All the horrors of their journey together condensed into one impossibly real moment when her body slammed the ground with its full dead weight. If only Rosa had come moments sooner . . .

"Tell me everything," Rosa said as they shot through a crossing on the raven sleigh. The sky shattered and resolved, the wide steppe behind him at last.

So he told her everything, and she told him in her turn, and he clutched her hands and allowed himself to weep for Em as the air split again and they found themselves above a deep woodland, night full upon the sky. Rosa commanded the sleigh to land, and soon they were building a fire in a broad clearing. The stars were quiet, but the trees whispered among themselves.

Daniel and Rosa sat together on the velvet seat of the sleigh, while the fire roared next to them. They ate pancakes, and Daniel amused himself watching Rosa's two shadows flicker in the firelight.

"You're so warm," he said to her, amazed by the heat of her shoulder beneath his arm.

"It's not me," she said. "It's this dress."

"I'm used to Em . . . she was so cold toward the end . . ." He trailed off, as the sadness stilled his tongue. Em had been cold in more than body. She had been incapable of love, but somehow he had grown to love her. He would miss her blunt practicality, her poised mannerisms, her games of numbered lists.

"You must have grown very close," Rosa said in a soft voice.

"We did. I mean, I did. I don't know how she felt, if she felt . . . but she was a good friend, and we looked out for each other. In the end, I didn't look out carefully enough."

"It wasn't your fault, Daniel," Rosa said, stroking his fingers gently. "Wherever she is now, she's happy."

Daniel gazed at her. She was so unspeakably beautiful, had such fire in her veins. She smiled at him.

"What is it?"

"I'm sorry, Rosa," he said. "I still love you."

Her eyes changed. Some of the fire dimmed. She fought with words for a few moments, then said, "It's all right, Daniel." She leaned in to kiss him. It had been so long since he'd touched her lips with his, and feelings both tender and violent rose in him. His hands moved into her hair and he pressed his body against her. Such sweet bruising warmth.

"Get me out of this stupid dress," she laughed, unpicking the soundless bells.

He stripped her and laid her in the cold grass on the bank. She smelled like heaven: warm skin and clean hair and musky female scents. She drew him down beside her and wrenched his clothes from his body, lips like fire on his flesh. Everything about her was laid open to him, he plunged into her and the brilliance of his desire sizzled through his veins and sinews. Grass tickled his bare skin. He pushed her head back and kissed her neck; her pulse thundered under his lips. The night enveloped them.

"I love you," he murmured against her ear. "I love you and the stupid words aren't enough."

"I know," she said. "They never are."

It was too cold for nakedness, and they dressed again, in time, and huddled together next to the fire, still in the dreamy weariness of lovemaking's wake. Rosa was fighting a dislocation, an anxiety that she couldn't name. So now she had to tell him everything. And telling was remembering, dragging up every detail and seeing the whole awful mess laid out.

"How soon can we go home, do you think?" Daniel asked.

Rosa fell silent, and could feel the unease stiffen into Daniel's shoulder.

"Rosa? We are going home, aren't we?"

She took a deep breath, released it. "It's confusing," she said.

"What's confusing? We take the bear to Grigory, then we go home."

"I'm not sure what we're going to do with the bear."

"But, Rosa—"

She continued, more forcefully, cutting him off, "And I'm not going home."

He sat up and pulled back so he could look at her. Seconds passed.

"What?" he said at last.

"I'm not going back to Mir."

He was frantic now, and the guilt soured her stomach.

"Why not? Why stay here? It's full of horrors."

"And wonders."

"Rosa, don't fuck with my head. You can't possibly mean to stay here because the sky's a pretty color."

Rosa turned away, and watched the fire. Shadows moved across her face. She searched for words. "I don't expect you to understand."

"Try me."

Anticipation prickled. The feeling of adrenalin that she ordinarily loved so much, now so unpleasant. She was afraid, but she tried to smile. "Oh, I'm sorry. I'm so sorry. Daniel. Last time I saw you, I promised to tell you something."

"Yes," he said slowly. "You promised you'd explain why we split up."

"It's the same reason. The reason I have to stay here in Skazki." She held out her hands, palms up, and shrugged apologetically. "I realize now that it's something I should have told you a long time ago."

A breeze shivered across the treetops. "I almost don't want you to tell me," Daniel said. "You're frightening me."

"I have to."

"I know."

Rosa paused. Where to start? Anywhere, she supposed. All roads led to the same awful destination.

"When my mother died she was only fifty-two," she said. "Her mother died aged fifty-seven. They both died of the same thing."

Daniel was puzzled. "Is that it? You think you're going to die young?"

"Wait," she said, holding a finger to his lips. "Wait. Don't say a word, not until I'm finished. Let me tell my story. I don't much like it, but it's mine to tell.

"Mama died at fifty-two, but she was sick for a long time. In fact, the first symptoms started to show up when she was only in her thirties. At the time, she put it down to the shock of Papa's death, but things got worse, not better. By the time she was forty-two, she had been diagnosed. The doctor who was treating her was the best we could find. Uncle Vasily funded it all. Dr. Howlett was part of a research project at a big Canadian hospital, and because of the family history, because of the early onset of the illness, he asked Mama to be involved in the research. He sequenced one of Mama's genes."

Daniel nodded, but she knew he didn't really follow. He'd always been more interested in art than science.

"They found a mutation." She realized her words were rushing out, flat and breathless, and tried to regain control. Fate weighed heavy. "A mutation on the PS–1 gene."

"What does that mean, Rosa?" he prompted.

"It meant that I could be tested too. If I wanted. Dr. Howlett was very keen, my friends were less so. I was young and cocky, so I took the test." Yes, she had once felt invincible. What a horror it had been to find out that she wasn't. She tried an ironic smile. "I had the same mutation. It's genetic fate. I'll die of it too."

Daniel shook his head. "You're going to die in your fifties? And for this you won't be with me now?"

Rosa felt then that Daniel could never understand. He probably thought she had inherited some romantic illness; something fitting for the raven-haired goddess he had always taken her to be, and she'd always encouraged him to imagine. A romantic wasting disease, a scented deathbed, perhaps, all covered in vines and rose petals. And then, an angel weeping on a headstone and two or three liquid-eyed children to console him. She could have laughed, but it would have sounded bitter and hard.

"Don't you want to know, Daniel? What I'm going to die of?"

Daniel shrugged. "Cancer?" he asked, probably because his own mother had died of cancer. He had been too young to see any of the mess and substance of her suffering.

"No, not cancer," she said, twisting the hem of her skirt between her fingers. "Nothing nearly so easy on my dignity."

Daniel shook his head, growing impatient. "Rosa, we might have thirty years together. That's enough time for love, and children, and holidays at the beach. What could be so bad that . . ."

The fire cracked and popped expectantly. An owl on a nearby

tree ruffled its feathers and swooped away. Rosa felt the pressure of fear, of embarrassment.

"Alzheimer's," she said, setting the word free at last. And, damn, here came the stupid tears.

"Alzheimer's?"

"Yes, yes. Forgetting who I am. Becoming a dead-eyed vessel." Her voice died off to a whisper.

Daniel was silent. A few moments passed, and she knew already that he was as repulsed by the illness as she was.

But then, "Rosa, Rosa," he said, reaching for her hand, "it might not be so bad."

She snatched her fingers away. "I know precisely how bad it will be. I nursed my mother through it. She didn't know who I was some days. Some days she threw things at my head. Some days she cried for hours and asked where my father was. Some days she just sat there like a zombie while I mopped up body fluids. I know *exactly* what I'm in for." Then, quieter: "What you're in for."

"I love you, Rosa. I'd look after you, no matter what happened."

Her mouth contorted and she reined in a sob, angry that she couldn't get her feelings under control. "Don't you understand? I don't want you to look after me. Not under those circumstances. I don't want you to see me so ruined."

"I wouldn't mind."

"I'd mind! This isn't about you." Her face grew warm. "This isn't about wanting to spare you the pain. This is about me. I want to stay beautiful and clever. I want to remember everything. I want to remember myself. I don't want to lose myself." The yawning chasm of fear opened up within her as she named it, the worst fear she had.

He reached out to touch her, but she shrugged him off, leapt to her feet and paced, swallowing her sobs and feigning composure. "That's why I'm staying here, Daniel. Here, my own death can't find me."

"Rosa, if you stay here you'll die horribly."

She shook her head, calming herself with her new exit clause. If Papa Grigory was telling the truth, there was a way out. *If* he was telling the truth. "No, no. You see, I've met Papa Grigory now. He keeps himself safe, and his little girl. I can live with them."

"And never leave his cottage? You? Spend forever in a tiny space like that? You'd go insane."

She hadn't yet imagined it, and Daniel's words deflated her. "Well, then, if I hate it after a hundred years, I can always walk out and be torn to pieces in the forest," she said flippantly.

"Just as long as you don't think you can walk out, back to Mir and find me. Because I'll be dead before the hundred years is up."

His serious voice annoyed her. She waved him away. "Don't talk like that. Don't make me feel guilty. This is my decision, my life, my brain." She tapped her head. "I'm staying here."

Daniel shook his head sadly. "Then I'll let you go," he replied, "but I will love you every day of my life."

Rosa returned to the fireside, folded her arms around him. "Daniel, I'm sorry. I'm so, so sorry."

He was stiff in her embrace. "You know, all of this is so . . ." Anger confounded his words. "I can't bring myself to wish I'd never met you," he finished, "but if I was sane, I would wish it."

She drew back to look into his eyes, and saw how tired he was and cursed herself for burdening him with this when he should have been resting. He had slogged for months through hostile countryside. "When was the last time you slept properly?" she asked. "You should lie down."

"I'm not going to sleep. Not now. How could I, after what you've just told me?"

"Then just lie down next to me." She encouraged him to lie down, his head in her lap. "We're here together now, Daniel. Let's enjoy it."

"I'm not enjoying anything. I want to know how—"

"No. I won't discuss it any further." She loosened the dreaming girdle from her waist. Without him knowing, she smoothed it across his shoulder. It would help him sleep, deeply enough to dream at least. She stroked his hair and gazed at the fire, muttering a little sleep incantation under her breath.

"Rosa?"

"Let's not talk anymore. There's nothing more to talk about."

One minute passed. Two. Then he was asleep.

Rosa watched the fire for a long time, thinking. Stars glimmered coolly above her, Anatoly bumped inside her. From time to time, she glanced at Daniel, his beloved face made childlike by sleep. She ached to be with him, to live out those fantasies that she knew he harbored as she did. But what choice did she have? If Anatoly had left her even a shred of her own magic to grow, she could return to Mir and then come back here in ten or fifteen years, before it was all too late. But she couldn't leave Anatoly inside her much longer. He would eventually choose his own death to imprisonment in the dark spaces under her ribs, and he'd be clever enough to do it without passing any magic into her.

Daniel was right in one thing. Living forever in Papa Grigory's little cottage was not ideal either. Eventually she'd be tempted out, longing for adventure, for sights and sounds as yet unwitnessed, and then she'd meet her death and wander revenant, a miserable confused soul forever.

Thoughts of Papa Grigory led to thoughts of the Golden Bear. Why had Perun and Veles told her a different version of events? What motives did each party have? It wasn't that she believed them over Grigory—he'd been more than generous to her—it was simply that something Veles had said repeated over and over in her head: *At least go to see the Snow Witch. Once you see her, all will be clear.*

Rosa thought that clarity might be precisely what she needed.

A dream at the edge of slumber.

A fair-haired girl. Pale blue eyes that turned to him, then deepened to the dark color of fathomless oceans. A shock to his heart.

"Rosa?" he muttered, half-waking.

"Shh . . . I'm here," she said.

"How long have I been asleep?" he asked, sitting up. A piece of material slipped off his shoulder, and Rosa scooped it up quickly.

"What's that?" he asked.

"You looked cold." She tied it around her waist and smiled. "Did you have sweet dreams?"

He frowned, remembering a dream only moments past that

had now fled from memory. "I can't remember." He met her eyes. What he did remember was the nightmare of last night's revelations. Her vanity, her stubbornness: two qualities he had always adored about her, but that now stood between them.

"You've only been asleep a few hours. Get some more rest if you like."

He ran his hand through his hair and yawned. "I'm fine. You?"

"I'm eager to get going. The sun's nearly up."

"Where are we going, then?" Daniel asked.

Rosa smiled cautiously. "You won't argue with me about it?"

"Would there be any point?" he asked.

She shook her head. "We're heading northeast," she said. "We're going to see the Snow Witch."

Thirty-three

What in the two worlds is she doing?

Rosa Kovalenka has taken my raven and is heading for precisely the place I don't want her to go!

I pace and I curse, and Totchka draws back from me, frightened. Why is Rosa doing this? Doesn't she know she is mine to control? My bogatyra, the heroine of my story. I put her on this journey, I dressed her in red, I furnished her with the secret weapons. Foolish, foolish girl.

Or am I a fool? An old fool, a desperate fool, a weak fool?

Totchka is alarmed. I've told her to play with her seashells outside, but she prefers to sit on her bed with her dolls, eyes turning up to me repeatedly, checking that I am not going to break the dishes and bite the table. I must collect myself. I must finally tell you why the Snow Witch can't have the Golden Bear. I have told you the rest of my story, there's no use in keeping the last from you.

You knew, I suppose, that it was me? That "Secret Ambassador" was one of my many appellations? You live long enough, you gather more names, as though identities proliferate the way memories do. It was I who negotiated with Olga, with Mokosha, with Sofya and Aleksandr. It was I who worked so hard for Skazki, to keep us attached to Mir by blood. The demons and spirits were too stupid, the old gods were too lazy. I alone, deathless wanderer, was suited for the task.

After Aleksandr's hasty half-promises, I resolved on spending more time in Mir, but away from court. The noble classes, after all, were a fraction of the population. I had to accept that I had done all I could in keeping Mokosha's blood on the throne, and now my real work was out among the people, encouraging them to pick up their old ways. I acknowledged, too, that Christ's religion was never going to leave Russia, but I had noticed how often the pagan and the Christian sat easily side by side in rural practices. A wolf-eyed sorcerer from Skazki offered little in the way of persuasion for Mir people, but a holy fool, who preached salvation along with superstition, did.

I first settled in the Tobolsk region, where I met a woman who needed a father for her three small children. I took her dead husband's name for convenience. It was Grigory Efimovich Rasputin.

I loved the peasant way of life. I loved its simplicity and its carnal nature. I reconnected with my baseness out there. I plugged as many women as would have me, I ate and drank to excess, I rolled in muddy puddles and worshipped Mother Moist Earth with my prick. When I grew bored with my new family, I began to wander in my high-cut peasant boots, with my loose shirt and long black coat, carrying a crooked staff. I wandered for years, and I met many good Mir folk, and I returned to them their old superstitions. I even spent time with Church hierarchs, learning as much as I could about this earthly religion and finding areas of doctrine that overlapped into mysticism, so I could later exploit them. I used my magic for miracles, for healing and enchantments, and tales of my passing reverberated around the countryside.

Word of my powers traveled far, and finally made it back to St. Petersburg, and to the Tsar Nikolai.

I was not unaware of his family, of course. I still had my magic mirror to watch them. In the entire time that Mokosha's blood was in Mir, and despite the intermarriages with other countries, that blood never flowed outside of Russia. It couldn't bear to leave its Mother. All I needed was a little Mokosha, warm in a beating Mir heart, to keep the worlds from slipping apart permanently. At least Aleksandr's promise had ensured that.

Two of Nikolai's children had it: the youngest daughter, Anastasia, and Aleksei, the little boy. Aleksei had inherited something else in his blood: it wouldn't clot properly. Little accidents became huge catastrophes. The boy was terribly ill, seemed doomed to an early grave.

Still, I did not force my hand. This time, I wanted to come to court as an invited guest, not as a sinister intruder.

When I came to St. Petersburg, it was at the behest of one of the Tsaritsa's closest friends, Anya Vyrubova. Anya was interested in mysticism, in prophets, mesmerists, saints, clairvoyants, rogues and madmen. She was a pretty moon-faced woman, doe-eyed and sweetly smiling, although there was something vain and vacant about her. She found for me a little room, and made sure I wanted for nothing. I was comfortable there for a time.

St. Petersburg was a thriving modern city. Motor cars shared the bridges with horses and carts; electric street lamps lit the roads radiating out from the admiralty; the finest homes always had a telephone. Anya paid me handsomely for a few magic tricks, and from there my reputation spread. I was besieged by supplicants: they wanted miracles, blessings, prophecies. Magic is physically demanding and, at first, I would lie exhausted on a shelf of the bathhouse after a night's work.

Then I grew canny. I gave very few of them what they really wanted. They were mostly happy to be divested of their money in return for some mumbling incantations and vague platitudes about God.

Those who couldn't pay in money paid in other ways. Sweets, alcohol, clocks, flowers, fish, anything. Some women, bored with their upper-class lives and drawn to my raw, bestial nature, paid with their bodies happily. Repeatedly.

I was humping one such woman, a baroness with stout ankles, on my creaking iron bed, when Anya burst into the room. She was flushed and her eyes sparkled. Without apology, she said, "Grigory! Exciting news! The Tsaritsa has asked to meet you!"

Anya and I were received in the Formal Reception Room of the palace at Tsarskoe Selo and told to wait. Anya sat on an upholstered French chair, while I circled the gold parquet floor. Seven huge windows invited in broad streams of sunlight. The walls, overlaid with white marble, seemed to glow. I paused in my pacing, gazing out the window over Aleksander Park. It was only October, but a light snow had fallen the previous night. Yellow leaves loosened and dived in the breeze, and with the sun glinting on the snow the effect was one of silvers and golds, as though the park was an extension of the extravagant grandeur inside.

"No need to be nervous, Grigory," Anya said. I hadn't realized she had come to stand at my side.

"I'm not nervous," I said to her with a smile. "I'm excited."

The door flew open, then thudded closed behind an imposing woman. Anya hurried to her side, offering her a kiss. "My dear Sunny," she said. "I have brought the holy man to you."

The woman turned to me. Her strong German face was beautiful, her blue eyes imperious, her red-gold hair gleamed in the sunshine. This was the Tsaritsa, Alix of Hesse-Darmstadt. The nickname "Sunny" had never suited anyone less. I never saw her brow without rainclouds upon it. I never saw her hands still, or her feet in one place. Even on this, our first meeting, I could sense a great disquiet in her. It wasn't my way to humble myself before these people, and I sensed anyway that I would make inroads with this woman if I avoided the simpering servility that kept all others at a distance from her. I walked forward, seized her elbows and enfolded her into an embrace.

"Mama," I said, "how you must have suffered with your little boy."

Sunny took a step back from me, alarmed but not angry. "Yes, I have. But how could you know?"

"I haven't told him anything," Anya interjected quickly.

"Your son," I said, "he suffers a bleeding disease."

Sunny pressed her hand to her mouth. "That is impossible for you to know. We have kept it secret from all but our closest circle."

"It is true though," I said.

Sunny lowered herself into a chair, her elbow resting on the ebony table beside her. "How can he know that?" she mumbled. "Anya, are you sure you didn't tell him?"

"I said nothing of Aleksei to him," Anya said, her round eyes agog. "I am as amazed as you."

I knelt in front of her, boldly taking her hands. "I know more than that, Mama," I said. "I know the trouble on your heart is guilt, that you believe Aleksei's illness is your fault. The bleeding is in your family, isn't it?"

Sunny's hand went to her breast, and she began to breathe rapidly.

"But I will tell you this now. The child will outgrow his illness. By the time he is a man, he will be well."

Sunny met my gaze, and her eyes were damp and her lips were trembling. "How can you say that will be so?"

I rose, smoothing my tangled hair. A few crumbs dropped out on the shoulder of my rough shirt. "I will make it so. If you will allow me to help you." I returned to the window, letting my promise sink in. From the corner of my eye, I could see Anya urging the Tsaritsa to stand, to approach me. I waited, and she came.

"My son," she said, "has just learned to walk. He stumbles and falls often. It makes me mad with worry. As though blackbirds in my head are flapping to be free." Here, she pressed her hand against her temple. "This morning, he hit his knee. It has already swollen hugely, and he has hardly stopped crying."

"Then bring him to me," I said, "and we shall see how it goes."

Sunny hurried to the door, throwing it open and bustling out. From a distance, I could hear her bellowing, "Maria! Bring Aleksei at once!"

Anya fell to her knees and touched my hand. "Grigory, you are a prophet."

"Stand up, Anya. We are old friends."

"I feel humbled. I have always been your most ardent supporter, but I did not know your gifts were so far-ranging."

I pulled her to her feet. "Now, now, Anya. Enough of that."

Anya clutched at my fingers still, shaking her head. "Do you not see? If you can heal Aleksei, you will be the most powerful man in all of Russia."

Precisely then, the scampering of feet rushed down the corridor toward us, and a little white dog raced into the room, with a little fair-haired girl in pursuit.

"Trushka, no!" she declared, hunting the dog to his hiding place under a table and firmly wagging her finger at him. "Bad dog." Then she looked up, saw me, and her jaw dropped. "Oh, my!"

I was puzzled. I knew that this was the Grand Duchess Anastasia, all of four years old but already remarkable for her pretty, mischievous face. Why should she react to my presence with such surprise?

"What is it, little girl?" I asked.

The dog ran past her and back into the corridor. Anastasia glanced after him only briefly, turning her gaze back to me. "I dreamed of you last night, sir," she said, "and now you are real."

I smiled, hoping the gesture would diminish the oddness of my wolf-like eyes. "Was it a nice dream?"

She shook her head slowly. "I don't think so. You were trying to steal my bear."

"Your bear?"

"I'll show you."

She raced off and I turned to Anya, feigning amused puzzlement. It was not odd to me that Anastasia should dream of me and the Golden Bear, especially the night before my arrival. Her Skazki blood gave her many gifts that she would probably never recognize or use.

In a few moments she was back, panting and flushed, with the dog scurrying at her heels. She presented for my inspection the Golden Bear. I took it carefully from her.

"She's very beautiful," I said. "Where did you get her?"

"She belongs to my family, but I love her the most and so she stays in my room. Though Aleksei stole her the other day, but I just stole her right back."

I was stroking the bear's familiar belly when Sunny returned, stern-faced.

"Get that dog out of here! You imp, I've told you no dogs in the reception room."

Anastasia collected the dog in her arms, and started, "But, Mama, this man—" Then she hushed when the nurse stole into the room with little Aleksei in her arms. The child was crying softly, hoarsely.

"I'll go, Mama," she said, leaving quickly and closing the door behind her.

I placed the bear on the table, and moved forward to lift Aleksei from the nurse's arms. She shrank from me, frightened. The child, however, relaxed as soon as he was in my embrace. No magic there. Sunny and the nurse were nervy women, always anxious and over-solicitous. With me, Aleksei merely felt that somebody strong and calm was in charge.

"Sit with me, my child," I said, lowering myself to the floor with my legs stretched out in front of me. I laid Aleksei across my lap and peeled back the bandage around his swollen knee. The blood was collecting under the skin. Fortunately it was only a minor bump, but a major injury would easily result in the boy bleeding to death. I understood the Tsaritsa's anxiety. It wasn't just for herself: it was for her country. Aleksei's death would leave Nikolai without a male heir.

I was still not sure what I would do, though I felt certain that somehow the sympathy of my Skazki nature, and this child's Skazki blood, would provide the key. I placed my hands on the swelling, and Aleksei whimpered but didn't flinch. Beneath my fingers, I could feel Mokosha's blood, strong and magical. The Mir weakness, which Sunny had introduced into Aleksei's body, was trying to drag it down.

The first thing I had to do was to ensure that the child wouldn't die while I performed my magic. He was very young, and there was no telling what effect powerful magic might have on him. I hummed softly, rocking him back and forth, preparing to store his soul outside of his body to protect it from whatever physical demands I had to place on it to heal him. There were no dogs, ducks or rats nearby. Ordinarily, I would have preferred to send his soul into another warm being, but on this day, I decided to send it to the Golden Bear.

With a breath and a muttered incantation, the boy's soul flew away, speared into the bear, and sat waiting to return. Aleksei still cried and whimpered, and I understood that an inanimate object like the bear could not hold a life completely within its dark confines, that the layer of the soul most closely linked to the physical had to stay behind in a warm body and continue to suffer. Suffering I could allow, but I would not allow this child to die.

I cupped the swelling on his knee with my palm, and closed my eyes and forced my mind down into the blood. Dark and red and moving around me like a powerful river. In it, I searched for Mokosha, for the familiar shadowy intensity of her magic; I pulled the shadows together, creating a tide, and with the tide, I pulled the blood back, out of the swelling, into his veins and heart. Below my hand, the lump began to shrink, Aleksei's sobs eased and his little body drooped and cooled. I had gone too far; I let go. His breath caught on a hook. Mine too. Then he breathed again, and warmth returned to his skin. I pressed him against me and hummed his soul back into his body, and he was restored to himself. He sat up and looked around, palming tears from his face.

"Mama?" he said.

Sunny, trembling, collapsed onto the floor next to me, kissing my hands and calling me Father. In those five short minutes, I had taken her in thrall.

My dealings with the Tsaritsa, indeed with the whole family, continued for many years after that. Every time Aleksei injured himself, I was summoned. If I hadn't heard from them in a long time, I would send some subtle magic through the air, and arrange a little mishap, a small crisis to keep them dependent on me. I took an apartment on Gorokhovaia Street, close to the train to Tsarskoe Selo. Sunny learned early to keep my visits secret, insisting that the children's nurse greet me as though I was her special visitor. The little girls adored me, though Aleksei never quite warmed to me. Perhaps he associated me too closely with his times of pain and suffering. The Golden Bear became his favorite object, though Anastasia fought him for it fiercely. I think he loved it as a peaceful keep for his soul in healing times, as well as for the blood memory of his magical heritage.

Secrecy or not, word soon began to circulate that I was close to the Tsar and Tsaritsa. Some took it to mean that I was God's own angel on earth, and they flocked to me for incantations and spells (though they called them prayers and prophecies), never leaving me alone in my little apartment for a moment. The opinions of some, however, were vastly lower. I had too much influence with the Tsar, they said. I was leading Russia into ruin, they said. My advice was being adopted over the advice of other, more qualified men, they said. Ah, what did I care what they said? They wanted what was best for Russia, standing at a narrow window of history that they hadn't the prescience to see beyond. I wanted what was best for the two worlds of Mir and Skazki, for all time stretching away to forever's edge.

I told him, and I told him, and I told him again. I said to Nikolai that he *must not* send Russia to the war. I feared something, something that I had started to feel but was beyond words. There were only two children left with Skazki blood . . . what if they should die?

He ignored my advice. How different things might have been had he listened to me.

When Nikolai came to me, when the Great War was already in full, terrible flight, it was late and I was sleeping. The doorbell rang and I ignored it, thinking it was another petitioner too stupid and self-absorbed to realize that even holy men sleep. When it rang again, I felt a prickle across my shoulders, a distinct feeling that I should go down and let this petitioner in.

I had been drinking heavily at the bathhouse before I'd come home to bed. Perhaps I was still drunk. The smell of cabbage and sheep's cheese hung heavily in the rooms of my apartment. I went to the door in my nightshirt to find the Tsar on the other side. He was dressed in a dark coat, with a fur hat pulled down over his ears. Nikolai was a slight man, pale and with hooded eyes. He had arrived incognito.

"Yes, Father, what is it?" I said, drawing him inside and closing the door behind him.

"I need to speak with you, Grigory," he replied.

"Then come upstairs and we'll be comfortable." I led him to the living room, and lit a dozen candles, which cast shadows on the grimy walls. The electric lamp was not working, and had been junked onto my desk along with bent icons, copper coins and a dozen old apples. Alcohol had dulled my sense of dignity: I wallowed in my own filth.

Nikolai pulled out a cigarette and lit it on one of the candles, before sitting in the heavy oak chair I offered him. He crossed his right ankle over his left knee—there was something effeminate about the gesture—and blew a stream of smoke into the air. Shadows hung under his eyes, and his small white hands trembled almost imperceptibly.

He was silent for a long time, watching me with his sad gaze. Then, finally, he said, "Russia is seething."

"What do you want from me?"

"I hear tales, and I don't know whether to believe them."

"Tales of me? Or tales of Russia's anger?"

"The tales of Russia's anger I know to believe. Human life has become too cheap, and yet Sunny still insists on fresh flowers every week brought by train from the Crimea. I can't stop her. I can't stop the tide that's rising. If only we could win this damnable war." He stopped, caught his breath. His lips twitched downward, and I realized he was trying not to cry. "No, it's the tales of you I have come to ask about."

"Go on."

"That you have known my family before. Impossibly, for you appear to be only a man of forty."

I dipped my head and pinched the bridge of my nose, thoughtful. How could he have heard this? "From whom do you hear these tales?"

"From my daughter Anastasia, who dreams of you often."

"They are but the dreams of a child."

"The dreams of a young woman, Grigory, because it is her approaching womanhood that has brought on this power of prophetic dreams which troubles me so greatly." He removed his hat and placed it on the seat beside him, and ran a hand through his hair. "How do you explain the engraving she found? You and Aleksandr? Or the old watercolor of your face, in the crowd behind Ekaterina the Great?"

I held my tongue on my opinion of Ekaterina, the fat German bully. Her insatiable lusts had nearly bred Mokosha's blood out of the family line.

"Well, it must be true then," I said. "I have known your family before."

"Anastasia said you helped Aleksandr. That the spirits of your magical homeland drove out Napoleon's Grand Army."

I understood, now, where the Tsar's thoughts were tending. Much had changed since Aleksandr's time: his broken promise would resound too loudly with the inhabitants of Skazki, and I doubted they would come to the Tsar's aid again. But, as always, the old hope rose in me again. *This time, perhaps, we will mend the breech for good.*

"I will tell you everything," I said. And so I did, starting with Olga and all the way through. Night faded and daylight glowed through the crimson curtains, and I explained to Nikolai his family's link to Skazki and the awesome responsibility that now sat on his shoulders.

After I had finished, I left Nikolai in contemplation, while I went to the kitchen and fixed some breakfast. I scraped mold off the cheese I'd left out too long, and found a crust of bread. In a jar on the bench where I sat to eat, handfuls of money were crammed to overflowing. I eyed it, making plans for a trip to the market which I knew I would never take. Sleeping, drinking, fucking: they were all I cared for. In time, he followed me in, leaned his shoulder against the cool tiled wall, and set his chin against fear.

"I'll do it, Secret Ambassador," he said. "If you can convince your people to come to our aid, I will grant you everything you want."

My blood flushed warm, and I put down my meal to steady myself against the bench. "Don't make empty promises."

"I will promise it with all my heart. I will put it in writing and sign it with my own blood."

"Your blood isn't worth much to me, Nikolai." I shook my head dismissively. "Allow me to return to my homeland, to assess the goodwill for the idea. It may take some time." Already I was outlining my plan: get the forest creatures on-side first; they were always more reasonable. Then the minor demons; finally the witches . . . and at the end of this process, Aleksei, nearly a grown man, would sit on the throne of two mighty kingdoms, reunited once again and invincible.

Nikolai left soon after. Pulling on his hat at the door, he turned to me and said, "Don't tell Sunny."

"Secrecy is my nature," I said with a smile, and watched him walk off into the dim, snowy morning alone.

Secrecy was also the agenda of the two men who watched him, who had followed him here the previous night, and about whom I had not known. Already there were a million suspicions about me, but the Tsar's midnight visit sealed my fate. I did not know it at the time, but I was about to fall victim to murderers.

I was made curious by Nikolai's visit. I was made curious by his talk of Anastasia's prophetic dreams. In days of old, when Mokosha lived as Ivan's wife, her name too had been Anastasia. Had some special sympathy of identity created a link between the Tsar's little girl and the pagan goddess I had loved so well? I remembered the first time I had met Anastasia, when she was a tiny child of four. Immediately she had recognized me, had felt a connection between me and the bear.

Nikolai had returned to his war residence. I took the train to Tsarskoe Selo.

Sunny received me, as she always did now, in her own room. Mauve curtains drifted over the windows; mauve wallpaper and mauve lace. Fresh flowers filled every flat space, and I remembered what the Tsar had told me, that these flowers came regularly by train at a time when food could not make its way to the front.

"Friend," she said, "I'm so pleased to see you. I hope you bring good prophecy, because I do not like my husband being so far from home and hearth."

"I predict all will be well, though it may be some time before you hold him in your arms again," I said, and this settled her fluttering hands a little, and brought some color to her cheeks. "Mother, it is not you I wish to see today. I had hoped to speak with Anastasia."

Sunny's expression was perplexed, perhaps even concerned. She loved me dearly, but she also knew the stories about me and my excesses.

"Only briefly, Mother," I said, "and you are welcome to stay while I speak with her."

Of course she consented. I was the man who healed her son, whose prophecy of Aleksei's recovery from hemophilia by manhood was already beginning to come true (which was not through my doing, but through the strength of Skazki blood, you understand).

Anastasia had bloomed into womanhood. She was, perhaps, sixteen at the time. Her pretty face was still impish, but her body had gathered curves. In truth, she was almost fat, but it didn't mar her beauty or her bearing.

"Mother?" she said, espying me waiting as Sunny ushered her in.

"Grigory must speak with you," Sunny said. "I shall wait here, and work on my cross-stitch." Sunny took herself into a corner and picked up her sewing. I stood with my back to the window, and the glass was cold. Outside, snow lay heavy around the bare, black trees. I was aware of Sunny's eyes, flicking away from her work and up to my face. She was worried. She was always worried. And all that worry couldn't save her from her awful fate in the end, so it was energy ill-spent.

I eyed Anastasia closely, and she giggled under my scrutiny.

"Grigory, what on earth is wrong? You look as though you expect my head to pop off and release monsters."

I chuckled, and touched her plump cheek. "I have heard about your dreams, little one. You are very busy when you are sleeping."

Sunny put aside her sewing and made no pretense of not watching.

"My dreams are very vivid, yes."

"And you often dream of me, or so I am told."

"Yes, I dream of you, and you are in stories from other places and times."

"What a creative girl! You should write them down."

"I started to, but Tatiana tore up my notebook, the swine. All because I stole her cream dress and ripped it accidentally." She laughed again. "I'm far too tired to be writing stories, anyway."

I pushed off the window and walked slowly around the room, aware of the two sets of eyes on me: Sunny's clouded with anxiety, Anastasia's with amusement.

"Well, you are being very mysterious today, Grigory," Anastasia said.

What was I to tell her? That I had a strong sense that the magic in her blood was the highest concentration since the babies grown in Mokosha's own womb? That her dreams showed that she was tied more tightly than any other ruler to Skazki? That, if I had my way, I would put her on the throne of Russia, ahead of her sickly brother, to rule it and the magic kingdom?

"Let's invite Anya up for tea," I said, forcing a smile. "I'm famished."

I was excited, standing on the brink of possibilities. A half-Mir witch queen, a new era. Time would tell if these dreams would come to be.

Living in Mir had dulled my wits. I drank too much and I cared too much about my prick and too little about my safety. When Feliks Yusipov invited me to meet his wife—with the inference that I would be welcome to fuck her—I took the invitation at face value. Why not? Yusipov was a known scoundrel, and he loved to dress in women's clothes and make merry. It crossed my mind that he may even want to join us. What didn't cross my mind was that the invitation was a front for a plot on my life.

Of course, as soon as they led me into the little downstairs room, I felt a twinge of concern. The low arches almost bumped my head. There were no windows. But there was a glorious feast of all my favorite things: little chocolate cream cakes, candied fruit and strawberry-iced pastries, and a decanter of madeira. I sat down, eager for the repast. The moment my fingers lit on one of the pastries, I sensed the poison within.

What was I to do? Yusipov and his cronies sat with me, smiling, nodding congenially.

"Irina will be here soon."

"Help yourself, my good friend. This food has been made especially for you."

I spied a candied apple on the table, reached for it and thrust it in my pocket. The men continued to urge me to eat. I smiled, took a moment to balance myself, then hummed a little tune.

"That's a lovely melody, Grigory," Yusipov said. "Would you like it if I played the guitar for you?"

"I'd like it very much," I said, reaching eagerly for the cakes. My soul was now stored in an apple in my pocket, so I didn't need to fear death. Moreover, I wanted to play a trick on these charming monsters.

I ate. I drank. The food smelled so bitterly of cyanide that I almost laughed at them. Any poor victim of these men would know he was being poisoned before he opened his mouth to eat!

The night wore on. Yusipov played his guitar. The men exchanged furtive glances; I pretended I didn't see. An hour passed, two. They were growing desperate. I asked them again where Irina was, just to see their reactions.

Yusipov nearly tripped over himself trying to get out the door. "I'll go upstairs and see what keeps her," he said. The other two followed him quickly. I put my feet on the table and picked my teeth, and tossed the candied apple up into the air and down again, waiting for the next act of the play.

The young rake returned with a gun. He shot me twice. I fell. They left. I lay there a long time, chuckling to myself about the merry game I was playing. When Yusipov came back, wanting to dispose of my body, I sat up and grinned at him. He shrieked and hid behind the table, and I walked out.

They got me again in the yard, another two bullets, slamming into my body. I fell again, and let them drag me to the river. I stilled my laughter as they heaved me into the water. This time, I intended to let them think the job was done. What a trick it would be to visit Yusipov the following day, inquiring after my coat! I sank under, bubbles fizzing through my beard. Their dark shapes waited above. I sank low, swam a hundred feet and surfaced. I began the walk home, cold and wet, chuckling over my intentions to upset Yusipov. I did not know that all my intentions were about to be foiled by an unexpected force.

Love.

I can explain it no more than any other fool can. I dragged myself out of Moika Canal, hummed my soul back into my body and quickly healed my wounds. Koschey the deathless fears no bullet or poison. I took a back route through dark, snow-lined streets, far from the electric lamps: damp stone, rotted vegetables dumped in alleyways, and the scent of fatty boiling mutton. An urban emptiness that is always inhabited by cold, and bad smells, and poverty. This is where I nearly stumbled over a bundle of rags that lay on a tiled doorstep.

As I sidestepped it, the bundle moved and whimpered. Perhaps the dramatic events of the evening had worn my nerves down. I jumped in fright. Then, when I realized the bundle was no more than some poor wretch freezing to death, I resumed my step and walked on.

"Papa?" a little voice wavered in the dark.

I turned. Everything changed.

The little girl was sick and pale, on the verge of death. Her eyes met mine and held them. A shiver of fate hissed across my body; some transformative power emanated from her.

"I'm not your papa," I said sternly.

"No, that's right," she replied. "My papa is dead."

"And where is your mama?"

"She is in the same place. And my brother. They are all dead. I was sleeping when you walked past, and something about your footsteps reminded me of my papa."

I swallowed down hard, and tried to make sense of these feelings. But I could not. It was as though my brain, so long the machine that drove my experience, now seized and jammed. A weight lifted off me: I was *glad* to feel instead of think. And I told myself that every man, no matter who he is and where he is from, is on a journey. Love is a part of every man's journey, why should I be different? I was weary—so weary—of machinations and calculations and schemes. Finding Totchka, I could see with stunning clarity, was the start of my new path, one which now beckoned with the sweetest promises. It did not pay to question such a revolution of feeling too directly.

"I must be on my way," I mumbled, with no conviction.

She raised her skinny arms, as though she assumed it perfectly natural that I would pick her up. "Will you take me with you, Papa?"

And when I did, it was perfectly natural.

In Skazki, the progress of Totchka's illness was halted. Her own death couldn't find her, but as she had been destined to die as a child she remained a child. No fate as a woman existed for her to fulfil. She was forever a little girl.

My little girl.

I did not enjoy my last laugh on Yusipov the way I had hoped. Never mind. I am certain, however, that he saw me climb out of the water that night. Why else would he have bothered to drown an old tramp, fill him with bullet holes and ensure his body washed up a few days later? They pointed to the corpse, bloated and death-eaten beyond the barest recognition. They said it was Rasputin. He told his co-conspirators that his plan had succeeded. In time he even managed to convince himself. It must have helped that I did not return to Mir.

Life with Totchka was simple and busy. I fed her, kept her warm, made her safe. I made the best of the fact that circumstances kept me in Skazki. I sent word to Nikolai that I would petition my fellow magical creatures, that he was to wait and hope for my return. I set up a stream of meetings and councils, all the while keeping Totchka safe and hidden in my cottage. Perhaps I wasn't as dedicated as I should have been to this cause, because I was unprepared to leave Totchka alone. Many of the hostile spirits of the far east didn't respond to my invitations, Baba Yaga refused to leave her home, and Perun and Veles sent to tell me to let it go, that life was perfectly acceptable to them without the weight of millions of worshippers. Perhaps if I'd been able to attend them in person . . . but it's too late for self-recriminations. Totchka's tearful anxiety at any suggestion of my departure was enough. I didn't go.

Support for a military alliance with Nikolai was thin. A year later, I was only just starting to win over the witches of the south. Then word came, from the bright lands of Mir, that a revolution had swept the land. The Tsar and his family no longer ruled in Russia, but they were still alive and well.

I took this news with mixed feelings. They were still alive, Anastasia and Aleksei. No separation was imminent. I had settled into a different kind of life with Totchka. Perhaps Perun and Veles were right. Perhaps this half-dream of life in Skazki was enough.

Yet, this half-dream of life was still dependent on Mokosha's blood living in Mir bodies. Aleksandr's stupid promise had made it so. If both Aleksei and Anastasia died without offspring, then everything changed. The final separation would occur, and Totchka would be ejected from Skazki, to die her own death in Mir.

Yes, I lied to Rosa. Would you not?

Nikolai and his family were imprisoned, at first in their own palace at Tsarskoe Selo. Then, by degrees, their circumstances grew more and more dire. From Tsarskoe Selo to Tobolsk, but still with a full retinue of servants. Finally, to Ekaterinaburg, to a house with bars on the windows, where their guards were loyal Bolsheviks who took joy in humiliating and frightening their prisoners.

I watched uneasily in my magic mirror, but always told myself that had the Bolskheviks wanted them dead, they would have killed them by now. As the spring bloomed into summer, I saw signs that all was coming undone.

What agonizing I endured, deciding what to do with Totchka. If I took her with me, she might die of her illness, but to leave her was to fear for her vulnerability, to miss her tender cuddles, to see her cry until her skinny body shook.

"No, no, Papa, no!" she sobbed, clutching at my knees. "I will die if you go. I cannot bear to be alone, what if something awful happens to you? Or to me?"

"Hush, Totchka," I said, peeling her off me and sitting her firmly at the table while I pulled on my coat. "Nothing will happen to me. I can't die. Nothing will happen to you so long as you stay here in the cottage, within the special circle of sunlight I have made for you."

She stretched out on the table and sobbed so hard I feared she would hurt herself. I tried to be strong as I tied my boots on, but her pale, terrified face as I picked up my staff nearly undid me.

"So you are going then?" she said, on a shuddering breath. "You are leaving me here all alone? Any monster could come from the forest—"

"No, child, you are safe in here."

"I fear I am not."

"Then I will make you safer," I said, and I put my staff down and closed my eyes and raised my hands above my head. I imagined extra layers of sunlight, building a shield around the cottage. I felt the magic moving in my body, aching in my muscles and weighing like lead in my bones. I gave it everything I had in those few moments, making Totchka's circle of light impregnable.

When I opened my eyes, Totchka was staring at me, horrified.

"What is it?" I asked.

"Look at yourself," she said.

I went to the mirror, and saw that my hair was now streaked with gray, my eyes had gathered bags and my skin had sagged under the weight of a dozen new wrinkles.

"Don't be alarmed, Totchka," I said, turning to her. "It only means that I have used as much magic as I could find in my body to make you safe. These lines are evidence that no harm will come to you. I wear them proudly."

Despite my reassurances, she was still wailing when I steeled myself and slipped through the veil, took two crossings and arrived in Ekaterinaburg. All I hoped was to convince Nikolai to allow me to take Aleksei and Anastasia with me back to Skazki, where I would keep them safe until the tense times had passed.

The night was warm. I shed my coat. Nikolai's home was three miles north of the crossing, and I was perspiring long before I arrived.

I did not know that which had already been set in motion: an evil scheme of assassination. A truck with a loud engine had been left running outside to mask the sound of gunshots, fifty gallons of sulfuric acid had been delivered to a deserted mine nearby, along with two hundred gallons of gasoline. The family, their cook, their footmen, their housemaid and their doctor had been ushered into a stinking basement room. They were told it was for their own safety. Anastasia, a young woman of seventeen, had dressed in a special gown. Inside its bodice were sewn all her jewels, which she hoped to take with her if they were forced to leave Ekaterinaburg. Aleksei, still only a boy, had brought his own treasure with him: the Golden Bear.

They waited for half an hour. Sunny's hands fluttered about, Nikolai's hooded eyes darted from side to side. The children argued with each other softly, keen for any distraction from the awful waiting. Then a uniformed man led a group of soldiers into the room.

"Nikolai Aleksandrovich," he said, striding over to the Tsar where he was sitting, "by the order of the Regional Soviet of the Urals, you are to be shot, along with all your family."

"What!" Nikolai said, but his exclamation was drowned by the sound of guns and screams of fear. Blood flowed, smoke filled the air. Aleksei, hit by one bullet in his shoulder, moaned on the floor. A soldier held the barrel of his pistol directly to the child's head and fired twice. Under the pile of bodies, Anastasia still cried. The same soldier seized a rifle and stabbed her with a bayonet: once, twice, three times. She fell silent.

The soldiers turned to each other, pleased with the sudden silence. They congratulated each other, and went upstairs to order the truck to come around.

This is when I slipped into the room.

Ah, it's not so hard. A little magic, a narrow basement window hidden behind a staircase. I could sense already that Anastasia was not dead. The jewels in her bodice had protected her from the bullets, and the bayonet wounds had missed her major organs, but she was dying, no doubt of it. Her body was catastrophically wounded.

For my purposes, though, she was still alive. I seized her poor broken body, and the Golden Bear, and I took her back to Skazki.

As for the rest of the royal family, they were butchered, burned and dumped down a mine. Of course the Bolsheviks knew that one of their victims was missing (why else do you think that so many legends have been able to cling to the name Anastasia?), but as long as all that remained were charred fragments, there was no need to tell their superiors. Losing a dead Romanov was probably unpardonable.

I expect you wonder what happened next. How I treated Anastasia, how I enlisted Morozko the father of the frost to aid me, how the Golden Bear arrived back in St. Petersburg. They are all stories for another time. Now is the time to act.

I have left Totchka only once, and only because so much depended on it. Now, I think you'll see, I need to leave her again. Briefly, only briefly. Long enough to negotiate the crossings to the Snow Witch's palace and stop Rosa Kovalenka before she does something we will all regret.

Thirty-four

Although the sense of vertigo never really left him, Daniel had to admit that flying was not the nightmare he'd once thought. Certainly, Rosa's company helped. While she was snuggled under his arm as they sped through the sky, he felt he was holding on to something safe and sure. He wasn't, of course: he knew that. Perhaps the fear of flying had simply become redundant. He had witnessed so many other horrors that falling from the sky seemed almost a pleasant way to die.

Not that he thought he would die. Not anymore. With Rosa, her magic, and the sleigh to travel anywhere, he believed he would get home again. For now, he didn't allow himself to entertain thoughts of how empty home would be without Rosa. Instead, he listed all the things he would do when he returned, all the things he hadn't been able to commit to before. Finishing his book, finding a job, making a life.

"What are you thinking about?" Rosa asked.

"About how cold it is," he said, "and how it's getting colder."

She reached up to adjust the hood of his new fur. "I'm warm as toast," she said smugly.

Below, a huge forest had given way to snowy hills. The last dots of dark green vegetation sped by, and the gray rocks wore white mantles. Ravines opened up in hillsides, and icy water poured into black pools below. The slopes grew steeper, the snow thicker. Voron swooped higher. The ground evened out. Gentle undulations under snowy brilliance. The sky was gray-violet; the sun, distant though it was, illuminated crystalline patterns on the snow. White, white and white.

Daniel squinted against the brightness. "I knew the Snow Witch would live somewhere snowy, but—"

"Do you think we're getting close?" Rosa asked, leaning over the bar to look below her.

Daniel's heart lurched to see her so close to the edge of the sleigh. "Rosa, careful."

She looked around and smiled. "I'm fine, Daniel. I can look after myself."

"I know."

He sat back, pulling his fur tightly around himself. He watched her leaning out, her hair streaming in the wind, her sweet mouth curled up in a delighted smile. What could he say or do to convince her to come home with him? If she didn't get sick until she was in her late thirties, that would still give them ten good years together. Ten years was better than nothing. Who knew? Before ten years was up, either of them might die crossing the street. She was giving up too much happiness to prevent unhappiness.

Not that he could say any of this to Rosa. Not now. But he would. He only had to think of the right way to phrase it. He had wandered for weeks in a dangerous magic kingdom . . . he was no longer afraid of Rosa's temper.

A sudden dip had him clutching at the bar of the sleigh.

"What was that?" he asked.

"I think Voron's taking us down," she replied. "Hold on."

He closed his eyes and braced himself for the descent, which was rough and fast. The seat dropped from underneath him, and he yelped. The sleigh caught him again, and he heard Rosa laughing. He opened his eyes and took a deep breath, and then he laughed too at the thrill of plummeting through the air on a magic sleigh. Something he would never feel again once he returned to Mir.

With a whoosh and a skid, the sleigh pulled up on a bank of snow. Rosa looked around, twisting in her seat.

"I can't see anything," she said. "No palace."

"Me neither."

"Then why has Voron brought us here?"

"I don't know." He climbed down from the sleigh. "Let's have a quick look around."

"Okay."

He put out a hand to help her, and she landed on the snow next to him. Against the white and gray backdrop, she was a gorgeous drop of colors: crimson dress, black hair, blue eyes.

"You go that way, I'll go this way. Meet back here in five minutes," she said.

"Got it."

He trudged up the embankment and saw only more snow. Carefully, he eased down the slope and began to walk across the white fields. The snow was thick, and his leg muscles had to work hard to move him forward. He left deep tracks behind him, and his shoes began to feel damp and cold. Up ahead, the edge of a ridge. From here, he could see down into a shallow valley. No palace. Between two banks of snow, though, he thought he could see a deep shadow. A cave? He let himself move down, following the curve of the bank.

A dark opening, about seven feet high.

"Rosa!" he called. "I've found something."

He hurried toward it, pulled up too late. Sinuous shapes moved at the edge of his vision. He turned. A bolt of adrenalin. Three snowy-white wolves closing on him.

"Shit!" he exclaimed, turning to run. The snow was too thick; he tripped. His breath was knocked out of him as he hit the ground, and the first wolf sprang forward. He saw eyes, teeth, paws advancing, and threw his arms over his face to protect himself.

"All the spirits of the snow, hear me!" Rosa's voice, ringing out over the snow.

The expected blow didn't come. Daniel uncovered his eyes. Rosa stood at the top of the ridge in her crimson dress, holding out her hand and sending her words across the frozen landscape. Her voice collected icy reverberations. The wolves had stopped, shocked, to listen. Their breath was visible on the crisp air.

"Tsar north wind, I invoke you! As your icy breath can churn the skies, so may I move these creatures. My word is firm, so it shall be." She swept her arm through the air. "Move! Move!"

Daniel turned to the wolves, who were scampering off into the snowy distance, tails bent between their hind legs. Rosa hurried down the slope and helped Daniel to his feet.

"Are you all right?" she asked.

"You just rescued me. Again."

"Did they hurt you?" She was feeling along his arms.

"No, I'm fine. But I have to rescue you next time, okay?"

Rosa frowned, irritated. "What nonsense, Daniel. We help each other. If you want a simpering princess for a companion, I'm not your girl." She brushed snow off his fur coat.

He shook off his embarrassment, indicated the opening in the snow. "A cave," he said. "I think the wolves were guarding it."

"Then that's exactly where we should go." She patted his side, feeling for the bear that was strapped against his body. Her nearness was the easy and familiar proximity of lovers, and it hurt him that it wasn't to last. "No matter what happens, don't give that bear to anyone or anything. Protect it with your life. Got it?"

"Got it."

She leaned up to kiss him, then said, "Follow me." She led him across the snow toward the cave, while he wondered what hope he had with a woman who could charm wolves.

Rosa caught her breath when she saw the inside of the cave.

At the entrance, it had appeared to be only a dark, rocky fissure, but around the first bend, it opened out into a frosted wonderland.

"Oh, my God," Daniel gasped, pulling up behind her.

The ceiling soared twenty feet above them, decorated with icicles that glowed silver-blue like crystal, lending the cavern an eerie half-light. The snowy walls and floor were studded with diamond-bright chunks of ice in swirling patterns. A latticework of ice was suspended from the ceiling. As the wind rushed into the cave, it whistled through the lattice. The music it made was eerie: tinkling and creaking in formless melodies, now shrieking and loud, now breathy and low depending on the force of the wind. Carved archways and alcoves gleamed with ice-blue treasures.

Ahead, two round tunnels sprouted.

Rosa turned to Daniel, her breath frosting on the air. "This is it. This is the Snow Witch's palace. Voron brought us as close as he could."

Daniel shivered. "It's cold."

"Hold my hand," she said, and tried to send him some of her warmth. She clutched his fingers to forcibly contain her excitement as much as for safety. "Let's take a look around."

"What are we looking for?"

"We're looking for signs that a Snow Witch lives here." The thought sobered her. "We must be careful. If we get separated, we meet back at Voron. Okay?"

"Okay."

Three deep blue shadows followed them in the icy corridor: Daniel's, Rosa's and the ever-present Anatoly's. Their footsteps were soft, the icy music chased their shadows. Sculptures in ice lined the corridors: wolves, foxes, owls. Dazzling wheels of icicles hung like chandeliers. For a long time, it seemed that they would hear and see nothing more than inanimate objects. Then Daniel stopped.

"Can you hear something?" he said.

Rosa tuned into her hearing, and thought she could make out a faint sighing reverberating down the corridor.

"That way," she said, indicating the entrance to a tunnel on the right. "It sounds like—"

"Somebody crying," Daniel said.

As they drew closer, Rosa agreed. "Crying, or moaning in pain." She remembered the magic mirror Grigory had been watching, the night she slept in his cottage. Similar sounds had come from its gleaming surface. "There, on the left. Do you see an opening?"

"I do, but it doesn't look inviting."

Away from the main thoroughfares of the ice palace, the ceiling was much lower, the icicles dimmer. Rosa's flesh prickled under the distinct sense that something unpleasant or unnatural was nearby. She squeezed Daniel's hand and realized she was holding her breath.

"Stay close," she said.

He nodded.

"Let's go and see her."

The doorway drew closer. The moans and cries grew louder. Heart in her mouth, Rosa tentatively peered around the threshold for her first glimpse of the Snow Witch.

"Oh," Rosa gasped.

No evil queen sitting on a throne carved of ice. Instead, a bed of stained straw laid on the frozen ground. Lying on it was the prostrate figure of a young woman in a champagne-colored dress. Rosa inched into the room, pulling Daniel behind her. She moved closer to the straw bed, gazing down. The woman's dress was torn and bloodstained. Blood was matted into her fair hair, her lips were blue and her eyes rolled back in her head.

"Is she alive?" Daniel whispered. His words echoed softly in the dark chamber.

In confirmation, the woman contorted and groaned, her eyelids fluttering.

"Ah, ah," she cried. "Ah, dear God, an end. An end!" Then she lapsed again into stillness, except for the rough rise and fall of her chest. She moaned softly, her breath misting on the air.

"I don't understand," Rosa said. "This is the Snow Witch?"

"Perhaps it's not. Perhaps it's one of her victims." Daniel moved closer. "She's only young, a teenager. How did she get these wounds?"

Rosa moved to Daniel's side, her heart contracting in sympathy with the woman's pain. Human suffering always made her feel stripped bare. No matter how many films and television shows worked to desensitize her, the real thing, with all its existential weight, always gutted her. Veles' words came back to her: *Once you see her, all will be clear.*

"No, no, Daniel. This is her. I'm certain of it." She released Daniel's hand and crouched next to the bed to touch the woman's wrist. It was ice-cold. "That's what Perun and Veles were trying to tell me. Grigory hasn't been honest. This is no nightmare creature."

Daniel met her gaze across the room. "This is no nightmare?" he asked. "Kept in a freezing room, injured and bloody, with no relief from pain?" Suddenly, his hand flew to his ribs. "Oh. Rosa. Something's happening with the bear."

"Stand back," Rosa said, hurrying to his side. "She's pulling it toward her."

"Why don't we just give it to her? It might stop her crying."

"Don't be foolish. We don't know the whole story. We should get back."

"Listen to Rosa!" This was a new voice in the room, and Rosa whirled around to see Papa Grigory standing at the entrance. Except he looked different. His hair was white and his face was haggard, as though he'd aged ten years since she had last seen him.

Rosa blocked Grigory's path to Daniel. "Leave Daniel alone," she said. "He has nothing to do with this."

"Pish! I'm not going to hurt anyone," Grigory said, advancing toward them. "Just give me that damned bear, and everything will be fine."

"Explain this first."

Grigory lunged, and Rosa thrust Daniel away, pushing him out the door.

"Run!" she shouted, doing the same thing herself, in the opposite direction to Daniel. Grigory paused in the corridor, trying to decide which one of them had the bear. Daniel was moving swiftly up the corridor. Grigory was turning his attention that way.

"The Golden Bear is mine to keep," Rosa stopped and called. He hesitated, turned to her.

"Rosa. What's all this nonsense?"

"I'm not giving it back," she said, and started to run.

Then he was barreling down the corridor toward her, his advanced age no handicap, and she was flying away from him. Her feet skidded on the ice and snow as she wove through the tunnels of the Snow Witch's palace. Up ahead, she could see daylight, so she ran directly for it, emerging from the icy half-light into full sun. Before her spread a frozen lake. She paused, wary.

He was right behind her.

She put her foot on the ice, and picked her way over it, toward the other side.

Grigory had pulled up on the edge. "Rosa, what are you doing?"

"Running away from you."

"You, of all people, know how dangerous the ice can be." *Crack.* A split in the ice fissured in a crooked line ahead of her. Its awful creak echoed in her memory, all the way back to the night her father died. She pulled up sharply, turned.

"Did you do that?"

In answer, another crack appeared beside her.

"Stop it," she said. "Let me go."

He had her trapped on the ice, and he moved toward her deliberately and unhurriedly. No matter. Daniel had the bear. He would climb into Voron and get away from here. Wouldn't he? Her body was trembling all over, even though the sarafan kept her blood warm.

"As I see it, you have three choices," he said as he drew closer. "You can die like your father, you can die like your mother, or you can listen to me and have your wish. Do you understand?"

"Who is she?" Rosa asked. She swallowed hard, thinking of the poor soul suffering inside the palace. She raised a hand and pointed back the way she had come. "Who is that?"

"That is the Snow Witch."

"Rubbish. You said the Snow Witch was a horrible monster. She's just a girl."

"Yes, yes, a girl full of bullet holes and bayonet wounds. She's a horror to look upon, wouldn't you say?" He pulled up in front of her. The bright light illuminated a thousand wrinkles on his brow. All of the centuries he had lived were now etched upon him: experience hanging heavy in his sagging skin, bottomless crevices scarring his cheeks, impossible networks of lines spreading from his eyes.

"What the hell happened to you?" she said, a cloud of fog rising from her lips.

"I had to reassure Totchka before I left. She made me reinforce the barricade. It's very demanding."

Rosa shrugged. "Well, you have me now. A captive audience. You might as well produce your explanations."

"They are not explanations," he muttered darkly. "They are *stories*."

"Go on then."

Grigory began his tale. "On a hot night in July 1918, I brought the wounded Grand Duchess Anastasia to my cottage in Skazki. I laid her in Totchka's bed, while Totchka sat frightened in a corner of the room, glad that I was home but unforgiving of the gasping, bleeding intruder.

"I was surprised. Foolishly, I had thought that the moment I brought Anastasia to Skazki, she would recover, sit up and look around. As Totchka had, two years past when I'd brought her back with me. Of course, it was not the death fated for Anastasia: it was a death not-her-own, the kind of death which Skazki could not save her from. So now I was burdened with the most serious problem Skazki had been faced with. Since Aleksandr's half-promise, Skazki's tie to Mir had been on the brink of disaster. As soon as the last of the magic blood had gone cold in a human body, the worlds would slide apart for good. With it, every Skazki creature would disappear from Mir, every Mir creature would disappear from Skazki.

"Morning was still hours away. The girl moaned in my arms, asking over and over for her mama, shudders of pain wracking her body. I could not let her die. Yet at any moment her body was going to give up its spirit. I could feel life ebbing from her.

"Sitting, just at my left hand where I had put her, was the Golden Bear. So many times, I had used it to store her brother's soul while I healed him. So easy. I hummed my little tune, lifting the soul from Anastasia's body and sending it rushing into the bear.

"This brought Anastasia no peace, you understand. Perhaps if I'd sent her into the body of a fox or a bird, her poor pained body might have fallen to rest, but I wasn't sure if that would work, if her soul in the warm body of another creature was enough to keep the worlds tied. I knew, from experience with Aleksei, that when the soul went to the bear, the heart in the body still beat.

" 'Papa, I don't like that dead girl in my bed,' Totchka said.

" 'She will be gone by morning, little one, I promise you,' I said. 'Tonight will be long. Be brave, and wait here for me.'

" 'You're not going again?' she said, her voice rising in panic.

"I leaned over her and grasped her head gently in my hands. 'No, no, sweet child. I go only as far as the edge of the circle. I must call a friend to assist me. This problem is too big for your papa to solve on his own.'

"I left the cottage, and the warm bubble which was its safe circumference, and stepped into the wild night alone. 'Morozko!' I called, sending my voice vibrating out over the veil, so that wherever he was he would hear it. 'Koschey needs your assistance. If ever you were a friend to me, come now.'

"Then I returned to the cottage and soothed Totchka in a pile of blankets on top of the stove, where she slept for a little while. As the firelight gleamed on the bear, I waited next to Anastasia's body. It was not easy. A corpse is unpleasant company, but a girl suspended at the moment of her painful death is far worse. She shuddered and cried, convulsed and cursed. Her wounds seeped blood and her breath came in trembling gasps. Two hours passed, then three. Finally, I heard a voice far away, calling me.

"'Koschey, if you want my help, you'll have to let me into this infernal bubble.'

"Morozko! You have met him now, Rosa, so I need not describe his firm physique, his cold aura, his snowy wings. Totchka woke as I led Morozko into the cottage, and she shrank under her covers and gazed at him with eyes saucer-wide, both frightened and amazed.

"I explained to him the situation, and why I had brought him here.

"'If the injuries are not too deep, perhaps you can freeze them closed,' I said. 'Then, her body and soul can be reunited and she can live here safely.'

"Morozko frowned, prodding her bloody wounds. 'She is full of holes, Koschey.'

"'But she was not yet dead when I pulled her soul out. Let us try it.'

"'If I do this, she will always be cold, from this day forward.'

"'It's the least of her problems. Go ahead.'

"Morozko leaned over the girl's body, and I could feel the waves of cold which rippled out from his body. He gingerly extended his index finger, and eased it into one of the bayonet wounds. Anastasia shrieked and convulsed, and Morozko withdrew his bloodied finger.

"'Did it work?' I asked, examining the wound. Already the girl's body was going cold, the wound had frozen over. No more blood oozed from it. 'Good, good,' I said. 'And now the rest.'

"One by one, Morozko froze the wounds, and Anastasia's lips

turned blue with cold. Her skin was icy, but beneath her wrists I could feel her veins pulsing. This body was alive. We still had hope.

"'Now, sit back,' I said to Morozko, 'and I'll attempt to tip her soul back into her body.'

"With my fingers still pressed into her wrist, I hummed my magic tune. Such a delicate operation. Have you ever cracked an egg, pouring the white in hope of keeping the yolk separate without it following all in a rush? So it was as I tipped Anastasia's soul back into her broken body, only to feel her pulse slow and falter. Death sucked at her soul, and I knew the instant it reunited fully with her body she was lost. I pulled her, slowly and carefully, back into the bear.

"'I couldn't do it,' I said. 'She will die the moment she is whole again.'

"'Then leave her separated,' said Morozko.

"'Forever? In so much pain?'

"A loud rattling stole my attention at that moment, and Totchka squealed and shouted, 'Papa, Papa, the bear is moving!'

"I turned to see the sight which had so terrified the little girl. The bear had rattled off the table, and was now suspended in the air between the table and Anastasia. The pull of the body on the soul, the pull of death over life was so strong. I seized the bear and jammed it firmly between my knees.

"'No, you shall not have it, Anastasia,' I said. 'Morozko is right. Your body and your soul must remain separate.'

"Morozko took Anastasia's body to the snowfields, where he built her a palace to live in. I sent the bear back to St. Petersburg, to a bathhouse I once practiced magic in, never dreaming that anybody would ever find it. The rest you know."

Rosa stared at him solemnly. "And this is the truth?"

"You are too clever for lies, Rosa. You have proven that."

"Anastasia has been lying in that cold place, in her death throes, for nearly ninety years?"

"Yes, yes," he said impatiently. "What is her suffering, Rosa, compared to mine? If I were to lose Totchka, I would die each morning when I woke to the emptiness in my bed."

Rosa closed her eyes, shutting out the bright snowy scene. Keeping the two worlds tied was the only way she could escape her own dreadful death, but for her happiness to be built on such misery . . . ?

"So, Rosa, it is time for you to choose your fate. Your father's death, your mother's death, or something else?" He held out his hand. "Come, you can join me on the safe side of the ice."

Rosa looked at his old fingers, and a feeling of dread weighed on her heart. Of standing at a moment in her life from which great happiness or great unhappiness might proceed, with only a hair's breadth of movement either way. Shadows gathered, expectant as vultures.

But then, were things all as they seemed to be? Was her choice really between Anastasia's suffering and her own? Grigory hadn't told her everything and, after what Perun had said to her, she suspected Grigory might not even know every piece of the puzzle.

"Rosa? Are you ready to make your choice?"

She nodded gravely. "Yes, Koschey. I am."

Daniel paced the circle around Voron for the hundredth time. Where was Rosa? Did she want him to take the sleigh to the sky and look for her? He didn't have a clue how to operate it. Nearly half an hour had passed and no sign of her. The wolves, still frightened by Rosa's incantation, sat off in the distance gazing at him. Only a matter of time before they grew bold and came back.

"Damn it," he muttered, trudging down the slope toward the cave. Rescuing Rosa was a complicated undertaking. There was a good chance she wanted him to stay away, was in the middle of some grand scheme that depended on him not being around. She'd asked him to guard the bear with his life, but he cared more about her than the bear. Back inside the icy palace, he retraced their earlier steps. The music sighed and creaked around him. His breath was fog and his heartbeat was rapid. The entrance to the Snow Witch's chamber loomed ahead. He clamped his arm down across the bear, took a deep breath and dashed past the entrance, grateful he didn't have to see the suffering woman again. Her moans followed him down the corridor, where he found footsteps in the snow.

Rosa's, then Grigory's. He tracked them toward an opening, then peered out into the sunlight.

Standing out on the lake, Rosa and Grigory faced each other, deep in conversation.

She didn't look like she was in danger. Perhaps he should just go back into the cave.

Then Grigory held out his hand to Rosa, and Daniel hesitated. Rosa's face was serious, sad. She reached for Grigory's hand, and he saw that the old man was helping her over a wide fissure in the ice.

"Rosa!" Daniel called.

He received neither an admonition, nor a gasp of relief. She smiled and waved, and he met her halfway across the ice, taking her hand in his.

"I am Grigory," the old man said, extending his hand. "It's good to meet you properly."

Daniel took his hand and shook it. It baffled him, that he should be standing here shaking hands with history. Grigory's wolf-eyes were narrowed and knowing.

"Rosa?" Daniel said uncertainly, turning to her. "What's going on?"

"Grigory has explained everything," Rosa said. "We were mistaken."

"But the girl?"

"The Snow Witch often poses as an injured young woman, to draw people into her trap," Grigory said.

"We were lucky Grigory came when he did." Rosa smiled up at the old man. "She might have killed us. He is here to protect us."

Daniel glanced from one to the other. Relief. Somebody to protect him in Skazki. Soon all the horror would be behind him. "And the bear?"

Rosa nodded firmly. "We're taking it back to Papa Grigory's cottage. From there, it's all up to you."

Thirty-five

In contrast to the lengthy journey Rosa had made alone in Voron, once Papa Grigory was in control they sped through crossings faster than an arrow. He explained that his role as ambassador meant that all crossings were open to him, all the time. Their distances collapsed to nothing. He said it smugly, with a conceited tilt of his head. Rosa recoiled inwardly from him. Since the story told to her on the ice, she found him abhorrent. How could she be anything but unhappy in his company? Especially with herself? For a lifetime, or more?

Luckily, an idea was already brewing.

Rosa turned her attention to Daniel, who nursed the bear in his lap, gazing at her strange face and trying not to look at the sky beneath them. Within hours, the bubble of sunshine over Grigory's cottage was visible, and they landed in the late afternoon light. Totchka waited anxiously by the door, launched herself into Grigory's arms and demanded he never leave again.

"I won't, I won't, my little one," he said, cuddling her so fiercely Rosa feared the girl's bones might break. "That is the last time we will be apart, I am certain of it."

"Hello," Daniel said, smiling at Totchka.

"Hello," she replied shyly. "Who are you?"

"This is Daniel," Grigory said. "He's going to make everything all right. Can he stay here tonight?"

"Rosa too?" She turned expectant eyes to Rosa, and once again Rosa was struck at the similarity to Grigory: was it just her expression, or was there more?

Grigory glanced at Rosa and back at Totchka. "Well, Rosa may stay a little longer."

After supper, Rosa walked out into the garden to savor her own company for a few minutes. She stood, right at the edge of the circumference of safety, and gazed out into the trees. It was an artificial contentment she felt. Life waited out there: movement, wildness, shadows and promises. It beckoned her. It might always beckon her.

She heard the door open behind her, and turned to see Daniel emerging.

"You see?" he said. "You're already longing to be out of here."

"Don't, Daniel," she said, turning from him and sitting down in the grass.

He sat next to her. "Rosa, if you come back with me, we'll have time together. There are no guarantees on anyone's future."

"I don't want to hear this."

"We could get a little place, have some babies . . ." He trailed off. He probably already knew that it was hopeless. "I do love you, Rosa."

"Back at the snowfields, you said you wanted to rescue me. You can. By going and not looking back. Okay? Forget this other stuff, this love stuff."

Daniel frowned, irritated. "Don't ruin our last evening, Rosa. 'This love stuff' is important."

"I know, I know," she said, immediately regretful. She sighed, stretching her legs out in front of her. "I have a lot on my mind."

"Do you want me to go back inside?"

"Can you stay and just not say anything?"

"I can."

So they sat, side by side in the grass, while the moon rose overhead and night deepened around them; and Rosa turned her idea over and over and decided that she would sleep on it.

"Whatever happens," she said, taking Daniel's hand and kissing his palm, "I did love you."

"I know."

Morning dew still clung to the clearing as Daniel waited for instruction. Rosa and Grigory were nearby, Totchka safely back at the cottage. If he squinted, he could bring on his second sight and see the veil moving, a multihued curtain drifting on the morning breeze.

"That will go," Rosa said, tapping his arm. "There's no way Anatoly will let you keep a shred of magic."

"What does Anatoly have to do with it?"

"You have to take him back with you." She touched his lips with cool fingertips. "He'll be cranky."

Daniel's skin cried out for her, but he kept silent.

Grigory stepped forward. "You have the bear?"

Daniel patted his ribs, where the bear was slung. "I'll be glad to get rid of her. I have bruises."

"You'll have more than bruises on the other side," Grigory said. "The crossing back to Mir might be brutal. The bear doesn't want to return, so I'll have to push you through very hard. You may find yourself dizzy. You may even faint."

"Anatoly will be there," Rosa said.

"Cranky Anatoly?"

"He's a good man underneath it all," she said. "And he owes me. He has all my magic. Did you hear that, Anatoly?" She smoothed her skirt across her belly, head drooping and hair trailing. It was similar to a gesture of a pregnant woman, and Daniel had to battle through more regrets, more discarded fantasies.

"What do I do?" Daniel said.

Grigory stroked his beard. "Nothing, just walk forward. I'll say the zagovor."

Daniel turned to Rosa. "And that's it? It's all over?"

"You have to return the bear to her hiding place," she said, distracted as she fastened the clasp on his fur cloak.

"And that's it," he muttered, his eyes drinking in her face for the last time. "That's it."

Rosa stepped forward. His arms closed around her, she felt her hands moving at his waist and wondered what she was doing. The bear. She was removing it from the sling, under the guise of a long good-bye hug. He wisely kept silent.

"Don't say another word," she said in a whisper. "Don't let go of another breath. Hold very still." She leaned in to kiss him, parting his lips with hers. He pressed his mouth against hers, and felt a sudden tickle and buzz. A bee in his mouth.

"Don't breathe again," Grigory said. "Not until you get to the other side."

Rosa drew back, pressing his lips closed with her fingers. He held his breath.

Grigory urged him forward, reciting his zagovor in an ominous voice. Daniel turned his eyes toward Rosa, but she was already looking away, surreptitiously curling the bear up underneath her jacket. He wanted to cry out to her, tell her how much he loved her, but the bee was buzzing in his mouth and he could say nothing.

So, instead, he did exactly what she had asked of him. He stepped into the veil.

Brutal didn't begin to describe the feeling. In the split-second he was in the crossing, his bones were rattled and his blood was shaken so hard it bubbled. Then he was falling through the other side, letting go of his breath. The bee escaped, there was a shadow looming over him, and he collapsed to the ground, unconscious.

Rosa turned to Grigory.

"He's gone," Grigory said. "Our troubles are over."

"Are they?" She withdrew the bear, forcing her hands not to shake. If she was wrong about this . . .

"Rosa!" he exclaimed. "What are you doing?"

With her free hand she removed the thunder arrow from around her neck. "You are wrong, Grigory. There is another way. It's right under your nose, but you haven't even seen it."

"No! Don't do it!" He leapt forward and she took a step back, bringing the thunder arrow crashing down on the bear's head. She thought she heard a howl, both distant in the forest and ominously close in her mind. Then the bear began to dissolve, turn to sand. A light, blinding and white, lifted into the air from her hands, then shot off toward the north.

"What have you done? What have you done?" Grigory cried.

Rosa watched the light disappear into the distance. "Good night, Anastasia," she breathed. Then turned to Grigory. "Who is Mila?"

"What are you talking about?" He looked around with panicked eyes, his impossibly aged skin pale with fright. "It will come. The undoing. Totchka, my Totchka! I must get back to her."

"Wait!" she said with as much power and strength as she could muster. "Who is Mila? Did you ever know a woman named Mila? In St. Petersburg, during your years in service to Sunny?"

He shook his head. "I . . . yes. Mila Stanislava. Wife of a wealthy merchant. He was always away, she was always crawling into my bed on Sunday afternoons."

Rosa recalled the memories she had stolen from Totchka, the night before her journey. A mother named Mila, a father who was only a shadow. And Perun's suggestion that Grigory had fathered a child, though he did not know it.

"Has anyone from Skazki ever spent so much time in Mir that they have become partly human, Grigory?" she asked. "Anyone who spent as much time there as you did?"

"Yes. Mokosha, Stasya. I lost her . . ." Realization was dawning on his terribly aged face. "What are you saying?"

"The world isn't ending, Grigory," she said. "Do you see? You, me, we're still here. The forest, the mountains. Anastasia is dead, and the world isn't ending. And that's because there is one half-blood child still remaining."

He nodded gravely. "Of course," he said. "My little girl. My Totchka."

He didn't want to let her go. Of course. But here in Skazki, she was never going to grow up. And she needed to grow up, she needed to become a woman, have a family of her own, create a new line to pin together the two worlds. And so Grigory learned one of the most painful lessons of parenthood: to let her go.

"She will die," he railed. "She is ill."

"Medicine is different now from ninety years ago. We'll find her a good doctor."

"Who will find her a doctor? Me? I can't walk among humans, I look like a monster. Are you willing to go back, Rosa Kovalenka?"

"I am, but not as Rosa Kovalenka."

"What do you mean?"

"It's easy," she said with a smile. "You just need to hum me a little tune."

Epilogue

Time blurred. Daniel fluttered in and out of consciousness. He understood that he was somewhere warm and comfortable, that hushed voices circled around him, that somebody with tender hands was caring for him.

From time to time a face would flash into his field of vision: a pale face, framed by snowy hair, with eyes . . . eyes that seemed somehow familiar but somehow not. He'd dreamed once of those eyes; or had he? The line between waking and dreaming was hopelessly clouded.

After a time . . . days or weeks, he couldn't tell . . . the voices became more distinct. Even snatches of conversation began to make sense.

Isn't it wonderful, Papa? He has made her well again.

You must rest, my darling.

But I love him, Mama. I love him.

Who do you think he is?

But when full consciousness came, it was all at once. In the first glimmer of dawn. He woke, and he was in a bed in a dim room. Across from him, another bed, with a snow-haired boy asleep in it.

Daniel struggled to sit. His head hurt, and he groaned softly.

The little boy was sitting up an instant later, eyes wide with excitement. "You're awake," he said. "You're awake."

"Where am I?"

The little boy threw back his covers and ran into the hallway. "He's awake, he's awake!" he cried. Soon, the room was full of people: a hard-faced woman who pushed him firmly back into his pillow and told him to be easy with himself; a hulking man with a sullen face; a thin, pale woman whom he recognized as the tender presence from his dreams; and the little boy, full of excited chatter.

"Who are you?" the boy asked.

"I'm Daniel," he said.

"I'm Makhar. This is my mother, Ludmilla, my father, Anatoly, who found you on your travels, and my sister, Elizavetta, who was sick and unconscious, and on the edge of dying before you came." Makhar sat on Daniel's bed and picked up one of his hands to squeeze. "Thank you. You saved her. Look how her eyes shine!"

Elizavetta turned away coyly, a smile repressed on her lips.

"I didn't do anything," Daniel said, understanding that this was the Chenchikov family, whom Rosa had mentioned. "But I can't stay."

"All in good time," Anatoly said. He took Elizavetta firmly by the shoulder and turned her toward the door. "Luda and Elizavetta will fix you some breakfast."

Elizavetta glanced at him over her shoulder, and he felt his heart lurch. Crazy. He didn't even know her. His fingers fiddled absently with the end of the cool sheet. The smell of laundry detergent and faint damp mustiness.

Makhar was dismissed too, and Anatoly sat by Daniel's bed and lowered his voice. He took a few moments, adjusting his collar and running his hand over his beard. Finally, he said, "Don't tell them anything."

"I don't intend to. I just want to get home."

"You need to recuperate first," Anatoly said. "Hush and listen. I don't want to stop you. I'm not a monster; you have left your monsters behind."

Daniel was taken aback, tensed himself to get out of bed and run if Anatoly was violent again. But then the older man dropped his head and pinched the bridge of his nose, and Daniel realized he was crying.

In time, he raised his head. "I am a man who has suffered," Anatoly said, collecting himself. "I am a man who continues to suffer, and is still not reconciled to certain recent events." He watched over his shoulder for a long time, and Daniel waited, completely confused.

Elizavetta was at the doorway again, this time she had her hand around the hand of a pale little girl. Daniel couldn't be certain—he had been through a great upheaval of mind and body—but the little girl looked to him like Papa Grigory's foundling, Totchka.

"Breakfast is ready, Papa," she said. "You promised I could take the child to the doctor again this morning."

Anatoly waved her away. "Yes, yes. Go. Do what you have to, you know I won't stand in your way."

Elizavetta took the opportunity of Anatoly's inattention to fix Daniel in her gaze, as though she was trying to tell him something with her eyes. Then the little girl coughed, and Elizavetta remembered herself and left.

Anatoly huffed. "I lost my daughter."

"Elizavetta? But she's . . . ," he started. "I'm afraid I don't—"

"Not all is as it appears to be, young man," Anatoly said, as though he hadn't heard him. "Some people will only ever see what they've always seen. Remember that. Now rest."

Daniel watched him leave, wondering at his cryptic words. His brain was tired, and he did still need to rest. He turned on his side, where he caught sight of a photograph on the bedside table. A young couple on their wedding day. He picked it up, read the inscription lettered in silver on the photo mat: *Nikita and Elizavetta.*

Elizavetta. He examined her in the photograph, and the sense of familiarity, of knowing her somehow, was gone. This woman looked different. She was plumper, that was for certain, but she had been ill a long time.

No, it was something else.

Her eyes.

The woman in the photograph had pale blue eyes; the Elizavetta he had just met had eyes of dark ocean blue.

Daniel flipped the photo facedown, and smiled.

Rosa Kovalenka was beautiful and clever, and almost nobody knew the truth about her.

But those who did, kept it to themselves.